DELUSION

DELUSION

Laura L. Sullivan

HARCOURT
Houghton Mifflin Harcourt
Boston New York 2012

Harcourt is an imprint of Houghton Mifflin Harcourt Publishing Company.

www.hmhbooks.com

Text set in Dante MT Std Regular.

Library of Congress Cataloging-in-Publication Data
Sullivan, Laura L.
Delusion / Laura L. Sullivan.
pages cm
Summary: "Two beautiful teenage sisters, Phil and Fee Albion, descendants of a long line of stage illusionists, are sent from London to the countryside during World War II, only to discover a hidden college of real magicians who just might help them save England from the Nazis."—Provided by publisher.
ISBN 978-0-547-68836-7
[1. Magic—Fiction. 2. Magicians—Fiction. 3. Sisters—Fiction. 4. World War, 1939–1945—England—Fiction. 5. Great Britain—History—George VI, 1936–1952—Fiction.] I. Title.
PZ7.S9527De 2012
[Fic]—dc23
2012028977

Manufactured in the United States of America
DOC 10 9 8 7 6 5 4 3 2 1
4500390696

For Reka

DELUSION

Chapter 1

Phil sprinted along the bank of the Thames, unbraiding her hair as she ran, so late she didn't dare ask a passing stranger the time. Even that small delay might be disastrous. This was opening night.

She'd been doing clever bits of magic for a wounded soldier at the hospital as part of the Women's Voluntary Service when she caught sight of his watch: six o'clock. With a hasty apology and a promise to return the next day to finish the trick, she dashed off to the Hall of Delusion. She didn't know the soldier's watch had stopped the moment the bombs first fell on his troop of the British Expeditionary Force in France, and that he kept it only as a memento.

Fee, dear Fee, was waiting for her when she slipped around the back of the theater. As always when they'd been apart any length of time, they embraced in their own peculiar way, forehead to forehead, leaning against each other, their long hair mingling in an alchemical blending. When they stood together like this — and they tended to linger, supporting and drawing support—they looked like a single creature. A magnificent portmanteau beast, said one of the old thespians who treated the Hall as his personal salon—a griffin, a chimera.

"I'm so sorry," Phil whispered to her sister. "Do we have time to dress?"

"We have all the time in the world!" Fee said merrily, and revealed that it was only a little before five. "Time enough to draw a crowd."

Phil groaned with the familial melodrama and separated herself from her sister. As always, they made a mutual soft murmur of regret that they must become their own unique selves again. With all that was going on in the world, they needed each other's sisterly solace more than ever, but were so busy that they rarely had time simply to be together, as they had almost every moment in their earlier childhood.

Maybe there'll be time tonight, when the show is over and everything is still, Phil thought as she ran inside to change. There was so much for them to talk over.

When Phil came out, disguised, the sisters tossed a coin with Hector and Stan for who would be the busker and who would be the shill.

"I hate being the shill," Phil said. "Anyway, by rights we shouldn't have to do a thing but get in our costumes and gather our powers. It is *our* night, after all."

"If we don't have an audience, it won't be much of a show," Fee said, coaxing Phil down the steps and casting an angelic smile at the two orphan boys her family had informally adopted. "Besides," she added, "they're much better at close-up magic than we are." They parted, going around opposite sides of the Hall of Delusion, the theater that had been in their family since the seventeenth century.

Phil might have preferred to sip tea (though not too much before going onstage, she'd learned the hard way) or, better yet, work out her nerves boxing with her brother, but she would never dream of shirking her duty — any duty. Her life, her calling, was the stage, but she had any number of lesser passions too, and she approached each of them with a single-minded dedication. Everything she did was, to her, the most important thing in the world, and she took herself, and her causes, very seriously.

She adjusted the severe lines of her dowdy wool suit. *Fancy, dressing like a spinster secretary at my age,* she thought. In addition to her inherited histrionics, she shared her family's obsession with clothes and generally managed to wear something that sparkled, even in wartime. Phil was seventeen but was disguised that day as a forty-year-old, complete with faint painted crow's-feet around her eyes. She came from a long line of performers and was ready to play anything from infant to sexpot to granny if it made the audience roar.

Now she looked respectable, practical, as ordinary as it was possible for her to look. A close observer might have noticed the lush curves that strained against the spare, rationed goods of her skirt, or the extravagance of flame-colored hair she'd tucked up under an efficient turban — she was most palpably made for the stage — but her family's business relied on the public's inability to closely observe anything, and Phil was, to the casual eye, just another pedestrian, one who would never believe in magic.

Which made it all the more impressive when this stodgy gray-clad secretary loudly exclaimed, "Merciful heavens, that fellow is flying!"

She let her mouth gape and her eyes bulge — an unattractive expression, but one she'd practiced at great length in front of a mirror. She looked like a codfish, but it got people to stop and share her amazement.

The instant she'd cried out, a young man in sprightly plus-fours who was apparently levitating a few inches in the air fell heavily to the ground with an apologetic grunt, as if to beg the public's pardon for doing something as frivolous as floating when there was a war going on. No fewer than five people stopped and stared.

"It can't be," the disguised Phil said, shaking her head. "I must be seeing things."

"What you are seeing, madam, is magic, pure and simple."

"I don't believe it," she said, for there's nothing more compelling than seeing a skeptic converted.

Another three people joined the gathering.

"Do it again," Phil begged, then settled back to watch Hector work his magic.

"Take care, please," he told a woman bending curiously to examine his shoes for wires or hydraulic lifts. He gave a self-deprecating little laugh. "I am only an apprentice, and sometimes I fall from the sky."

A clever new touch, Phil thought, *suggesting he could soar to the heavens if he trained a bit more.* If you lead someone to consider the impossible, they're that much more likely to accept the merely improbable.

"And you, sir, with your fine watch, please step back a bit. The antigravitational forces are such as to occasionally disrupt timepieces."

Phil nodded in approval. He had them positioned exactly right, clustered and facing traffic so the passing motors and pedestrians too single-minded to stop would create a blurring backdrop to the trick and add to the distraction. He turned so they looked at his heels from an angle, placed his feet just so, raised his hands with a flourish that brought all eyes but Phil's briefly away from his feet, then, trembling with the mighty effort needed to control the forces of the universe, raised his entire body three inches off the ground.

Except, of course, for the toes of his right foot, which the astonished crowd couldn't see.

Gravity pounced upon him again, and he landed with a stagger, out of breath and grinning. "Come back in a year and see how high I can go. Or you can see what a master magician can do this very afternoon." He gestured to a brightly lit marquee that would be extinguished when blackout began at dusk.

"Experience the powers of the House of Albion, possessed of the secrets of the ages. This family of magicians has been at the royal command for four hundred years." This was not strictly true. Legend had it that an Albion once cast Charles I's horoscope, predicting a short life and a sore throat, and occasionally a prince and his entourage filled a box at the Hall, but they had no royal charter. "For mere pennies" — well, quite a few of them — "you too can see the wonders once reserved for kings and emperors. See the visible vanish and unseen spirits forced into flesh. See a man have his head sawed off, a woman drown and be reborn." His voice had lapsed into a hawker's dramatic wheedle, and he instantly lost half the crowd. They liked the show, but they didn't want to be sold something.

That was careless of him, sounding like a carny at a fair. He knew his business better than that. Come to think of it, he was off his game in his levitation, too. He'd done the lazy version, not the more difficult — and much more impressive — variation that required clandestinely removing his shoe and picking it up between his heels while standing on his hidden bare foot. You could deceive a much larger crowd that way, and get better altitude.

She watched him awhile as he set up a little table and began card tricks. Again, he stuck to the most basic palmings and switches — and was so clumsy that Phil heard a little boy say, "Mummy, I see the queen in his pocket!"

Hector wasn't an Albion, but he'd been training with the family for five years, since arriving as a scruffy twelve-year-old with a black-haired gypsy-looking boy in tow. He knew the business almost as well as those who had it in their blood, so it surprised Phil that he would put on such a ham-handed show.

Not that they needed to boost the audience that night. It was Phil and Fee's debut, and their parents had called in every favor to fill the seats on their daughters' most important night. It was a graduation of sorts — the first time they'd be performing an elaborate illusion entirely of their own device — and their parents were as nervous and proud as mother eagles watching their chicks' maiden flight.

And now, Phil thought, *I have something to distract me on the most important day of my life.* There was only one reason Hector would be dropping cards and losing his ace: he was planning to propose.

It was a logical match, and Phil was an eminently logical girl.

He'd been devoted to her since the day after showing up at the Albion doorstep, when she'd pulled a piece of chocolate from his ear and deigned to share it with him. At first she refused to teach him any magic tricks — they were family secrets, after all — but he managed to spy on them while earning his keep sweeping the aisles and scrubbing the loo, and one day he surprised them all with a quite passable transformation of a beetle into a flower. From that day on, he was allowed to sit in on magic lessons, and he attached himself particularly to Phil. He continued to spy on her, to ferret out the few spectacular illusions the family refused to teach him, but a year ago he let himself be caught, accepted Phil's furious lecture, told her how lovely she was, and kissed her.

Hector's courtship had progressed with increasing confidence, and Phil tolerated it with a good humor. At first, indeed, it was something of a joke, and when she curled up in bed with Fee every night, they'd giggle over his imbecilic love poetry and misguided attempts at gallantry. But—and maybe it was simply force of habit—she eventually stopped laughing and tentatively accepted his advances. They never progressed beyond kisses and a bit of pawing. Neither had time for much more than that, what with the theater and their studies under a tutor (who gave his services in exchange for the use of the venue every Tuesday to put on his avant-garde plays.)

As soon as he'd planted that first kiss, he began talking about their future together in such an assured manner that she didn't quite have the heart to correct him. He was a dear friend—and she couldn't kill a dear friend's dreams. But when his dreams seemed to include her as his wife, she became uneasy.

Well, it's only sensible, she told herself. *I'm a magician, I mean to remain a magician, and I can't see myself married to a greengrocer or publican. Magicians marry magicians, or at least entertainers.* Phil's own heartrendingly beautiful mum had been an opera singer when she married Dad, but one stage is very like another, and she knew how to wear false eyelashes and take direction. Phil knew she would marry a magician and bear magician children, as her ancestors had for hundreds of years, and it was all very proper, very suitable, that she should marry Hector.

Then why does it put me off my game to even think of him proposing? she wondered.

Because I don't love him. I'm very fond of him. I always have a good time when I'm around him. We work well together. It would be an ideal marriage, without passion, perhaps, but who needs that? Leave that for Fee, who falls in love every ten days like very romantic clockwork.

So she told herself, but though she could generally convince anyone of anything when she set her mind to it (though it's true they sometimes gave in from sheer weariness), Phil still had her doubts.

Hector was having difficulty holding the crowd's interest, and he flashed her a subtle signal to help. But she was annoyed at his presumption to think of doing something so silly as proposing on her big night, so she abandoned him and drifted over to the cluster of people gathered around little Stan.

After all, Phil was a master of escape.

As if the buildings around the Hall of Delusion had been a pagan temple constructed to mark the passing of the seasons, there were a very few evenings of the year when the declining sun squeezed its molten light directly into the narrow crevice between the walls, casting the street in a buttery glow. The light seemed to seek out two objects: a haze of a girl in the softest red and gold, and a small dancing crystalline orb. The boy who manipulated the orb was himself in shadow. He carried the shadow with him, in his dark skin and hair, in his very being, as if he both cast his own darkness and hid in it. His opacity served as a foil for the brilliant glass ball he danced over and under his fingers, defying gravity as surely as Hector but without, as far as Phil could ever see, using any tricks. It was pure dexterity, the dint of countless hours of practice, and was in itself a kind of magic of concentration. The sun made opalescent fire flash in the clear glass as it floated over his knuckles, slipped between his fingers, and leaped up in the air, only to roll down his suddenly arched back and caper once more on his waiting fingertips.

Stanislaus Bambula spied Phil and flashed a smile, a candle in the darkness. He was solemn and solitary by nature, and Phil sometimes believed there was so much on his young mind, he simply could not think with other people around him too often. Nonetheless she knew he was blissfully happy curled up in the welcoming bosom of the Albion family, fed, sheltered, and taught the arcane arts without many questions asked. They knew he was an orphan but never quizzed him about his past. His future was clear. At ten, his was the most natural talent the family had ever seen, and he was destined to be a great magician.

Near him, absently oohing when the ball miraculously ducked under Stan's hand and righted itself, was the dreamy Fee. While Phil had received her mother's extravagantly red hair unadulterated, Fee's hair combined Mum's improbable scarlet with Dad's bright gold ("A preposterous complexion for a magician," Mum always said. "Ought to be raven-haired with black flashing eyes."), creating a strawberry mist of waves that seemed on the verge of evaporating. All of Fee seemed caught in the middle of a spell, on the verge of transfiguring to another state, as deliquescent as the moment before the dew falls.

Her skin was very pale, her blue-gray eyes elsewhere. Her favorite expression was wistful, her favorite activity was love, her favorite utterance a sigh.

She was, as might be imagined, a master of vanishing.

Phil walked deliberately past her sister without acknowledging her, a sign that Fee was to follow her. A moment later Fee joined her in their dressing room.

"Hector's going to ask me to marry him tonight. After the show, I think." *Please, please not before it.*

"You've perfected mind reading?"

Phil chuckled. That was a lark. It was their constant joke that magic was real. How nice that would be, they often said, if all you had to do was mutter a few archaic words instead of practicing a thousand hours in an icy tub learning how to hold your breath for three minutes while wiggling out of handcuffs and a straitjacket.

"No, but he's clearly nervous about something, and what else could it be? What should I say?"

"If you have to wonder what you'll say, the answer must be no." Fee believed in True Love. Phil believed in a Good Match.

"I think I'll tell him I have to think about it. For two years at least." Fee sighed.

"Or maybe when the war's over. It can't last much longer."

Fee covered her elfin ears. "Don't talk to me about the war, please." She had never quite grown out of the childhood belief that if she did not acknowledge something, it did not exist. Fee, who could hardly bear to see a worm writhe its last on the pavement, grew faint if she thought about the good, beautiful, kind young people who were killing one another in horrible ways. Because they all would have been good, she said, if people had just left them alone and never told them to fight. What about Hitler? Phil would ask. Well, perhaps he wasn't raised quite right, Fee would equivocate. There must be good in everyone, somewhere, I know it.

"Maybe I can just avoid him. He'll be busy with the lights throughout the show, and if he fouls up The Disappearing World, I'll murder him. There's no second show today, so afterward it will be hours of congratulation, if it goes well, or commiseration, if it fails, but in any case lots of people and food and drink, and he can't exactly propose in front of everyone, can he?"

"Wouldn't that be romantic?" Fee said. "A declaration of his love before all the world?"

"No," Phil said adamantly, "it would not." Because the only thing worse than breaking Hector's heart in private would be breaking it in public.

No, she amended. The worst thing would be to accept him out of embarrassment and obligation and kindness. For she liked Hector so very much, she did not quite know how to tell him that she didn't love him.

Their part didn't come until the end, the finale that would have to be particularly grand to overshadow the masterful illusions of their parents and older brother Geoff. Fee appeared onstage early in the act, to be cut in half vertically with an unbearable sound of sawing through her skull, then scurried back to their dressing room to pour herself into her sequined oil-slick costume.

They watched from the wings as Geoff hammered a spectator's Patek Philippe watch to bits, then resurrected it, polished, better than new. Dad levitated a woman from the audience, while Mum sashayed and gesticulated and flourished. She was really quite a good magician herself after twenty years as an Albion, but she preferred the less demanding role of stage beauty. She was still striking even in natural light, but just old enough that she enjoyed the heavy makeup and feathers and stage lights that worked a glamour to defy her years.

Then the lights went out, and Dad's voice, forced down an octave, said in a cavernous boom, "Now, for the first time ever, experience the wonder of the cosmos, the primal forces of the universe, as two of the most powerful magicians in England make not just a person, not just a building, but *everything* disappear."

The lights flashed on blindingly, then dimmed so the two girls in their shining obsidian sheaths were disembodied heads and hands. The audience thought that was a pretty good trick in itself and was always willing to cheer attractive girls. But these girls did not shimmy or undulate or even smile (which had been the hardest thing for Fee in rehearsal). They stared over the audience with kohl-shadowed eyes and spoke in perfect unison in voices of doom, an oracular chorus.

"Imagine . . . everything you know, everything you love, vanishing in the space of an instant."

They paused, letting the fear begin to build. And it did, even in those people who went to the Hall of Delusion only to scoff and try to spy the mirrors and false bottoms.

Cold air began to flow gently through floor vents, making legs shiver.

The lights grew imperceptibly darker.

"Imagine, the person next to you suddenly gone, the husband, the stranger. Imagine the walls of this theater flying apart into their separate molecules. Imagine this planet as it was at the dawn of time, every atom alone and apart in the void of space."

Phil and Fee had argued about this for a while, wondering if science would throw the audience off, but Geoff told them it wasn't proper science anyway and would work, so long as everyone knew that an atom is pretty small and not a thing you'd like your loved ones to be reduced to.

A low percussive heartbeat began to thrum, just within the range of hearing.

"If you were gone too, it wouldn't matter. You wouldn't know the world had ended. But today you will be alone, utterly alone, the only living thing left in the vast emptiness of space. Ladies and gentlemen, experience . . . The Disappearing World!"

It almost would have worked without any special effects. The buildup, the public's perpetual fear of invasion and destruction, combined with a sudden darkness, would have made half the audience scream.

But Phil and Fee had devised a way to do it in full—more than full—light. A blaze erupted from the darkness. Strobes and mirrors at just the right intervals and levels blinded and dazzled and confused so that, for the space of five seconds, though the room was preternaturally bright, no one could see the person in the seat next to him, the very walls of the theater, his hand before his face. The recorded heartbeat crescendoed and was echoed by a terrible high-pitched whine and then a thunder crash that shook the building. Every light went out, and even the people who had come alone grabbed the nearest hand.

Phil and Fee stood together in the blackness, their shoulders just touching.

"What happened?" Fee whispered. "That boom — it wasn't in the rehearsal. Is Hector improvising?"

One coherent thought emerged from Phil's confusion: *Maybe that was what Hector was nervous about, and I don't have to deal with a proposal tonight after all.*

Even when the lights failed to come up thirty long seconds later, and the audience wondered if the trick was still going on, Phil could only feel relief.

Then someone began to open doors to the lobby, fire escapes, delivery bays, letting the evening haze float in. Only it was brighter than it should have been, flickering, and came with a choking chalky dust. There was a faint sound like angry buzzing bees, and then . . .

Phil hardly believed those volcanic sounds could be bombs. Nothing made by man could be so powerful. There was another explosion quite close by, then one slightly farther off, and though they retreated in a steady rhythm, the ground continued to shake. She heard a voice from outside cry, "There are hundreds of them!" People started to call for help, from a human, from a god, but they were cut off by a blast that was sound and touch and light and heat, all at once. Another wave of bombs began to fall, right outside the Hall of Delusion.

Phil and Fee could see the ghostly shapes of their audience rushing outside, tripping over one another, showing their best and worst as they pushed grandmothers out of their way or stayed to help people they'd never met.

The sisters had been trained from infancy to let nothing distract them while onstage. They could handle heckling and inappropriate laughter, broken props, torn costumes, and fires that refused to be swallowed. Now, because they were performers and the show must always go on, they stood stupidly on the stage while outside the world disintegrated.

Hector barreled out of the dusty half-light and dragged them underground. Mum and Dad rushed down the aisles, shouting over the confusion that their cellar was a shelter, but only a few people heard them. They were running for the nearest tube station or, more likely, just running.

The city had prepared for bombardment for slightly more than a year, since the day war was declared. The munitions plants and airfields had received steady strikes, and several cities had been hit, but though she carried her gas mask everywhere and nagged her neighbors, with the power of her WVS badge, to install their Anderson shelters in their petunia beds, she never really thought the Germans would bomb civilians in London. One small contingent had dropped a few bombs on the city a month before, but even the most adamant Hun haters admitted that was probably a mistake made by green or disobedient pilots on the way to bomb a port. There was an immediate retaliatory attack on Berlin, and then all had been quiet, aside from the expected attacks on military targets.

Phil staggered down to the cellar, past the mirrored boxes and human-size aquariums, past the chests and presses full of costumes going back generations. Her parents had gathered up a handful of people, mostly those too slow to join the others in their mad career into the inferno, or too world-weary to much care if this was their last day on earth. There was a little boy separated from his mother, and a middle-aged man with his empty sleeve pinned up, sitting on the floor, rocking, remembering the Great War that had taken his arm and half his generation.

Coming slowly out of her shock, Phil looked around the lantern-lit room for those most important to her. Miss Merriall, the wardrobe mistress, was calmly heating water over Sterno for tea. Dad was pacing rather dramatically in his purple star-spangled cape, and Mum was wheeling all of the standing mirrors into an alcove where they wouldn't cause deadly shards if they shattered. Hector quivered in a tension of fury like a setter at point, spots of pink on his pale cheeks, looking as if he desperately wanted to punch someone but didn't know who, or how. Geoff was passing around spare gas masks . . .

"Where's Stan?" Phil shouted. The shriek and boom of the bombs was muffled now. Even the end of the world couldn't last forever.

"He was outside during the performance," Fee said, her eyes widening. "You know how he hates watching the shows."

Almost before Fee had finished, Phil was dashing past her family and up the stairs. Fee was right: though Stan enjoyed quiet training, he could never stand to watch the magic onstage before an audience. No one knew quite why, but when the show started, he would either wait outside the theater, letting his crystal ball run like a pet over his body, or more likely, take a walk down to the nearby Thames.

Phil opened the stage door and entered the disappearing world.

The Luftwaffe didn't bother using flashing strobes where a blazing holocaust of incendiary bombs would do. They created terror not with chill breezes and subtle sound effects but with craters and corpses, screaming and explosions. And they removed the world Phil knew not with trickery and illusion but with the brute force of physics, leveling building after building, reducing the world inexorably to atoms.

She could hear bombs falling somewhere far away, but for the moment there were no planes overhead. The theater had been spared, but the dress store three buildings away had suffered a direct hit and was utterly gone. The café beside it was rubble, and the bookstore next door was still standing but with one wall blown off and the roof crumbling. Down the road was a deep pit with a charred bus dangling on its lip, and the entire row of buildings across the street was on fire. Farther away she could see masonry skeletons of buildings that had been gutted by the concussive force.

"Stan!" she screamed, but everyone was screaming for someone.

Geoff came up behind her. "Phil, don't be a fool. There might be more bombers on the way."

"Stan was out here. He always walked by the candy store." It too was engulfed, exuding a sickening burnt-sugar smell. "It's gone. He's gone!"

She staggered into the chaos, to tear through rubble looking for Stan, to weep helpless tears and curse the Germans when a second wave of bombers came in after nightfall, following the trail of fire across London they'd blazed earlier.

All around London, millions of citizens were rallying. Their fear fled quickly, replaced by anger and then at last by something far more useful: grim, stubborn determination, a rocklike resolution to endure.

Soon Phil's family joined her on their devastated street, and the Albions began to account for the fallen and treat the survivors. Fee found Phil a few hours later with rills of tear tracks running down her sooty face, sitting on a curb, exhausted with work and weeping.

"I can't find Stan anywhere," she said as Fee collapsed beside her. She sniffed, then sneezed from the mortar dust hanging in the air. "He's gone, Fee. Our little brother is gone."

Chapter 2

When they dragged themselves, wild-eyed and shell-shocked, in for breakfast at noon, Dad and Mum told the girls they were being sent to the countryside, someplace nice and safe.

"Not bloody likely!" Phil replied. "I'm not running away."

She had a barrage of further objections ready, but before she could lob a single volley, her parents revealed their own astounding news.

"We meant to tell you last night anyway," Dad said. "Hush, that's only part of it. It's been in the works for ages and was going to be our big surprise after your show." He bowed his head. He'd been so proud that the Albions had been chosen for such a great—if dangerous—honor, but there could be no celebration now that little Stan was gone. Still, it made what he had planned all the more imperative. "We're joining the army," he said.

"What, the Home Guard?" Phil asked. Popularly known as Dad's Army, it was mostly made up of men too old to go to the front.

They trained as best they could with limited support and hardly any weaponry against the day Germans would land on English soil.

"Pah! I mean the real army, a special division—but hush!" He looked around with staged drama. "It is top secret! Winnie—Mr. Churchill, that is—was most insistent that no one outside of the squad know of its existence. But of course I except fellow Albions, and Albions by association." He nodded to Hector. "We are accustomed to keeping secrets."

Phil was so used to her father overacting that she didn't take him very seriously, until he said, "We are joining the Magic Squad."

He leaned precariously on the back two legs of his chair, arms folded, and waited.

"You mean, to entertain the troops?" Phil asked dubiously.

"We mean nothing of the sort," said much more practical Mum. "It is a unit comprised of illusionists and stage technicians and painters and engineers whose job will be to deceive the Germans."

"And the Italians, and the Japs, and whoever else dares to threaten dear old England," Geoff said, jumping to his feet. "Any one of us can make a building disappear with a few tricks of light. Just think bigger. Imagine making a whole railroad disappear when the bombers come in! Or creating a false battalion of tanks to divert the panzers! Or those tricks we do with liquid nitrogen—we could make an entire town believe it was under a gas attack. Just think what trickery and illusions could do to help win this war!"

Until that moment, Phil had been able to see nothing beyond mangled bodies, spilled blood by inferno's light, collapsed apartments where families were trapped, crushed, maybe still alive, for a while. Most of all, she saw a small empty space where Stan was supposed to be. And against all that, her own paltry efforts, the pull of her small muscles, the insignificance of her comfort. Now, suddenly, she saw how she could use her own unique skills to make a difference. How clever of the army to see how the Albions could be put to use. Above all else, Phil needed to be useful. She could see it now—how to turn a destroyer into a fleet of innocent fishing ships, how to hide an entire canal. If she could create illusions onstage, she could do them in the theater of war!

"When do we start?" she asked eagerly.

"*You* start for a farmhouse in Sussex by the next train," Dad said. "We head for parts unknown shortly thereafter." Oh, how he wished he had implemented the plan just one day sooner!

What followed was an epic battle that Phil fought valiantly, though she knew she was defeated from the outset.

She'd been allowed almost absolute freedom in her seventeen years; she didn't see why now all of a sudden her parents got protective. If she could stay out until midnight while a Shakespearean roué friend of the family introduced her to Tom Collins, why couldn't she parachute into France and dazzle the Germans with her illusions?

Her parents returned a flat no.

"The Auxiliary Territorial Services then," Phil insisted. If she couldn't join her parents and brother, at least she could join the armed forces in some capacity. She simply had to do something useful in this war.

"You're too young."

"I'll stay in London and keep volunteering. Or I'll work in a munitions factory. Anything! It isn't fair that you three get to save England while Fee and I get shipped to some comfy country retreat."

"Oh, I daresay it won't be all that comfy," Mum said.

Phil's eyes lit up. "Oh Mum, do you mean the Land Army! It won't be fighting Germans, quite, but if I could be a Land Girl, then at least I'll free up some fellow to go and fight them for me." She didn't know a thing about plows or cows but had seen the posters featuring staunch, hardy girls in clingy khaki jodhpurs and even clingier forest-green sweaters.

"You can't be a Land Girl at seventeen, Phil," Ma said gently. "You're still a child. You have to be kept safe."

"But—"

"You're *my* child," Mum said. "I couldn't bear it if anything happened to you."

"What about you, Mum?" Fee asked. "What are we going to do if anything happens to you?"

"Nothing will happen to any of us," she said with that facility for lying that all parents learn once their children develop the power of speech. "But our country is in danger, and we must go where we are most needed."

"Precisely, which is why I should be allowed—"

"Enough!" Dad said brusquely. "Miss Merriall was kind enough to arrange for lodging for the four of you . . . I mean three . . ." There was a terrible moment of silence, then Dad found the strength to go on. "It's at her sister's farm, a place called Weasel Rue."

He unfolded a worn map and searched Sussex. "The town's called

Bittersweet. Apples and hops, farm country. Where is the ruddy thing?" His finger wandered over the map, to no avail. "Well, it's not on the map, but Miss Merriall assures us it's there. You'll be expected to work a bit, no doubt, but it is a well-to-do establishment, and you'll be safe there."

Safety was exactly what Phil did not want. She wanted privation and hardship, to feel like she was giving something of herself for England.

"If it's all the same to you," she sniffed, "I'm going to pretend to be a Land Girl."

She was brought out of her own sulky egoism by Hector's ragged voice. "I'm joining up, too."

Dad sighed. "I understand how you feel, Hector, but you're simply too young."

"I've been considering it for a long time, ever since I turned eighteen. Last night cinched it."

Phil looked at Hector in amazement. Until that moment she'd always thought of him as a boy, although he was a year her senior. Now, miraculously, he was a man, full-fledged, and she did not know whether to be proud of him or tell him he was a young fool.

And all this time I was only thinking about myself, she realized with a pang of guilt. *Worrying about my own feelings and future, when Hector was planning to go off to fight, maybe to die. Of course Hector wasn't going to ask me to marry him.*

Mum, being a mum, knew exactly what she thought. "No! I absolutely forbid it. I understand how you feel, but you're just barely of age, and there's no point in being cannon fodder when you can leave the work to us. How on earth do you expect us to do our jobs if our children aren't safe?"

"They killed my brother," Hector said between gritted teeth. "I know he's not really, but we've been together for so long. Ever since that night at the orphanage when he took my hand, I've taken care of him."

Phil noticed that Hector's nails were torn and bleeding, and she realized he must have been digging through masonry all night, looking for Stan.

"I've been thinking about joining up for a long time. Now I'm sure," he said with grim resolution. "Mum, Dad, I'm sorry, but you can't talk me out of this, and you can't stop me."

"Sharper than a serpent's tooth . . ." Dad said, and hugged his adopted son tightly.

There was a terrible heavy silence. Then with a visible effort, Fee said with forced brightness, "I, for one, will love being in the countryside. We all have to fight the war in our own way. The only way I can fight it is by pretending it isn't happening. By pretending as hard as I can that England is still the lovely tranquil land of bluebell woods and sheep fields it has always been. Hector, I'm awfully proud of you. I'm proud of you all."

She flung her head down on the kitchen table and burst into tears. When her golden red hair fell forward, Phil saw a small bloody handprint on the back of her sister's neck. Fee might hate the war, but she'd been out there too amid the death and despair. That was the mark of some little child she'd comforted, one who had perhaps lost her house, her family, at the very least that childhood certainty that the world is a safe and loving place. Phil's faint contempt for Fee's pacifist nature vanished. Fee might not have shaken her furious fist at the German bombers, but that was only because she was too busy looking down to care for the smallest victims.

Did Hector propose before he left?" Fee asked as they sat in the train, watching their beloved city recede in a cloud of fog and smoke.

"Thank goodness, no. What with everything going on, I might have said yes without noticing." Phil thought he'd been close, though, and might have, had she given him a little encouragement. He'd taken her hand in a very formal manner and promised he'd return to her. Not just return, but return to her, which by extrapolation sounded very like a commitment. Then he seemed to wait, but she'd said nothing remotely binding in return, just a stoic, maternal plea that he be safe.

He laughed at that. "If I wanted to be safe, I'd be with you in Sussex."

Piqued, she said, "When the Germans come, they'll probably parachute right into Weasel Rue. No doubt I'll see more action than you will."

He'd kissed her then, promised to write every day, shouldered his duffel, and marched resolutely from the Hall of Delusion.

Now her joking words came back to her.

"Fee," she said, still staring after London, "it's only a matter of time before the Germans invade us. Do you think it's possible they could come through our part of Sussex?" There was a strange gleam in her eye. "Not that I want them to, of course, and it stands to reason they'd come through far to the north of us. But they might, mightn't they? If they do, we need to be ready. Even out here we can help win the war."

Fee turned deliberately away from distant London, now little more than a sooty smear in the sky, and looked out over the placid, rolling sheep-dotted hills. She knew her sister would have willingly stayed in London through every bomb Germany could lob at them, but she was frankly relieved to have all that horror out of sight. Not so much for her personal safety as to save her from the overwhelming, crushing pity she felt for her fellow man even under the best of circumstances. She still didn't know how she'd gotten through last night. Adrenaline and some vital essence stolen from her stoic sister, no doubt. She knew she was a coward, but she could never, never go through that again. That little girl who'd lost everyone she loved had clung to her as if she'd never let go . . .

"I think we're doing our part simply by being here, Phil. We're freeing up Mum and Dad and Geoff to do what they have to do. You know what Milton said."

Phil gave her a withering look. "Of course I don't." She loved her sister, but really, poetry was the limit.

"'They also serve who only stand and wait.'"

"Bugger standing and waiting. What do you think a German with a bayonet would do to you if you stood and waited? What we need to do is find a way to help the local Home Guard." She had an inspiration. "We can do the same thing Mum and Dad and Geoff are doing—right here in England!"

"How?"

"I don't quite know yet, but I'll talk with the Guard. Sussex is between the coast and London, so there's bound to be a huge auxiliary force. Old men and invalids, to be sure, but still, they'll know how to organize. Forget about being a Land Girl. Who wants to hoe mangel-wurzels when they can be fighting!"

"You can't exactly box the Germans," Fee pointed out.

Geoff, a conscientious big brother, had tried to make sure his sisters' virtues would remain intact for exactly as long as they wanted them to, and had done his best to teach both to box. Fee had only sighed at her gloves, but Phil had taken to it like a bantamweight Beau Jack and repaid Geoff for his pains by regularly trouncing him (but only, he always said, because he was too much of a gentleman to fight back).

"If I can hang upside-down in a straitjacket with a hundred blokes trying to see up my skirt, I can do anything."

Then, as she often did when agitated, she took a pair of handcuffs from her purse, clamped her hands together behind her back, and practiced her escapes, much to the consternation of a trio of nuns who shared their compartment.

Fee sighed. Her dreams and daydreams had always been full of wildflowers, butterflies, and long rambles over moors. All, of course, with an as-yet-unknown Someone at her side. She'd brought along her entire collection of Jane Austen, and if she could only manage to hurt herself rather badly and then be saved by a dashing romantic young lord, like her heroine Marianne Dashwood, life would be perfect. She was just enough of a realist to know this probably wouldn't happen, but rereading *Sense and Sensibility* in a pastoral setting would be nearly as good. As long as she never, ever had to hear another bomb falling . . .

A genial conductor told them theirs was the next stop, and the girls pressed their noses to the window for a look at their new home.

"Oh!" Fee said with delight. "It's out of Shakespeare, or Hardy!" She was literary, but not architectural, and knew only that the little village was picturesquely lovely. "And the yellow roses! How are they still blooming this late?" She wandered away from the station, abandoning her luggage. "Do you see the little dragons in the ironwork of the streetlights? Oh, I can almost forget . . ."

Phil looked the village over with a critical eye. "Those roses should be dug up and potatoes planted in their place," she said. "And do you see a single shelter? These lights are pretty," she owned, "but they ought to be out by now."

"It's still an hour until dusk, at least," Fee said.

"All the same, the air raid warden will want to know about it. Better safe than . . ." But *sorry* seemed too inadequate a word after the carnage she'd witnessed the night before, and she let her platitude drift away.

It was such a small town that they were surprised to see more than fifty people debouch from the train, cheerful groups of women, whole families shepherding children. "Did the entire town go on vacation?" Phil asked. "There can't be that many people in all of Bittersweet."

"This way, please," someone called out, though Phil and Fee couldn't see who spoke. The crowd made its unhurried and disorganized way to a motor lorry and two open farm carts. When the masses scrambled in, the girls could see they were being directed by a small, sharp sparrow of a woman in a floral chintz dress and Wellingtons. The breeze blew her dress up a bit, and Fee nudged her sister. "Did you see? Bloomers!"

"Don't dilly-dally," the woman chirped at the group. "Got to get the lot of you settled so you can be up with the sun. 'A bushel before sunrise' has always been my motto, and it's served me well so far. Step lively now, the hops won't wait."

"I'm ever so sorry," Fee said, "but we're looking for Weasel Rue Farm. We're to stay with . . . oh, I can't remember what her married name is, but she used to be a Miss Merriall."

The little woman cocked her head and peered at them with her very bright eyes. "You'll be the theater girls. I must say you look it." They weren't sure what she meant by that but decided to take it for a compliment. "Weren't there supposed to be four of you? I only agreed to take you because I thought there'd be a pair of boys to help with the hops and the apples."

"Hector joined the army," Phil said, "and Stan . . . he . . . just last night . . ." She leaned into Fee and gathered enough strength to say stoically, "Stan died in the bombing."

"Sorry to hear that," the woman said, though her eyes wandered over the people loaded into the wagons, and it was evident she wanted to get back to her own business as soon as possible. "I'm Mrs. Pippin, that's Miss Merriall as was. No one troubled to tell me your names."

"I'm Phil," she said. "Philomel, really, but who could stomach that."

"Quite," Mrs. Pippin said.

"And I'm Phoebe, but everyone calls me Fee. That's with an F-e-e, not a P-h-o-e, because if you just wrote Phoe, who on earth would know how to say your name? They'd call me phooey."

"Have you got surnames?"

"Of course. Albion."

"Good. I had a notion you might really be my sister's children. I always feared the worst when our Rose ran off to London." She gave them a very canny look. "The dear knows what goes on backstage."

("She speaks as if *backstage* were a code name for a brothel," Fee whispered to her sister later that night.)

"Well, there's bound to be one bad apple in the barrel, I always say," Mrs. Pippin went on.

"Oh, no, Miss Merriall isn't a bad apple!" Fee insisted. "She's our wardrobe mistress, and she can sew anything in about half an hour, and you can't imagine how useful that is when your father decides at the last minute it would look better for a ballerina to be cut in half than a flamenco dancer."

All Mrs. Pippin said was "Mistress, humph! No truck with mistresses at Weasel Rue."

("Can you imagine dear, plump, dowdy Miss Merriall being anyone's mistress?" Phil asked when they were alone.

Fee sighed and said doubtfully, "Perhaps there are some men who'd find her . . . comfortable.")

"Come along, girls," Mrs. Pippin said. "The stationmaster will see your things are sent on. For now bundle into the cart, and I'll drop you off at the farm before I unload this lot." She gestured with absolute disdain to the chattering band in the back.

They climbed up next to Mrs. Pippin and were off with a flick of the reins.

"What a charming village," Fee said, preparing to gush.

"Half the drains are bad. The houses haven't been updated since the Old Earl's time."

An Old Earl implied a Young Earl, and Fee immediately had romantic designs on him. "Does he live very close by?" With petrol rationing, any possible love must be within a five-mile radius. Unless the Pippins had a spare bicycle, in which case Fee could stalk her prey as much as ten miles in clement weather.

"The Old Earl's been dead and gone these forty years and more. Died at Mafeking."

"His descendants then?"

"Not a one. Don't know as he had any children."

Fee frowned, then brightened, one sort of romance replacing another. "It must be a lovely estate, though. Who lives in it now?"

"There is no estate. There was a castle, once, but it's gone."

"Ruined, you mean?" Ruins were, if anything, more romantic than stately homes, particularly, she imagined, by foggy moonlight. Even if your only company was Jane Austen and dreams.

"I mean gone, every brick. Weasel Rue is the largest house you'll find for twenty miles."

While Fee wondered how a castle could simply vanish, and then, following her expertise, pondered how she'd go about *making* it vanish, Phil quizzed Mrs. Pippin about the local Home Guard.

"Home Guard? What on earth do we have to guard? Here in Bittersweet there's just hops and apples and sheep. We're at the back end of everything. Mr. Hitler wouldn't dream of coming here, and if a bomb fell accidentally, it would take one look at the place and turn around again." She nickered to the horses to speed them along, her hands tight on the reins, her jaw set.

("She called him Mister," Fee said to Phil when they curled up in bed to discuss the day. "Do you think she's—"

"Never. If Hitler came near her hops, she'd eat him alive. Don't you remember what she said about German beer? 'It tastes like piss from an asparagus-eating pig.' Now that's patriotism if I ever heard it.")

"There's no war here," Mrs. Pippin said at length. "The war is for them out there. Folks who stay in Bittersweet never have to worry about such blights as wars. Bittersweet's safe."

Before long they turned down into a navel of land between gently rolling hills and got their first look at Weasel Rue.

Chapter 3

Look at it, sprawled like a sleeping dragon," Fee said.

It was an old golden stone building without a single pretense to any architectural style. Someone had built part of the house when they had money, and added another wing when they had more. Bits jutted out here and there when some feature of geography or habit made it easier to put a kitchen at odd angles rather than move the pigsty. It was a large house, or rather a long house, winding, as Fee said, in a serpentine fashion, and it was very much a farmhouse, with chickens and geese promenading on the grass and an omnipresent yet strangely pleasant scent of manure in the air.

Phil shook her head. "Impossible to defend," she said when Mrs. Pippin hopped down. "Why on earth didn't they build it on a rise like anyone sensible?"

"It's nestled," Fee said. "I like it. It feels safe and cozy."

"Lots of things feel safe that aren't," Phil said sharply. "The Hall of Delusion felt safe."

There were several flocks of sheep barricaded within the thorny hedgerows that divided the gentle hills. "From inside the house it must look like you're in a boat being tossed on waves of sheep."

"Really, Fee, aren't you taking it a bit far? It's just a nice farmhouse."

Fee sighed. She never quite gave up trying to sway her prosaic sister.

"You get yourselves settled. My son Algernon will show you to your room. I'll be back in a jiff after I get this lot squared away."

"What are they all here for?" Phil finally managed to ask. "Are they evacuees?"

"Heavens, no! Do you think I'd saddle myself with all these beastly Londoners for good? No, these are just hop pickers here for a few weeks. They come from the East End of London every year."

"And they all stay here?" Phil asked. The farmhouse was large, but not large enough for fifty or more people.

"They stay in the hopper huts, and thank the lord my grandfather had sense enough to build them far away from Weasel Rue. Londoners are worse than tinkers, and though I forbid it, they seem to have a bottomless stash of gin. If they drank cider or beer like any civilized person, I wouldn't mind, good wholesome beverages that they are, but I don't trust them that drink hard liquor. Now, scurry inside, and I'll be back in an hour. There's always one that balks at the earth closet and has to be told it's that or a bucket and you better not dump it in the open. I've known sows cleaner than Londoners."

"My," said Phil as she watched Mrs. Pippin lead the caravan away, "I never knew I was worse than a sow, and a sot to boot."

"She can't stand London," said a low-pitched voice from the farmhouse door, making them start. They turned and saw a young man, not much more than twenty, with tight-curling chestnut hair cut short and a tall, lithe body. "Can't stand any place other than here, really. Are you the magician girls?"

"We are," Fee said, intensely interested by what little she could make out in the doorway's shadow. "And we haven't brought an ounce of gin, so we hope to win her over."

"You don't stand a chance unless you've lived here all you life. She never really loves anyone unless they can claim five generations in Bittersweet. Lucky for her social life, not many people move away."

"Her sister did."

"Yes, and as far as I know they've never spoken or written since, until she asked if you two could stay for a while. It was like that with me, when I left. Not a letter, like I stopped existing."

"Oh, were you in London? Maybe you saw our show?" Fee always felt she had a better chance of captivating a man if he'd seen her in her body-hugging sequins. Appearances shouldn't matter to true love, but she was quite sure they did anyway.

"I was only there briefly, on my way to army training. But don't stand out there with the dew about to fall. Get your things and come in. I'm Algernon."

There was a brief awkward pause as they waited for him to come and help them, but he just stood in the threshold, smiling, waiting, and at last they hefted their bags. He slipped into the house just before them, holding the door at least, and they trudged in, weary from the trip, and the terror and work of the night before. Inside, it was impossibly peaceful, dark, and warm, with a succession of fading prints and more recent photographs of monarchs lined up as if they were Mrs. Pippin's own ancestors.

"I'm Phil," she said, holding out her hand. "And I can't help but notice there are no blackout curtains. Miss Merriall sent along two trunks of material from the theater for safekeeping. If you don't have any coupons left, I'm sure we can find something heavy enough, though she'll want it back one day for costuming."

Algernon made no attempt to shake her hand. He stared at her fixedly, still faintly smiling.

"I don't mean to offend you, I'm sure, but there's a war on. No one around here seems to know that." She let her hand drop.

"*I* know it," he whispered.

"I've been here all of half an hour, and I can already see it's a disgrace. Look at that window, with nothing but lace curtains over it."

He turned his head so he faced a spot a few feet away from the window.

"Why, if a German bomber—" She broke off. When Algernon turned toward the light, she could see the striations of scars cross his face, as if a giant clawed paw had raked him right across the eyes and down to his chin.

"Phil," Fee whispered, and crept up to touch Algernon's arm.

"You can stare," he said. "I won't know. It happened at Dunkirk. It's funny, a physicist told me how it works. It wasn't the shrapnel that blinded me. The concussive force got to my eyes first and ruined them a fraction of a second before the metal got there. By then my eyes were squeezed shut. The shards never touched them. Amazing things, nerves, when they still work."

He groped behind him for the settee, and Fee was immediately there, supporting him. In an instant she saw the possibilities: a lifetime of dedication and sacrifice, evenings spent reading him poetry, being his eyes on their rambles, the way other senses (touch, she hoped) would be enhanced now that he'd lost his vision. Fee was always a sucker for lame dogs and birds with broken wings. In the space of a breath she was half in love with him, and it is fortunate that before the other half could construct itself, an irate female voice snapped, "He doesn't need your help!" A girl with a pretty, hard-set face and sulky mouth came from another room laden with tea — for two.

The Albion girls introduced themselves, and she told them, "I'm Diana, Algie's fiancée."

Fee sighed. Well, there must be plenty of other prospects nearby.

"Darling," Algernon protested gently, "I've told you the marriage is off."

"No," Diana said, plainly resuming an old argument. "Do you think I'd change my mind just because you're blind? Would you, if it were me?"

"That's different. I'm a man. I'm supposed to run this farm, support my family. How can I do that now? Now that I'm useless, I've freed you to find a better man."

"I don't want a better man, you idiot. I want you."

Phil and Fee exchanged quick looks but managed not to laugh.

"Perhaps we should go to our room and freshen up," Fee said.

"Yes," Diana said, glaring at them, at Fee in particular. "Why don't you do that. It's the last room, down there." She pointed absently. "I'm sure you can find your own way."

Having received their marching orders, they walked down the narrow, winding hallway to their room.

Fee unpacked her books, commandeering the single nightstand between their twin beds, while Phil started to hang up her clothes. She'd packed her most practical things—dungarees starched by Miss Merriall and ironed into a razor crease, shirts swiped from her brother, sweaters in her most utilitarian colors—though of course, being an Albion, those colors were bright canary (on the theory it might blend in with fields of grain) and deep claret with rhinestones sewn on. To these she'd added opera gloves for warmth, silk scarves to tie up her hair, and her few remaining silk stockings. Both girls brought some of their stage clothes, too, show dresses with beads on the bosom and feathers on the nethers, mementos of the life they'd left behind.

Their parents, such sticklers for discipline on the stage, had never bothered to extend that authority to the rest of life, and the girls were allowed to wear—and for the most part do—exactly what they liked. Of all the girls at the city school, only Phil and Fee glittered on a regular basis.

Phil didn't consider herself vain. It was just that she would never wear beige when she could wear fuchsia, or wool when silk was available. And even when cloth, along with practically everything else, was strictly rationed, there were always yards and yards of rare and beautiful material neatly folded in Miss Merriall's many cedar chests. During times of plenty, she bought every lovely fabric that caught her eye. And it was a good thing, too, for Dad was always changing up the show. He'd decide in the morning that what the audience really needed was for them to all dress as a pasha and his harem, and Miss Merriall, fingers flying, would comply with coin-studded bodices and puffed gauze trousers by the evening performance.

Phil, taking inventory, suddenly gasped. "Boots!" She held up a pair that were bootish in only the most nominal sense that they came up over her ankle—soft white leather, overlaid lace, a spool heel. "How could I have forgotten to pack real boots? Fat lot of good these will do me when I'm digging a trench or pouring concrete for a pillbox bunker."

"We're staying in farm country. I'm sure someone can lend you sturdy boots."

"Of course," Phil said, jumping up, filled with nervous energy and the fervent need to perform some patriotic act immediately. "That Diana's too puny, and for some reason I don't think she's eager to do us any favors, but there must be some old boots in a closet that no one will miss. Back in two shakes."

She went in search, leaving Fee to curl up with *Sense and Sensibility* and wonder if Willoughby was really so bad after all. She rather fancied finding a dissolute seducer to reform.

Leery of bothering the engaged-or-perhaps-not couple, Phil tentatively searched the rest of the house, hoping to find a storage closet where she could equip herself. The house was dark by now, which pleased her because the Germans couldn't see them, but it made navigation rather difficult, not to say frightening. *Not,* she told herself, *that I can let myself be frightened of anything ever again. I mean to be a soldier now, like Hector, even if I can't be in any official organization. I'll know in my heart I'm a soldier for England, and a soldier never quails before anything.*

Still, she was thinking of getting a candle when she heard a low ghastly groan coming from the nearest room. She froze, desperately wanting to run, and told herself that with so many real terrors, she'd be a fool to believe in ghosts.

The sound repeated, and she heard a grinding, low and repetitive, and a metallic rattle that was somehow familiar. Ghosts, she seemed to recall, sometimes wore chains . . .

Whatever it was, it couldn't be a line of German soldiers, so she had to be brave and go in. What was the worst it could be? A rat? An old lady in a rocking chair?

A dead old lady in a rocking chair?

She clamped her teeth together and opened the door.

A second later she ran, not quite screaming but certainly gasping, back to the parlor, where Algernon and Diana stared at her, he in amazement, she in irritation.

"There's . . . there's . . ." she panted.

"Calm down. What is it?" Algernon asked.

"It's a giant bug, tied up, in terrible pain!"

"She found Uncle Walter," Diana said. "You should have warned her. Good night dear, I'll be back tomorrow." She leaned in to kiss his scarred face, and he moved to evade her as soon as he felt the brush of her lips.

"You don't have to."

"Shut up," she said, and left.

"What's Uncle Walter?" Phil asked, catching her breath. *What*, for that thing back there could not possibly have been a *who*.

"Another one who left the farm," Algernon said. "He went away to the Great War—the war to end all wars, they called it—a happy young buck who rode to the hounds and had quite a way with the ladies. A few years later they sent us home that. You must have seen him in dim light. That's the gas mask. He's wearing his old helmet too, I'm sure. He always does."

"He was hunched over and rocking, and I heard a chain. I thought maybe . . ." She was too embarrassed to say what she'd thought.

"He's handcuffed himself to the radiator. In cold weather he locks himself to the bed so he doesn't get burned—he's mad, not stupid—but he prefers the radiator. He's sure he can't get away from that."

"Is he dangerous?"

"He says he is. He only handcuffs himself on the bad days, though. Sometimes he's almost normal."

"What happened to him?"

"They called it shell shock, but we all know a shell had nothing to do with it. This," he said, wiggling his fingers at his ruined face, "is shell shock. What Uncle Walter has is pure human-induced insanity, self-chosen, as the least of all available evils. Shall I tell you? You seem pretty gung ho, and I don't want to put you off war."

"Please."

"He's talked about it a few times. You can't imagine how it was. Half his friends blown to bits in the most horrible ways. Not that there's any particularly good way to be blown to bits, but when I was in France, people seemed to die cleanly. Better guns these days, I suppose. In the trenches back then, it was all leaking intestines and gangrenous legs and screaming for days stuck in no-man's-land."

"That would be enough to drive most people mad," Phil said.

"No, he got through that part. He said every second he thought about running away, but he didn't. He said he was so scared, he vomited ten times a day, hid his face in his helmet and cried, and didn't bother to learn anyone's name because they'd be dead the next morning. He was terrified of dying, yet he thought about strolling out on the battlefield and letting a sniper take him cleanly, just to get it over with. He thought about all these things, went quietly crazy inside, kept it to himself, and soldiered on.

"Then one day they caught another boy, just like him. A farm boy not even seventeen, who got so scared and lonely he crept off to an abandoned barn to hide and fell asleep while his friends were killing and dying in droves. When they found him, he had his thumb in his mouth and was cuddling a letter from his mother under his cheek. They charged him with desertion and court-martialed him within days. While his unit was still at the front, they drove him a mile back behind the lines, tied him to a post with a red X on his chest, and picked twelve men for the firing squad. Uncle Walter was one of those men. He shot the boy, then allowed himself to go mad at last. At least the boy died fast, not holding his guts together in the frozen mud. He had ten bullet holes in his chest, and one between his eyes. Uncle Walter was a sharpshooter, you see."

"But the man deserted," Phil said slowly, trying to puzzle out her feelings.

"He was a boy, not a man, and you don't know what you're talking about." Algernon's easygoing jocularity was suddenly gone. "If you shoot a human being for being afraid, you might as well shoot him for being cold, or hungry. You can hide fear, like Uncle Walter did for a while, but you can't help it. Pray God you never have to find out."

"I'll do my part in the Home Guard."

"You can't. You're a girl. Besides, there isn't one here."

"Then I'll make one. Even if I'm the only active member. Now, I need sturdy boots please."

He laughed at her. "What do you think you're going to do?"

"Whatever I can to keep the Germans from conquering England. It's their fault, then as now, that innocent boys aren't allowed to be quietly cowardly in the bosom of their families where no one need ever know. And that is why," she added, striking a dramatic pose she didn't realize was ludicrous, "I will fight to the death to keep them out of England."

Algernon shook his head. "You should go out with the hop pickers. Earn your keep here and maybe take your mind off things for a while."

Phil's withering look was lost on the blind man, but her silence was not.

"Very well. You can wear Uncle Walter's old boots, I suppose. He has several sets of them. They're in his closet."

She didn't want to go back in that room with the poor madman in the gas mask, but she had to be brave, about everything.

"Why exactly is he wearing handcuffs?" she asked.

"When it was time to shoot the boy who deserted, he thought about shooting his commanding officer and as many of the other ranking men as he could get instead. He still isn't sure he made the right decision, and he wants to be sure he doesn't do something rash now. And then, as he will surely tell you one day if you get a bit of cider into him, he's the bloodiest murderer in the county. He was a sharpshooter, remember. He killed a hundred men at least. He says he never knows when he might kill again."

"Did you kill anyone?" Phil asked.

"I didn't kill anyone, and I didn't save anyone. I was just there, like a tourist. A tourist with one hell of a souvenir. Good night, magician girl."

Chapter 4

Phil meant to get straight to business at dawn, but her theatrical life had conditioned her to late hours, and she didn't stagger into the dining room until nine. Mrs. Pippin had been awake since five to chivvy the hop pickers into action.

Algernon took care of the cows, making his halting way to the milking shed, where they let themselves into their stalls and waited patiently. There were only four, but it still took him the better part of the morning to milk them by feel. The farm cats had learned to follow close behind, because he spilled a quarter of it, and he always had trouble with the steam sterilizer, but he was determined to do what he could and only laughed at the thought of the additional damage a steam burn could do to his face.

"Everyone's gone. Except Uncle Walter, that is," Fee said. "Algie left these for you." She indicated a pair of boots under the table. They were old but impeccably polished and looked only slightly too big.

"They're Uncle Walter's. Algie thought you might not want to deal with him yourself."

What he'd actually said was "Uncle Walter used to be quite the ladies' man, back when he had all his marbles. The sight of a girl like Phil might shock him out of his insanity, and frankly we're all used to it by now. Having a genuine madman in the family lends a certain panache."

But the boots, bolstered with two pairs of socks, did admirably, and Phil turned this way and that before the slightly foggy old mirror, as happy as if she had a new part to play in the Hall of Delusion. Her outfit was a bit plain, though, so she cinched in her waist with a gold-dyed alligator belt as wide as her hand. And because a magician is always thinking about her craft, she repaired to her room and took a needle and thread to the back waistband of her brand-new dungarees, transferring something from one of her too-showy outfits.

"Are you coming with me?" she asked, hoping Fee would decline. Fee was fine on strolls, useless on walks. She had a distressing tendency to stop every ten feet and marvel at some perfectly bland piece of nature, and with imminent battle on her mind, the last thing Phil wanted was to be forced to praise a thistle.

"No—if you don't mind, I'll stay here and take care of the chickens."

Mrs. Pippin had offered Fee a chance to pick hops, proffering no money but hinting that she could earn her board. Fee had been about to reluctantly agree when a flock of speckled Sussex hens strutted by the window, led by a ginger-colored rooster and flanked by a small brownish chicken with a fierce red eye who pecked anyone who got too close to her. Sprinkled among them were what looked to Fee like tennis balls with legs, perfectly round fuzzy yellow chicks.

"Oh, the darlings!" Fee had said with an emphatic sigh.

Mrs. Pippin, spotting opportunity, had said, "Or would you rather be in charge of the poultry while you're here?" The chickens were the bane of her existence. She could tolerate the lone pig, who sat in one spot and grew fat for the sole purpose of being eaten—it knew its place. She harbored some actual affection for the decoratively anonymous sheep who, if they didn't kill themselves with their own stupidity, provided bountiful wool. And the cows were soothing, predictable. The chickens, however, were clever, inquisitive, vindictive, and worse than rats about getting into things. They left great green-black viscous droppings everywhere and destroyed the new peas.

And so Fee became mistress of the chickens, the geese, the small flock of ducks, and the ridiculously scaled-down bantams. She became like a mother hen herself, coaxing them off their eggs, arbitrating their many quarrels, and cuddling their chicks even when they grew up to be roosters with deadly spurs.

Phil walked to the village first. She didn't quite believe the insular Mrs. Pippin or her sarcastic son and wanted to find out what sort of home defense already existed. What she found disgusted her.

"Siren?" said the postmistress. "We've got the church bells if there's an emergency."

"But don't you know the bells are supposed to be used to relay warnings in case of land invasion, not for air raids? There's a prohibition on bell ringing so as not to send false alarms."

She only laughed. "The church bell rang ninety-five times when Old Granny Braeburn passed on last week. Wouldn't she be tickled to think she'd started a rumor of invasion! A greater gossip there never was."

Mr. Henshawe, owner of the tiny grocery store, was no more help.

"Guns? Pah, who needs game with a mouthful of lead in every bite when they can get a nice bit of tinned meat here?" He held up a can of Spam.

"But you need them to fight the Germans if they invade!"

"Why on earth would they come here? We're in the middle of nowhere. They'll come from the east coast, or parachute on London. They won't call upon us on their way. Whatever happens, it won't concern us."

I hope they ration every single thing you sell and you go out of business, Phil thought viciously as she left. *Not concern you!* she wanted to shout. *Not concern you, when a Hun has your head on a bayonet?*

She looked for young men to rally but found only one, who just sniggered at the word *duty.*

"You'll find slim pickings in young men," the vicar told her as he swept the church steps. "We lost so many to the Great War, and to influenza, that there were very few children born here for a decade or more."

"You then, vicar—will you take up a rifle and defend England?"

"You're joking, of course. But do you know I boxed in the seminary? I was quite good in my day." Phil's eyes lit up, and she almost challenged the vicar to a friendly bout then and there. "But no, I will not take up a gun. I only punched people who asked me to and were close enough to punch me in return. If the Germans come, I will try to make peace."

Shades of Neville Chamberlain, she thought as she left the church and headed back to the farmland.

She passed the oast house with its great pointed foolscap bells for drying the hops. Beyond that, on the flatter land, were the hop fields themselves, acres of towering vines supported on trellised wires. Nearby, and stretching in vast orchards to the south of Bittersweet, were the lush-bodied apple trees, their hard fruit slowly mellowing.

As she walked, she burned with fury over the villagers' utter indifference to the state of the world. Bombs might not be falling on their own heads, but they were still English and owed it to their country to do something—anything. No one was saving scrap metal to make planes or old bones to make glycerin for explosives. No one followed blackout protocol, and there were no night patrols or plane spotters.

"I won't let them be indifferent," she swore aloud. "I'll drag them out of their complacency and *make* them train. If any Germans parachute here, they'll get the surprise of their lives." She could see herself mounted on one of the old shire horses—so what if she couldn't ride, they looked broad-backed and steady—holding a Tommy gun and leading the pugilist vicar and the rest into battle.

She saw it almost as a stage setting, herself illuminated with brave orange light. It would be a beautiful scene.

Furious, scheming, dreaming (and if she had understood herself properly, acting, more than anything), she strode across the hills. She was mostly burning off her nervous energy, assuaging her need to simply do something, but she told herself she was searching for a place to train on the day when she finally assembled a force for the Home Guard. "A big open flat field for maneuvers—one that isn't covered with hops or hay or apples or sheep."

She walked doggedly for an hour, and it wasn't until her feet in their overlarge boots began to ache that she realized what a fool she was. Of course the villagers would never hike all the way out here for their maneuvers, and with petrol and even tire rubber rationed like everything else, they couldn't drive either. She was envisioning leading an entire army of farmers, but all she could probably hope for was a ragtag smattering of old men she could guilt into joining her, and a handful of lazy farmhands too backward to even qualify as cannon fodder, with perhaps a lad or two attracted by her looks. For that reluctant rabble, she might as well use the village green.

And even that, she finally admitted with dismay, was being optimistic. More likely they'd just ignore her rallying cry or, worse, laugh at her.

The land rose, and she was giving serious thought to heading home to soak her poor feet in Epsom salts when she heard voices just beyond the rise. Deep voices, male and young. Perfect, she decided, sight unseen, for her newly organized Home Guard. Her spirits, ever buoyant, began to rally. *I can do it,* she thought. She tugged down her wine-colored sweater, fluffed her long loose hair (because she knew how effective advertising is in wartime), and marched upward to recruit them.

She broke off from humming "The Bear Walked over the Mountain" and gasped. The men were suddenly inconsequential. Beyond them was a wonderland, a Xanadu, of trees that towered to the clouds, flowers in such profusion that she felt giddy with their scent, silvered rills that snaked calligraphy through it all. She caught her breath—it was all too much, scent and sight, the cacophony of a thousand songbirds.

Could it be an open-air zoo? She spied something striped and sinuous creeping through a heavy-blossomed thicket. *It cannot be a tiger,* she thought. Another movement caught her eye, and on the far shore of a twisting, maple-fringed lake, she saw a summerhouse sprout like a mushroom, all in the space of a moment. A movie set, perhaps? A tent? She herself was skilled at quick prop-work. It must be inflatable.

At the center of it all, on a slight rise, stood the most lovely building she could imagine, shimmering golden under the noon sun. Was it a castle or a cathedral? It was extravagantly Gothic, a riot of arches and buttresses, of great mullioned windows with red and gold stained glass.

Fee, seeing it, would have dreamed of loving the young heir, of fairies in the garden and lost treasures buried on the grounds, of maidens drowned in the mere and gypsies camping in the meadow, filling the estate with their wild music.

Phil, seeing it, thought that whoever could afford to spend such vast sums of money on exotic plants and beasts must surely have the money to provide weapons and training for the Home Guard, and probably a slew of gardeners and gamekeepers to volunteer. She marched up to the two men—young lords of the manor, no doubt—on the other side of a ha-ha and prepared to plead her case.

One of the young men spoke first.

"Are you certain, sir, that she cannot see us?" He looked like a beautiful shepherd, just the sort Venus or Inanna would admire, with fair curling hair springing tenderly behind his ears. He was dressed, incongruously, like a particularly outré Oscar Wilde, in an aubergine velvet jacket and extravagantly spotted yellow silk neckerchief, above which his innocent face peered, a lamb in wolf's clothing. He looked at Phil curiously, then turned back to his companion.

"Not us, nor Stour. Have you so little faith in your masters, lad?" This man was a bit older, dark and severe, with black hair pulled back in a tight queue and eyes deeply shadowed by heavy winged brows. He wore tight riding breeches and boots. He didn't trouble to look at Phil at all, but took the other man's arm and began to stroll along the border of the sunken, walled ditch that separated them from the interloper.

Phil looked after them, frowning, then began to follow. Apparently they believed her beneath their notice. Well, she had her own opinions about class structure, but she'd keep them to herself long enough to secure their patronage. Why, a man rich enough to own that Gothic monstrosity might buy the village a tank.

"I could swear she looked right at the castle, and then at me, sir."

The dark man sighed. "It is entirely possible that the more sensitive commoners might feel a certain . . . awareness . . . of this place. They may feel themselves compelled to pause and admire the prospect, but mark my words, they will never glimpse so much as a stone of Stour. The magical protection is too strong for that. Stour has been hidden from the world here for forty years so far. I doubt the spells will come undone the first day you take your place on the watch."

"Why have the watch then, sir?"

"Because we dare not let anything interfere with our sacred mission. You know what would become of the world if we failed."

The lovely boy kept looking back at Phil over his shoulder. "I think she's following us."

"Nonsense!" the other said, annoyed. Really, prentices were so woefully stupid, confusing coincidence with purpose. "She cannot see us, or the castle, or even the ha-ha, but the magic ensures she sees a barrier nonetheless. Swampy ground or cow droppings, whatever is necessary to keep her from prying. Like any creature, she walks along the obstruction to see a way past. Any moment now she will give up and turn away." He stopped and faced Phil, looking at her with such little interest that she might be a sheep.

Phil smiled at them and said, "Hello!"

"Sir!"

"I heard her. Coincidence. It was used as an exclamation, not a greeting. Perhaps she sees some rare bird behind us. In the nesting season there are a great number of collectors out here looking for eggs—"

"Excuse me, but I'm not looking for eggs. I'd like to speak to the owner of the house. Stour, did you say? It's about the Home Guard."

She waited, looking as pleasant as she could. The nerve of them to ignore her for so long—and what was that hogswallow about not being able to see the castle? Perhaps it was one of those stately homes closed to visitors. Well, she didn't want to tour their ridiculous gardens (which should be plowed up and sowed with carrots) or buy a souvenir stamped with the family crest. She just wanted rifles, radios, and oh, wouldn't it be heavenly to have her very own antiaircraft gun? Her dreams, so recently crushed, rose phoenixlike from the ashes of her doubts.

"Prentice, fetch two or three of the other masters. I should be able to deal with this, but"—the dark-haired man swallowed hard—"it is possible that something has gone seriously wrong. Don't alarm anyone, but hurry."

"Yes, Master," the young man said, and hastened through the wooded lakeside toward the house.

"You see," Phil went on hopefully, "the village is wholly unprepared, and something really must be done. If I could just talk with whoever is in charge for a moment?"

"It can't be as it seems," the man said.

"Oh, but it is. Hardly anyone has blackout curtains, and can you believe it? There's not even a siren."

"Can she be mad? Or rehearsing for a play? Of course, that must be it. I'm as bad as a prentice, believing I see meaning in random events." He leaned over the ha-ha and peered at Phil. "Yes, she certainly is a commoner. Not a spark of magic about her. Coincidence, nothing more." He chuckled to himself. "Imagine, a commoner suddenly able to see past the barriers. Still, couldn't hurt to check."

He squatted on his haunches and placed his hands on the ground, his fingers digging through the thick grass until they reached dirt. He closed his eyes, and for a fleeting moment a look of ecstatic joy crossed his face as a vibration of power surged up from the earth. Under his touch, the deep emerald grass brightened to a neon hue, as faintly incandescent as a glowworm at noon. But Phil didn't notice, for she was looking at the young man's intense face, wondering why the good-looking ones were always nutters.

The man stood, brushing off his hands. Just as he thought—the barriers were firmly in place. No one would be able to see anything beyond the ha-ha save a stretch of bland, uninviting countryside, and if he tried to traverse it, he would find his feet always turned in the wrong direction. Stour was perfectly concealed from anyone but a magician, and it was clear this girl was no magician. There was no charge of earth-force around her. She was as anonymous and uninteresting as an animal, as common as the starlings that settled in a dark murmuration in the meadow behind her.

"Everything is just fine," he said with smug complacency.

"But it isn't—that's the problem," Phil said, and leaped across the ha-ha.

The man staggered back and gave a cry that, since Phil was feeling uncharitable, she would have almost called a scream. It startled the flock of starlings into flight, and they wheeled madly overhead. He went ghastly white and shook his head in disbelief, plainly terrified. She whirled around. Was it a bomber? A paratrooper? Only an invasion could make a grown man so distraught. But there was nothing—just her.

"If you'll only let me explain," she tried again.

The man seemed to gather his courage. He planted his feet squarely, stared her fiercely in the eye—and Phil was certain he was about to sic his bailiff on her. *Oh well,* she thought. Perhaps he'd give a few pounds, but all hopes of her own personal antiaircraft gun flew away on the breeze. The man looked angry enough to loose the dogs on her, and she was glad that even though he was evidently a lord, he didn't have medieval rights over those on his land. He'd probably send her to the dungeon, all for trying to save England. *All nobles,* she thought, *should be sent to the front lines.*

The man closed his black eyes, concentrating deeply. Very faintly, so subtly that Phil began to rub her eyes, colors began to coalesce from the air and gather around him. Amber deep as honey rose in a pulsating swirl from the earth, and emerald and ruby lights danced like sparks in an opal, whirling faster and faster until he suddenly flung open his eyes in a manic stare and shouted, "Die, intruder!"

Behind her, speckled starlings began to fall from the sky, hitting the ground with soft feather-muffled thuds like dud artillery. The grass around her withered, and the purple clovers grew ashen.

Phil, looking at his intense, handsome face, didn't notice. She blinked at him, wondered if it was possible to have sunstroke in the crisp fall weather, and said, "That's not very hospitable."

He stared at her, aghast. "What are you?" he breathed, as from behind him came the scurrying steps of men who seemed unaccustomed to hurrying. Two were portly and dressed in velvet smoking jackets. The third looked like an aging film star, perhaps eighty, but tall and lean with a steel-gray goatee. He wore tweeds with leather patches on the elbows and held a drooping unlit ivory pipe.

They may not be the most martial material, Phil thought, *but at least they are men. The portly ones can be plane spotters, but that fine old gentleman should be leading drills.* He was clothed like a professor, but there was an unmistakable military air about the way he stood in perfect parade rest. She addressed herself to him. The young dark fellow looked ill.

"I'm awfully sorry to have disturbed you, but I've come from the village on important business."

He ignored her. "What have you done, Master Arden?" the old man said.

"Headmaster Rudyard, I . . . the commoner crossed the divide and I feared—"

Phil pressed her lips together in smug satisfaction to see the arrogant young man taken down a peg. Abashed and stammering, he stared down at the dead starlings and looked as if he wanted to sink into the earth.

"In fear, and not with thoughtful purpose, you used the forbidden magic. You sought to kill a human."

"But she is only a commoner, and somehow she can see us. She can cross the divide!"

"Silence! The only saving grace is that you failed. I do not know what shames me more—that you attempted the taboo magic, or that your powers were not equal to it. Perhaps we were too hasty in advancing you from journeyman. Arden, you are henceforth in durance, and forbidden to draw from the earth until we have decided your punishment."

Phil smiled. This distinguished old bloke was evidently in charge and was putting that Arden fellow properly in his place. She didn't understand half of it, but any minute now the gentleman would apologize, and to make it up to her, he'd be obligated to help with the Home Guard.

"Will you fuddle her at once, Headmaster?" one of the plump men asked in a stage whisper.

"I shall, and she'll be quickly on her way, none the wiser." He looked steadily at Phil for a moment until she felt uncomfortable. Again, the air grew heavy with translucent color, and she blinked heavily in the intense sunlight, wondering what on earth was wrong with her eyes.

"It's men we need, and weapons, too. Or money, I suppose. Sir? You have been a soldier, sir?" The stiffness of his spine and an intensity in his eyes made her certain.

He flicked a disdainful glance at Arden, then spread his fingers parallel to the ground and assumed a look of intense concentration. After a moment he stopped with a sigh. "Not a single thing. She should be bound with all the force of the Essence—but nothing. The power is here, in me, but it has no effect on her." The other men looked frightened, but the old gentleman only said, "Curious."

"I knew my magic wasn't faulty!" Arden said, and Headmaster Rudyard frowned him into silence.

He addressed Phil at last. "As for you, my lady, will you come with me?" He held out his arm.

Phil had scarcely been listening to their conversation. She saw herself facing down a troop of German invaders, so well equipped that they surrendered on sight. She placed her hand in the crook of his arm and marched through that writhing Eden of vines and flowers toward Stour Manor as proudly as if she were taking her third curtain call after a death-defying escape. *Some men,* she thought, *know how to treat a visitor—and a lady.*

As she passed, she surreptitiously stuck her tongue out at Arden and mouthed, "Beast!"

She was not quite so pleased when, at the great arched entrance, a half-dozen men in the oddest assortment of clothes seized her and carried her off, kicking, clawing, and cursing like a sailor, to a dark room, where they bound her hand and foot with hemp ropes and tossed her onto a chaise.

She felt slightly better when Arden was brought into the room, too, where he submitted to being tied to a chair.

Her mood improved considerably when she let her breath out and found that the ropes were just slack enough to work with. The considerate men had bound her hands behind her, so it was easy enough to reach the tiny pocket she had sewn into the back waistband of every garment she owned — a sensible precaution for a girl who makes her living by letting herself be tied up. She bypassed the handcuff key and the two slivers of metal, pointed at one end, cocked at the other, and plucked out the razor blade.

And when she was free and her eyes had fully adjusted to the gloom, she was practically ecstatic, for the fools had locked her in a sort of armory. Amid heads and horns and stuffed beasts hung fowling pieces and rifles and impossibly long-barreled muskets, all quite old but clean and oiled. There were swords and daggers, pikes and flails — all manner of deadly, pointy things. She shrugged off the ropes, snatched up the deadliest, pointiest thing she could find — a curved Rajput tulwar sword — and pressed the tip to Arden's throat before he could think to call for help. She looked as if she'd done it a hundred times before. She hadn't. She'd done it a thousand times at least, rehearsing for the grand decapitation scene the Albions so often used for their finale.

"Now," she said in her most thrilling stage voice, "tell me what the bloody hell is going on here!"

Arden wished with all his heart he'd managed to kill her after all, even if it meant his demotion back to journeyman or, worse yet, his expulsion from the College of Drycraeft, the English school of magic.

Chapter 5

I don't fear death!" Arden said, lifting his chin to expose his throat more fully to the blade. All the same, his neck was tight with tension, its sinews standing out. In the saltcellar hollows above his collarbone where his white shirt gaped, Phil could see his pulse beating, swift and strong.

"Of course you don't," Phil said sweetly. "But you do fear pain. Or you'll soon learn to." She pushed the tip a fraction harder against his skin. "Tell me why they tied me up. What is this place?"

She fervently hoped he'd say something, because she really had no idea what to do next. On the stage, this was her cue to swing the blade back dramatically, angling it to catch the blue light aimed by a hidden stagehand, and then with a ululating battle cry chop off his head. Well, not his head, exactly, but a waxwork simulacrum with a balloon full of viscous blood-red syrup that was substituted at the last instant. And of course the sword was flimsy foil that would hardly cut a blancmange. She knew in her heart she was all show. There was no way she'd hurt someone who was tied up, not even this arrogant nutcake who'd blathered on about magic and killing and . . . Oh! That must be it. He was crazy, just like Uncle Walter. Well, that explained him. *What a shame,* she thought, pulling her blade back and cocking her head to study him. He was rather good-looking, if you liked that black-haired, arrogant, surly sort . . .

Perhaps it explained the others, too. Yes, this must be an insane asylum. Because the things the other men had talked about, things she'd barely heard at the time, lost as she was in her own dreams of guns and arms, were now slowly coming back to her. And they only made sense if this was a house of lunatics.

What Arden said next confirmed it.

"We are magicians in the College of Drycraeft, servants of the earth and ministers of the Essence that flows through her. And you, whoever you are, are an unnatural aberration who will no doubt be killed as soon as the masters have time to confer."

Privately, he hoped they would not confer too long, though given the glacial pace of most of the college's decisions, the girl's ridiculously red hair would go gray before they came to any conclusion. It was one of many things that irked him about the college, but now that he was a master, he hoped to institute certain reforms.

"If you're a magician, why don't you get out of those ropes? Or don't you do escapism?"

Arden glared at her. "I've given my word not to draw from the Essence. I can do no magic until the Conclave of Masters decides my punishment."

"Hmm. Convenient, isn't it?" She lowered the tulwar and went to the door, listening intently. "Tell me how to get out of this place. Is this an official asylum, then, or does your family just have an unfortunate gene?"

"You think I'm insane?"

"They say if you have wit enough to ask, you aren't. I'd supposed that's why you aren't at the front. If you aren't crazy, you ought to be ashamed of yourself, a big hale fellow like you. You should be fighting for your country instead of playing children's games. Magicians, indeed! You should have picked your shill a little more carefully. I'm one of the Albions, and what I don't know about magic you could fit on the head of a pin." She tossed her hair and made a *humph* sound. Arden, against his will, liked the one but not the other.

Albion? Albion! Godric Albion, the Traitor! Realization upon realization rushed at him, overwhelmed him, and suddenly he was screaming for help, pulling against his ropes until his skin peeled away.

"Shut up!" Phil hissed desperately. If he brought all those madmen running . . . even with her weapon, she might not be able to hold them off.

Arden ignored her. It all made sense. If this girl was who he thought she was, her ancestor was stripped of his magic almost three hundred years ago. The textbooks said that made him a commoner, devoid of any ability to use the Essence. But there were whispers that it had made him something even worse than a commoner. What if he, and his descendants, were utterly separate from the Essence, immune to it? If she was here to attack them, there was nothing their magic could do to her. An Albion had almost destroyed the college before. He wouldn't let this one do the same.

He shouted for help until he hardly had breath. What this girl's sudden appearance meant, he could not say for sure. All he knew was that something very close to panic had seized him. She must be put down, like vermin.

"Be quiet, now, or I'll—" She raised the tulwar, this time aiming the spiked pommel at his head. A hard blow might knock him unconscious. Or it might kill him.

She couldn't, not quite. Puffing an exasperated sigh at what she called her weakness, she ran to the door and listened again, then slipped out and down the portrait-lined corridor. Arden's yells echoed behind her.

Holding her tulwar high—she had visions of impaling herself in a headlong fall, and wouldn't that be a pretty way to go?—she dashed around corner after corner, getting ever more helplessly lost. It wasn't until she chanced peeking behind a closed door and caught a glimpse out a window that she even realized she was on the second floor. She could see the lake and the blushing maples and tried to keep that orientation in mind when she resumed her search for an exit. She barreled past a line of little boys who looked at her in thrilled amazement, though not fear. Racing, armed, red hair flying, Phil was like an air raid siren shrilling through their rote lives.

Were there no stairs in this damned place? It was all hallways and rooms. She checked more and more doors. Some led to empty bedrooms, some to vacant classrooms, but none led to egress. Nearly at the end of her tether, she flung open one more door and found a man just stepping out of a claw-footed bath. Phil was about to retreat in shame when she decided, no, this had gone on far too long. Pointing her blade at his chubby pink and white nakedness, she said, "Show me how to get out of this madhouse."

He fumbled for his spectacles, gave a girlish shriek when at last he saw the interloper clearly, and dove for the nearest garment he could find, which, alas, was no more than a polka-dotted necktie. Still, it covered the vital bits if he didn't walk too fast, so Phil gritted her teeth, torn between mirth and mortification, and urged him with gentle pokes out to the corridor.

He led her silently, with nervous backward glances, to an ornate double door carved with spiral patterns. There he stopped, trembling.

"Oh, very well," she said, and pushed both doors open herself. But instead of a rush of sunlight and freedom, she saw a spacious, windowless, torch-lit room with a massive wooden table in its center. Seated around it, in chairs only a step down from thrones, were some twenty men and one little boy half-hidden in the shadows.

Phil turned on her nearly naked guide with a snarl, but before she could flee, he gathered the last, perhaps only, drop of his courage and shoved her as hard as he could, propelling her into the room. His momentum sent him after her, and he collapsed in a dead faint, his necktie, unfortunately, askew.

The doors closed behind them, apparently of their own volition.

She tugged at the doors, but they wouldn't budge. Whirling, she glared at the conclave. "How dare you treat me like this! I'm an English citizen and a representative of the Home Guard"—a lie in a good cause—"and my sister and my . . . my father will be coming in search of me." Her voice, which had started out stage-strong, began to falter, and she felt like she was on the verge of tears. *Whatever happens,* she told herself, *I'll never let them fall. If you can't be brave, at least you can act like someone who is brave.* She'd acted like an executioner and a mer-girl and a snared fox and a queen onstage. Surely she could act like someone who felt no fear.

She steeled herself as one of the men rose. It was the gentleman she'd met earlier, whose arm she'd taken so trustingly. Well, she had a thing or two to say to him!

Unfortunately, with all those eyes on her in the flickering torch-light, she couldn't quite recall what they were at the moment.

"You are a resourceful girl," he said, walking a step or two nearer but stopping when she made a motion with the sword. He turned to one of the men still seated. "I say, Barnaby, did you by any chance tie her up in the *Game Room?*" His tone was affable, but Phil noticed an edge to it.

"It is the only room that's never in use, Headmaster Rudyard, and I thought —"

"You thought you'd put our prisoner in a ROOMFUL OF WEAP-ONS!" For a breath he looked furious, and most of the people in the room, including Phil, cringed, but the next moment he was all smiles and bonhomie again. *Like correcting a dog with a sharp word,* Phil thought. And like a dog, the man who had erred looked abashed but slavishly eager to please the next time.

The Headmaster turned again to Phil. "You see, we are so un-worldly here at Stour that we forget some of the subtleties of life. Such as, do not arm your enemy. Particularly when it may not be in your power to disarm her."

"I'm not your enemy," Phil said.

"No? Is not the mongoose the enemy of the krait? The little snake may bite and bite, but the mongoose is immune to its deadly venom, you see. Immune." He let the word linger.

"I just want to leave," Phil said desperately, reaching back to try the door again. She knew she could pick the lock—doors or chains or handcuffs, it made no difference to her—but it would take her a few seconds at least, perhaps longer if it was a tricky device, and she couldn't turn away from these men. Maybe she could do it one-handed behind her back, as she did the handcuffs and the simple pad-locks they used onstage, but she couldn't do it left-handed and didn't dare shift her sword.

"I'm afraid that isn't possible, young lady. You've stumbled on a secret organization."

"Are you Nazis?" she gasped, electrified.

The Headmaster frowned in puzzlement and bent to confer with one of the men in a brief whisper, then shook his head. "No, we are not Nazis. We are . . . something else."

"If this is an asylum, I understand you don't want word to get out. Is this where the nobility sends their batty sons and crazy cousins? Fine, that's none of my business. But surely you know that you can't keep me here. I'm sorry I came onto your property, but the worst you can do is have me before the magistrate on trespassing charges." She hoped that if everything she said was rational and practical, this might all somehow start to make sense.

"We are not mad," the Headmaster said, smiling gently within the shelter of his neat silver goatee. "It is only that we ought to kill you."

He said it so calmly, it actually slipped by her for a second. *Oh, well, if that's all* . . . Then the full force of her dire situation struck her.

Even if she was brave enough to hack through some of them, she'd be overpowered by sheer numbers. This was her finale, and she had to decide how to face it. This was the water tank escape in the third minute, when her lungs were burning and her brain was screaming *breathe!* and at any moment her mouth would obey and gulp in a deep breath of death.

She gripped her tulwar tighter and narrowed her eyes at the Headmaster. She would launch a preemptive attack, and he, their leader, would be the first to fall to her blade. She hoped that might throw the others into such disarray that she could make her escape.

At least, she thought with a brief melodramatic return of her usual stage theatrics, *I will take a few of them with me when I die!*

She took a step toward the Headmaster, over the prone fleshy form of her erstwhile guide, and pointed her sword tip at his chest.

"We *ought* to kill you," he said, without moving or seeming the least concerned. "But we cannot. One of our number has spoken for you. A prentice, it is true, but our laws are ancient and unequivocal. Any objection to a death sentence must be honored."

A small figure materialized from the flickering torch-shadows at the edge of the room.

Phil dropped her sword with a clatter and had the boy in her arms in a heartbeat. She wasn't afraid anymore. Madmen and murder—they couldn't count for anything in a world that allowed miracles.

Her little adopted brother Stan was alive.

She hugged him fiercely, burying her face in his dark shaggy curls. She kept her eyes closed for the longest time, only feeling him, afraid to look at him directly in case she'd been wrong. But no, he smelled like her Stan, too. When he came to the Albion family, he had had nothing more than a spare shirt and a string of sandalwood beads, tied up in a handkerchief. The beads never lost their smell. He kept them between his folded clothes, and their sweet warm spice always hung about him. Phil took a deep breath and opened her eyes.

"Stanislaus Bambula has joined our order in the College of Drycraeft as a junior prentice. He claims—he swears—that you are no threat to us, and so we must let you live. Against our better judgment, I might add. Against *my* better judgment."

She looked into Stan's otter-brown eyes, eyes so dark they were almost black, but with an earthy depth, a softness, that black eyes never quite attain. Black eyes glitter—they reflect, like glass or obsidian. The darkest brown eyes draw you in.

"Why did they take you?" she asked, kneeling and gazing up at her brother.

"Don't worry, Phil," he said, and she felt her heart catch at that familiar voice, the strange mix of Shakespearean precision and Cockney and some vague central European accent he'd picked up in his short but varied life.

"Don't worry?" she asked, incredulous. "Come on, we're leaving right now." She glared over his shoulder at the gathering of men, daring them to stop her.

"I can't," Stan said gently. "I won't. This is where I belong."

"You're confused. What happened? Were you hurt in the bombings? Did they bring you here?" Her fingers traced spider steps over his skull but found no injury.

"I wasn't hurt," he said, enduring her fussing with a little squirm.

"And yes, they brought me here. But as soon as I arrived I knew — oh, Phil, this is home. Or as close to home as I'll ever have, without my own mum."

Phil frowned. He'd never said a word about his family, and she'd always assumed they'd died or abandoned him when he was too young to remember them.

"Our home is at the Hall of Delusion," she said firmly. "At least it was, and it will be again as soon as it's safe, but in any case your home is with us." She rose and took his hand, giving it a tug, but he stood firm, surprisingly stolid for his size.

"This is where I belong," he said. "I would have been here long ago, if only I'd known, but my mother always told me . . . well, that doesn't matter now. Believe me, I'm safe here, and happy."

"You don't know what you're talking about. These men — lunatics or perverts or whatever they might be — have kidnapped you and . . . and tricked you! I'm not leaving without you." She gave his hand another pull, but before it could dissolve into a battle, Headmaster Rudyard stepped nearer.

"As well to be hung for a sheep as a lamb, they said when I was a boy. It is clear that she won't leave without further assurance of your safety, Prentice Stanislaus. We may not kill her, we cannot contain her with magic, and I'm sure we can only toss her back over the ha-ha so many times before she decides to make herself a true nuisance. You say she is safe, prentice? Well, you may hold the future of the College of Drycraeft in your hands. If you think she can be trusted to hold her tongue, why don't you tell her about us."

Stan nodded. "And about her, sir?"

The Headmaster's silver caterpillar eyebrows twitched upward. "No. We know nothing about her, lad. We only suspect, and that is no better than the wagging tongues of old gossips. Go someplace you can be alone. The solar, perhaps. If we are very fortunate, she'll tell the world and end up locked in an asylum for the rest of her life and will trouble us no more."

Phil snaked out an arm and recaptured her sword. "Somewhere outside the manor, if you please."

The Headmaster chuckled. "Of course, of course. You are no prisoner—anymore."

"Neither is Stan," she retorted.

He did not answer her directly, only studied her for a long moment before saying, "Don't leave the grounds too quickly. There is still a matter I must discuss with you."

The doors clicked behind her, unlocking and swinging ajar. Holding Stan tightly, she backed out, telling herself that no matter what Stan might say, she was taking him back to Weasel Rue with her, even if she had to drag him all the way.

Stan led her through the woods, past vines growing as fast as twining snakes that reached for her arms. Unseen in the shrubbery, something large moved, making a sound between a purr and a growl. When the landscape opened near the lake's mossy bank, she glimpsed a flash of prancing white. A horse, she assured herself, wide-eyed. For there was no way she could have seen a horn.

"What is this place?" she breathed. If Rousseau had painted a madhouse, it would look like this. But Stan seemed to have no fear, so she clung to him and kept her terror secret when a golden bear lumbered across their path, ignoring them as it reared up to eat pink lychee nuts.

They sat together under the Japanese maples, on a high bank overlooking the lake. For a long moment Stan gazed over the water, watching the reflection of passing clouds until the surface was shattered by the stout, olive-colored body of a hunting pike. When at last he spoke, he didn't answer her directly.

"My mother never danced for me, but she told me of the nights when the campfires were so bright they blinded the moon, when fiddlers played songs that would lure gods from the heavens and ghosts from below, when the caravans looked like palaces. On those nights, she told me, she would dance, and it was beyond the power of any eye to look away from her. They took her when she was heavy with me, away from her family, away from her lovers, and locked her away in a place they called a university, in Dresden. It was a prison. There she bore me, and there we stayed for five years."

His voice was far away, and he spoke as if he had seen those womb-times with his own eyes.

"I don't understand. Who took your mother? Why?"

"We are Romany, Gypsies. She was a sorceress, renowned among her people. We were in Poland when they found her. They had taken members of our clan before, over the generations. It runs in our line, you see. They came from nowhere, and in an instant we were behind beautiful, cold stone walls. I know I can't remember—how could I?—yet I know there was a time when all the warmth and light fell out of the world. I was born a month later in the Universität Zauberhaft."

"But *why* did they take you?" Phil asked, knowing she was missing something crucial.

"Magic," he said. "Haven't you been listening?"

She had been, but in her mind there was only one kind of magic, and these people didn't seem to practice it. Any other definition would not be logically possible. She shook her head.

Stan smiled, a beacon in his shadowed face. "Look. Tell me what this is, if not magic."

He closed his eyes for a moment, and Phil thought he must be thinking of his favorite thing in the world, for every care in his serious young face seemed to vanish. He opened his eyes, beatific, and the ground began to shimmer beneath his crossed legs. It stirred some memory within her, like a recollection of a delicious smell, or the ghost of a loving touch from infancy, something so irrevocably lost it might never have been, yet so precious it made her heart hurt. Pale green light rose like a mist to envelop Stan, and he stretched out his hand to bestow a benediction upon the earth.

Then, at their feet, a flower began to grow.

The ground stirred and cracked, heaving from below as with a miniature incipient volcano, and then a spearhead of green cleft its way to the sunlight. In a matter of seconds it sprouted stem, leaves, and curving cat's-claw thorns, and at last a gaudy scarlet flower budded and blossomed and unfurled itself in sanguine glory.

"It's from Madagascar," Stan said as the jade glow faded. "I saw it in a book once."

Phil nudged his feet aside, first one, then the other. "There's a button, right, and a pneumatic device?"

Stan grinned.

"A projection then?" But she knew no smoke and mirrors could produce such a perfect illusion at close range. She could smell the damned thing! Already little flies rose from the lakeside mud to investigate its novel nectar. "A trapdoor?" she asked desperately.

"Magic," Stan said.

"It's not a real flower, then." She chuckled with relief. "All of this is an illusion. Thank goodness! I admit I was a little worried about the bear and the tiger. But if they're not real—"

"They're perfectly real—as long as they last." He waved his hand, and with an opalescent wave of light, a curtain of vines dissolved, revealing a nonplussed tiger, which vanished in turn a moment later.

Stan touched one of the delicate flower petals. "I created this, from nothing, using the powers of the earth. Nearly everything on these grounds was created by the magicians, drawn up out of nothing, here for a breath, and gone again, like everything that lives. We're all part of the Essence. I knew what it was even before I came here and they gave it a name. I could always summon the earth's power, though when I was in Dresden, I hid it as best I could. It was easier there—there's hardly any Essence outside of England."

She stared at him, dumbfounded. "You mean, it's *real* magic?"

He nodded.

"And this place—they can all do it?"

"It's a school. They call it the College of Drycraeft. The college of magic, in other words."

"That's what that bastard said, the one who mumbled nonsense about . . . ." She gasped. "Do you mean when he glared at me and told me to die, he was really doing magic to kill me?" Her hand went to her throat.

"That's what he meant to do, yes. That's why he's in so much trouble. It is absolutely forbidden to use the killing magic. I've only been here a few days, and I know that much already."

"But I'm alive!"

"Mm-hmm . . . well . . ." He shifted his gaze away. He wasn't supposed to talk about it, but this was his sister, practically, and maybe she had the right to know.

Phil saved him from any further conscience wrangling. "Ha! Is he the class dunce? I wish you could have seen his face when I didn't oblige him by dropping dead! Well, I hope they leave him tied up all night. Serves him right!"

Stan didn't mention that he'd likely get much worse than that.

"What happened to you and your mother, then? In Dresden."

"It was a terrible place." He shuddered. "For five years she pretended docility and obedience and schemed to escape. She taught me to hide my powers as best I could, but I couldn't—I couldn't!" He squeezed his eyes shut and went on. "They can't draw on the Essence there as they can in England, I don't quite know why. They are mad for power, though. They suck it from the earth, from beasts, and make use of anyone with even a hint of magic to help them gather more. It is hard to explain. I'm only just learning how my own powers work. The Germans, they used my mother like a milk cow, draining her daily for their own use. And they would have used me likewise, if we hadn't escaped.

"We couldn't go back to her people, and they'd think to look for us in Eastern Europe, so we fled west, to England. But they found us.

They found me. I was just coming into my power. I didn't know how to shield it, and they tracked us down. My mother gave herself up to help me get away. They . . . they killed her."

Phil put her arms around him and let her flaming hair fall over his face, while his small body shook with silent sobs.

"I soon learned to hide my powers," he said when he grew calm, "and for a time I lived in an orphanage."

"Where you met Hector."

"But I couldn't conceal my magic entirely, and eventually they found me again. I had to run. I made Hector come with me."

Magic — real? Phil could scarcely fathom it. She twirled the sword she held point down in the dirt. She'd thought it was a formidable weapon, but imagine being able to change a person's mind, to make him fall in love, to kill him, all with a thought.

Why, powers like that could win the war!

For either side . . .

"Then — was it only three days ago? — I was walking down by the river, and someone put a cloth with something nasty over my face. The next thing I knew, I was here. I thought it would be like the German school — Mother always told me to do whatever I could to stay out of the clutches of magicians. So I drained the Essence out of five masters before they convinced me that they were different. I realized this is exactly where I want to be. Where I need to be."

"You killed them?"

"Oh, no, just made them unconscious. We all have Earth Essence in us. Every living thing does. It's like energy, a life force. If you have a little taken away, you weaken. If you lose too much, you die."

She pictured entire battlefields of Germans falling unconscious.

She pictured Hitler, dying, just because someone willed it. Why, to have even one of these magicians fighting on England's side could turn the war.

Before she could think it through, Headmaster Rudyard picked his way through the ferns. She gripped the tulwar more tightly but didn't raise it.

"We have something very serious to discuss," he said, pacing like a general, hands clasped in the small of his back. "One of our number—the man you met before, Master Arden—committed a crime against you."

"String him up," Phil said casually, tossing her hair.

"By which you mean hanging? No, that is not our way," he said. "Had he succeeded in killing you, without authorization from the conclave, we would have little choice but to kill him. But it would not be by hanging. The entire college would have joined to drain him of his Essence. His life would pass through us and thence to the earth."

Phil stared at him, wide-eyed. "Just like that? What if . . . I mean, obviously I'm no threat . . ." The Headmaster pulled a wry face. "But if I had been, say, coming at him with a sword, wouldn't he be justified in fighting back?"

"No, certainly not. We are peaceful. To take a life, a human life, is blasphemy against everything we stand for."

"What exactly *do* you stand for?" Phil asked.

"There is no time for that at the moment. Your arrival places us in a delicate situation. Master Arden tried to kill you."

"And thank goodness he's at the bottom of his class, eh? I'm glad he's incompetent."

"Master Arden may be rash, may even be criminal, but he is a Master of Drycraeft, and his magic does not fail. What he did would have killed anyone, even another master. Even, perhaps, me. But it had no effect on you. Do you know why?"

She shook her head.

"I'm told that you and your family are stage magicians, illusionists. That you have been for centuries. I believe that generations of practicing the very antithesis of real magic has in some way made you immune to our power."

Phil saw the Headmaster's eyes flick fleetingly to meet Stan's. It sounded fishy to her. She hadn't really paid attention in school, but she gathered that the theory of acquired traits had been put to rest some eighty years ago. Giraffes did not get long necks by stretching them daily, and people did not become immune to real magic simply by actively not believing in it.

On the other hand, until recently she thought it was a proven fact that the only kind of magic in the world was the sort the Albions practiced. Perhaps facts needed to be rearranged.

"You mean, you can't cast a spell on me?" Phil asked.

"They aren't spells — there are no incantations or words of power. There is only the Essence. But yes, it seems that nothing magical can touch you. Arden could not kill you. I could not chain or fuddle you to make you forget you ever saw us. Stour has such magical barriers around it that no one who is not a magician can set foot on the grounds, and yet you hopped past the safeguards." He gave a little laugh. "Do you see now why you worried us?"

"Honestly, the only reason I came here was to get volunteers for the Home Guard."

"And now that I've had a moment to think about it, I see that you're no threat to us. Even if you told the world and led an army here, they couldn't breach our defenses. They could bump their noses against the very walls of Stour and never know it was there. Ah, but here he is. The criminal."

They turned to find Master Arden with a four-man escort. His arms were bound behind his back, and his face was so ostentatiously stoic, with such a terribly stiff upper lip that is was obvious he was concealing great distress. Fear was there, Phil could see it plainly, but hatred, too, and something even more bitter.

"You!" he spat, and half-lunged, half-stumbled toward her.

"Peace, Master Arden," the Headmaster said. "If she had been any other, you would even now be lying cold in the ground."

"If she were any other, I never would have—"

The Headmaster stared steadily at him, and as a barely seen bolt of crystalline lightning arced through the air, Arden fell suddenly silent, magically robbed of the power of speech. The ropes that tied his arms unknotted themselves and coiled at his feet. He looked like he desperately wanted to run, or to hurl himself at Phil, but he stood, trembling, his sharp-cut cheeks flushed.

"Given the peculiar circumstances," the Headmaster went on, "the conclave has decided not to punish you."

Arden let out a breath he didn't know he was holding. Death, severance from the Essence, banishment—one was as bad as the other. And yet, there was a part of him that had almost hoped . . .

"We have decided rather that the crime was not against our order but against the girl. She will decide whether you live or die for performing the killing magic."

Arden opened his mouth to protest, but he still couldn't speak. At the mercy of that Medusa, with her snakes of red hair and terrible sword and absurdly flippant manner? Didn't they see what a danger she was, with her traitor's blood? What if there were more like her? What if she brought them into the college with more swords, or guns? The order had been secret, utterly concealed from the outside world for centuries. The girl might be nothing, true, merely a fluke or a freak, but what if she was a harbinger of an invasion?

The Headmaster turned to Phil. "You have his life in your hands. What would you do with it?"

Then she did the most hurtful thing of all. She laughed. "His life? What would I want with that useless thing?"

Arden hated her as he had never hated another human being before. Not his father who beat him, not his mother who wouldn't protect him, not even Ruby, who had laughed at him, too, called him a small fish, and gone to a backstreet doctor as soon as she found out she was pregnant.

"You release him, then?" the Headmaster asked.

Phil tapped her dimpled chin with one finger, contemplating. "No . . . no, I don't think he should get off that easy. Let him owe me his life. I'll claim it when I want it."

Arden managed to make a choking sound, but the Headmaster nodded. "Very well. Go now, and do not return until you claim him."

"I'll go," Phil said, "but I'll be back sooner than that. I've got to look after my little brother, don't I?"

She gave Stan a swift kiss and ruffled his unruly curls.

"And I'll be taking this for the war effort," she added, swinging the tulwar perilously close to Arden's throat. He flinched.

"Don't worry, magician," she said with a wink. "Not yet, anyway."

Chapter 6

Phil ran home, past the waiting oast houses and the fields of mingled grumbling and laughing from the hop pickers.

Stan's alive! She sang it to herself as she jogged. She had to write to Mum and Dad at once, and oh, Hector, too. Could they get leave? And wouldn't Fee be thrilled! The thought of seeing Fee's face light up was in itself almost as good as the fact of having Stan back again.

Then she stopped dead in the middle of the path, flanked by apple trees laden with nearly ripe red-checked fruit. Should she tell Fee?

That there could even be any doubt startled her. She shared everything with Fee—her first kiss, her irrational fear of fresh figs, her doubts about Hector. Fee was her confidante, her second self. There was no trivial pain or worry with which she didn't burden Fee, nor yet any poetic fancy or romantic whim Fee failed to inflict on her. They shared everything.

Of course she had to tell Fee that Stan was alive.

Only, was there any way to do it without revealing the existence of the College of Drycraeft?

It was too strange, too confusing, and for all that she was apparently immune to magic, and her sister presumably would be as well, too dangerous for Fee to be involved. Phil felt herself to be perfectly capable of dealing with masses of men who may or may not have wanted her dead, but she knew Fee wasn't made of such stern stuff. What would she have done if she'd been the one tied up? Wept or fainted or quoted Tennyson. And although they said they meant her no harm, well, who could guess what might happen? Better to keep Fee well out of it.

She trotted off again and was still undecided as Weasel Rue came into sight. She was usually good at off-the-cuff lying—she called it improvisational acting—but try as she might, she couldn't think of any way to tell one piece of news without the other.

She came to a panting halt in front of Fee, who sat on a bundle of hay, cuddling and cooing to a rooster that eyed Phil balefully. Phil did everything she could to school her expression. She bit her tongue, clenched her nails into her palms, thought of an audience full of critics from the *Daily Mail, London News,* the *Times,* and the *Guardian,* all expecting her to keep a straight face. For any other audience, it would have worked.

Fee flew into her arms, pressed herself to her sister's damp forehead, squealed when the rooster tried to stab her with spurs he forgot had been removed with a hot potato the week before, and threw her heart and soul into the breathless words, "Tell me!"

And so, against her better judgment, Phil did.

Fee pushed her sister's hair out of her face and stared at her, eyelash to eyelash, for a long moment. Then she rolled her eyes elaborately skyward and sighed.

"Fee, I know it sounds impossible, but you have to believe—"

"Hush," she replied, frowning.

"I'm not crazy."

"Of course you're not," Fee said absently, doing a fair pantomime of lunacy herself by pointing straight upward and ticking her arm downward ten degrees at a time, all the while making faces like a monkey doing math. "Bother! I don't know how explorers and natives and such manage it. She said get the fowl in at six, but I can't remember if I ever set my watch to summer time, and I always used to set it fast so I'd be on time for our shows, then I set it ahead another half-hour last night to make sure I'd get up early, and now I don't know if its noon or midnight." She squinted up at the sun. "What time does that sun look like to you? Do you think it would put the hens off their laying if I shut them up a little early?"

"Have you heard a word I said?" Phil asked.

"Oh, more than one!" she said, catching her sister's hand. "And if you'll just help me get the chickens shut up, we can be on our way to see Stan."

"You mean you believe me?"

Fee gave her sister an odd look. Belief—in anything at all—had never been a problem for her. If any of her favorite authors had made a little brother vanish in a bomb barrage only to reappear under the most extraordinary circumstances, she would have accepted it without blinking. She'd always known her own life was destined to be a story, and was rather surprised it had waited until now.

"And you did understand?" Phil asked, thinking perhaps her sister was lulling her until she could summon a few hardy men with a strait-jacket (from which she could escape within thirty seconds). "Stan, alive? Magic, real?"

"Mmm-hmm," Fee said absently, twitching her apron at an errant hen. She'd rather hoped that when her life took a literary turn, it would involve a male protagonist, but still, Stan and magic were a good start. Anything might follow. "Mind the bantams. They're tricky. What should I wear?"

Phil just grinned at her darling sister. Grief might crush Fee, but she took even the most shocking happiness as no more than her due. Every good thing in her life simply confirmed her immutable faith that the world was a lovely place. Bombs and death had shaken her, but she was still the eternal optimist.

When the chickens were cooped and settling nicely, the rooster strutting in the dusty confines like a thwarted martinet, the two girls set off hand in hand together down the rutted path toward the open hills. Along the way, Phil told her more of what she'd gleaned from her time at Stour. One matter was apparently the most important, because Fee kept returning to it.

"Do you mean there's not one woman at the college? Not a single one?"

Phil managed to suppress both a grin and a groan and told her for the dozenth time, "All I saw were men. Men and boys, from eight or ten, to eighty."

"But, er, enough in between, right?"

"I distinctly remember kicking a fellow of about twenty in the stomach when they were tying me up, so yes, I'd say there are a few eligible men there. But you're not to go falling in love with any of them. Or all of them. I know you, Fee! These aren't normal men."

Fee gave her hips a little shimmy. "We'll see about that."

"You know what I mean. They're odd. And dangerous."

"Oh, Phil, you don't really know me at all, do you?" she asked, most unfairly. "I only fall a *little* in love with every man I meet. Just the tiniest, littlest bit, just for fun. I can't help that. But I'll only fall *truly* in love with one man, and odds are I won't meet him in the College of Drycraeft. There's a world full of men, and only one right one for me. So a girl has to shop around a bit to find out who he is, you see? I'm there to see Stan. If flirtation happens, I promise it will be completely accidental."

But the shimmy stayed in her hips as they walked across the gloaming. She'd chosen a jade-green shantung that was far too summery, but it had the advantage of twitching seductively with her every move, so she made the supreme sacrifice of warmth for style and was pleased with the results. Her gas mask, bouncing against her swaying hip in its cloth-of-gold drawstring satchel, spoiled the lines somewhat, but neither sister ever left home without hers.

They ascended the last promontory, and the grand prospect of Stour spread before them.

"Oh," Fee breathed, "it's right, so exactly right." She'd been desperately afraid that it would be a dowdy brick lump in the middle of a manicured lawn, without romance or charm, but its extravagance left her briefly speechless. It was better than ruins! The baobabs and banyans, the milling herds of delicate antelopes, the perfumes of Araby in the air—she took them all as only her due.

Anything could happen in a place like this, she thought. Duels for her honor, quests to win her hand, and poetry galore! The gloaming was pinkening where the sun lowered just behind the hills, while from the leaden clouds on the far horizon, a swift wind was wuthering. A bird that might well be a nightingale sang a dulcet melody into the imminent twilight, and one bright heavenly body that Fee firmly told herself was Venus hovered in the sky. Nature and architecture were conspiring to give Fee exactly the setting she craved. Even without romance, it was almost good enough. Almost.

Phil, unaffected by the picturesque glories around her, said, "Now stay close to me, beware of bears, and if anyone tries any funny business, you run away and leave me to handle it."

"That's what Lord Grumley used to call his indiscretions with chorus girls — funny business." He was the Shakespearean roué whom the girls good-naturedly allowed to believe was corrupting them. "Do you remember he'd pull his cravat over his eyes before every grope, on the ostrich theory? 'Sin unseen ain't sin at all,' he used to say, the old dear. How that man loved the blackout."

"There won't be any of that kind of funny business," Phil said firmly.

She led Fee to the ha-ha and leaped the gap first. Fee, more hesitant, paced the edge and made a few false starts before she jumped. She looked like a silky gazelle . . . until the landing, when her ankle turned in the soft earth, and she crumpled to the ground with a gasping "Oh!"

Phil had little patience for a girl who wore heels and a shantung frock cross-country, so she didn't rush to comfort Fee, on the principle that those who ought to know better must take the consequences, even beloved sisters. "Are you hurt?" she asked.

"No," Fee said pathetically, her abalone-gray eyes welling. "But look! My very last pair of decent stockings!" She raised one slender leg until her skirt fell well above her thigh, revealing a rosy garter belt. There, on the knee, was a hole that descended in a ladder down to her ankle. "I can clean the dress, if I'm lucky, or turn it into a blouse or tunic, but the stockings are hopeless, Phil! Hopeless!" She let her leg fall and flung herself back dramatically on the soft turf, making her hemline inch higher.

Phil, knowing her sister was in jest — mostly, anyway — was about to laugh and drag her to her feet, when a figure dashed out of the shadowed landscape and scooped Fee into its arms. *His* arms, for the interloper was broad-shouldered and narrow-hipped and said in a strong baritone, "Be still, gentle maiden, and I will succor thee."

Fee began to scowl, knowing it would be like Phil to arrange such a ridiculous act and script with someone just to mock her romantic sensibilities. No one had said such a thing in the last several centuries — outside her own fantasies. Angry at having her secret dreams teased, she struggled and looked up at the man who held her, ready to launch a tirade. Then she stopped, mute and spellbound.

Venus had fallen in love with such a man and welcomed him to a bed of lynx fur. Sleeping Endymion looked so, and comely, foolish Paris. He was a classical statue given breath and life, chiseled and soft all at once. Fee had never seen anyone quite so handsome, and she considered herself something of an expert on masculine beauty.

But where the faces of most good-looking men plainly say, *look at me,* his only begged, humbly and sincerely, to be allowed to look on her.

"Dry your tears, my lady," he said, staring, staring, as if she were the first of her kind, a sublimely rare creature born into his hands. "Where is the pain? Be still, and I will heal you."

He set her down again in the springy grass and began to feel her ankle.

"There?" he asked.

"No," Fee gasped. "Not there."

He moved higher, his amber eyes anxiously watching her reaction. "There?" he asked, caressing her knee.

Fee's breath began to come fast. "No," she murmured. "Not quite . . ."

His hand crept up to her thigh, pressing gently just beneath her silken hem, checking for tenderness, and Fee gave a hysterical little pant while Phil watched, wondering if the boy was going to be seduced or smacked.

"Whatever you're doing up there, Prentice Thomas, it's not healing," said a voice, cold and harsh. Arden stepped from the shadows. "She's another unnatural monster whom the Essence can't touch." He glared at Phil.

"Nothing monstrous could have such a lovely form," Thomas said, and Arden laughed sharply.

"You know nothing of the world, prentice. If danger and evil were hideous, everyone could avoid them. The wickedest things are cloaked in beauty."

Gentle disbelief clouded Thomas's face. "You're wrong, you must be, Master Arden. I read in a poem, beauty is truth, truth beauty."

Slowly, like a man waking to a revelation, he turned away from his master to look again at reclining Fee, and they regarded each other with the promise of everything in the world hanging in the space between them, the unheard melody, the unbestowed kiss, the sweetness and the wild ecstasy. Fee found her own echo in his eyes, and she loved, and he loved, like Arcadian innocents.

Of course, Fee was in many ways more of a satyress than a shepherdess, and she knew she was prone to falling in love—just a little bit in love, mind you—at the drop of a hat. But this—why, he sounded like something out of Scott, or even her dear Jane! Though she couldn't imagine even the wickedest Austen seducer creeping up her inner thigh . . .

"You spend far too much time in the library, prentice," Arden said. "Time you should be using to perfect your magic. Why aren't you with the others at the Exaltation?"

"I'm on guard duty," the young prentice said, losing his chivalric tone.

"Then escort these intruders off the grounds."

"We're here to see Stan," Phil said, "and you know you can't make us leave."

She saw his big fists clench at his sides, and for a moment she was afraid of what he could do. He might not be able to use magic on her, but he looked like one of those Hungarian fellows in storybooks who turn into wolves at the slightest provocation—and she'd left her sword at home.

Arden closed his eyes for a moment, controlling himself. Headmaster Rudyard said Phil was to be allowed on the grounds, and while he wasn't quite ready to openly defy the head of the College, he wasn't happy about it.

"Prentice Stanislaus is otherwise occupied," he said.

"He's participating in his first Exaltation," Thomas said dreamily. "We couldn't possibly disturb him at such a moment."

"We'll wait," Phil said, and Arden made a growling sound.

"I'll take you there." Thomas helped Fee to her feet, forgetting to release her hand. "It's such a beautiful experience."

"You're wasting your time with these two, prentice. They don't have a spark of Essence in them. They won't feel thing."

"But everything on earth has the Essence within it. How can they be without Essence? They are alive, aren't they?" He squeezed Fee's warm hand. "Yet I can feel nothing in her." He cocked his lovely head at Fee in perplexed pity. "How do you bear it?" he asked. "You must feel so lonely, so empty. There is some part of you waiting to be filled."

Fee cast a look at her sister, saying in their own telepathy, *That's what Lord Grumly would say!*

"I know!" Thomas said. "I will fill that place for you!"

Fee pulled away and fell on Phil's shoulder, giggling uncontrollably. Phil looked over her sister's head and inadvertently caught Arden's eye. For one unguarded moment, they smiled knowingly at each other at Thomas's earnest innocence. Then Arden caught himself, scowled, and looked away.

"They'll be a nuisance," Arden said. "I'd better go with you, to make sure they don't interrupt the Exaltation. If they do, I'll throw them off the grounds myself, whatever the Headmaster says." His hands tightened into fists again and stalked away. "Come along!"

The boy took Fee's hand as naturally as breathing and led her as a child leads another down a happy path.

Phil followed in their wake, marveling that Fee had done it again. Of course, it was easy with a young man who probably hadn't seen a woman for years. Well, let Fee have her fun. She knew her sister wouldn't take it seriously. She never did.

Thomas guided them to a cluster of large flat-topped rocks perched on a rise. "The Three Dwarves," he called them, explaining that they were supposed to come alive and wander at night. "Not that we believe it," he quickly added.

Oh no, thought Phil. *Magic is quite enough without dwarves being real, as well.*

"Here," he said, settling Fee and helping her tuck her skirt away from the furry absinthe-colored moss. "You'll have a perfect view."

Phil looked over the broad lake basin and surrounding landscaped lawn and saw perhaps four hundred men scattered over the grounds, silent and still, surrounded by a mercury-colored mist. "What are they doing?" she asked. Here were men, fighting men, wasting their time looking at stars or meditating, when they could be preparing for invasion—saving England!

"They're keeping the world alive," Thomas said matter-of-factly.

Phil laughed, and Arden stepped swiftly to her side and said sharply, "Be quiet. You don't know anything." He was so close to her, so quickly, that again she felt a little afraid. It embarrassed her, so she forced herself not to flinch away.

"Then tell me."

"Why? So you can laugh some more?"

When she saw his face, she bit back her tart reply and said, even more gently than she meant to, "Tell me."

He did, and was so intent on his tale he completely forgot to step away from Phil. He spoke in a hushed murmur in her ear, just loud enough for Fee to hear, too.

"The earth is a body, through which the Essence flows," he said. "Like blood, it swirls to every corner of the globe."

She desperately wanted to point out that a globe has no corners, but she held her tongue, lest he stop his lesson.

"But like blood, the Essence would grow sluggish and stagnant if it did not have a heart to pump it. England is that heart, and we help the Essence circulate throughout the world. England exists because of us, and the earth could not exist without us."

"What do you mean, England exists because of you?" The whole thing struck her as supremely arrogant.

"There have been hearts before England existed, other islands that have been raised by magicians and sunk by indolence or treachery. Tir Na Nog vanished almost before memory, and after it, Atlantis and Lyonesse were cast beneath the waves. Each time the world was almost lost, but each time the greatest from among the magicians who survived gathered their powers and the Earth's Essence and raised a new sanctuary, a new center of the world. They put their magic, their selves, into it, so that the islands became, each in turn, repositories of power. In this age, it is England. There is Essence everywhere, but vast amounts course through English soil, far more than anywhere else. We tend it, we guide it through its channels."

"That's what they're doing?" Phil asked.

Arden nodded. "It is the Exaltation, the drawing-up of the island's power. The Essence flows through them and thence through the world. It is the most—" He broke off abruptly, and she saw from the corner of her eye that his face was contorted in anguish. "You can't imagine it. When you surrender yourself to the Exaltation, when you're a vessel for the powers of the earth, there's no fear left in you, no loneliness, no sorrow. It is intimate and vast, all at once. You're held oh so tenderly, and you know that nothing bad can ever touch you again."

He wasn't speaking to her. She doubted he even remembered she was there. He was gazing out over the lake, the lawn, with the yearning of a lover for his beloved.

"Why aren't you with them?" she asked.

He started, recalling where he was, who he was with. "I'm in disgrace, remember? Because of you. They may never let me draw the Essence again." He lowered his voice to the barest whisper. "Damn it, kill me or release me. I cannot live like this!"

"The Essence sounds like a drug," Phil said. "Or love."

"It's nothing like love," he spat. "Love is a corrupt thing, a lie. The Essence is pure. Ah!" He pressed his temples distractedly. "See your brother and go, and don't return. Please."

"What harm can we do?" Phil asked.

"You're disrupting everything!" he said between tightly clenched teeth. He'd worked so hard to find his serenity again, and now it was beginning to crumble. He felt like he had as a child, helpless in the face of screams and beatings, until the Essence had risen up in him, given him peace and power. And he felt as he had, not so long ago, when he thought he found something even better than the Essence and had been crushed for his blasphemy. He'd always been able to find refuge in his power. What if he was never allowed to use it again? What if he was cursed, as Phil's ancestor had been, stripped of his power and cast out, empty and alone? It would be worse than being a commoner. He'd be like an Albion.

He watched Phil watching the Exaltation, her brow knitted, her full lips pursed. She could feel nothing of what was going on down there. Even though he was forbidden to use his power, his skin prickled with acute awareness of the massive amounts of Essence surging up from the ground. It was like a teasing, intimate touch that promised no fulfillment.

He couldn't imagine what it must be like for Phil and her sister, to feel none of it.

Yes, he could, he decided, with a flash of sympathy for the girls. It must feel like death.

On the stone beside them, Thomas was telling Fee in hushed ecstasy what was happening. He would touch her arm to bring her attention to one thing, then lean into her strawberry waves to whisper in her ear.

"The colors are lovely," Fee said. The mercury mist had thinned, and the air around the men seemed charged with prismatic colors.

"You can see them? Most commoners can't. Drawing Essence from different sources makes different colors. Green from plants, red from animals, and see those swirls of amber and gold? They're from the Earth. From near the surface, anyway, where there are living things. It gets darker, the deeper you go. Of course," he added confidentially, "very few can draw up the black Essence from the Earth's heart. And look here."

He placed his hand over Fee's, enveloping it in a glittering white glow that sparked with sudden jewel accents. "This is the Essence of my body. We have everything in us, you see, parts of all the world. We can feel a trace of everything the Essence has touched." He closed his eyes. "I feel roots, mushroom spores, worms. You really feel nothing?"

"I see the glow, but I feel nothing."

"There must be something I can do," he said, gazing at her as a physician might look on his patient on her deathbed, wracking his brains for a cure. "Let me try. Let me fill you, please! It won't hurt."

Fee, who a second ago had been completely under the romantic spell of the moment, broke into giggles again.

"Let me fill you with my Essence," Thomas said again with throaty passion. "I don't know what's keeping you from feeling it, but I'm sure I can thrust through. It might be difficult to break through your barrier, but once you know how splendid it feels—"

At that point Fee had to stand up and walk away.

Confused, Thomas looked over his shoulder at Phil. "I don't know how you live without the Essence, but you both certainly seem to be exceptionally jolly girls. Fee's hardly stopped laughing since I met her."

When she'd regained enough of her composure, Fee sat at Thomas's side once again and they fell into easy conversation.

("I don't know what I would have done if he'd tried to put his Essence into me," Fee told her sister when they were in bed that night. "I honestly think I might have let him."

"What, right there in front of everybody?" Phil asked, forcing her face to be very serious.

"Well, all those men were doing it, weren't they?")

Phil sat on another of the Three Dwarves, and Arden remained standing nearby, his arms crossed, his feet braced in a wide stance. Full night fell, and at length the magicians rose without ceremony and went their separate ways.

"Even though I couldn't feel anything, it was still lovely, wasn't it, Phil?" Fee said. "Like watching monks do a very quiet magic show. Proper magic, I mean — our kind. Do you think we could get colors like that in the Hall of Delusion?" She sighed. "It makes me happy to think there's still a quiet, peaceful place in the world. The war's not really here, is it?"

"The *nation* is at war," Phil said. "And no matter how well these men hide themselves, they are part of England." She turned to Arden. "You say England is the heart of the world? Well, the heart is under attack."

"Those are commoner matters, for commoners to settle amongst themselves," Arden said. "There'll always be an England . . ."

In the starlight, Fee began to hum the popular Vera Lynn tune.

" . . . And we'll always be here, guarding it, helping the Essence to flow, keeping the world alive."

"But what if the Germans invade? What if they win? It won't be England anymore!"

"Do you think it matters what kind of rabble are scurrying around out there?" he said with a contemptuous glower. "Do you think the race of people who huddle there now have lived there forever? When we raised this isle," he said, as if he had been intimately involved in it himself, "we, the Masters of Drycraeft, were the only inhabitants. Others moved in, Celtic tribes, Vikings, Romans, Saxons, all waging their silly little wars, all killing one another, all conquering and immediately thinking they'd been here since the dawn of time. Through all of it, we have been the same—untouched. It doesn't matter to us."

Phil drew breath to shout him into sense, when Thomas asked, timidly, "What is war?"

It stopped her cold. *It's explosions and screaming,* she thought, remembering the first night of the Blitz. *It's pain and loss and blood, resignation and determination. It's being steel and jelly all at once.*

"It's . . . fighting," she said inadequately. "It's when two nations, or many nations, fight each other. When their soldiers kill one another, and they bomb cities."

"Why?"

"Well, Germany invaded Poland."

"Why?"

The details were a little hazy, but she thought she understood the generalities. "For land and power. He—Hitler, that is—wants to build an empire."

"So those countries are at war?"

"Poland was defeated, and England and France declared war in its defense. Then France fell, and now it's mostly us. England against Germany, and Italy, and Japan, too, I suppose."

"But," Thomas said, his perfect brow tragically crinkled, "*why?*"

"Well, Hitler started it all. He killed thousands, tens of thousands in Poland. Soldiers and civilians."

"With his own hands?"

"No, no, with his army, and tanks and planes. And he's still killing. He's been bombing England. Just the night before we left, they dropped bombs all over London. It was . . . it was . . ." She shook her head and looked away.

"Others kill at this man's bidding?" Thomas gasped, leaping to his feet. "Master Arden, does the Headmaster know about this? There should be a conclave. The masters should drain this madman's Essence, return it to the earth."

Arden looked not at the young prentice but at the girls. "Do you see what you've done? You and your disruptive Albion blood. We don't interfere in the outside world. Commoners' futile scrabbling for power, their politics, their hatreds and their . . . loves . . . are nothing to us. We tend the Essence. We keep the earth alive. The College of Drycraeft doesn't need to know about your paltry little war. You've muddled this young fool's head with a few words. Do you see why you shouldn't be here?"

And he found, to his surprise and chagrin, that Phil looked at him with pity, much the same pity with which he'd regarded her when he realized what it must mean for her to lack any connection to the Essence. Like he was the monster, the ignorant, inadequate one.

The war was nothing to him. England, as a nation, was nothing to him. In the end, the earth would be the same, no matter how many millions were slaughtered. The war would be over one day, and the College of Drycraeft would continue its service, untroubled, forever. It had to.

Chapter 7

I still don't know if we should leave Stan there," Phil said to Fee the following morning.

"You mean Prentice Stanislaus?" Fee asked with a chuckle as she rinsed suds from the breakfast dishes. "He was so happy, couldn't you see? He has to be someplace for the duration of the war. If he has real magic, shouldn't he be allowed to learn how to use it properly?"

"I suppose," Phil admitted, drying with a clean rag. "But they mean to keep him there forever! Do you know, they're not even allowed to leave the college grounds. It's a prison. They're indoctrinating them. And why aren't there any women there, eh?"

"All the better," Fee said.

"Fee, it isn't natural. They'll teach him to hate his own family because we're commoners. Commoners! Ugh, I just wanted to slap that Arden's smug face whenever he used the word. Like they're nature's nobility. I ought to claim his stupid life after all."

"Phil!"

"Oh, I don't mean it, of course. But it's such a *wasted* life, isn't it?"

"They say they keep the world alive."

"I can't believe those magicians are so vital that the world would die without them. It's like any gentlemen's club—they make up secret histories and obscure rules to make themselves feel important and exclude others. If they all enlisted, the world would muddle on, same as it always has."

"They're not doing any harm," Fee said, always willing to see the best.

"But they aren't doing any good. And the trouble is, they're so convinced they are. A quarter of them are of an age to join up, and the rest should be doing something useful. They could be in a munitions factory, or planting potatoes—not to say what they could be doing with their magic. Only think, our family's magic, which is all falsehood and illusion, is doing more to win the war than real powers that could kill Germans. Between them and the villagers, we're handing Germany a victory." Phil closed her eyes. "I feel like I'm in a dream. Am I the only one who knows what's happening?"

"Maybe they're right. The war might never come here."

"But if it does, we have to be ready! They're like little chicks, watching the fox and thinking they're too fluffy and cute to be eaten."

She heard a chuckle behind her. "Try telling Eamon Dooley the mechanic he's a fresh-pipped chick," Algernon said, feeling his way to the kitchen door. "That might goad him into volunteering, if you're still on that fool's errand."

"I am, actually, and I will. Who else can I get?"

"I was joking. No one in Bittersweet will train or drill or save rubber and scrap. Not if a panzer unit rolled through. You're wasting your time, kiddo."

She might have been satisfied with scowls and rantings, but the *kiddo* pushed her over the edge.

"You would do it, wouldn't you? If you could see, you'd form a branch of the Home Guard, wouldn't you?"

"If I could see, I'd be at the front now."

"You know what I mean. You're not like everyone here. You've seen war. You *know.* Would you help me, if you could?"

He was seeing something with those sightless eyes, she was sure of it. The sea walls at Dunkirk, the harbor churning and red.

"I would," he said at last.

"Good," she said smugly. "Then you will."

"I . . . no . . . I can't."

"You were in the British Expeditionary Force. You're a soldier. Even if you can't see, you can tell me what to do. Damnit, all you have to do is stand there, being a hero, and you'll shame and inspire 'em into action."

"You're a fool if you think I'm a hero."

"You enlisted. You did your duty. You're a hero. Please help me. Bittersweet has to be ready for invasion, and it has to do its part for the war effort."

"It's a Sisyphean battle, and there are cows to be milked."

"I'll milk the damned cows! Just please, tell me how to organize an army!"

He shuffled awkwardly away, and Phil's hopes deflated. Then

without turning back, he said, "What the hell. I'm no use on the farm. Yesterday I tried to milk the bull."

"You'll help?" Phil squealed.

"For all the good it will do. I might as well be useless at one thing as another."

Phil had her speech prepared, just the right balance of inspirational patriotism, bullying, and the promise of tea and biscuits (Fee's contribution to the scheme). She rapped at the mechanic's door and was greeted by a red-bearded giant.

"Good morning," she said pleasantly. "If I could have a moment of your time, I'd like to talk with you about—"

"This girl here says you're a great fuzzy chick who's too far tucked up his ma's feathers to learn how to fire a rifle or dig a trench like a man," Algernon interrupted. "That true?"

Phil blushed pink; the mechanic flushed bright scarlet and looked on the verge of apoplexy. "Who's been spreading such bald-faced lies!" he demanded.

Algernon cocked his head at Phil. "She heard you wouldn't join her Home Guard because you were afraid you couldn't thrust a bayonet as well as a girl. She said if you care to, you can sew blackout curtains and roll bandages instead."

"I didn't—" Phil began, but Algernon nudged her.

"Why, I . . . Now, missie, don't you go listening to rumors. It ain't true. Look at me—you think I can't dig a trench? Strong as an ox, I am." He twitched his pectorals and then curled his arm to reveal a bicep as big as a shire horse's hoof. "Feel it, missie, just feel it, and tell me you'll not have me in the Guard."

She felt it. It was like the turnip that won first prize at the agricultural fair.

"Oxen are strong, but we won't take them in the Guard," Algernon said. "What else can you do?"

"I can fix any car on the road."

"The last thing we need in an invasion is Germans commandeering our cars and tractors. The important question is, can you disable a car?"

"Why, missie, you stand right there and watch."

He stepped brusquely past them to where a muddy Morris coupe rumbled down the cobbled street. With his bulk placed squarely in front of the grille, the driver had no choice but to stop.

"What's this all about, Eamon?" asked Mr. Henshawe, the little grocer.

"For the war effort," the burly mechanic said as he opened the bonnet, fiddled a moment, then tossed a small bit of metal into the languishing yellow rosebushes across the street. "There," he said, rubbing engine grease on his already-stained overalls. "Let's see a Nazi drive that to Buckingham Palace!"

And so Phil added the first name to her roster of informal Home Guards.

As she helped the grocer search for his missing bit of motor, she tried to solicit him, too.

"Pah, Germans!" he said, scrabbling through the loam. "Might as well say the fairies will be coming through Bittersweet. Now help me find that engine gizmo. I've a missing shipment of tea to account for. Not a drop of leaf on the shelves, and the delivery was supposed to be yesterday."

"You don't have to march and fight, you know," Phil said. She found the missing part but kept it hidden in her palm. "In a place like this, you should be able to get most of your food locally and save your coupons. I'm sure as a grocer it isn't good for business, but as an Englishman you ought to encourage your customers not to buy anything that's rationed. Leave those things to the people in London and Birmingham and Leeds, where they can't grow their own food. If all your customers left their ration books at home—"

"Their what?" Henshawe asked.

Thus it came out, after a great deal of incredulity on Phil's part and indignation on the grocer's ("What! Tell a body how much he can eat and how much he can buy with his own honest money!") that the townspeople of Bittersweet had never been issued ration books.

"How is that possible?" Phil asked as she tossed the engine part back under the bush and took Algernon's arm to lead him to the next likely prospect for civil defense. "*Everyone* is issued food coupons and a gas mask and—"

"No gas masks either," Algernon said. "Except Uncle Walter, of course."

Phil stopped dead in the road. "I don't believe it. Does the government even know about Bittersweet? Is it invisible? Oh!"

She remembered the moment when her parents had first told her she'd be going to the country. Dad had tried to find the village on the map—it hadn't been there, though it was a very detailed map that listed the tiniest hamlets.

If the magicians could hide all of Stour, could they do something similar with an entire town? For a group so concerned with staying hidden, it was a natural step, and they were probably capable of it. Could they make every bureaucratic eye in London skim over the village's name when doling out supplies and conscripting recruits?

Those wretches! thought Phil. *Bad enough that all those able-bodied men huddle in their manor and don't do their bit fighting Nazis. But to steal away an entire village from its duty of national defense—it's unpardonable!*

She fumbled in the side pocket of her gas mask pouch and counted out her shillings. "Come on, we're going to the post office."

She bought a pack of nearly transparent paper and drafted three quick letters. She had no addresses, but she chose recipients who were so well known that her letter would either be automatically delivered or else tossed away by a postman assuming it was a joke, rather like letters addressed to Father Christmas. One went to Lord Woolton at the Ministry of Food, informing him that no one in Bitersweet had ration cards. Another went to Winston Churchill, stating how eager the village was to help the war effort, if only someone would tell them how. The last she simply addressed to the Ministry of Defense, asking that a recruiter pay the town a visit.

Not wanting to be sent to Bedlam, she didn't offer any theories about magicians. She signed herself "A Concerned Englishwoman," affixed the stamps, and sent them into the void.

As soon as they were in the box, she had misgivings. What could one small town really do, with its old men and pugilist vicars? Would it be best to leave things as they were? Perhaps, with her interference, she was condemning men to death, men who otherwise would have lived long, happy lives, solved scientific problems, contributed to the birth of geniuses and saviors.

No, she told herself firmly. All over England and in distant battle-fields, men who had at least as much right to such possibilities were fighting and dying. Everyone had to do his part.

She and Algernon spent the rest of their day recruiting, with dismal results.

"Isn't that thing over by now?" one housewife asked when Phil encouraged her to take in evacuee children.

"Give up my saucepans!" gulped another, barring the door with her considerable bulk as if Phil meant to launch an immediate assault on her cupboards. "Not on your nelly!"

One fellow in his forties seemed on the verge of volunteering for Phil's Home Guard, albeit not quite for the right reasons. "Red-heads," he said, looking her up and down, lingering longest in the middle. "Plenty of spunk, you redheads." Phil, dragging and disappointed with her day's work, was ready even to accept recruits with dubious motives, when a ginger-haired slip of a woman gripped him by the ear and hauled him inside. She glowered at Phil.

"My Enery's got room for one red-headed woman in his life, and I ain't about to step aside for a London piece like you. Off with you now!"

One old man did agree to dig up his zinnias and plant cabbage and silverbeet, but only because his flowers had gotten the blight.

When she tried to tell the deaf, grandmotherly Mrs. Abernathy about rationing and food shortages, she accidentally gave the ancient woman the impression that she herself was hungry, and Phil and Algernon weren't allowed to escape until they'd choked down two cups of tea and some excruciatingly dry seed cake.

"It's no use," Phil said as they backtracked down High Street.

Algernon, starting to answer, stumbled, and Phil caught him with an arm around his waist.

"What do you think you're doing?" came an indignant feminine voice from behind. Phil turned and found Diana bearing down on them. Hastily, Phil disengaged herself from Algernon and explained.

Diana's eyes lit up. It had been so long since Algernon had taken any real interest in anything. If this project, however foolish, could give him a new passion for life, she was all for it. But she'd be damned if she'd let that curvy, wiggling slut of a London girl do it at his side.

Thrilling with enthusiasm, she said, "Oh yes, just what the village needs, a war hero to shake it out of its lethargy."

Algernon tried for the second time that day to protest the word *hero,* but Diana easily talked over him. "I know *exactly* what to do," she said brightly, flicking a glance at Phil that clearly said *and you do not.* "The ladies of the knitting circle will make nothing but socks for the poor soldiers, and every farmer will double his egg production so we can send more to the starving Londoners."

"They aren't exactly starving," Phil began. *Honestly, she makes us sound like beggars and guttersnipes.* "What we really need is people for the Home Guard. And rifles, or any other kind of weapon."

"Yes, yes," Diana said dismissively. "I'll arrange all that."

"We've spoken with practically everyone in the village," Phil said. "No one is interested."

Diana looked at Algernon with burning devotion, seeing him coming back to life. "I'll *make* them be interested!" she swore.

$\mathcal{S}$he did it, too. Phil wasn't sure exactly how — whether it was simply that they were more willing to listen to a local than an outsider, or perhaps that Diana knew their secrets and hidden fears, the better to bribe and bully them. But by afternoon she'd recruited some dozen men and the red-haired woman for paramilitary training and had almost everyone else reluctantly agreeing to save scrap. It was easy to find volunteer fire wardens once she hit on the idea of letting them work in pairs. Several teenage couples relished the idea of being allowed out all night, ostensibly to watch for incendiaries.

Even steely-eyed Diana might not have had such luck, if the war hadn't happened to hit close to home for the first time since its declaration.

Bittersweet had run out of tea.

Phil had never seen anything like it. An Englishwoman deprived of her cuppa is a fearsome creature. After the poor little grocer had to deny the first housewife her weekly supply, word got around, and soon every able-bodied woman was crowding inside the store, demanding her soothing and stimulating leaf at once.

Now there, thought Phil, as she watched them rant and storm in their house dresses and aprons, *is my army of volunteers.* She'd rarely seen such passion, even in the London Women's Voluntary Service.

After scurrying to safety to place a few frantic calls, the grocer stood trembling before the seething, bekerchiefed masses and explained that he could not get a shipment for at least another week.

This was terrible news, but they were a cooperative community and, after some mumbling and grumbling, agreed to divvy up their stores until things returned to normal.

Then, quaking, the grocer admitted the worst: when at last supplies did arrive, the quantity would be so severely limited that there
would scarcely be enough for each person to have a scant spoonful of
tea each day.

"But I need tea for breakfast, and elevenses, and lunch," Mrs.
Enery said. "And an afternoon pick-me-up, not to mention teatime
proper, and like as not a cup around the fireplace before bed. One
spoonful of tea won't even tinge the water!"

"It's Hitler's fault!" Phil shouted, absorbed in the mob.

Since the crowd was evidently primed to tear *someone* limb from
limb, the grocer was only too happy to turn their aggressions elsewhere and echoed this resoundingly. "Oh yes, it's because of the war,
and submarines torpedoing tea ships from Ceylon, and . . . and . . .
Hitler hates tea!"

Angry people are always willing to seize upon an object for their
spite, and as soon as Diana stepped in and redirected their energies,
nearly everyone agreed to do whatever she could to defeat the horrible tea-hating Hun.

Chapter 8

Luckily, Phil knew that Weasel Rue had plenty of tea (and Mrs. Pippin didn't know about the shortage yet), so she told the Home Guard volunteers that the first meeting would be that very afternoon over an outdoor tea. She rushed ahead to make the preparations, with the dozen recruits to follow in an hour.

"Fee! Tea!" she ordered as she ran into the farmhouse. She had hoped to have Algie's help, but Diana had snatched him away. Then, with what Phil could have sworn was a malicious gleam in her eye, she'd told all the volunteers in her resounding sergeant's voice to bring their broomsticks to stand in for rifles and spades for knives, for they'd be starting military practice straight away.

Phil had no idea what to do, but she wasn't about to disappoint them. Men could be lured with food and the promise of looking at a pretty girl, but they could be held only by either duty or excitement. Their sense of duty was so tenuous that she had no faith in it.

"Fee!" she cried again, checking outside. She needed her sister for her opinion but mostly to play hostess. Phil had to be the man of the family, so Fee had better be prepared to pour tea and be the woman. "Where the devil are you? Fooling about in the hay with the bantams?"

Fee was in the hay, all right, but her companion was hardly a bantam. Phil stifled a giggle with her fist.

Thomas—what Phil could see of him—lay stretched out on his back while Fee kneeled over him, her abundant red-blond hair making a misty tent over them both. She kissed the side of his neck, the hollow at the base of his throat, and then, tossing her tresses back out of the way, fell upon his lips in her fervent, practiced manner.

"Ahem," Phil said.

"Mmm," Fee replied, looking up, and in that instant of sisterly telepathy, Phil's eyes widened in alarm. She was used to her sister's many amours, which came and went faster than a Thames tide. Fee played at love, enthusiastically and heartlessly, practicing, she always told her sister, for the real thing. She gave her affections—which, physically speaking, never went beyond kisses and admittedly rather daring caresses—lightly and took them merrily back when the game was done. She left broken hearts in her wake, but spared less pity for them than she did for a desiccated worm on the sidewalk (which always made her weep and try her hand at worm nursing), for she never made any promises, never let them think they had a chance at owning her heart.

There was no laughter in Fee's face now, though, only a determined, serious sort of bliss. It was the same look of concentration she had when she was mastering a new vanishing trick, her against the world and all the laws of nature, determined to make her illusion work. Invariably, she succeeded. Fee might be soft and yielding in many ways, but she had steel at her core.

"No," Phil said.

Fee sighed. "Yes, I'm afraid."

She didn't look afraid. But Phil was, for Thomas and for Fee. It would end in heartbreak, sure as the sun sets. And Thomas, well, he was like a newborn lamb, gazing at the world in fresh-eyed innocence. Fee surely must know what it would do to this young man to let him love her.

For Phil could see at a glance that if such a thing as love existed, this foolish pair were gripped firmly in its teeth. And she very much feared it was a death grip, unbreakable.

"You're not supposed to be here," Phil said, forcing her voice to be harsh. "Go back to Stour where you belong."

"I had to come," Thomas said, sitting up and managing a half-bow from his perch on the hay. "I was lured to her as to a siren on the rocks."

"Yes, and you know what happened to those stupid sailors. You'll be in hot water with the Headmaster if you're found here. Go!"

"He came to ask about the war," Fee said. "And since you were the one who said that every one of those magicians should be fighting at the front lines, I thought you wouldn't mind if I told him a bit more about it."

"Fee, kitchen. Now!" Phil stomped off, wondering why it was just her luck to have a family crisis when she desperately needed to be on her game. In her mind's eye, she could clearly see all of England falling simply because she did not get her recruits organized quite in time. Why, one fortification, one alert signalman spotting a paratrooper, could mean the difference between victory and defeat.

"What in the world are you up to, Fee?" she asked. "Wait, get the tea things together while you're telling me. Twelve or thirteen are coming, and most of them men, so don't bother cutting the bread thin. Oh, butter! Thank goodness we're in the country. I'd never sway them with marge. Sardines, do you think? Get rid of your magician first, though."

Fee made a pretty pout. "But we have so much to talk about. I feel like I've known him all my life."

"Ha! You got that out of a book."

"Maybe, but it's true. I look at him, and all I want to do is be with him."

"And kiss him, and—"

"Well, yes, of course, but it's so much more than that. This is it."

"It?" Phil asked, knowing, dreading.

"I'm in love. Real love."

"Codswallop! You met the boy under interesting circumstances, he's clueless enough to make you feel like a woman of the world, and because he hasn't seen a female since he left his dam's teat, he thinks you're the bee's knees. You're flattered, it's fun, but you know that being involved with one of those magicians is downright foolish. It's not love, Fee. It can't be, not so soon. You've spent, what, two hours in each other's company? I've known Hector for years, and I still don't know if I love him."

"You know," Fee said. "You might marry Hector and be happy, but you don't love him. I might marry Thomas and be miserable, but I'd love him. That matters more than anything."

"Then love's a damned stupid thing!" Phil said, slamming down a stack of sturdy saucers. "Be sensible, Fee. You might as well say you love a priest, or a monk. He lives for that Essence nonsense, and he will his whole life. Members of the College of Drycraeft can't have sweethearts."

"He says he wants to leave the order."

Phil grabbed her sister by the shoulders and pulled her into their forehead-to-forehead embrace. Usually it was a position of solace and affection. This time, though, Phil stared at Fee until her eyes merged into a single Cyclops orbit, and she tried with all her silent influence to force her sister not to be an idiot.

Fee stroked her sister's hair, slowly, rhythmically, as she might to calm a riled cat. At last, Phil pulled away and said angrily, "Fine! You win!" At this, Fee's smile grew infuriatingly smug. "You're the only person in the world who actually falls in love at first sight. You're a perfect romantic novel. But don't you see? You're going to get hurt."

"The magicians can't hurt either of us."

"You know that's not what I mean."

"Isn't it? Thomas doesn't just want to sneak out to visit me. He wants to leave the order, for good."

"They'll never let him. They'll find him, like they found Stan. Like the German magicians tracked down Stan's mother. Do you know that they've arranged for the entire country to ignore Bittersweet, and manipulated everyone in the village so they don't care about England or the war? Just to keep attention away from Stour. They'll do anything to keep their order secret. Why, they'll probably kill Thomas if he runs away, drain his Essence and—"

"No!" Fee gasped, blanching deathly pale. "They wouldn't!"

"They're fools and cowards and sticklers for their own arcane laws. But most likely they'll discover he's sneaked out today and lock him in the dungeon until we go."

"I'll never leave him."

"One bit of triteness after another."

"It's only trite when it isn't real," Fee said stubbornly. "Just wait until you're in love. You'll see."

"I'd like to see the day love makes me such a confounded fool. Damn! They'll be here any minute. Biscuits, you think, or just the bread? I hope Mrs. Pippin doesn't flay me for pillaging her food. She will when she finds out there's no more tea."

"She won't care. She only takes rose hips and hyssop. May I go back to Thomas now?" Fee folded her hands in schoolgirl primness.

"Why not? Just make sure your handkerchiefs are clean. You'll need them for all the tears that will come tomorrow."

"I'm ready for tears," Fee reassured her. "After all, tears are a natural part of love."

Phil gathered her volunteers in a little fallow field within sight of the house. In canvas overalls and leather aprons, in grease-stained trousers and, in one case, a polka-dotted pinafore, they clustered around her. They were skeptical, naturally enough, that a seventeen-year-old girl could teach them anything about warcraft, and assumed they'd receive little more than a lecture about not talking to strangers with German accents, or be told to buy war bonds. They still largely felt that the war was none of their business, but life did get boring sometimes, and hiking out to Weasel Rue to see what the Londoner had to say was as good a distraction as any.

Plus, there was food.

Phil faced them as she would a hostile audience on those nights when the first five rows of the Hall of Delusion were filled with tipsy university students. When met with hecklers, she stared them down and amazed them into silence and, later, applause. She fully intended to do the same with her Home Guard volunteers.

Only, she had no idea what to do.

Oh, she could rant about their ostrichlike, head-in-the-sand ways, or tell them horrific tales about the first night of bombing. But the former would only make them resentful right now, though in time she knew she could rouse their guilt. And the latter, while sensational enough to be stirring, was, after all, only words. She had to do something spectacular, something to make them feel, intimately and personally, that they were in real danger.

Boxing, maybe? No, not dramatic enough.

"Wait right here," she suddenly said, and whirled and ran back to the farmhouse. When she returned, she carried a clanking satchel.

"Volunteer, please," she said. "Thank you so much, Mr. Dooley. Now if you'll clamp these on me." She handed him a set of handcuffs and put her hands behind her back. "Tighter. Now, when the Germans come —"

"Who's to say they'll come?" asked Mrs. Enery.

"Hitler says they'll come," Phil said. "He's got practically all of

Europe, and we're next. Now say the Germans get as far as Bitter-sweet—"

"No German will ever set foot on English soil," the baker said with absolute certainty.

"You bloody fool! They already have! The Channel Islands have been invaded and occupied! D'you think that's not English soil?"

Thirteen pairs of eyes showed their whites, to cries of "No!" "Never!" and "Blimy!"

"You mean, you hadn't heard? It happened last June."

Heads shook and had the decency to look a bit embarrassed. "We don't have much truck with the rest of the world out here."

"The Germans have been bombing London every night, and what can it be if not preparations for a land invasion? They will strike the beaches and fight through from shore to shore. No place will be safe—and every place, even the tiniest village, might prove the decisive battleground that keeps invasion from turning into occupation."

"We could never fight an army," the baker said.

"But we can slow it down. We can sabotage tanks and keep the enemy from getting food and supplies. We can mislead him. Who knows what the course of war might bring? If our troops were massing for a counterattack, but couldn't muster for another day, don't you think blocking a panzer line for a few hours in Bittersweet might make all the difference? There are a thousand things any one of us can do, that might mean nothing but might mean everything. Together you and I are going to learn everything we can to prepare for the worst day. First, today, I'll teach you something that will come in handy if you're ever captured—the art of escape.

"Now, supposing you were German soldiers come to interrogate me. Why, as soon as you were distracted, quick as anything, I'd . . ." She undulated her shoulders, gave her body a little twist, and within two seconds the nickel-plated handcuffs clanked to the turf.

"Impossible," they cried, and "How'd you do that?" "Oughtn't to be allowed," said a man she later learned was a part-time constable.

"Show me how to do that," said Mrs. Enery keenly. "Show me right now, missie!"

So she did. Breaking them into groups and dividing her three sets of handcuffs among them, she showed them how to pick the locks with a bent piece of wire, how to shim them open by sliding a bobby pin along the ratchet teeth. She taught them how to bend their wrists to keep the handcuffs from tightening all the way, and convinced them that, if the situation were dire enough, they could curl their hands into a narrow tube shape and pull until enough joints dislocated that they could slip free.

"My own dad had to do that once, when he was learning the trade."

"What's his trade, then, and yours, come to mention it?" asked the sometime constable. "Burglary?"

Phil laughed. "Don't you people gossip? My family are magicians."

She had them now, and they hung on her every word as she told them about life on the stage, about crowned heads she'd entertained (and on one memorable occasion, threatened to cut off, an act that was surely becoming her forte). Then, smoothly, she segued into the first night of the Blitz.

"I never knew," the baker said in wonder as he practiced shimming his cuffs. "What was this, only a week ago?"

"Not even. You didn't hear it on the wireless?"

"Only the postmistress and your Mrs. Pippin have a set. Neither of them ever said anything."

"And no one takes the paper?"

They looked at each other, shaking their heads.

"We all knew there was a war, Miss Albion," Dooley said. "It's just . . . we thought it was far away."

There was no use in blaming them, Phil decided. The only thing to do was start from scratch.

"Next time we meet, I'll teach you how to get out of ropes, and we'll start civil defense lessons proper. Thank you so much for coming." On cue, Fee burst from the farmhouse with the first tea tray. Thomas drifted in her wake with a cutting board of toast and big lumps of farm butter.

Phil felt a sharp nudge in her ribs. "Who's he?" Mrs. Enery asked admiringly. Phil thought perhaps she'd been forgiven for attracting Enery's attention—the nudge didn't break any ribs. "Another magician?"

"You might say that," Phil admitted, and followed her troops to the benches nestled under ash tree shade.

Fee, playing hostess, and Thomas, in the role of her devoted slave, handed around tea and toast and slivers of a ginger cake that had once been undercooked in the middle but had staled to biscotti-like perfection. Fee charmed them all, miraculously without flirting, Phil noticed.

("I think I promised we'd put on a magic show for them," Fee confessed later that night.

"You what! We don't have time for that."

"You told me to be charming, and I was smiling and saying yes so much, I didn't even notice what I was agreeing to. Don't worry, they'll forget."

Of course, they didn't.)

When the volunteers had all gone home to supper—the English being capable of near-perpetual eating, with a meal for practically every hour—Phil and Fee sent Thomas home and began to clean up. While the dishes were still piled in the sink, they were accosted by Mrs. Pippin, fresh from the hop gardens and full of righteous ire at all outlanders.

"I'm sorry I used so much of your food. I had some . . . people over."

"Never mind about the food. You took it from the slops cupboard, from what I can see."

To the sisters' chagrin, Mrs. Pippin pointed out which cabinets held food for human consumption, and which contained stale bread, slightly moldy cheese, and sour milk, provender for the vastly pregnant sow.

"If they can take that, they can take the Germans," Phil said, after Fee admitted she'd scraped a bit of mold from the loaves.

"I met your lot of ragtags on the way back," Mrs. Pippin said as she rewashed the dishes the sisters thought they'd already scrubbed spotless. "Dooley says there's Germans on Guernsey. That true?"

Phil nodded. "Starving, too, from what I hear, both sides."

Mrs. Pippin looked over her suds to some long-ago time, her busy little hands falling still. "I went to Guernsey when I was a girl. My mother took ill one summer, and my father had the farm to tend, so I was sent to a relative there. They were goat herders and lived up on the crags, but when I climbed high enough, I could see the sea all around. Blue above, blue below, and me, five years old, on a rock in the middle. The goats there are golden, you know."

She broke off and a said brusquely, "A shame Guernsey's been invaded, but it's hardly proper England. Practically France." She dried her hands as if she were wiping the years away, and turned her attention to supper.

"You see," Phil said when they'd migrated to the parlor, "even Mrs. Pippin can feel the war now. Just give me a few weeks, and I'll have the town whipped into shape. Only, I wish I knew the best way to go about it. What if the Germans really do come? I know how to fight a man." She held up her deceptively delicate fists. "But I don't know how to fight an army."

"I thought you said if you could hang upside down with a passel of men trying to peer at your knickers, you could do anything," Fee reminded her.

Phil was about to tell Fee to mind her own knickers when a hoarse voice from the sofa said, "That, I'd pay to see."

Phil almost didn't recognize Uncle Walter without his WWI gas mask on. Hunkered in his room, chained to the radiator, he'd been a ruined hulk, a decrepit shell sunk in his memories. She'd thought of him as Mrs. Pippin's uncle, but now she realized he must be her brother, and Algernon's uncle. He was in his late forties at most, with a long nose and small, bird-bright eyes. He hadn't been out of his room since the Albions arrived, but now he sat on the sofa. It was evidently one of his good days.

"I saw you out there with them," he said. "You're wasting your time, you know."

"Yes," Phil said, "that does seem to be the general consensus."

"It's not just Bittersweet, though. People don't think about things, if they can help it. Especially when it comes to war. People rush into it without thinking, and they hide from it without thinking. I've seen ten thousand boys run straight into enemy fire without thinking a single thought. Do it, someone says, and they do. And then ministers and men dither and mutter with empty pates when a few minutes of violence would stem a lifetime of bloodshed. They don't think, you see. Ah, but where does that get you most of the time? Crazy or dead. Well, everything gets you dead, doesn't it. Eventually. Can't win."

Perhaps not such a good day after all, Phil thought. She backed up a step.

"War's like tennis," Uncle Walter went on, perched on the edge of the sofa with his elbows on his knees. "You lob the ball to me. What can I do but knock it back, then you to me, over and over? If I don't, I lose. You won't put down your racket, for then you'd lose. One man who stops to think in the middle of the battlefield is dead. Ten million men who stop to think in the heat of war are a generation of angels who will make a heaven on earth."

Phil didn't quite grasp what he was saying, but Fee drifted to sit at his side and asked, "What's the answer, then?"

"Ah, but that would require thinking, pet, and I gave that up with my marbles and my gun. Let's speak of pleasanter things. Which of you used to hang upside down in her knickers?"

"That would be me, and the answer's easy," Phil said. "You defend yourself and what you love. They started it. We stop it."

He cocked his head up at her. "Spoken like a true heroine."

"War's not nice, but I won't feel guilty for thrashing someone who threatens me."

"They lob the ball, you return it. *Ad infinitum, ad nauseam.*"

"Better that than getting whacked in the loaf with a tennis ball," Phil said, and Uncle Walter gave a laugh that sounded perfectly sane. "Look here, I want your help."

"Anything to oblige, my dear." For a moment she could see the man he'd been, gay and insouciant and twenty, charming the local ladies in the years leading up to the War to End All Wars.

"I need you to help me drill my Home Guard volunteers."

All at once his eyes glazed over, and without a word he stood, brushed past them, and shuffled down the hall. The girls stared at each other for a moment, then followed him. By the time they got to his doorway, he had already chained himself to the radiator and was struggling with shaking fingers to pull his old army-issue gas mask over his glistening brow.

Phil squatted beside him and pulled the mask away. "Look at me. No—look at me!" She threw the mask across the room. "I know you're not crazy. Not really. It's just a dumb show to escape reality. You saw terrible things. Maybe you did terrible things. But can you be so selfish as to hide in your room when England needs you?"

"England doesn't need another man to shoot metal into meat."

"We have to make sure the best side wins."

"There is no best side."

"How can you say that? *We* don't round up people and call them undesirable. *We* don't work people with different opinions to death in labor camps. *We* don't try to take over the world."

"Only because it hasn't occurred to us. Or because it wouldn't be useful to whoever's in charge. Believe me, all humans are beasts. Go away."

"Pick up a gun and teach us how to fight!"

He closed his eyes, stuck his fingers in his ears, and began a sing-song chant. "Hit the ball, lob it back . . . hit the ball, lob it back."

However Phil shouted, however she shook him, he wouldn't acknowledge her after that.

"I'll get through to him somehow."

Fee took her sister in their familiar embrace, forehead to forehead. "Hasn't he suffered enough? Let him be, Phil."

"I have to do what I can, and more than I can, even if it comes to naught," Phil said at last. "Maybe I'm going about it all wrong."

"What do you mean?" Fee asked. She pulled her sister down onto the bed and began brushing out her hair, curling the tips around her fingers.

"This morning the villagers didn't care a fig for the war, and now I have twelve volunteers for the Home Guard, and half the rest of Bittersweet is at least thinking about doing their bit. It wasn't my doing, I know that. I have tea and Diana the Green-Eyed-Monster to thank."

"Mostly tea, I think."

"Exactly. Everyone has something that will spur him to action. I just have to find it."

Fee looked perplexed. "You mean, for Uncle Walter?"

"No, you goose—for the magicians! Why should they be any different from the villagers? Blind, stupid, closed-minded, parochial

—until you give them a damned good reason not to be. I just have to find their tea."

"But you said it yourself — all they care about is their college."

"Out of the hundreds of men there, surely a few would care about England, given the chance," Phil said. "Think what just one real magician could do. Here I am, teaching bakers and mechanics to slip handcuffs, when the magicians could pluck bombs from the sky!"

"But how will you convince them?"

"We just have to figure out what they need, what they long for, what they lack."

"They need women," Fee said promptly. "But if you're not up for seduction . . ."

"Well, I don't have to seduce them, but maybe I could show them something they haven't seen in a while."

Fee giggled.

"I didn't mean *that*," she said.

"Not even to win the war?"

"Well, certainly then. Now there's a thought. Flashing bosoms on the battlefield to distract enemy soldiers. You know they can't resist staring."

"It would never work. Our side would stare, too. Oh, we should tell Uncle Walter! Bosoms might bring about the ten million angels on the battlefield, all laying down their arms at once."

Chapter 9

Phil was still contemplating the conundrum the next morning —what does a man who can make anything with magic really need? She determined to grill Thomas that evening when he sneaked back to Weasel Rue as promised. If she could separate Fee from his lips. Honestly, you'd think the girl had never bussed a fellow, the way she went on.

True to his word, Thomas crept up to Weasel Rue farm near dusk.

"I can't stay long," he said. "I'm supposed to be out feeling the star Essence, which is the most boring thing on earth because no one can really feel it, but we all pretend to, faintly, and then look smug. May I have another kiss?"

Phil rolled her eyes, but Fee obliged, and soon she was so involved in this pleasant pursuit that she hardly flinched when Master Arden emerged from the gloaming and cried, "Ha!"

"A regular boys' night out," Phil said. "And you pass yourselves off as such models of monklike decorum! Off to the pub for a pint, are you?"

"I'm here to collect this wastrel before he's discovered missing," Arden said. "Take your hands off that hussy and come along, prentice."

No one called Fee a hussy, unless it was Phil herself. She swung for his face at exactly the same time Thomas charged him, shoulder first like a rugby forward, and barreled him to the ground. Once Thomas had the master pinned, he was like the dog who caught the car, having no idea what to do with his prize.

"Take it back," Thomas said.

"How dare you, you insolent—"

"Take it back, please," Thomas said calmly. "I won't let you up, else."

Arden hooked his foot under Thomas's hip and pushed him off. "Come with me now, or I'll—"

"I love her!" Thomas said, trying to hold Arden down.

"Love doesn't exist!" Arden said, and punched Thomas's naïve, angelic face, knocking him back onto the turf. Arden stood, looking ashamed, and brushed himself off, while Fee flung herself onto Thomas, covering his face with kisses (not realizing that's the very last thing a freshly punched person wants).

Phil stood between the men with her arms crossed. "You're not welcome here."

"This boy is my responsibility. Come, Thomas." His voice was paternal—stern and gentle—and Phil could tell how sorry he was.

Thomas got unsteadily to his feet. "I understand it now," he said softly.

"Understand what?" Arden asked.

"War," Thomas said. "I know now why someone will fight, why someone will kill. I love her, Arden. There is no love in the college, but I've found it, on my own. You can't take it away. I won't let you." He steeled himself and squared his broad shoulders, while Fee cooed and petted his battered face. "I won't let you," he said again, in deadly earnest.

"You know you have no choice," Arden replied. "You belong to the College of Drycraeft for life. You can't have a lover, or a wife, or a family. You're deluding yourself with this . . . oh, very well, she's not a hussy," he amended, seeing Thomas's eyes glitter dangerously. "But it's a fleeting experience, a passing physical sensation, nothing as enduring as our link to the Essence."

"You don't know," Thomas said hotly. "It's far better than the Essence."

"I *do* know. I—" He broke off. "Leave it for your journeyman year, prentice. Then you can dally with all the women you like, and be serving the college at the same time. Return to your studies, and in a week this girl will be nothing to you."

"I won't go back. You can't make me!"

"What a child you are," Arden said, shaking his head, and then the air began to glow with opal fire.

"No!" Thomas shouted, going suddenly stiff. "You can't take me back! I won't! I want to leave the college. Please!" He began to rise off the ground, his body tense and frozen. His next cry was cut off as the immobilization reached his mouth.

Fee dodged around her sister and fell at Arden's feet. "Please let him make his own choice," she begged him. "Forget about love. I know you despise it. Only think of him. Don't keep him a prisoner. If your Essence is the joy you say it is, shouldn't it be a pleasure to be at your college, not a punishment?"

"You don't understand. You couldn't. It isn't up to me. The other masters would track him down and bring him back—or kill him."

"No!" She clung to his trousers, and Arden looked embarrassed. "Can't you hide him, or—or—"

"There's nothing I can do. Particularly after the trouble I'm already in. Thomas is my prentice, bound to me. I'm responsible for his training and his conduct. If the other masters couldn't find him, I'd be punished in his stead." He gave a sardonic laugh and looked at Phil. "If you mean to make your claim on my life, you'd best be quick about it. There may be others clamoring for it, even if Thomas returns."

"How can you stay in that terrible place?" Phil asked.

She expected him to staunchly defend the college again, but he only said, "Cloistered peace is better than the fever of the world."

For a moment, Phil thought he looked like Uncle Walter, in that instant before he sank into his episodes of madness, voluntary or real. *Arden has suffered,* Phil realized, *and he shuts himself into the College of Drycraeft as others lock themselves into lunacy or the bottle to escape their pain.* She felt a fleeting tenderness that was rare for her, a Fee-like desire to offer comfort.

Arden turned on his heel, and Thomas, hovering, immobile as a trussed and frozen carcass, drifted behind him.

"Phil, do something!" Fee said.

"What can I do?"

"You can knock him down."

"He'd only get up again."

"Not if you knocked him hard enough."

"I can hear you, you know," Arden said, stopping, arms crossed. "Can't you two just let it go? Everything you've done has caused change and disruption. All we want is to be left alone. The college has endured for hundreds of years, after the last Albions tore it apart." He stopped short.

"What did you say?" Phil asked sharply.

"Nothing."

"You mean, there have been other Albions who knew about you?"

"That's not for me to say."

"Phil," Fee whispered urgently into her ear, "what about Thomas?"

"Oh, fine, we'll go with them and see what we can do."

"I forbid it!" Arden said.

"You might be able to do your hocus-pocus on that poor boy, but you know you can't touch us."

"I could knock *you* down."

If she didn't know better, she would have sworn he was starting to find this all just a little bit funny.

"Let Thomas go, and we'll all go to Stour together," Phil said.

Arden looked doubtful.

"He won't try to run," Fee said.

"And you could stop him if he did," said Phil. "You know it's wrong to keep someone against his will. Your college might as well be a prison. Let us talk to your headmaster. I'm sure he'll listen to reason."

"He'd die to protect the college."

"Yes, yes, I know that. You'd all die for your Essence, but you won't lift a finger for your fellow Englishman. But letting one boy leave isn't going to tear the place apart."

They're like gadflies, Arden thought, looking at the girls. Wisps of things with their hair like sunset, commingling in the evening breeze as they stood shoulder to shoulder, insignificant beside him, a master of the Essence, and yet somehow he could not rid himself of them. They buzzed their arguments and darted in with their incandescent emotions, stinging him until he thought he'd go mad. Short of pummeling them—and despite his peaceful vows he was sorely tempted—there was no way to evade them. He was skilled enough to open a portal and go directly to Stour in an instant, but what would that avail him? They'd just hike there and be pounding at the door within an hour and would never, never go away until they'd turned the entire college on its head.

There was a time when he'd firmly believed the college needed to be shaken up. Once, when he'd laid his head on a creamy breast and dreamed of a different future, he'd rehearsed the very words he'd say to Headmaster Rudyard. *I'm devoted to the Essence,* he would have said, *and will be all my life. But now that I'm trained and trustworthy, why not serve the world in the world. I would never use my abilities for power, or to change the course of events that don't concern me. Please, Headmaster, let me be free to love, to live, to—*

But he'd never had the chance to speak those words. His dreams had dissolved in Ruby's mocking laugh, the future he imagined washed down the drain of some back-alley clinic.

Now—he couldn't help it—he wondered if the fault had been

not with love but with its object. Seeing those two fools together, part of him wanted to say it was no more than the lust of young blood. But another part thought, *What if it is real? What will the college be killing by keeping them apart?*

And even if it was as false as saccharine, shouldn't they be allowed to discover it for themselves? If there was no pain at Stour, neither was there joy, save that which was to be found in the Essence. And that could be had anywhere, from Cornwall to Kent to Northumberland.

The Headmaster would never allow it. All the magicians were drilled from their first days at the college, when their home lives and kidnapping were still fresh, in why they were forbidden to leave.

Gently, he eased the boy to the ground and freed him from his magical bonds. Thomas rubbed his stiff limbs. "I didn't stop to think that you might be punished, too, master," he said meekly. "You've always been so kind to me. I'd never do anything to make you suffer." He turned to Fee. "I cannot leave the college if Master Arden will be punished."

"But—"

"Would you follow me if it meant your sister would come to harm? Don't lose hope, my love," he said when her eyes silvered with tears. "When he sees I'm in earnest, Headmaster Rudyard will have to let me go."

"You're forgetting the lessons of the past, prentice. He'd never risk another Schism. That was the fault of one man leaving."

"Yes, but—"

"Save your breath for the hike, prentice, and for kissing your sweetheart goodbye."

"You would let him go, if it were up to you?" Fee asked.

Arden didn't answer.

Thomas and Fee walked slowly ahead. His arm held her shoulders, while both of hers encircled his waist, and her head lay on his breast. How they could locomote like that was beyond Phil, but she supposed that love made people insensible to comfort and practicality.

Phil and Arden walked several paces behind, a suitable distance apart. "I thought you weren't supposed to use the Essence," Phil said as they strolled along the rutted track.

He'd forgotten. It was such a part of him that he'd used it as naturally as blinking.

"I suppose I'll be punished for that, too."

"The very idea that they can discipline a grown man like a schoolboy," Phil scoffed. "Flogging?" She sounded hopeful.

"No, you know we don't condone violence of any kind."

"Hmm, like punching your prentice?"

"I—I made a mistake."

"You shouldn't have done it to the poor boy, but I like that you have it in you. Not a bad right hook."

He gave her a slantendicular glance.

"Are all the others like you, then? Keeping up a pretense of pacifism but full of pent-up rage? You tried to kill me with magic, and you knocked the snot out of Thomas, who by the way took it like a champion and knocked you down cleanly enough before. It strikes me that the currents run deeper than they appear to among you magicians. So what will they do to you, then?"

"If Thomas got away — if I allowed him to get away — they might well drain me. But for using the Essence when I'm under prohibition, they'll likely add to my current sentence."

"But obviously you can still use the Essence. They just trust you not to?"

"There must be trust with the kind of power we wield. Trust, and control." *But not enough trust,* he thought. *And too much control.*

No! he chided himself. *I've resigned myself to the way things must be. I must not think like that ever again.*

"When I was in school, we did whatever we could to get around our punishment. There was a girl who kept herself in candy money by selling prewritten sheets saying *I will not* a hundred times. In French and Latin and German, too. Cut our punishment in half, just having to fill in the crime."

He gave her a puzzled look.

"You know, the standard punishment, one hundred lines of *I will not* whatever. Dip Edith's pigtails in the inkwell. Make spitballs. Pass notes."

"I was only in school for a year. I started late, because . . . my mother was ill."

"And you started once she was well again?"

"I started after she died."

She didn't want to picture the little boy he'd been. She didn't want to feel sympathy.

"Mum kept me home until I was seven. She knew she was dying.

Then when she was gone, my father sent me to school. The College of Drycraeft took me when I was eight."

"Your poor father! He must have been mad with grief when they stole you away."

"He was dead by then. When they found me, I was living on the street."

It was getting harder and harder to fight the sympathy, and she really wished he wouldn't tell her about his childhood. He was so easy to hate that kind thoughts about him were unsettling. "How terrible, to lose father and mother both. How did he die?"

He was silent for so long, she thought he wasn't going to answer. *Of course, he hates me, and regrets he's said so much.*

Then, as they came within earshot of the griping and giggling hop pickers in the hanging trellised gardens, he said in a very low voice, "I killed him."

"What do you mean?" she asked, hoping he was being metaphorical, suffering from some misplaced guilt that his father suffered a heart attack while working hard to provide for his son.

"What do you think it means? I came into my powers, and I drained him of his Essence."

"It was an accident?"

"By no means. I had no idea what I was doing, mind you, but you couldn't call it an accident."

"But why?"

"He was a son of a bitch who beat me since I could stand, and beat my mother on her deathbed when she tried to protect me," he said. "He died in under a minute, and I ran away. If I'd known what I was about, he would have lasted a month, writhing and screaming all the while."

One magician, at least, was no pacifist, but a tiger in chains. Oh, but what a thing for a small boy to endure, first the abuse, and then the terrible responsibility of ending it.

Phil slowed, and Arden shortened his steps, too, so that they fell even farther behind the loving couple. From the darkening hop gardens came familiar London accents, coarse jesting, and cigarette smoke, hidden behind the row of hopper huts, tempting beckonings of her past life. It was the patter that filled the streets of her memory, the voices of charwomen and servants and East End housewives, as omnipresent a background there as birdsong was here. She wished she were home, then remembered, home might be a pile of rubble, now or in a day's time. This was a new world, where babies were bombed to oblivion on the day of their birth, and little boys executed their fathers with magic. She didn't understand it. Something had gone so horribly wrong, somewhere . . .

"It's not your fault," she told him, and almost reached out a hand to touch his shoulder but caught herself. He saw the gesture, though. "In any case, he deserved it, didn't he, for what he did to you and your mum? Maybe not the writhing and screaming bit—"

"The college believes that all life is equally valuable. The Essence within is what counts. The Essence is incorruptible."

"Do they know what you did?"

"Of course. It's a common enough story. When a child comes into his powers, he doesn't know how to use them. Without training, without control, he's a danger. That's why we always have journey-men out on search. Usually we get them just as they're budding, be-fore they do any inadvertent harm."

"Or advertent harm," she added, not sure if there was such a word.

"I've been absolved, and that chapter of my life is over now."

"You don't regret it, though."

He left the answer unsaid, and in the heavy silence of the unspo-ken, they walked the rest of the way to Stour.

Chapter 10

$\mathcal{S}$ay goodbye to me now," Thomas said, stopping at the barrier between the mundane and the magical and catching Fee's hands.

"You're giving up? You're not even going to try to leave?"

"I'll try, dearest, but if the Headmaster refuses, I dare not disobey. Our happiness is not the only thing at stake. For you, I would risk everything. My life would be nothing, sacrificed to my love for you."

Fee sniffed and was lost to sight in his embrace.

"I don't know why the Headmaster insists on keeping sentimental novels in the college library," Arden said in an aside to Phil. "Fills their heads with such utter nonsense. How could that fool think giving up his life would serve the cause of their love?"

"That's a step. You admit they're in love now?"

"Oh, I suppose they think they are, and that's as good as the real thing for now. It's all Romeo and Juliet and young Werther in his head, though."

"And Jane Austen and the Brontës in hers. At least her fantasies have a happy ending."

"Thomas's a dreamer, but he's got a practical streak in there somewhere. He knows he can't leave. He just should have known sooner. For both their sakes."

They watched Thomas push Fee far enough back to look into her eyes. "I would give up my life to be with you," he said, and Phil suppressed a snort. "But I can't hurt Arden. He's my teacher, and my friend. It is a matter of honor. I could not love you, dear, so much, loved I not honor more."

"Ugh, honor!" Fee said with absolute contempt. "I wouldn't mind if you left me to go to war, but this? Sealing yourself up in a nunnery? If you want Richard Lovelace, remember, stone walls do not a prison make, nor iron bars a cage. You've all walled yourselves up with fear. They want to confine you, but you've made your own dungeon of your mind, all of you, thinking you have to be shut off from everything that is wondrous about the world. You let yourselves be pent. If you all objected—"

"But we won't. And I can't. Oh, sweet, sweet love! I wish I'd never beheld you. My heart is rent from me, and my soul. Farewell." And he held her, tangled in her hair and fettered to her eye.

"Isn't there anything you can do?" Phil whispered to Arden.

He shook his head. "It will be like the pulling of a tooth—pain, but only for a moment, and then an empty place that one gets accustomed to. They will live. I did."

"You were in love?"

"We'd best go. They'll be gathered in the great room for the conclave. Hell. I ought to drain him unconscious and put him to bed. Prentice, are you certain you want to ask the Headmaster? You know how it will end."

"I do. But I have to try." He released Fee and marched resolutely off, leaving the others to follow him into Stour.

Magic or not, I don't see how anyone could miss this," Phil said as they walked on a gently undulating carpet of morning glories that reached their tendrils toward the massive pointed arch of the entranceway. She hadn't properly appreciated Stour's grandeur before, having been seized by a multitude of hands the last time she passed through, but now she couldn't see how any kind of magic could make Stour invisible. It was a fairy-tale creation—either that or a nightmare ghost-castle, she couldn't decide which. It was as if some impulsive child had been given an army of masons and told them, Towers! Stained glass! Points and spires! Higher! More!

Perhaps, she decided, it stayed hidden because it was simply too improbable. What the eye cannot believe, it often refuses to see. That thing with a horn cantered past them, and she resolutely closed her eyes until it was gone.

"Cathedral air," Fee said, breathing deeply once they were inside. She wasn't religious, but she liked to be in big churches. She would stand in the middle of the nave and throw her head back, so that some people assumed she was a student studying the architecture of the vaulting, while others thought she must be a budding young saint in the first ecstatic stages of beatification.

They followed Thomas's echoing footsteps though the deserted halls until they heard a door open and slam.

"He's inside," Arden said.

"Aren't we going in?" Fee asked.

"No, better not. They mistrust women, and you two are prime examples of their worst fears. You wait here. I'll go in, and if I don't come back—"

"We'll say a kind word at your memorial," Phil said.

Before the door banged closed again, they caught a glimpse of masses of men in all sorts of outlandish costumes from the last three hundred years, standing packed together in what might originally have been a ballroom or banquet hall.

"I do like their fashion sense," Fee said, leaning against a bas-relief in the wall. "Thomas told me they make all their clothes with their magic, according to pictures in books, and everyone picks whatever style appeals most. Imagine not having to follow trends, but wearing a chiton one day and a farthingale the next. Oh, I wish we were magic, too!"

"We are, just as much as we need to be. I wonder what happens to the magic women, anyway."

"Thomas said they have their own school, somewhere, but they don't have to stay there all their lives."

"That's odd."

"Right. So it doesn't make sense that the men have to be—"

They heard a muffled shout from within, cries first of indignation, then of fear.

"He can't be fighting them!" Fee said, and surged toward the door.

"Wait!" Phil said, catching her sleeve. "There are hundreds of men in there. What do you think you can do against all of them?"

"What can you do against the German army? But you still try. Let me go!"

"I'll go first, then. You'd only faint."

"I only faint at appropriate times," Fee answered. It was true. Fee had gotten through the first night of the Blitz without weakening once, but she'd been known to swoon from a too-vigorous foxtrot and fall into convenient arms, assuming the arms belonged to a handsome young man.

So they went in together, prepared for anything from incriminating stares to manhandling.

Not a single magician so much as noticed them. Which, for girls like Phil and Fee, was astounding.

Every eye in the torch-lit room was turned toward a raised dais at one end, where a black-clad figure stood, alert but relaxed, with his hands loosely clasped at the small of his back.

"It can't be!" Phil whispered.

The sable uniform of the Schutzstaffel, or the SS, the dreaded Nazi paramilitary unit, had all but been phased out by that time, replaced by suits of gray or brown. But the sinister image of a man in black flared breeches and glossy jackboots, a peaked cap and a crimson armband like a bloody wound, would live forever in English memory as the picture of the quintessential Nazi. The man who stood at his ease on the raised platform wore an immaculate SS uniform complete in every detail, from the emblazoned swastika on the armband to the death's head insignia at his throat — complete, that is, except for an incongruous deep purple turban that stood in place of the black cap. It was pinned in the front with a large opal and a fluttering aigrette, and spiky tips of corn-blond hair jutted from the back.

The room had gone quiet, shuffling feet and uncertain murmurs the only sounds in the vast hall. Phil and Fee edged along the wall to get a better look.

The man spoke. "I deeply regret that such an action was necessary." His voice, impeccable public-school English with German vowels, echoed through the room. "They will recover, in time. The next man who opposes me will not share their good fortune."

The sisters, pressing forward, saw a clearing in the crowd at the strange man's feet. Some dozen magicians lay splayed on the ground, Renaissance robes flung haphazardly atop Victorian greatcoats. The air around them crackled in staticky aftershocks of faint color. They did not move, and Phil couldn't tell if they were still breathing, though she could see no wounds.

"I thank you for your attention," he said, as though he were an honored guest speaker. "We will be comrades in the near future, and killing a great many of you would be an ill start. I am Herr Kommandant Klaus von Hahnsberg of the Universität Zauberhaft."

"The Schism faction," Phil heard someone say. "The Dresden school," said another. One man—Phil thought it was the plump fellow she'd intimidated on her first visit—simply fainted again, which told her more than anything.

"The time has come to heal the deep divisions that have separated our houses for so long. We have quarreled, true, but three hundred years is ample time for forgiveness. I have come to you with the intent of rejoining our two groups."

Headmaster Rudyard broke from the crowd, a splendid figure who made seventy seem like the prime of life, and this young buck of thirty a mere stripling. "You are not welcome in the College of Drycraeft. Three hundred years or three thousand, we will never accept you into our order."

The Kommandant threw back his head and laughed. "Us, join you? Masters of the Essence join this nunnery full of sniveling, cowardly old women? You mistake me. I offer you — or some of you, who might prove yourselves worthy — the chance to join our order at the university."

Gasps and denials, a few hushed cries of "Do something" and "Banish him, drain him."

"The Essence has no master," Rudyard said. "We are its servants. The separation has corrupted your understanding of drycraeft."

The Kommandant's voice rose to a frenzied pitch. "You are the ones who have become corrupted, you indolent, lazy wastes of power! Here you sit, in your pile of stones, doing nothing but playing with the Essence when you could be using it to rule the world!" He began to gesticulate wildly as he spoke. "We are the elite, masters among men, yet you lot live almost like commoners, doing nothing with your great gift, while the lowly crawl unhindered through the world like rats. We who control the Essence are supermen, gods, beside those — those vermin. In Germany, they understand that some people are aristocrats by virtue of birth, while some are no more than parasites. Magicians are the flower of humanity. All others are like worms beneath our feet."

He locked his fanatic gaze on first one, then another magician.

Most of the faces he met were full of disdain and incredulity, but a few, mostly younger, looked up at him with unconcealed interest.

"Join us! Assume your rightful place in the world. The commoners are doing our work for us—see how they've conquered all of Europe with just a little prodding on our part? Your island is next, then Russia, then the globe. You don't have much time to decide, my brothers. Soon it will be too late. The brave new world will be here—and you will be excluded from it."

With great dignity, Headmaster Rudyard said, "You've trespassed on our home long enough. Go, before we make you go. Or perhaps it will be too late for *you*."

Phil caught sight of Arden's sun-browned neck and thick queue of black hair. He had moved to stand beside the Headmaster, and when the threat was spoken, he gave a fierce, satisfied smile.

But the Kommandant only smirked. "Idle threats. I know your pacifist ways, old man. Using the Essence to harm another is a capital offense. Go on—I defy all of you together to try to drain my life. You cannot do it, and I'll tell you why. You fear your power. I wish you would put all of your wills together and drain me, just to have a taste of what you could be. It would be worth it, if it convinced all of you to join us. But you won't." He searched the group to find the young men who had looked so eager for his words. "Because I've convinced many of you already. Try it, old man, and you'll find half your students have turned against you."

"That's a lie!" Arden shouted, when the Headmaster said nothing. "We have a code, and not even a degenerate traitor like you will goad us into misusing the Essence."

"You'd be well advised not to try," the Kommandant said. "Your power is nothing compared to ours."

"We'll see about that," Arden said, and shook off the Headmaster's grasp.

"Are you challenging me?" the Kommandant asked with a slow smile.

"I'm telling you to leave," Arden said, stalking toward the dais. "Or we'll make you, one way or another."

"Ah, you will be an asset to our university," the Kommandant cried, delighted. "Such fire! You know your rightful place in the world, unlike these others with the weak, watery hearts of disgusting commoners. Shall we duel, then, as commoners do with blades? Single combat, you and I?"

"Master Arden, you forget yourself," the Headmaster warned.

But Phil could see Arden's face in profile grow focused and intense as he called upon the Essence to battle the intruder. His body began to glow, pearl soft at first, brightening a moment later, until it sparked orange-gold as he drew power from the earth.

The Kommandant narrowed his eyes, and it seemed as if some unseen hand laid a cloak across his shoulders, a red so dark it was almost black. Red, Phil thought, for Essence drawn from living things. The opal in his turban shone with incandescent fire.

For a long moment it seemed to Phil that nothing was happening. Beads of sweat blossomed on Arden's brow and dripped into his eyes, but he didn't blink. Then suddenly the Kommandant smiled, and the deep red glow snaked out to Arden's throat.

Arden's eyes bulged, and he clutched his neck, struggling for air.

He lunged for the intruder, then fell at his feet with the other stunned magicians. But he wasn't stunned—he was dying.

No one made a move to help him, and the vital sparking light hovering over Arden's skin flickered and expired.

"All right then," Phil said under her breath, and slipped away from her sister.

"Oi!" After Phil had proved such an adept at boxing, the Albions had briefly incorporated her skills into the act, with a bumptious Cockney-flavored script, but her twill trousers and cap, coupled with her fists, proved less of a draw than sequins and a sword, so the act was soon abandoned. Now that she was planning to resurrect her skills, she thought it would be best to get into character.

"Bugger off to a kraut house, Jerry," she said, and vaulted onto the dais.

The Kommandant looked at her as if she were a particularly pungent piece of offal. "You let your commoner whores speak? How novel! This one will have her tongue ripped out for her insolence."

The Essence surged through him, and he called upon the molecules of her tongue to violently disengage themselves from her body. Instead, to his surprise, the molecules of his own nose found themselves violently disarranged when her fist slammed into his face. A second punch knocked him down, breaking his concentration, and Arden gasped a grateful breath. By the time Phil had the presence of mind to save her knuckles from splitting by kicking him in the ribs, the Kommandant had managed to open a portal and vanished. Phil aimed a last kick at the empty air, just in case he was not gone but merely invisible, then sat down abruptly, shaking.

Fee was at her side in an instant, curling around her. "You were brilliant, Phil," she whispered. "The bravest person I know."

"Now that it's over, I don't feel so brave," Phil said. "Why do they always say to keep a stiff upper lip, Fee? My upper lip's fine, it's the lower one that's quivering like an aspen."

The stunned magicians were starting to revive. Some looked bewildered. "We were only going to contain him, Headmaster, I swear," one nonplussed middle-aged man in loud tweeds said. "Why did he do that to us?" Others looked positively militant. "How dare he!" an elderly magician spat as he hauled himself up with his cane, while another, rubbing his head, confessed in wonder that he'd never felt such power in one man. How had the German magician harnessed enough Essence to stop a dozen powerful magicians at one blow, and then proceeded to bring one of the most skilled young masters to the edge of death? The Essence itself was limitless, but there was certainly a limit to what one man could capture and use at any given moment.

"Everyone, to your quarters immediately. Journeymen, see that the prentices are secure. Elder masters, remain here with me. And you too, Master Arden," he added to the junior master.

Arden was still on his knees, gasping ragged breaths.

When the room had mostly cleared (except for Thomas, who lingered unnoticed by the door), Headmaster Rudyard climbed the stairs to the dais and stood behind the girls, ignoring them as if they were no more consequential than house cats. "Now, more than ever, we masters must maintain cohesion and calm. I do not think we should give much credence to this rogue magician's actions. Tomorrow I will address the college for a few moments, and then I want that to be the end of it." He made as if to step down from the dais.

"Not one of you helped me," Arden said, laboring to his feet. "Not a single one of you was man enough to help me."

"You know better than to engage in a duel," one of the other masters said. "Just because you choose to blatantly misuse the Essence, you can't expect us to follow suit."

"I am one of you!" he roared. "I am a master of the College of Drycraeft. That magician attacked us! He threatened our college, injured our brothers. He almost killed me!"

"If you hadn't—"

"You, Master Jereboam, are reputed to be second only to the Headmaster in your ability to channel the Essence, and yet you let that Dresden traitor knock you to the ground. Now you defend his actions, and condemn mine?"

"We have our laws for a reason."

"Times change," Arden said passionately. "He invaded our home, attacked us, and you would sit back and let him?"

"We have no intention of—" the Headmaster began, but Arden cut him off.

"Didn't you hear him? He and his magicians have meddled to start this war we've been hearing about. A world war."

"A commoner war," Master Jereboam spat derisively.

"A commoner saved my life when my friends and colleagues stood by watching me die, all because of an archaic code!"

He looked at Phil for the first time since the attack and gave her a barely perceptible nod. Fee would have demanded a flowery speech of contrition, perhaps delivered in full prostration, but for Phil, it was enough. She nodded back, and in those twin gestures was far more than Fee could have found in all of her dear Jane's books.

"He has declared war on the college," Arden went on.

"I'd hardly say —"

"Shut your mealy-mouthed yammering, Jereboam! Rudyard, you know what is coming. It's what we've feared for the last three hundred years. They should have killed the traitors when they left the college. That one man was almost enough to defeat us, as we are now, placid as cattle. More will come, and when they do, we must be ready to fight them!"

"We do not use the Essence for violence."

"You do if the conclave votes for it. Vote — right now. Let us resolve to drain them if they dare set foot in Stour again."

"There are other ways," the Headmaster said. He looked tired now, and old.

"What, appeasement? You've heard what the returning journeymen have said. The German commoners may be here any day, and with them the German magicians."

"They honor the Essence, the same as we do," Jereboam said. "Perhaps they have gone a bit astray in the years apart, but if we could only reason with them —"

"The Kommandant was right," Arden said bitterly. "You're all cowards. At least he will fight for what he wants."

"I don't think we *can* fight him," Jereboam said. "Did you feel the currents running though him? He's so much stronger than us. He certainly bested you."

Arden flushed. "I'd rather die fighting than show my belly like a cur. Maybe I can't fight him, but—"

"I can fight him," Phil said softly.

"—I'll be damned if I turn over the College of Drycraeft to him. We'll train, we'll get stronger, we'll practice using the Essence for combat."

"Never!" the Headmaster shouted. "We will never desecrate the sanctity of the Essence by using it for violent ends. Given time, I'm sure we can make the Dresden magicians see the error of their ways. This much is certain—if you use your power to do another harm, you yourself will be drained."

"How ironic," Arden said. "Headmaster, you've seen war yourself. Did negotiation save you in Mafeking? No, it was arms and blood. You killed your share in the siege, with the Essence, too, no doubt."

"We're getting ahead of ourselves. We don't know what the Dresden magicians will do. He might not represent all of them."

"We know the Germans are taking over the world, piece by piece."

"We will do our best to keep them from Stour, but the war is none of our concern. And we will not, under any circumstances, use the Essence against another human, be he magician or commoner."

"Then we are lost," Arden said, and turned away from his master in deep disappointment.

"I can fight them," Phil said again.

Arden turned on his heel. "What?"

"It doesn't matter how strong their magic might be—it won't hurt me. And you saw he had no inclination to fight me. He didn't block, he didn't react—he just ran. Or popped out." She didn't like to think what she would have done if the Kommandant had proven more adept. The only living things she'd struck were her brother Geoffrey and his boxing friends. She'd never had someone really try to hurt her.

"We don't need any commoner interfering—" Jereboam began, but Arden interrupted.

"You'd help us?"

"My little brother is here," she reminded him. "The German magicians killed his mother and hunted him. Do you think I'm going to let them take him now? Bad enough you lot have him. And if the German magicians are behind the war, and I can fight them, don't you think I will?"

"Even if we allowed you to help, there may be hundreds of them," the Headmaster said. "What could one girl do, albeit a girl immune to the Essence?"

"Two girls," Fee said, casting a quick, loving look at Thomas.

Phil squeezed her sister's hand, grateful.

"We have to let them help, Rudyard," Arden said. "And what's more, we should learn to fight ourselves. To hell with the Essence. There's more than one way to kill someone. There's nothing in our laws keeping me from binding someone with the Essence and then pummeling him with my fists." He recalled Phil in her glory. "Or chopping his head off with a sword."

"We are against all forms of violence," the Headmaster said.

"No, *you* are against all forms of violence, Rudyard. Nothing in our code prohibits fighting or killing, only using the Essence to do it. Phil, you'll teach us, then?"

"What I know," she said. "But I have a price."

"What is it?" Arden asked warily.

"I want your weapons. The guns, the swords, everything from the room where I was tied up."

The elder masters argued about it for the better part of three hours, politely debating while Arden shouted and thundered and paced and finally, in frustration, put his fist through a stained-glass window. The Headmaster calmly repaired both flesh and glass and resumed his placid deliberation.

After several informal votes, Master Jereboam was the only hold-out. Finally, near midnight, he threw up his hands and said, "Oh, for goodness' sake, yes, no, I'm far beyond caring. Let the little twits have their weapons, let the commoners fight their wars, let our masters become pugilists, so long as you let me go to sleep!" He gave a pro-digious yawn, voted yes, and left to tuck himself into bed, where he slept the deep, blissful sleep of the blameless.

Chapter 11

Y ou mean, you never got to ask?" Fee said as she leaned happily on Thomas's arm.

"No, the Dresden magician came before I could say a word. Oh, you should have heard the speech I had prepared. It would have melted the heart of a stone."

Luck favors young love. Headmaster Rudyard had put Arden in charge of coordinating the Albion girls. "Might as well be of some use," he'd said, "since you have another two weeks added on to your sentence." Arden needed an assistant, so he chose his young prentice. He was against Thomas's affair with Fee and didn't quite understand why he'd made their dreams come true when he knew they'd be in for a rude awakening soon enough. He had a glimpse of an answer when, as soon as they cleared the college grounds, Fee gave him a swift peck on the cheek, full of pretty, breathless gratitude.

Maybe happiness should be seized, he thought, *even if it won't last.*

Now the two escorted Phil and Fee back to Weasel Rue, loaded with swords and rifles. The prohibition on using the Essence didn't seem to bother Arden at all now. His eyes gleamed with a new passion, and the loss didn't hurt nearly as much. Betrayed by his comrades, he was feeling rebellious and knew how easily he'd defy his punishment if it proved necessary, or perhaps even merely convenient.

"Was he really at Mafeking?" Phil asked, shifting the brace of swords she carried over each shoulder.

"Oh, yes."

"But how? I thought you were captured—"

"Admitted, if you please."

"Certainly. Sounds more like an insane asylum that way. In any case, I thought you were admitted at an early age. How did he get to war?"

"Rudyard was an unusual case. He was a lord, taken young as the rest of us were, but he escaped and didn't rejoin us until he was much older. Most of our magicians are poor foundlings."

"Why?" she asked.

"Most of them have single mothers, so they're much more likely to be put up for adoption or grow up in poverty."

Phil crinkled her forehead in puzzlement. "But why on earth would more magicians be born to single mothers?"

"Because most of them have a magician father and a commoner mother. Journeymen in their period of travel father the children, then—"

"Return to the college, of course, leaving behind the poor woman who fell in love with them. Or is it rape?"

"No, no. How could you think that?"

"Ah, so only seduction, lies, and abandonment. Did you sire any children when you went out into the world, then?"

"I . . . no."

She looked relieved. "At least one of you has some morals. But if you're allowed to live in the world for a while, why not forever? Think of all the good you could do!"

"We have a strict tenet prohibiting us from interfering in the outside world. We have a sacred duty to perform the Exaltation, to circulate the Essence and keep the world alive. There's no room in our lives for anything else, not when the price of negligence is so high."

"Loyalty is all well and good, but what about love? For, um, children, I mean."

"There is no place for it."

"What a sad, sorry lot you all are," Phil said. "But what were you saying about the Headmaster?"

"He was one of the few magicians born to two commoners, the Lord and Lady Stour."

"So not quite commoners, then," Phil said.

"Even monarchs are commoners, to us," he said unflinchingly.

"And I'm a subcommoner, right?"

"You are . . . something else." He remembered his early disgust at the mere thought of her—cursed to be utterly without the Essence—and felt ashamed. She was hardly responsible for her lineage. He was starting to think he'd been wrong about her.

"Our journeymen found Rudyard at the usual age, around eight. But he wasn't a poor boy glad to be rid of hunger and disgrace. He was heir to Stour and even at that age was absolutely dedicated to his birthright. He was at the college for a little over a year, learning all he could, and then he escaped. There was such a sensation in the papers about it that the Headmaster at the time decided not to pursue him. He must have stayed mum and continued to practice using the Essence, because by the time he met up with members of the college again, he was much more powerful than any of them."

"Because he used it instead of just fiddling with it like you do."

"He'd joined the army and wound up in besieged Mafeking in the second Boer War. He was gravely wounded and sent home to die. A wandering journeyman was drawn to his power, as he lay on his deathbed, and saved his life. Grateful, and no doubt weary of war and of the world, he rejoined us and gave us Stour Manor for our new college."

"You haven't always been here?"

"We have to move every hundred years or so."

"So you don't get caught?"

"You make us sound like criminals."

"No, only kidnappers and traitors to your country."

"Hmm, well. Mostly we move because we have to spend time circulating the Essence in each part of the island, to keep it healthy."

"I don't know much about geology, but I bet there are fellows who could prove that you didn't raise England from the sea, and the earth is doing just fine without you."

"They'd be wrong," he said flatly, and having argued herself red in the face with fanatics before, Phil wisely let it drop.

When they neared Weasel Rue, Phil said, "It's odd your Headmaster would say he doesn't believe in interfering with the outside world, when it's plain he's cast a spell over all of Bittersweet."

"Ah, yes—that. But it's for our protection, not to exert any influence or control."

"You're keeping hundreds of people from doing their part. Bad enough you all are cowards—well, not one of you, maybe—without manipulating an entire village into being cowards, too. How do you do it?"

"The Headmaster reaches inside them and directs their thoughts. Here and in London, too."

"But that's a violation!" The idea of someone changing her thoughts was as bad a physical assault. "And why on earth, if you can do that, can't you reach across the Channel and meddle with Hitler's brain?"

"It's not as bad as you think," Arden assured her. "We can't actually make anyone do what he doesn't want to do; we only make it easier for him to do the easy thing, you see? People will always prefer to ignore the unpleasant parts of life, so it's simply a matter of making the people of Bittersweet turn away from anything that doesn't immediately concern them."

They both leaned against a tree while they waited for Fee and Thomas to bid each other farewell. Phil heard a sigh close to her ear and felt warm breath on her cheek, but when she turned her head, Arden was staring at the stars. She was profoundly glad that she was immune to the Essence and couldn't be manipulated into doing something she suddenly wanted to do, quite badly.

"I wish I could have persuaded Rudyard to let you live at Stour," Arden said, as the lovers' murmurs drifted from the darkness.

"You certainly have changed," Phil said, and leaned her cheek on the rough bark, wondering if he'd turn his head toward her, too.

But Arden, remembering his last doomed love affair, said stiffly, "It's only practical. If you have a guard dog, you don't bring it to visit, you chain it in the yard."

Stung, Phil stalked away.

Arden, alone, wondered why he was such a fool.

When I heard we were going to a farm, I worried we'd be with some strait-laced stickler who would impose a curfew and look askance if we wore makeup," Phil said to Fee as they crept into the pitch-dark house. "But I like Mrs. Pippin's laissez-faire attitude toward boarders. Bed, meals, and independence."

"She *does* look askance at your makeup, Phil, but then, so do I. You wear a bit too much lipstick."

"So do you, only you kiss it away. Well, has the shine rubbed off your romance?"

"Thomas is as heavenly as ever, thank you. He recited all of *The Lady of Shalott.*"

"How romantic. To be cooped up in a tower and then die the moment you escape in search of your true love."

"Phil dear, you've read more poetry than you let on."

"No, I've been kept awake too many nights with your reciting. Even German began to make sense after Mr. Somerset droned it into my ear for a few years. Oh, what a waste that was. I wonder if he's interned?"

"He wasn't German, silly. He was as English as you. Oh, damn!"

"What on earth?"

"The chickens!" In a flurry, Fee dashed out into the night to see if her feathered charges had settled themselves without her assistance. (They had, and she only succeeded in convincing them all that she was an invading fox and sending them into a squawking terror.)

Chuckling, Phil cut herself a thick slice of bread—not from the slops larder this time—and sat down at the kitchen table to spread it with butter and honey. She was proud of herself, proud of her swollen knuckles and the slightly sick feeling lingering in the pit of her stomach. *I fought a German!* she thought. She knew full well that instinct and adrenaline rather than any real skill had saved the day, but it was enough to encourage her.

I'll get the boxing vicar to help me give lessons, she thought, *and now that we have a few guns, surely there's someone in Bittersweet who knows how to shoot. I'll train with the villagers and do what I can for the magicians. And before long, they'll be willing to help me—with far more than weapons.*

Finally, she knew what the magicians needed: the very thing they despised her for, her invulnerability to the Essence. If she could help them in their struggle against the German magicians, surely they'd return the favor by helping England against the German army.

She heard a click and the whisper of the back door swinging carefully open.

Licking the last honeyed crumbs from her fingers, she called out softly, "I'm going to take a bath, Fee. See you in bed."

In the small morning hours, the house was hushed and still. Phil felt her way down the hall to the bathroom, which stood between their room and Uncle Walter's. *What a shame he's become a pacifist,* she thought as she turned on the tap. Still, she didn't entirely blame him.

After the Dresden magician disappeared, all she had wanted was to be somewhere nice and safe where she never, ever had to do anything remotely like that again. It was only when her nerves settled that she was sure she could do it all over, if she had to. If she could just convince Uncle Walter—the only real soldier in Bittersweet, except for Algie, of course—to teach her real military tactics.

"Of course he's antiwar," she murmured as she ran her hand under the hot water. "Who wants war? But he has to see that when someone attacks, you defend, and not only defend, but crush them. What rot about a tennis match! You don't keep the game going forever—you win it, as fast and as hard as you can, and do your best never to play another. Oh, thank goodness they haven't heard of the five-inch rule here," she added, guiltily filling the tub with scalding water to the rim.

The rest of the country was urged to take infrequent, shallow baths, to save on fuel and water. She'd meant to comply, even when not compelled, but "Oh, how heavenly!" she sighed as she sank to her chin. Steam rose from her skin, and she closed her eyes, thinking about Arden.

For the life of her, she couldn't figure him out. Did he hate her or not? And if so, was it because she couldn't feel the Essence, or because she was a woman, or because she was a troublemaker? It was as if he were an actor who kept slipping out of character, being kind, honest, even sentimental for minutes at a time, then remembering his role and putting his mask back on.

Or was the cold arrogance his real self, and the warmth no more than an act?

She was glad she'd have ample time to find out for herself.

"And if I don't like what I find," she whispered, her lips, just above the water line, making ripples, "then I can always claim his life." Not that she ever would, but she rather enjoyed the idea that she could hold it over his head like the sword of Damocles.

The bathroom had no window, so she was permitted the luxury of light at nighttime without any fear of alerting overhead planes with the slightest glimmer. Suddenly, the room went black.

She sat up and heard the door open. "Damn fuses," she said. "Fetch a candle, Fee, and I'll get out. It's still piping hot, and I didn't do anything unpleasant in it, I swear." She started to stand but slipped on the soap and splashed down on her backside just as the room seemed to explode around her. By the flare of muzzle-flash, she saw a hulking form in an olive field tunic reacquire its target: her.

She screamed, and since there was no retreating, she slithered out of the tub, clumsy as a seal on land, and tried to lunge past her attacker to the door. She hit his knees in the darkness, and they both went down, tangled, on the slippery floor. Another shot went wide, into the ceiling, and in the blaze of gunpowder incandescence she saw a face at least as terrified as her own. In a language she couldn't understand, he chanted what sounded like a paean of sorrow and resignation. Somewhere in the house, a light flipped on, and as the man hauled himself up and aimed a final shot at her chest, she could see tears streaming down his face.

"Es tut mir bahng," he wept. "Es tut mir vai."

She tried to push herself into the hall, but her bare feet skidded on the pooled water, and she squeezed her eyes shut as a gunshot filled her ears.

She opened them a moment later to see Uncle Walter clad only in a pair of boxers standing over her, a pistol in his hand. Her attacker bled out on the tile, convulsed, and was still. His countenance was oddly calm, as if he had expected no different end.

Uncle Walter stepped over the corpse and handed her a towel, averting his eyes until she was wrapped. She was shaking so badly that she fumbled it, and by the time she was covered, one corner was soaked in blood.

Not quite coherent yet, Phil said weakly, "You're not chained to the radiator?"

Uncle Walter knew what she meant, though, and said, perfectly steady and sane, "There are times to kill. This was one of them."

The front door slammed, making Phil take a quick terrified breath. But it was only Fee coming in from her chicken checking. "Oops," she said softly at the bang, then, as she came into the hall, "Oh no, I woke you all!"

Then—though later she always tried to deny it—Phil succumbed to mild hysterics, babbling incoherently about German assassins.

Mrs. Pippin ran from her room, took one look at the situation, made exactly the same sound she made when a sheep did something foolish and fatal, as sheep so often do, and bustled the girls into their room.

Algernon, cursing profusely at his blindness, stumbled into the hall with a shotgun at his shoulder. "Will someone point me in the right direction!" he shouted.

"You stand guard over the girls," Mrs. Pippin told her son, figuring a blind man with a shotgun had a reasonable chance of success against a potential enemy trapped in a doorway. "And you, Walter, at the front door. I'll ring for the constable, and I suppose the doctor, too, though I've seen stuffed Christmas geese on the table with more blood left in them than that man. Who is he? Looks a desperate wreck, to be sure."

With the same efficiency with which she coordinated a harvest or butchered a rabbit, she marshaled the household into action.

She should be the one leading the Home Guard, Phil thought in admiration when she'd calmed down. *And how is it that everyone seems to have a gun? No one volunteered theirs when I was looking for some to train with.* It never occurred to her that people, well-trained soldiers in particular, might not trust teenage girls with their weapons.

The constable arrived, bleary-eyed and mussed. "A stranger to these parts," he said when he'd examined the body. "Any of you know him?" No one did. "Perhaps he's some disgruntled city boyfriend?"

"Phil said she'd never seen him," Algernon told him. "She thinks he's . . ." It was almost too silly to say aloud.

"Out with it," the constable said.

"She thinks it's a German assassin."

"Why on earth would a German assassin be here, and if he was, why come after a girl in her bath? Did he offer her insult?"

"Aside from trying to shoot her? No."

"Then he must be a lunatic who broke into this house at random," the constable theorized. This was his first deadly crime, and he wanted it wrapped up swiftly and neatly.

"I think she believes he was trying to stop her from organizing the local Home Guard," Algernon said. "She was a bit beside herself, but she went on about her being the only one who could fight them."

"Germans on the brain," Mrs. Pippin said dismissively. "As if any would come here."

"He *is* German," Uncle Walter said, coming out of the girls' room. "A German Jew. I heard him speak. We had several Yiddish-speaking German Jews working as agents for us in the" —he gulped, and steadied himself —"in the last war."

"What did he say?"

"That I don't know."

"Are we sure the girl doesn't recognize him? Let's bring her out for another look."

"That wouldn't be wise," said the doctor. He'd just come from the girls' room. "She's had quite a shock and is still overwrought. It will do her no good to see a bloody corpse again."

But the constable, sensing his authority was being undermined, insisted, and Phil was brought out without much resistance. Truth be told, she wanted to see the man again. Something about him was bothering her.

"You don't have to go with me," Phil told Fee. "I can manage, and you don't want to see him."

"I *do* have to. What happens to you happens to me, too. You know that. If I see it, I can share it, and then it will be it easier for you. You shouldn't be alone in this pain."

It is *a pain,* Phil thought. *How well Fee understands. I ought to feel frightened, or panicked, or relieved, or angry, but somehow I'm only sad. Why is that?* she wondered.

One look at her attacker, and she understood. She'd been in no condition to notice before, in the flash and thunder and terror of the gunshots, but now, in the deathly quiet of the crime scene, she finally got a good look at the man who had tried to kill her.

Looming in the darkness in his baggy fatigues, he'd seemed a giant, as big as Orion in the sky. But in death, it seemed as if he'd hastened the transformation into skeleton. His face was gaunt, with deep-sunken eyes and dry white lips. His wrist looked too fragile to bear the weight of his gun. She could just barely see something moving in his hair: lice.

"He's starving," Phil said.

"If it's food he wanted, why ever didn't he steal it from the pantry?" Mrs. Pippin wondered. "There's a wheel of cheddar on the table that would have fed him for a week."

And suddenly Phil knew, with a sick feeling in the pit of her stomach, why this man had been sent to kill her. With the realization fled the last remnants of terror, replaced by a seething fury she'd never felt before, not even when the bombs fell on London.

"Is it all right if I go to sleep now?" she asked, her voice trembling.

"Of course, poor child," the constable said. "I have enough for my report."

The doctor fetched something from his black bag. "Here," he said, slipping two pills into her palm. "Take these, one for each of you, and you'll be out until noon tomorrow. Best thing for you."

Phil nodded, and the girls went to their room.

As soon as the door closed, Phil pounced on Fee in a flurry of furious tears. "He's a prisoner!" she said. "A German Jew, Uncle Walter said. He's from a forced labor camp, I know he is! Oh, the beasts, the filthy, filthy brutes! I could see it in his face, how much he hated what he was doing. He was weeping, Fee—weeping! The Dresden magicians must have threatened him, or his family . . . or promised him freedom if he did what they ordered. The poor man. They work them to death in those camps. He was no more than bones."

"You can't be sure," Fee began.

"I *am* sure," she said, pounding her fist on the bed. "And I swear to you, I will make them pay!" Her face was a mask of animal rage.

"Maybe you should take a sleeping pill," Fee said.

"No, there's no way I can sleep," Phil said, tucking the pills into a pocket of her gas mask satchel. "I have to talk to Uncle Walter."

"You're not going to tell him about the magicians, are you?"

"I might."

"He'll think you're as crazy as he is."

"He's not crazy," she said. "He proved that tonight. He just thinks war is the most inhumane thing in the world. After he hears this, he'll know there's something worse than mere war. People just need a good reason to fight. I was his reason tonight. When he knows about that poor man, he'll have another."

She slipped out, and before long Uncle Walter heard urgent knuckles rapping at his door.

Chapter 12

Phil, with the resilience of youth, really did sleep until noon, even without the pills. When she woke, the corpse was gone, the bathroom scrubbed clean, and the bullet holes were patched. Soon the only sign of the fray was the fresh, slightly damp plaster at the level where Phil's head had been.

"Did you have any luck with Uncle Walter?" Fee asked over tea and oatcakes. She'd been asleep by the time Phil returned.

"Yes and no."

"Don't tell me he believed you?"

"I'm not sure. I don't think he particularly cares whether it's true or not. I think the idea that it *could* be true is enough."

"Like when I read about bamboo slivers under the fingernails—ugh!"

"Er, yes, something like that. What he actually said was, 'It's a crime against nature to shoot pretty girls. Any reasonable civilization tosses 'em in the harem. These Germans must be worse than I thought.' In any event, he offered a compromise. He agreed to train me, but not the Home Guard or the magicians. I was a little vague, and I think he prefers to believe they're an academy of stage magicians like us."

"Good thing you didn't press it. I don't think his sanity could take it. I know mine hardly can. When do you start?"

"After tea I have my first shooting lesson."

"Then you'll train the rest?"

"I'll do my best. Do you suppose our teachers did it this way —cramming the night before to stay just one step ahead of their students? I wish I'd known. I wouldn't have felt so stupid all those years. Are you coming to Stour with me?" She was going to collect more guns, teach a passel of pacifists how to make their very first fist, and of course tell them about the attempt on her life.

"Naturally," Fee said, and to Phil's disgust, she simpered.

"Are you aware that you look like an utter nincompoop every time you so much as think of Thomas? If I ever fall in love, I promise I'm going to be sensible about it."

"Speaking of which, heard from Hector?"

"Bugger all," Phil said, and ran to her room to dig through her pile of dirty clothes. She emerged, a bit disheveled, a moment later with the letter she'd received two days ago and promptly forgotten amid all the bustle and excitement and danger.

Guiltily, she tore it open.

"What does he say?" Fee asked.

Phil skimmed through. "Training is going well. He gave his sergeant a black eye during hand-to-hand combat training, but he didn't get disciplined because the sergeant said it was better than a bayonet in the gut, and he might get a medal out of it, or a pension. The sergeant, not Hector. Let's see . . . he doesn't know where they'll be posted to, and he couldn't tell me anyway, but he has a feeling those French lessons might pay off. Hopes to go to Poland, though, to . . . oh!" She bit her lip. "To see if he can find any of Stan's Romany relatives and let them know what happened. I didn't write to tell him yet, did you? I'll do that right away, and Mum and Dad, too. It's inexcusable of me—and of you, too, so that makes me feel a bit better. Love to you, of course, and that's it."

Fee deftly plucked it out of her hand.

"Here! Give that back!"

"If that's all there is to it, why not let me read it," Fee said, dancing out of the way. "Oh ho!" She read aloud as Phil chased her around the table. "'One of the lads from Shropshire, who I don't think ever saw the inside of a schoolroom, asked Sarge if he could have three days of "passionate leave" because his sister was sick. Sarge said if he needed passionate leave for his sister, then everything he heard about Shropshire was true. Tell me, Phil, are you missing me too terribly? Should I ask my sergeant for passionate leave to visit you?' Oh, Phil! If you really don't care for him, you have to tell him." She sniggered. "Before he requests passionate leave."

"Oh, he's just joshing, and you know he means *compassionate*. Anyway, I never gave him any reason to think it would be anything serious."

"Didn't you? I remember you two being late to rehearsal, you with your hair mussed and him with a goofy face."

"You're a fine one to talk!"

"I adore Hector, but you know he isn't the one for you."

"He might be. If not him, who else?"

"Perhaps a certain Master of Drycraeft who stares his eyes out whenever you aren't looking."

Phil blew a raspberry. "Arden? He doesn't know what he wants, about anything."

"Oh, men have a way of figuring these things out, given time."

"Listen to you—you fall in love, and suddenly you're the voice of wisdom."

"I might be wrong about Arden, but you know I'm right about Hector. You have to tell him you're not in love with him."

"Just what he needs when he's about to be deployed—a Dear John letter."

"Better than letting him think he's coming home to you with a veil and orange blossoms."

"And I'll get a letter in return saying 'When did I ever propose?' No, better to just say nothing."

Fee shrugged and did just that. A few minutes later, after she'd painted her lips in a pretty pink pout, they set off for Stour.

The found the college in an uproar.

Arden—who would never admit he'd been watching for them for hours—ran out the door to meet them. "Another German magician came," he said, breathless after dashing down four flights of stairs.

"Was anyone hurt?" Phil asked.

"No, she opened a gateway to the journeyman dormitory, and—"

"She!" Fee shrilled in indignation.

"So the lads say. Several resisted, and she drained them insensible, but she managed to whisper promises to a few. Of course, they all said later they only listened to gather information for the masters to use, but one of the young louts — a journeyman named Bergen — has been spouting about parasite races and supermen and lord knows what rot."

The girls exchanged looks. "That's Nazi talk," Phil said.

"But what would the magicians have against the Jewish people?" Fee asked.

"*All* people," Phil said, bristling. "Isn't that what she meant, Arden? We're the parasites, the nonmagic."

"We had to confine him to his room after we caught him lecturing the prentices about magicians being the master race, and crushing the undesirables under our heels. To think that such a thing could take hold here in the college, after everything we've drilled into them."

"Drilling makes for parroting, not belief," Phil said. "Besides, I gather *you* think magicians are superior to the rest of humanity."

"We are," he said, not noticing Phil's expression as he scanned the grounds for any more disturbance. "But that's beside the point. Because we're better, we stay separate. Our only purpose is to tend the Essence. Any talk of being masters is fundamentally against our creed. We could rule, easily, but we have more important things to do with our power."

"Ah, so you're fine with the racial superiority part of Nazi ideology," Phil said archly. "Just not the world dominance part. Very reassuring."

"It isn't a question of race," he said. "It's a question of ability. I am more powerful than you, by virtue of my ability to control the

Essence. Therefore I'm superior. It's only logical. But I don't need to dominate you."

"I'd like to see you try," Phil said under her breath, but Arden had looked away again.

"Where is Jereboam? He's supposed to have to the journeymen gathered for your lesson."

"I don't think there will be a lesson," Phil said, taking Fee's hand and turning away.

"What? Of course there will. Just give me a moment to gather them. That Dresden magician was right about one thing—we're weaklings and cowards. To think we'll have to rely on crude instruments like knives and guns and fists when, if we only trained in practical use of the Essence, we could wipe those traitors from the face of the earth. Where are you going?" he added imperiously as the sisters walked away.

"We vermin would rather leave things to the supermen, if you don't mind. Just a few more meetings, and I'm sure you'll all be good little fascists, using us commoners for forced labor."

"Phil! I never meant—"

She whirled to face him suddenly, scarlet hair flying, hands on her hips. "My people—my parasitic, subhuman, commoner people—are fighting a war against the very idea of superiority. You have some turbaned fop and a German siren pop into your school—we have tanks waiting across the Channel, and planes dropping firebombs on us every night, and a madman controlling all of Europe! And you have the nerve to tell me you're superior to the rest of the world, but it doesn't really matter because you're too goddamned noble to rub it in our stupid little commoner faces? You, who won't lift a finger to stop millions of people from dying, have the gall to think you're better than my Mum and Dad and brother, who are risking their lives to keep the world sane and safe for everyone?"

"I never meant—"

"I was almost killed last night, just for helping you!"

"What!"

"And do you know who they sent to kill me? Someone both you and the Nazis think is subhuman. A nonmagic Jew. A Jewish prisoner. A starving, desperate, probably tortured man who was weeping when he pulled the trigger."

"My God!" Arden cried, in his distress unconsciously falling back to his eight-year-old self, for there was no religion at the college. "Are you hurt?"

"What do you care? I'm just an inferior commoner. Oh, that's right, I can be useful to you. Slave labor to teach you how to protect yourselves, when you won't do a thing for my people. Come on, Fee."

She tugged her sister along. Fee allowed herself to be led, a bit reluctantly, perhaps, because she was desperate to see Thomas, but family came first.

Arden ran after them. "Wait, you don't understand." He grabbed Phil by the shoulder to stop her.

She knocked him away with the back of her hand, then slapped him across the face. "You're either an isolationist superior magician, or you're part of the world. Make your choice. You can't have it both ways."

The girls stormed off (well, Phil stormed, Fee drifted like a misty morning rain) as Arden, gaping, watched them.

"Weren't you a little hard on him?" Fee asked, once they were out of earshot.

"Don't you dare start on me!" Phil snapped.

"Aren't you shooting yourself in the foot, just a bit? And I do hope saying that doesn't jinx you with Uncle Walter tonight, but really, fighting Germans is fighting Germans, and if those Dresden magicians are helping Hitler—"

"Arden and the rest could do it themselves, so much better than I ever could. Oh, what I wouldn't give to have their power! I damned well wouldn't let it go to waste like they do."

"If there's a chance they'll help, you better go back."

"No!" Her pride had been stung, and she wasn't ready to yield. "If they want my help, let them come to me."

How foolish Fee is, Phil mused as they walked, *thinking Arden has any interest in me. And how foolish I am, to be intrigued by the possibility.*

Good lord, woman, do you want to shoot your own head off?" Uncle Walter ranted. "No! Now you'll shoot me instead. Toward the target, please."

"But in movies they always hold their pistols up next to their heads, pointing at the sky."

"That's cinematography, not shooting. Did it ever occur to you that real life might be different?"

It had, but only recently, when she'd seen how terribly, viscously red spilled blood was.

He drilled her for an hour with the pistol, then introduced her to the rudiments of riflery. He reviewed the few firearms she'd gotten from the magicians. "They'll do," he said. "Archaic, but the principle's the same: gunpowder, lead, and blow a hole in the person you don't care for."

Saving her life seemed to have brought Uncle Walter out of his shell shock, real or feigned, for the time being.

"I'd forgotten," he said, "that there's fighting, and then there's fighting *for* something. In the trenches, it all gets blurred. When someone tries to kill a pretty girl, though, you remember that there are sometimes good reasons to do very unpleasant things. The problem is when kings and generals tell you to fight; when you're fighting to hold an imaginary line, not for a damsel in distress."

"Uncle Walter," she asked later, as she broke down the pistol to clean and oil it, "do you really believe me? About the magicians, I mean?"

"Seems an odd sort of thing for you to make up. I can think of a thousand more convincing lies. It's not significantly more likely that a starving refugee would break into a farm in the middle of nowhere and try to murder you in your bath, than it is that German magicians are trying to assassinate you."

"But still."

Uncle Walter shrugged. "I believe you about the magicians. I've seen one before, I think."

Now she was sure he was losing his tenuous hold on sanity again.

"It was in the war. I was holed up in a sniper position on a rise, while a skirmish was going on below me. The Germans were hopelessly outnumbered and outgunned; it should have been an easy victory. Then—and I could see it quite clearly through my spotting scope—a long-haired young man in a sort of parody of a uniform, rough olive wool, but cut in wide-legged flowing trousers and a puff-sleeved jacket, with a great shining opal necklace at his throat, raised his arms, and all at once our men began dropping like flies. Nearly the whole battalion was wiped out in the space of a minute. Gas, the report said, but what kind of gas picks and chooses its victims by uniform color? The Germans were in among us, but not one of them succumbed."

"It didn't affect you?"

"Well, I was hidden, up above the fighting, picking off officers, and no one had noticed me. I put a bullet in the fellow's brain, and the survivors, no more than a dozen or so, escaped."

"Did you tell anyone?"

"Ah, no. I was still gung ho then and didn't want to be marked as unfit for duty. And now you say you're trying to get England's own magicians into the war? Glory, can you picture it? A silent war for once, death without the booms and bangs."

She tried but still couldn't convince him to train either the magicians or the Home Guard himself. "I'm teaching you to shoot so you can protect yourself and your sister, that's all." He'd dipped his toe back into the waters of the world, but he wasn't willing to take the plunge.

As he left, he said, "Next time, if you're a good girl, I might even let you have bullets."

Alone in the field, Phil pantomimed the things she would teach her Home Guard the next morning, and so she was in a particularly militant frame of mind when Arden came tramping over the hill. Why then, she wondered, annoyed with herself, did she feel a surge of relief? Why did her heart give a leaping little flutter when he appeared?

When Phil finally found her tongue, she was not at her most diplomatic. "Come to apologize?" she asked sharply.

"No," Arden said, swinging a heavy satchel from his shoulder. "I've come to remind you about your part of our bargain. Our weapons in exchange for your training. We never promised to help you with your war. We can't, you know that. And our personal beliefs don't matter when we each have our own war to fight, do they? You need what I can give you, and I need you. Er, we need you."

He unzipped the elongated bag and drew out five matched and gleaming rifles.

"Where did those come from?" Phil asked. "I'd swear they weren't in the game room." Their stocks were made out of some burnished, leopard-spotted wood, the metal components were the shining blue-black of a raven's wing, and though her experience with rifles encompassed all of one hour, she knew, the moment she picked one of them up, that it was perfectly balanced, light, true.

"Some of the younger masters and I have been tinkering," he said, as Phil checked to see if it was unloaded, raised it to her shoulder, and dry-fired into the distant shrubbery. "We copied the rifle that seemed the most modern, and improved it a bit."

"So you made these with magic? The Essence, I mean?"

"Well, I didn't, because I'm still not allowed to. But my friends did."

"Can I use them, then?" Phil asked.

"Haven't you figured that much out yet?" he said. "The Essence doesn't touch you, true." He fixed his gaze steadily on her. "See, nothing, no matter how much Essence I draw."

"What did you try to do?"

"Change that ridiculous hair of yours to something a bit quieter."

Phil felt compelled to pull a lock over her shoulder and check, just to be sure. "Don't do that anymore," she warned.

"You know it won't work. Why should you mind?"

"It just gives me the willies to think you could change someone utterly against her will, make her do things she doesn't want to do, feel things she doesn't want to feel."

She almost wished she could blame some of what she was feeling on magic. It would make things far less confusing.

"But the Essence can also be used to make things, real things," Arden said. "And once they're in the world, there's no difference between what we create and what comes about naturally." He gave a little chuckle. "You can see the jungle and the wild beasts at Stour, right? We created them, too."

Phil marveled at the rifles a moment longer, still half-expecting them to dissolve in her hands. Arden took advantage of her distraction to glare at a serpentine tendril that tumbled on her cheek. It annoyed him, and he wanted very much to tuck it behind her ear. When she finally looked up and caught him staring, he coughed and stepped back.

"Well," he said brusquely, "does our agreement still hold? I've done my part, and I'll get you a few more rifles if you like. You'll come tomorrow morning?"

"I suppose," she said grudgingly. In her heart she was relieved that he'd made it easy for her to come back.

I guess an apology was too much to hope for, she thought as Arden strode away.

Then he turned, and her heart gave another one of its ridiculous dickey-bird leaps as he walked back and stood close, too close, oh lord, far too close, did these magicians have no sense of propriety?

"I *am* sorry," he said.

And before she could renew their conflict by belligerently pinning him down as to exactly what he was sorry for, he left.

Chapter 13

Don't you think it's terribly hard on him?" Fee asked as she leaned her head awkwardly out the window, letting the sun's last rays dry her strawberry masses of waves as she combed them into smooth obedience. "He must be pulled in a thousand directions. Well, three, at least." She knew Phil was, in her own way, as emotional a creature as she was, but she fought it so hard that it was always easier to stick to facts and certainties than feelings and exaggeration.

"A person should know what he believes," Phil said stoutly.

"Yes, people should," Fee owned, "but how can they, sometimes? I keep thinking of those little German children being raised to think the Hitler Youth is the best thing since the Girl Guides. All their friends are doing it, they have cute uniforms and get to wave flags, and everyone tells them they're wonderful. I wonder what we'd do, if we were ten years old and someone told us we were the master race and gave us little swastikas. Our parents taught us to make doves disappear and glue on false eyelashes, and we never questioned whether that was a normal lifestyle."

"And what does that have to do with Arden?"

"He's been indoctrinated in the ways of the college for more than half his life. You can't expect him to suddenly throw everything off. Part of him wants to be what they tell him to be, a passive custodian of the Essence, removed from the world. Part of him wants to defend what he loves, even if it goes against the rules of his order. And part of him wants to . . ."

"To what?"

"Oh, you know."

"You mean, do what the Dresden magicians want and rule the world with his magic?"

"Silly. Can't you see the poor man's half in love with you?"

Phil laughed. "Stop kidding around, Fee, and get ready for supper. A brace of geese tonight, Mrs. Pippin said."

"Oh no! Not Millie and Betsy!"

"I think so. Just don't make friends with the new piglets. We'll probably be having one next Easter, with an apple in its mouth."

Fee had a little weep—then at supper found the geese to be delicious. At around eight, there was a knock at the door. Everyone looked up in alarm, thinking the same thought.

"Nonsense!" Fee said. "If someone is going to attack, he doesn't *knock*. I'll get it." She hoped against hope it might be Thomas come to tell her he was released at last . . . or at least to give her a good-night kiss. She flung the creaking wooden door open and found a large craggy man pointing a pistol at her chest.

She couldn't tear her eyes away from the barrel's black maw, couldn't move, couldn't utter a sound. *Scream*, she told herself. *Even if he kills you, at least the others will have warning.*

Then the man reversed the pistol and handed it to her. It promptly fell from her nerveless fingers and landed with a thud, but fortunately not a bang.

"Oh dear," she said, finding her voice at last as the man pushed his way in. "Phil!"

As soon as Phil came in, licking goose grease from her fingers, the man pointed at her hair and began speaking rapidly in German. Fee could write lists of German nouns and verbs, but conversation was wholly beyond her. Phil, though, had begun reading Goethe (albeit against her will) by the time most German classes in England were canceled and could at least make out a word or two, here and there.

"Ich ergebe mich" was the phrase he repeated most frequently, in tones of utter weariness.

"What is he saying?" Fee asked, looking with moist eyes at the man's gaunt frame, his haunted visage. She wanted, more than anything, to make him a snack.

"I surrender," Phil replied.

He was another labor camp assassin sent by the Dresden magicians, only this time they thought they'd be clever by sending, not a middle-aged cobbler, but a warrior, a militant Zionist who'd been training to reclaim a different homeland before the Nazis had gained power. He'd fought the Germans with urban guerrilla tactics ever since the passing of the anti-Jewish Nuremberg Laws, until at last he was captured and, much to his surprise, not executed but sent to Dresden.

While there, he was . . ." Something or other," Phil said with a helpless shrug. "Something was done to him . . . acted upon him. I don't know what. Oh, damn! If only he'd quote something from *Faust*. It was bad, living death, I gather that much."

"They tortured him, I'm sure," Fee said.

"But it was something more, something worse. I wished I'd kept my German-English dicker, but I felt like a traitor owning it."

"In the meantime, don't you think we should give him dinner and a place to sleep?" Fee asked, finally succumbing to her nurturing nature.

After concealing the gun, they called in Mrs. Pippin and explained with a simulacrum of truth that he was a wanderer looking for work. They didn't let him talk, thinking there was probably no lie that could cover the coincidence of two Germans appearing in such a short time.

Though Mrs. Pippin was happy to offer a filling meal in the barn, she shooed the man out of her house as if he were an errant barnyard fowl. "Shan't have a lot of vagrants and tinkers in the place," she said. "Be sure and run him off when he's done. If he asks for odd jobs, tell him we have none."

"I suppose it wouldn't have done for him to stay here, anyway," Phil said later. "They're bound to send someone else after me, and if they find him here living high on the hog—"

Fee looked at her sister in amazement. "Aren't you even frightened that the Dresden magicians are sending people to kill you?"

"Of course I'm frightened," she replied. "But it doesn't do any good to bellyache about it, does it? Anyway, I'm not half so afraid now that I have a Luger." She slipped the gun out to admire it. "I finally have something small enough to carry with me all the time. Besides, they're sending people who don't really want to kill me, which is an entirely different thing."

They took him to the barn and stuffed him with every delicacy they could find, quizzing him between bites and understanding about half of his replies. "Rapp Schnur," he said at least a dozen times before they figured out it was his name. He had no family living—a sister had been taken to the Dachau concentration camp and died, of typhus, officially, but most likely from a combination of starvation, beatings, and overwork. There was therefore no one whose continued well-being could be used to blackmail him.

When he was taken by the men in the opals and turbans ("Thank goodness those words are the same in German and English," Phil said later. "We certainly never learned them from Mr. Somerset") and was tormented in that mysterious way they could not quite translate, he'd thought he was finished. Then a woman with *Sonnenschein* hair made him what sounded like a preposterous offer: go to England, shoot a girl, and be free.

"I remember her cursing that they couldn't use a Nazi soldier for the job," he said. "But the Führer wouldn't consent. Apparently their technique was still experimental, and the first people they sent didn't make it."

Of course Rapp had said yes, thinking that if he was given a gun, at worst he could use it on his captors and then on himself, or at best, he could surrender to English authorities.

"We're not much in the way of authorities," Fee said as she ladled plum preserves onto his bread. Rapp shook his head incomprehendingly but smiled.

"What I don't understand," he confessed, "is why they wanted me to kill you and not Winston Churchill."

"Oh, we English girls are more dangerous than mere politicians any day."

After some debate, they decided to take him to the college. "*Was ist das?*" Rapp Schnur asked when they came to the ha-ha bordering the vast starlit wilderness of Stour.

"You can see it?" Phil asked.

"I don't know how it is," Rapp Schnur said, as if in a dream. "Since they sent me to England, I've felt my vitality returning. They sent me to do evil, and look, I have received a blessing. And now, here—I feel as if my heart had stopped, only to begin beating again just now."

Phil translated the parts Fee couldn't catch, and they watched the tall man easily leap the ha-ha and walk toward the castle as if under compulsion. They followed and were met halfway by a cadre of magicians, led by Arden.

"Halt, traitor!" he cried.

"I thought you'd decided I was trustworthy," Phil said, frowning at the sudden shift.

"Not you—the Dresden magician. How are you keeping him captive?"

"Oh, he's no magician. He's another assassin they sent to do me in, but they picked someone sensible enough not to turn murderer under duress."

"He's a magician," Arden said, giving the habitual glower Phil was beginning to think attractive, if a tad overused. "I can feel the Essence radiating from him."

"Well, that would explain why he could see Stour," Phil said. "You have to take him in now."

Fortunately for everyone's sanity, if not their patience, the Stour library was the best collection in the county, and it wasn't long before they all had repaired to that dusty, drafty room and clustered over a century-old German-English dictionary.

"*Drained,* of course!" Phil said when they finally managed to decipher the word the man had used for the particularly horrible thing that had been done to him. "Stan told me the Dresden magicians used his mother like a milk cow. Do you think Rapp and Stan's mother were drained of their Essence the same way you tried to do to me?"

"Of course! That's how the Kommandant was so powerful—how he could best a roomful of magicians." Arden knit his brow and began to pace.

"The Essence contained in a magician is a far, far different thing than that contained in a commoner. From a commoner, we could only drain the Essence, but from another magician, we could borrow actual *power,* for a short time at least. There's the Essence, and then there's the ability to *use* the Essence. Could these Dresdeners be stealing other magicians' power? How else could they have defeated the strongest of us?"

"You among them," Phil said with what she intended as sarcasm, but one of the other young masters spoke up.

"Indeed, Master Arden here may have more intrinsic power than even the Headmaster. When we tried, four of us together could not take Arden."

"Hush!" Arden hissed, while the another master kicked him in the shin and a third called him a prentice-headed idiot.

Phil's eyes danced. "You mean, you've been defying house rules and practicing fighting with the Essence?"

"Please, lower your voice," Arden said. "The walls have ears."

She felt greater admiration for him than she ever had before. "You *will* fight!" she said warmly. "I was so sure you—" She'd been going to say *wouldn't*, but Fee's sharp elbow reached her ribs just in time and she edited it to "would."

"I've decided—that is, we've decided—that if we are willing to risk our lives to protect the College of Drycraeft, we must also be willing to forfeit our lives as punishment. Die in battle, or be executed afterward, it matters little, so long as we save the college."

"I seem to recall someone once mocking people who would die for what they love."

"I think that someone was you, Phil," Fee murmured.

"It gives me hope in mankind," Phil said, ignoring her.

"Magician-kind," Fee said.

"Oh no, they're still just men, after all. Now who was it said that, hmm?"

All this time, Rapp Schnur had been thumbing furiously through the dictionary. When there was finally a lull, he said haltingly, in English, "May I stay here?"

"Of course," Phil said.

"No," said Arden simultaneously.

"Where, then, if not here? He's a magician, you said so yourself."

"A German magician. The enemy."

"Idiot! Your enemy was torturing him. You have an obligation—"

"Fine, fine, if only to get to the bottom of what the Dresden magicians are doing."

"Making your own decisions, too?" Phil asked, amused.

Arden looked very grave. "We've decided the laws of the College of Drycraeft are not perfectly constructed to meet this unforeseen situation. We've taken it upon ourselves to mount a guard on the grounds and defend the college and our fellow magicians in any way necessary. We knew the moment the German magician set foot here—even if he wasn't quite the magician we were prepared for. And we have empowered ourselves to make certain decisions for the college's welfare, without consulting the elder masters in full conclave."

"Sounds perilously like mutiny," Phil said.

Fee, who had read books about mutineers and knew they didn't meet pretty ends, said, "Thomas isn't involved, is he? Oh Arden, please don't let him!"

How odd, Arden thought as he looked at her beseeching face. *Those eyes, so like her sister's, do nothing at all to me. And yet if Phil ever looked at me like that, pleading . . .*

"You don't have to worry," he said brusquely. "We won't have any giddy prentices spoiling our work. Now, can you come in the morning? We have a lot of work to do."

"While Rudyard and the other oldsters cogitate in their studies about whether to propose a vote to discuss the mere possibility of using the Essence to save their lives," another smirking young master named Hereweald added under his breath.

The other masters laughed, but Arden only pressed his lips together and stared hard at the table.

From that day forth, Phil settled into a regular, if exhausting pattern. Algernon reminded her about her promise to milk the cows in exchange for his help, so her days began and ended with udders. In between came Home Guard in the morning, and what the magicians had come to call Phil's muster in the afternoon. She was wearing herself to a frazzle hiking to Bittersweet and Stour every day, but she was content at last, convinced she was doing everything one girl could do in defense of her homeland.

Headmaster Rudyard, while not actually forbidding his magicians to train in physical fighting, made it clear he strongly disapproved of the muster. There had been no further incursions on college soil, and though he officially deplored the two attempts on Phil's life, he pointed out whenever he had the opportunity that commoner matters were not college matters.

Phil started them on boxing and escapes first, along with a general encouragement to lift heavy objects and hit things with sticks. Many of the magicians were woefully out of shape. It wasn't long before they all demanded rifles and pistols, too, and soon one journeyman or another was always on noise-supression duty, ensuring that the crack of firearms didn't draw unwanted attention from the locals.

Arden kept his circle of mutineers small, no more than four or five other masters near his own age who, like him, were loyal to their traditions but dismayed that a rule that was on its own a capital thing couldn't be bent in the interests of self-preservation and world preservation. Thomas, as Arden's personal prentice, was of course on the fringes and knew all about his master's activities, though he was ordered to pretend not to and was refused admittance to the secret cabal. Arden was determined to keep him safely out of it. *For the boy's own sake,* he told himself. *Certainly not for Fee's, and most assuredly not because Phil's happiness depends on her sister's.*

But though the core of rebels was small, nearly half of the college wanted to train with Phil. Most couldn't, because the Headmaster suddenly arranged new, stringent schedules and invented seemingly arbitrary assignments almost daily. Each afternoon, though, at least a dozen magicians gathered on a hill behind Stour and trained. Different men came different days, and all together Phil thought about fifty or sixty learned the rudiments of what she had to teach.

Which was, gradually, and thanks mostly to her motley assortment of Home Guard volunteers, steadily increasing.

Each morning the Bittersweet guard either trained outdoors on the village common or repaired to a low escarpment outside the village for target practice. Since the magicians manufactured a perpetual supply of ammunition, they gained quick proficiency

One day the vicar showed up with two teenage wastrels in tow. "It's hard labor or jail," he told her, introducing the elder Joey and younger Peter.

"I suppose they can dig holes."

"Won't take orders from a girl my own age," Joey said. "Can't make me."

"I imagine she can, actually," the vicar said.

"I hope you don't mind," he told her later. "I'm at my wit's end what to do with them."

"Not at all—on one condition."

"Give me strength!"

And so the vicar agreed to offer boxing lessons. Not for the purposes of aggression or even defense, he adamantly insisted at every opportunity. Only in the name of physical and mental conditioning. A sort of physical prayer, he called it, to turn the mind and body away from sin.

Joey and Peter soon proved their true worth when they took advantage of a rare moment of quietude to shove an improvised firecracker down a gopher hole in their backyard.

Fee happened to be on a trip to town, hoping against hope that a stylish and inexpensive frock might have miraculously found its way to the general store. Ever more frantically in love with Thomas, she'd begun to worry he might get sick of her wearing the same old clothes over and over, never dreaming that, though he wrote sonnets about her earlobes and odes to her toes, he never gave a passing thought to her clothes, aside from a vague feeling that, if circumstances were just right, they might perhaps one day be off entirely. And so Fee spied the boys crouched near the hole just as it exploded and showered their gleeful faces with dirt.

When accosted, they freely admitted they were after gophers. Not realizing that the pests competed with them for their dinner, that every onion or carrot the gophers ate meant bland cabbage soup for the boys, she slapped them both and called them nasty beasts. Then she felt sorry, gave them a chocolate bar she'd been specially saving, and sermonized for half an hour on the need to be gentle and loving to all creatures. She walked away with their store of firecrackers and handed them over to Phil.

"You say they *made* these?" she asked.

"Yes, from fertilizer and such."

Phil tracked them down immediately and took them to the firing range outside Bittersweet and let them show off their pyrotechnics. When the last thunderous echoes died away and she could hear again, she asked, her eyes shining with excitement, "Can you make anything *bigger?*"

And so Phil acquired her own pair of sappers.

Chapter 14

The people of Bittersweet got themselves ready for a war they hardly believed was there.

Then the war came for them.

It was nearly October, and the hops were all in, drying comfortably in their oast houses, waiting to become beer. The guest pickers had gone home to their bombarded city. It was in the lull between hops and apples that life in Bittersweet changed. To Mr. Henshawe's amazement, he received an official document requesting the names and ages of all his customers.

"Cheek!" he said, and tossed it.

The following week he received another, this time accompanied by a stern sheet listing the scheduled fines for rationing violations, including being an uncooperative shopkeeper. This time, with great grumbling, he complied, and not long after that the first ration books arrived.

Unlike the rest of England, Bittersweet was well fixed for meat, butter, cheese, and eggs. Everyone had a vegetable garden, and besides apples there were damsons and sloes growing wild. There was no danger of starvation.

There was, however, great risk of grumpiness.

"Ten ounces of sugar a week?" Mrs. Enery gasped when Mr. Henshawe handed over her ration book. "Belt tightening indeed. My Enery will have to give up his roly-poly if I'm to have spotted dick for the gels at bridge. Still, to win the war . . ."

"That's ten ounces of sugar a *month*," the grocer said, and ducked behind the counter as Mrs. Enery vented her wrath on an unfortunate turnip.

And tea, the prop and support of the English people, barely trickled into Bittersweet.

There is some comfort in communal grumbling. It was mild misery, but it was shared misery for a good cause, and for the first week of rationing, everyone was well pleased.

But there was no comfort to be had with the first draft notice.

There were four young men between eighteen and twenty-five in Bittersweet. In the space of a few days, three of them were called up, and the fourth, deprived of his lifelong friends, signed on to follow them.

Their mothers wept unashamedly at the train station, draping themselves in a moist, gelatinous way over their embarrassed sons and then, when the engine pulled away, falling into one another's arms as the town's three-man band played "God Save the King" and "Apple Blossom Time."

The whole town had turned out, tight-lipped (save the mums) and doing their best to make the boys believe they were full-fledged heroes off to save their nation, while each was sure they were sending their young citizens off to die.

The train that carried the recruits off brought day-old papers, and those who subscribed grimly took their copies. Now that Bittersweet cared about the war, everyone read the news. Several families had even ordered wireless sets and invited their neighbors in to hear nightly reports—Churchill's gritty reassurance and cheering patriotic music, interspersed with baffling phrases that may have referred to the latest exhibit of surrealist art or may have been coded messages to the resistance. When they wanted to be particularly riled up, they fine-tuned their sets to catch the voice of the traitorous English citizen, Lord Haw Haw, broadcasting on the Nazi propaganda program, *Germany Calling.*

Once talk had been of hops and apples, of sheep and lumbago, of rusts and mites and scales. Now everything was War.

Walking through the dispirited village after the young soldiers had departed, Phil felt desolate. She looked at the nearest yards, their botanical beauty disrupted by the half-subterranean corrugated steel arches of Anderson shelters. Windows that had once been open and bright with borders of starched white lace curtains were now dark and forbidding. Hanging curtains couldn't stifle all the homefire glow, so most people tacked the edges down and never bothered to unpin them in the daylight.

"I *was* right to open their eyes, wasn't I, Fee?" she asked, frowning anxiously. The image of those four boys going off to war haunted her. She knew the odds were, at least one of them wouldn't return. "Maybe I should have left Bittersweet alone. What's the harm of a hundred or so people living in peace and ignorance, with plenty of sugar and their windows ablaze at midnight? What battle is lost for being four soldiers shy? Oh, I know, I know — I did the right thing. But it almost feels wrong!"

From the edge of the training field, Arden tried to put his finger on the proper metaphor for Phil. He knew he was at a profound disadvantage, having read none of the right books from which he could crib. He had never been to Arabia, had no idea what a burning oasis might look like at sunset against golden desert sands. He really could not say whether Phil, in her tight goldenrod sweater, her fiery hair unbound, most resembled a doubloon-laden treasure ship with billowing crimson sails, or a tropical island volcano erupting magma from a mountain of frangipani.

A flame, he decided at last. A flame that ignites what it touches. This girl had blazed through the village, undoing the subtle befuddlement Rudyard had orchestrated, and she had singed every student at Stour.

And consumed me, he confessed to himself.

"View haloo!" Phil cried across the field when she spied him, and sprinted over before he could retreat. "Caught you before you could go to ground. Why do you always lurk, eh? Afraid of a bit of fisticuffs? Come on, spar with me. I promise I won't beat you too badly."

"No, I —"

She shrugged before he could make a coherent argument and

flopped on the ground at his feet, suddenly boneless. "Oh, but I'm weary!" she said. "You'd think, being a teacher, I'd just shout advice from the sidelines, but somehow I seem to do twice the work. Do I ever ache! Here, do me a favor and press right there." She contorted her arms until she pointed to a hollow between her shoulder blade and her spine.

"I really don't think—"

"Don't think, just *do*. It will hurt me like the dickens, so you ought to enjoy it. Use your knuckles, or better yet your elbow, and dig right in. It's too tight for words. Ah! Oh! Yes! Harder! Ow! Not quite so hard. Ah, you're liking that now, aren't you?"

At those words he abruptly stopped, for he had indeed very much liked his fingers grasping the rough yellow wool of her shoulder, the nearness of his body to hers as he worked her tight muscle loose, the taste, the crinkled texture of the single flaming hair that wafted its way into his mouth.

"You've done an amazing job with them," Arden admitted.

"Well, they've been pining for action. You can't keep grown men cooped up and impotent. Even monks make Benedictine and get up to lord knows what behind their walls. How on earth did you keep the boys from rebelling for hundreds of years? Hey! Rapp!" she shouted as he sparred. "Don't cuddle him—kill him!"

"There has been rebellion before," Arden said. "Led by your ancestor, Godric Albion."

"You said there had been other Albions here before, but I thought you were being metaphorical. Other annoying commoner girls who frowned at you and called you cowards."

He looked down at the sunburned part in her hair and fought the urge to trace it with his finger.

"There was a clique of five or so journeyman going about their wanderings in the seventeenth century. Now they are forced to split up, but back then they traveled in groups. They made their way to the court of King Charles I and found the noble life so congenial they never left. Godric Albion was a favorite of the king, a sort of court jester and sage adviser combined, using the Essence to charm one and all. They were granted titles, land, political appointments—knowing all the while they'd have to disappear and return to the college for the rest of their lives. And they might have gone back placidly, if the Civil War hadn't begun. They were friends of King Charles, you see. Godric persuaded the other four journeymen to stay and fight, and he sneaked back to the college and recruited more, until the college was torn apart. The Schism, we call it."

"But they were stopped, right?" She had great gaps in her historical knowledge, but she knew the story of the first Charles's execution because she was always fascinated by his son, the romantic second Charles, he of the black curling lovelocks and a thousand mistresses.

"Aye. They were hunted down and dragged back to the college, to be publicly drained. Every magician, down to the youngest prentice, was forced to drain a part of the criminals' lives, so none would never forget what happened to traitors. A few escaped and fled to the Continent. Their descendants, and those they trained, are the Dresden magicians."

"And Godric?"

"They caught him, too, but they didn't kill him. They wanted him to suffer unspeakable torments for what he'd done, so they took away his link to the Essence."

"They made him a commoner? Oh, a fate worse than death!"

"He thought so. He tried to kill himself after, throwing himself out a window. Only it wasn't high enough, and they saved him, then turned him over to Cromwell. He spent the rest of the war in prison, and then the college lost track of him."

"And he's really my ancestor?"

"Presumably. I'd always wondered about him. It didn't seem to me that it was possible to simply turn someone from magician to commoner. But when I figured out what you are, it made sense. I thought you'd come to Stour to do what your ancestor did. I thought you knew, that your family had plotted through the generations to destroy us, or lure us back into the world."

"And what's wrong with that?"

"We need to use all our magic for the Exaltation. Out there we'd go mad with power, and the world would die."

"Hogwash. *You* wouldn't go mad, I can tell that."

"We all do, when we're on our Journeying. In one way or another, we're drunk with it. Then most of us become disgusted with ourselves and crawl home, repentant."

"Most of you?"

"It's a dangerous world out there. Journeymen sometimes meet with accidents if they let themselves get carried away."

"You mean—"

"Not such a peaceful order after all, are we? They're hunted down.

I never knew it happened until I became a master myself. One of my friends, a journeyman a few years my senior, never came home. They told me he was hit by a bus." He blinked quickly. "But it's necessary," he said, as though trying very hard to convince himself.

Phil jumped up suddenly, unnerved by his talk. When she was on edge at home, she sparred with Geoffrey. Now she needed to punch something, and Arden was the closest object at hand. "Put up your hands," she said, and hardly giving him time to brace himself, punched his cupped palm as hard as she could. "Now hit me!" she ordered when she was out of breath. As he swung, and she blocked and dodged, he made his confession.

"It could have been me," he said, narrowly missing her with an uppercut.

"You were in love," she said, remembering, and wondered why she was assaulted with a splinter of jealousy, sharp and insidiously probing. She stopped simply evading and went on the attack, jabbing him in the stomach. It made her feel a little better.

"I thought I was in love. An entirely different thing."

She shrugged and danced out of his range. "I wouldn't know. But I imagine it feels about the same, at the time. For her, you would have left the college?"

"I would have, once."

She looked at him, expecting to find anguish, regret. She saw only anger. His attack became fierce.

"You thought I couldn't go mad with power?" he asked. "I loved her. I lied just now. I didn't *think* I loved her. I *loved* her, with all my soul. I was wrong to love her. No, she was the wrong person to love.

But I did love her. She came to me one day and told me she was pregnant. I told her I'd do anything for her, work my fingers to the bone, be her slave, all to make sure she and our child were happy. Do you know what she did? She laughed and said all she needed was fifty dollars so she could get rid of it. It. Our child was an *it*. She was a singer, you see, on the make, looking for a patron. 'You're a swell kid,' she told me, 'but you're small time. I've got prospects.' She patted me on the cheek — it was worse than a slap — and slipped away. I thought I'd die. And then I decided to punish her."

"Like — like you did your father?" Phil panted.

"I might have, I was so hurt. But I wanted to hurt her, too, and make the punishment fit the crime. She'd found someone else right away. Or she'd had him already, I don't know. A rich man, a merchant, with a diamond on his pinky and another on his tie. He would have set her up in her own show. She was really quite good, you know. Only I made her come back to me."

"I thought you couldn't make anyone do something they didn't want to do."

"That's so . . . but it was easy enough to make her want to do it. I can make a lump of coal with the Essence, and I can make a diamond, too. I made her think I was rich, that she'd thrown a good thing away. And then . . ." He looked away. "Then I made her crawl. I made her grovel and debase herself as no woman ever has before. I, who would have been her slave, forced her to be my slave instead. And when I was thoroughly disgusted with her and myself, I left her in the gutter, weeping for me. Oh, don't worry," he added bitterly. "I'm sure she bounced back within a week. Probably told her merchant she was caring for her sick mother and took up with him again."

Phil's hands suddenly dropped to her side, and Arden barely had time to check his next punch. When she said nothing, he asked, in challenge, "Well, what do you think of me now?" He didn't know what had possessed him, telling her that. She'd despise him—as well she should. He despised himself for it.

Strange thoughts were filling Phil's head, things she wouldn't even tell Fee. But all she said, as the sun sank to the rim of the western hills, was, "She did throw a good thing away, the silly chit." And then, coach and drill sergeant again, she bellowed, "Felton! Forget Queensberry. If he's open below the belt, *hit* below the belt!"

Arden argued with himself for the next half-hour and almost won. Finally, by a supreme effort of will, dredging up some distant memory of what might be the proper thing to do at the moment, he asked almost angrily, "May I walk you home?"

Chapter 15

The setting alone would have been enough to make Fee fall in love—the sky, twilight purple and deepening by the moment to star-pricked charcoal; the froggy churr of a nightjar like a trembling heart; and a man, darkly vital and obviously brimming with a thousand unsaid things, beside her.

Phil, however, might just as well have placed a naked sword between them to keep them chastely separate. She walked beside Arden but kept a measured distance, almost intimate but not quite. He would have to make the effort to surmount that little extra gap between them.

"We . . . I . . . we can't thank you enough," he said.

"I thought I was the disruptive influence that was set to bring down the college," Phil countered, mentally kicking herself. *Why do I have to say these things? Fee would have sighed dreamily, and that would have been that.*

Of course, the last thing I need right now is for that particular thing to be that.

Then why on earth didn't I say "No, you can't walk me home"?

"You're really very . . . strong. For someone your size, I mean," Arden said, realizing what a conversational wasteland his life had been until now. The college certainly hadn't taught him how to make small talk or pay compliments. Strong for her size? Was that what a girl wanted to hear? He should have asked Thomas, if he hadn't been ashamed. In this, the prentice had surpassed the master.

"I have to be strong," she said. "My kind of magic is very physically demanding. I'm getting out of practice, though. I haven't escaped from a straitjacket in weeks. Maybe one of these days you can tie me up and—"

No, no, no, don't lead him there, she fumed. *Of course, he's the only man in the world who wouldn't make a randy joke about it.*

"I will if you like. I wouldn't mind seeing how you do it. I couldn't, really, that first day we met. You were so well tied up, and you got out of it so fast. Like magic."

She looked at him quickly enough to catch the tail end of his smile.

"Oh, that wasn't even a trick—that was good planning. I always have a pick or two and a bit of razor sewn into my clothes, just in case."

"That's how you do it onstage, then, at the—what was it—Hall of Illusion?"

"No, onstage it's the real thing. Well, the real fake thing. It's all trickery of one sort or another. And it isn't Illusion—it's Delusion."

He looked at her quizzically. The small talk was coming more naturally now, creating a comfortable buffer between all the things he wanted to say and shouldn't.

"An illusion is a creation that you know can't exist, but you see it, experience it anyway. You let yourself be fooled—you're complicit. A delusion, on the other hand, gives you something that you ought to know could never be real, but presents it so convincingly that you have no choice but to believe it. Other magicians just do illusions. The Albions are so great they can force people to believe what they know isn't real."

"Are commoners—forgive me, are people really so gullible?"

She shrugged. "People trust what they see, what they're told. Tell an audience that you're going to make the Victoria Memorial disappear, and though they'll claim they don't believe it's possible, they'll be primed for it. Oh, you can make people accept all sorts of outlandish things."

Not me, Arden thought stoutly. *A Master of Drycraeft can see through any deceit.*

"You might get a chance to see some of what we do," Phil went on. "The Home Guard has been asking Fee and me to put on a magic show for their Christmas celebration. We don't have any props, of course, and we'd have to requisition every light and mirror in town to make it really spectacular, but we should be able to put on a fairly good show. You're welcome to come, if—"

"There are a lot of *ifs*, aren't there."

"There always are, it seems. If the war isn't over and I'm not home. If we're not bombed to smithereens by then."

"If Rudyard still lets me sneak out of Stour. If you haven't decided to claim my life."

They were nearing Weasel Rue. The nestled farmhouse somehow managed to look cozy and inviting even without a candle in the window or a light under the door crack. Well blacked out, Phil thought with satisfaction. She stopped at the rustic post and rail fence that nominally separated the farmhouse grounds from the farming acres proper.

Foolish to get attached to a place, she thought, looking at the unlovely, snaking house. It wasn't home, it was only where she happened to live. Or if it was home, it was because Fee was there. Just as foolish to get attached to people. Phil had made such good friends here, though. She wished more than anything that the war would end and she could return to her normal life in London, and yet . . . *How perverse of me to almost be glad if it lasts just a little while longer.*

"Arden, are we friends?" she asked suddenly.

She had turned and was leaning her elbows back on the fence, hips canted forward, searching his face.

This is the moment, he thought. *Now is when I decide if I will follow Thomas's unwise path, or be sensible. My only purpose is to help the Essence flow through the world. Love has proven itself a worthless thing, and the fact that a beautiful, passionate, generally insufferable girl is gazing up at me in the darkness, mere inches away, is no reason at all why I should touch that preposterous red hair of hers.*

He did touch it, but only because that perpetually stray lock was about to go in her eye, and it was annoying him. There, now that it was safely tucked behind her ear, there was certainly no reason why his hand should linger on her cheek.

Though, somehow, it did.

"I didn't think it would be possible," he said, letting his fingers slide along the strong line of her jaw, while his thumb found eternal solace in the dimple of her chin.

"Most things are possible."

Not this, though, Arden told himself, even as his thumb, restless after all, touched her parted lips . . .

The front door of Weasel Rue opened, and the bright light streaming from within drew shadows from their bodies, entwined, for an instant, then abruptly separate.

Damn, each thought.

The person in the doorway couldn't see clearly out into the night. "Phil, is that you?" a familiar voice called.

Silhouetted against the cheerful farmhouse light stood Hector, manly in full uniform, grinning like a schoolboy.

"Who is that?" Arden asked, trying and failing to keep the jealousy out of his voice.

"He's my . . . brother," she said, which was true enough. "I should go." She tore herself away, the phantom of Arden's touch still on her lips. "Tomorrow?"

"Tomorrow," he promised.

She ran off, and he lingered at the fence watching her, glad beyond belief that he'd made the unwise choice after all. Tomorrow. Oh, tomorrow!

With an indulgent grin, happy for her happiness, Arden watched

Phil's brother race out to meet her . . . catch her up in his arms and whirl her around . . . kiss her . . . kiss her again, hard and lingering on the lips he'd only this very moment decided were his forever.

I was right, he thought bitterly, turning away. *Love is a lie.*

Phil, surprised, confused, and too polite to do what she really wanted to do, which was to shove Hector away and explain in a word that she had no desire to marry him, stayed in his arms because she couldn't immediately bring herself to crush someone she did, sincerely, love. Finally her lack of response gave him his first hint, and when he pulled away, still smiling, more tentatively now, her face told him the rest, and his smile trembled and collapsed.

"I got two days of 'passionate leave,'" he said, drawing himself up and forcing himself, as the army had taught him, to be indifferent and brave and oh so very English. "I thought I'd surprise you."

"You did! I'm so . . . of course I'm so happy to see you, darling." He winced at the word. "Come inside and tell me absolutely everything. Only . . . you go in, I'll be there in a jiffy." She sneaked a look over her shoulder into the night. Had Arden seen? She had to explain.

Hector allowed himself to be guided into the house, and Phil sprinted back to the fence. "Arden!" she called in a hoarse whisper. But he was gone.

She started to run after him but caught herself. She couldn't treat Hector like that. Despite their misunderstanding, he was still, as she'd told Arden, her brother, her own dear brother home on fleeting leave, and she had to spend every possible moment with him. Arden would surely understand. Perhaps, in the shadows, he had not seen that unbrotherly kiss. *Tomorrow,* he'd said. She caught her breath, the possibilities tingling through her body. Tonight she belonged to Hector, as his loving sister. But tomorrow! Oh, tomorrow!

Arden stormed into Stour with such ferocity that the little prentice who'd been set to watch for him trembled with dread as he relayed his message: Report to Headmaster Rudyard immediately.

"Tell him I'll see him in the morning," Arden snapped, and the little prentice burst into tears.

"Please, master, if you don't go, he'll think I didn't do my job, and he'll—"

"Oh, very well," he said, sweeping majestically past the sniveling child. He wanted to be alone, to hit something, to curse something, to set the world ablaze with the Essence and burn out the shameful feelings that—even now, even knowing her perfidy—ravaged his breast.

"I know what you're up to," Headmaster Rudyard said as soon as Arden entered his office.

For a moment he thought this must mean his uncontrollable passion for Phil, and with an angry flush rising to his cheeks, he was about to tell the Headmaster it was none of his damned business, and get the fight he was looking for. But Rudyard forestalled him.

"The secret meetings, training to use the Essence for violence. Did you really think you could hide it from me, Arden? Do you really believe I don't know everything that goes on in the bounds of Stour?"

(*Not everything,* Rudyard admitted to himself. *Not everything,* Arden thought with relief.)

"By rights I should call the college into full conclave now and see you and your cohorts condemned for this gross act of rebellion."

"The others aren't at fault. I ordered them, coerced them, threatened them—"

Rudyard held up his hand, and to Arden's amazement, his lips twitched in the faintest smile. "I know it doesn't take much to coerce a young man to action when his aged superiors seem to be doing nothing. I was your age, too, once." The mirth vanished. "In another time, we would not be having this conversation. You would simply be drained before your peers."

"Or in secret."

"Yes, if it was for the good of the college. But I need you. You above all. You, who came so close to not returning to the fold."

"You knew!"

Rudyard nodded. "But you did come back. The one who was sent to dispatch you reported that you'd abandoned the girl and were more than willing to return, after all. More than any other man here, you've shown that you can resist temptation, however pressing. And now, though what you're doing is in defiance of all our laws, a capital offense, I know you do it with an honest heart. You would die for the college. You would die for the Essence. Very likely, you *will* die for the Essence."

Arden's red-hot anger turned to ice.

"We are attacked on two fronts, Arden—by an enemy from without, and one from within. The Dresden magicians have returned to Stour."

"Impossible! We've . . . I've warded the place more heavily. I would have known."

"You are a child in cunning, compared to them. With their corruption of the Essence, they are capable of things we're not even aware of yet. They have an accomplice inside Stour who is manipulating the protection we've established, making a way for them to enter undetected."

"Then how do you know they've been here?"

"Even with help, they can only stay a few moments before being detected. One, at least, has managed to come here repeatedly."

"If they're here, why haven't they attacked?"

"They *are* attacking. They're attacking the minds of our magicians."

Aghast, Arden asked, "They can turn a man's mind against his will?"

Not for the first time, Rudyard wondered if it had been a mistake keeping the magicians fundamentally innocent all these hundreds of years. To be so ignorant of human nature . . . And yet their methods had kept the world safe and whole, so far. Who was he to question the old ways? And even among the sheltered men, there was always one who was a bit more worldly, a bit cannier, balancing right on the knife-edge of tractability. Rudyard had been such a man in his youth, and Arden was, in many ways, another. Had things gone otherwise, Arden might have one day succeeded him.

"They are not turning our magicians' minds against their will. They are telling suggestible men things they like to hear, about being special, and worthy, and powerful. What man does not want to be told he is of the master race?"

"But they know it already. What can the Dresdeners say that will sway them? Everyone here knows his duty. No one would betray the Essence. They all know what would happen to the earth."

"No doubt the Dresdeners are vowing they'll continue the Exaltation and all of our work and promising them more besides."

"What could they be promising? What could a magician possibly want that he couldn't conjure for himself with the Essence?"

"That is for you to find out. You must uncover the traitors, and you must find out what the Dresden invaders are planning."

"But how?" He thought he'd been so vigilant, yet one of the enemy had still gotten through. What more could he do?

"One discovers a traitor by becoming a traitor himself."

"No!"

"No one but you can do this task. You're known to be rebellious, and the threat of death already hangs over your head—a fine motivation for betrayal."

"Everyone knows I'm loyal."

"To the Essence, yes, but you will make them believe your loyalty to the college is fading. Let it be known, and she will come to you."

"She?"

"I believe the woman who visited the journeymen shortly after the Kommandant came is the one infiltrating the college now. I don't know how many have fallen under her sway, but if it continues, we may be faced with a war from within. Only you can stop it."

"Why not you, or Felton, or—"

"They say the Dresdener is very lovely, and young, with hair the color of the sun."

"Again, why me?"

Rudyard laughed, shaking his head in disbelief. "You have faults, Arden, but vanity is not among them. When you return to your room, look at yourself in the mirror, and you will see why you must be the opponent of a beautiful woman. You will seduce her. You will let her believe you are devoted to her. You, who have had such success in the world of love, will do this with ease."

"Success?" he asked weakly.

"You seem to inspire feminine devotion. That singer you had in London was so mad for you, she killed herself when you left her."

A deep chill settled into Arden's bones, and for a moment he couldn't breathe.

"Are you surprised? According to the one I'd set to watch you, she adored you. Jumped off a roof. And those Albion girls are always making eyes at you. The fierce one pretends not to, but the pretty, soft one, don't you see how she beams at you? You have a way with women, Arden. Time to put it to use for the good of the college."

You stupid old man, Arden longed to say. Fee, love him? Couldn't Rudyard see that she was simply joyously happy, that because she loved Thomas, she loved the world? And Phil—treacherous minx—no, he was being too hard on her. *She never said she loved me, never gave me reason to believe she did. There was no faith betrayed.*

Ah, but Ruby! All at once his injured, embittered heart melted. The thought of her supple soft limbs flung broken on the pavement, of that pert, sweet face shattered, dead . . . Had that been his fault? He hadn't meant to hurt her, exactly, not like that, only to make her *feel.* Poor Ruby. For the first time he remembered her without rancor, the way she'd climb and twine and press herself to him like an eager little capuchin, the old melancholy songs she'd sing after lovemaking—"Barbara Allen"; "My Lodging It Is on the Cold Ground"; "Early One Morning" . . .

His eyes grew heavy, and he blinked and looked away. It was as well Phil had not stayed in his arms, as well that she did not love him, or pretend to. *Because even if she did love me,* he thought, *I'd still have to seduce this Dresden magician with her sunshine hair. Now, it will be easy. I will be like Ruby was and make love without feeling love. No, I will certainly never feel love.*

"Learn their plans, Arden," the Headmaster went on. "They want to take over the college—I must know how! I don't know who the traitor is yet, but it would be wise to get closer to some of the journeymen she first approached, those who have begun to parrot her sacrilege and seemed to repent almost at once. Bergen was one, and Lightbody, and Jasper, though he's so good-natured and stupid, he always agrees with whoever's nearest. I heard him concur with a magpie, once."

Chapter 16

Hector stayed until noon, putting on a good face the whole while, such a very good face that Phil was caught off guard when, just before catching a ride with a corporal friend returning from Brighton, he pulled Phil aside.

"I know things are topsy-turvy. Us, and the world. You don't have to decide anything now. I know, you've decided already. Your lips told me, even without words. But it's a woman's privilege to change her mind, right? I just want you to know that, if you change yours, I won't say a word of reproach, only 'yes.' I love you, Phil. Always have, always will. I want you to be my wife, but if you won't be that, you'll still be my friend. Like it or not, eh?"

The news about Stan had certainly softened the blow of rejection. After a hasty conference, the sisters had decided to stay as far away from the truth as possible. They told him that Stan had been found, insensible, and taken to a country sanitarium where, the doctors were hopeful, he might regain his memory in a year's time.

"It's enough," Hector said, giving Phil a brotherly peck on the forehead. "I suppose *two* miracles would be asking a bit much of the cosmos."

As soon as he'd gone, Phil ran to Stour, but Arden was nowhere to be found, and she held her classes on the field as usual, bludgeoning her students without mercy, catching a tap on the cheek from the instantly contrite Rapp on one of the frequent occasions when she glanced hopefully over her shoulder toward the castle.

He came, as before, when the training was nearly over. He would have done his utmost to avoid her, but Rudyard had counseled him to keep to his former patterns as much as possible, so as not to arouse suspicion.

When she spied him at last, she lit on him like a hawk to her master. The words tumbled out, and she scarcely knew if she was coherent. "He *is* my brother. Stan's brother anyway. I mean . . . not quite that, but they came to the Hall of Delusion together, and he's lived with my family and we taught him, and it seemed quite natural for a time that we should marry one day, and I never really thought about it, but when I did think about it, I knew I wouldn't, and like Fee always says, you don't have to *think* about love, do you?"

She looked up at him expectantly.

"I don't think about it at all," he said, looking anywhere but at her.

"Oh!" she gasped, thinking he meant one thing, and then said, "Oh . . ." realizing that perhaps he meant something else entirely.

But no—last night, when his large sun-browned hand had been on her face, Phil knew, for a fleeting instant, what Fee had known every moment of her life since finding Thomas. He felt it, too, of that she was sure.

I deserve his coldness, she thought miserably, *because I didn't know my own mind when I should have. I know it now, Arden. Look at me!*

But he wouldn't. He couldn't. Even from the periphery of his vision, her face, her entire body were filled with such thrilling anticipation that if he looked, he would be lost.

Confused and hurt, she sat beside him and turned her attention to the last sparring magicians taking final playful jabs at each other as they drifted back to Stour in preparation for the evening's Exaltation.

"Coming, Arden?" the sweaty Master Felton asked, rather sloppily as he sucked on his bruised knuckles. "We only have half an hour or so until the Exaltation. Oh! I forgot you're forbidden. Forgive me." He stammered apologies until he was out of earshot.

Phil and Arden watched bats fill the gloaming as they fattened for their winter sleep. Night insects indulging in their last hurrah droned from the hedgerows. Phil pulled her sweater tighter across her chest against the crisping air, and Arden fought the urge to put an arm around her. *I've made up my mind,* he thought. *Why am I still here?* He pretended to adjust his jacket and in the process inched closer.

This is an interlude, the last one, he told himself. In just a moment, his work would begin in earnest. Already, he'd made contact with the traitor. It had been ridiculously easy — the journeyman was so eager to share what he was sure was the perfect truth, so flattered when, after hearing murmurs of heresy from Arden, the young master had listened to his ideas, had frowned, then nodded.

Tonight, when nearly all the rest of the college was at the Exaltation, Arden would commit his first traitorous act. "You may have to do terrible things," Rudyard had warned him. "Things that will make you despise yourself. When this is done, you may be so despoiled in spirit as to be unworthy of the Essence, and if that is so, I promise, I will drain you myself. Or it may be that the Dresdeners will kill you. Or if you are the man I take you for, you may well do away with yourself when it is over and done with. There is no shame in the peace of death, once you have done your duty."

(*You do not know what I can endure, old man.*)

"But you must do whatever is necessary to save the college, to serve the Essence, to keep the corrupt German magicians from taking over. Do you swear it?"

He had sworn, life and soul, to save the college.

Now, by the side of the girl he knew he loved, he allowed himself one last dream of happiness. *I could take her hand now.* "*Run away with me,*" *I'd say, and she would, I know she would! Let the college take care of itself. Damn Rudyard, and damn the college, and damn the . . . no I cannot damn the Essence. That at least is pure. But oh, how can their rules stop my heart? How can they tell me not to love? The German magicians let women in their order. Maybe . . . maybe . . .* No, for a thousand other reasons, but ultimately because despite her heritage, she was a commoner, and the Dresdeners despised commoners like vermin, like a disease.

But if there was a way to restore her powers, what then? He'd been talking with Thomas, who had a theory that what they'd done to Godric Albion, what his descendants had inherited, was reversible. Phil seemed to have no particular interest in restoring her birthright, but Thomas was obsessed with giving Fee back her link to the Essence. He'd been poring through college history, scouring the library for any hint, and he thought he almost understood what had been done, and how, perhaps, it could be undone.

If Phil was a magician, like him, and the Dresden magicians came to power . . .

Ah, he understood now what Rudyard had meant about not bending the magicians' will, but simply giving them something they want. No, he could never do it. But even if it was only in his thoughts, he'd come close enough to know that another man might yield.

The gap between them had almost closed, but Arden could waste no more time. The Exaltation was nearly half over.

"I have to go," he said, tucking his feet underneath him and rising.

"Oh," Phil said, and he searched her voice for regret.

"There's something I have to do. But tomorrow? You're coming again, right?" Tomorrow. Just last night, that word had held such promise. Now Arden sounded cold, angry, impossibly distant. "I come every day."

"Well, yes. I'll see you then."

She watched him walk toward Stour, all elongated shadow and mist, and felt, inexplicably, that she'd just lost him.

No, she amended, *I never had him. We're not of the same world, there's no possibility of happiness. He won't forsake his order, and I can't join it. Not that I would, even if I had his powers.*

Could it really be true? she wondered. *My ancestor, a magician? And if he hadn't rebelled so many centuries ago, I could have been one, too?*

No, silly, of course not, she chided herself. *Magicians can't have families, so the Albions wouldn't have been the Albions. If I even existed, I would have been conceived by some randy journeyman and raised without any knowledge of my father. Oh, Dad, how I miss you and Mum!*

She hadn't gotten a letter from them or her brother yet, but they'd told her to expect that—their group was top secret, their mission and location classified, and it was unlikely they'd be able to get any mail out for quite some time. "Don't fret about us," Mum had whispered to her with her goodbye kiss. "We're too valuable to be put in harm's way."

If Godric Albion hadn't had his magic stripped from him, Phil thought, *Mum and Dad and Geoffrey could defeat the entire Axis force all on their own. I could smash every German bomber against the Dover cliffs and keep London and Hull and Manchester from being bombed. Or perhaps I couldn't. They seem to believe girl magicians aren't worth much. Then again, I think they're wrong about a few other things.*

She dozed and dreamed, lulled by fiddling crickets and the drone of half-frozen cicadas, knowing she should be getting home but reluctant to leave the spot of earth that was still faintly warm from Arden's body. She held her palm over the radiating heat, a bit of his life still hovering beside her, and thought, *That's as near as I'll ever come to feeling the Essence for myself.*

"I'm close," she'd told Fee that morning. "I can see their opinions changing daily. Arden and his five followers are willing to do anything to save the college, but soon, very soon, I'll convince them to go a step farther. I've had to tread carefully, but they have had a taste of rebellion now, and they like it. And I know exactly what to test them on."

She would have that evening, if Arden hadn't left in such a hurry. Because, she told herself, her own desires were nothing to the needs of her country, and however her fantasies about Arden might shatter, there was still England to be saved.

Like very reliable German clockwork, the insect drone intensified, as if a great cicada god loomed in the heavens. Then the creatures of the ground fell silent, in awe of the mechanical monsters flying overhead.

For the past week Bittersweet, which hadn't seen a German plane even at the height of the Battle of Britain, was witness to steady convoys of German bombers and supporting fighters making their way to London each evening. Other routes had become too heavily guarded by the RAF and its spectacularly improved radar array, so they sneaked through the relative safety of the agricultural corridor, of which Bittersweet was the isolated heart.

There had been pandemonium the first night they were spotted. Joey, on watch, had run through town blowing a bugle until he was breathless (they hadn't invested in a siren), and villagers tumbled from their homes in their flannels and nightshirts and, in the case of the well-fashioned mechanic Eamon Dooley, in nothing at all but his Home Guard armband and his stirrup pump, much to the delight of his female neighbors. Buckets were filled to douse fires, sandbags slit to dump on incendiaries, and the villagers, forgetting their shelters, stood on the main street, watching squadrons of planes fill the skies.

No bombs fell; Bittersweet was too small a target.

"What's the matter, ain't we good enough for you?" shouted a furious Mrs. Enery as she shook her fist at the diminishing aircraft.

Now, on schedule, a wave of bombers passed overhead, and Phil cursed them as she did every night, wishing them fuel leaks and gremlins galore. If only Arden had stayed, she was sure she could have convinced him tonight.

"There's one sure way," Fee had told her a few days ago. "A man in love will do anything for his sweetheart—if he knows she loves him back."

"Love him? Why on earth would I get myself as hopelessly tangled as you? Your love is doomed. No, don't sniff at me, you knew it from the start. There's no future in it."

"But oh, what a present."

"Why should I love someone I can't have? If I don't want good, safe, practical Hector, why would I want Arden?"

"That's your problem, Phil. You *think* about love. A person can't decide to love someone, she just does, because she has no other choice, and damn the consequences."

Alone in the heavy silence of the planes' wakes, the spot beside her grown cold, she knew Fee was right.

How had it happened? There had been no revelation, no epiphany, only a slowly breaking dawn. No, she thought grimly—not dawn, but a descent into night, a love born of crepuscular shadow and imminent blackness.

I love him, but that doesn't change a thing. We can't be together.

I'm a soldier, as much as a girl on the home front can be, and this is war. There is no place for love.

An unintelligible cacophony of shouts came from Stour. The Exaltation must be over, and the magicians, the younger ones at least, were like students freed from class.

The sounds grew louder, and their tenor changed. She couldn't make out any words, but something was wrong, she was certain of it. Tying her hair into a double knot at the nape of her neck (she'd loosened it automatically when Arden had approached, which she only now dimly realized was a symptom of her feelings), she ran for the college.

She grabbed the first magician she recognized. "Hereweald, what's going on?"

"Rapp Schnurr's been murdered!"

She went cold, felt faint. "German magicians?"

"No. At least . . . there's no sign that anyone opened a portal."

"You could tell, even afterward?"

"Oh yes, it takes an awful lot of Essence. You couldn't miss it—it would be like missing a gunshot. We've all been on alert."

"Maybe you didn't feel it because of the Exaltation?"

He shook his head. "There was no portal. Someone here at Stour killed him."

Phil dug her fingers into the interstices of the golden stone walls, keeping herself upright with sheer force of will.

"But everyone was at the Exaltation, right?" she asked.

"Not Rapp. He wasn't ready for it yet. A few of the youngest prentices were inside Stour, and one or two people who were ill."

"And Arden."

"And Arden. But how could you think he would—"

"I didn't mean that!" Phil cried, appalled. "Only, is he safe? Have you accounted for him yet?" One look at her blanched, desperate face, and Hereweald knew her secret. *Lucky devil that Arden,* he thought. He'd spent more than a few nights rehearsing and discarding romantic speeches for Phil himself.

"Stay here. I'll find him."

Only Phil, being Phil, did not stay there. She paced, she stopped and interrogated every magician she knew by sight, and finally, driven to distraction with worry, she plunged into the heart of Stour.

She'd been inside the college a few times by then and knew her way around. The magicians' dormitories were in the east wing, with masters on the ground floor, mere collegians who never earned the name of master on the second, journeymen on the third, and prentices on the fourth and clustered in the attic rooms. Rapp, because of his age, had been placed with the journeymen, though he was classed as the greenest prentice.

She went to the third floor first. Surely Arden would be there, determined to find out what had happened to poor Rapp. It was easy to find his room. Magicians of all ranks filled the chamber and milled in the hall. Arden wasn't among them. She pushed her way through.

Headmaster Rudyard stood at Rapp's bedside, looking solemn but not overly disturbed. Phil could see Rapp's bare feet hanging over the edge of the bed. She stepped closer.

I'm not ready for war, she told herself, barely breathing. The neat, round seared-edged bullet holes in paper targets; the pheasants dying like blissful martyrs, expressionless, with a sacred heart of blood on their breasts; the glove-cushioned punches—she thought they had sufficiently prepared her for violence. She'd seen a man die, shot before her very eyes, and still, it was nothing to this.

She stared, but somehow she was more aware of things at the periphery of her vision than she was of her bludgeoned friend. At the window, a diaphanous curtain swelled in the chill breeze. In the corner, sudden movement when a middle-aged master bent and was sick. A very tall, beefy blond journeyman, standing on the edge of the crowd like a centurion, a head taller than anyone else, staring, not at the body, but at her.

Then, steeling herself, she forced herself to look, to really look at her murdered friend.

He hadn't been drained—there had been nothing peaceful about his final moment. He'd been beaten to death, and the heavy stone that was the murder weapon lay discarded on the floor, half under the tumbled bedclothes. Rapp's face was . . . gone. Whoever had done this had not been content merely to kill him.

"Who did this?" she whispered to Rudyard.

"One of the Dresden magicians came through a portal."

"No, that's not possible. Hereweald said—" She broke off. To speak of it might reveal Arden and the other masters' rebellious activities. "He told me the night the Kommandant came that you can tell—almost hear—when a portal is opened."

"And I did sense a portal opening," Rudyard said gravely. "Now go. This is a college matter, no affair for commoners."

There were disgruntled noises from the other magicians.

"It's *her* affair," one muttered.

"She's the only one who can properly fight the Dresden magicians," another said.

An elderly collegian on frail shaking legs said querulously, "If you'd made her welcome, she might have been here, stopped this abomination. No magicians killing magicians in *my* day."

"This will be discussed tomorrow in a Conclave of Masters," Rudyard said smoothly, emphasizing the last word to exclude the old man, who had never graduated to that august level. "For now, assign a detail to bury the body and . . ."

"That's it?" Phil asked. "Bury him and talk behind closed doors? Why aren't you opening a portal in Dresden and smiting all of *them* in their beds? You have to do something. He was my friend. He was killed because he refused to kill me."

"Then perhaps this is your fault," he said brusquely, and quit the room, leaving Phil stunned.

Several other magicians left with him, but the few who remained patted her on the shoulder and spoke words of sympathy.

"He's merged with the Essence now," the ancient collegian said, squinting at her with kindly, rheumy eyes. In his journeyman days he'd loved a girl who, in his fading memory at least, resembled Phil. But he'd returned to the fold. "Don't weep for him. The pain is gone now."

But when she looked again at the bloody pulp where Rapp's face had been, she knew the old man was wrong. Pain like that echoes through the world forever.

Wearily, she descended the stairs to the masters' floor and sought out Arden's room. She knew it was near the climbing wisteria, for he'd complained about the stubborn, clinging branches blocking his view.

On the third try she found it, an austere room with its window flung wide open. Thick creeping branches clawed their way in like cadaverous hands, rooted to the inner walls. The window had not been closed for months, at least, and the air had a cathedral chill.

Arden—oh, alive, thank heaven—stood with his back to her, washing his hands in a basin. He was scrubbing them with such a peculiar ferocity that he didn't hear her enter, and he turned with a start when she softly called his name, splashing a spray of russet water across the floor.

"You're safe?" she asked, standing perfectly still so she didn't throw herself into his arms.

"I—I cut myself." He held up his hand. Blood welled sluggishly from a slice on his finger.

She was ashamed that for an instant Arden's small wound caused her almost as much heartache as Rapp's death.

"I thought they might have gotten you, too," she stammered. "Please, may I sit down?" Without waiting for permission, she collapsed onto his rumpled bed, and when her knees gave way, so did the rest of her. "I'm sorry," she said between sobs. "It's just . . . his face! And you, alone here. I thought . . ." She sniffed, and tried to pull herself together, and wondered why he didn't wrap his body comfortingly around hers and tell her everything would be all right, even if it was a lie.

But he did not come to her, and she sniffed again, a self-pitying sniff that again shamed her. To her surprise, she caught a whiff of something familiar—almost, she would swear, the Jean Patou scent Mum wore when Dad took her dancing, Adieu Sagesse, Farewell Wisdom, the heady melange of neroli and spicy carnations, with animal base notes. She thought of Mum, glowing, on Dad's arm. Where was she now? An office in England or a trench in France?

No, it was only a ghost scent, the longing for Mum's comfort in lieu of Arden's. Only the dried dead flowerheads of Stour's gardens.

She drew a deep, shuddering breath and told him about Rapp Schnur.

"And Hereweald says there was no portal, but Rudyard says there was. What does it mean, Arden? You said he would . . . eliminate certain magicians. Could he have killed Rapp?"

"No, it is not possible," Arden said, but he crossed to the window and gave her his back.

"Who, then? It must be someone in Stour, someone who lives here. Or they could have opened a portal outside of Stour and sneaked in on foot, couldn't they? But you've told me you and your friends have wards on all the borders, beyond even what they usually have. You'd know if someone came in, right? Arden?"

He wouldn't look at her.

"You should bring in the constable. Oh, I know, but couldn't you fuddle him afterward? If it was one of the magicians, someone from the college I mean, he could find fingerprints, or clues, or—"

"No. There are enough commoners wandering through Stour already."

"But someone killed him—horribly. Please, won't you do something, Arden? The Headmaster, he just wants to bury him and have done with it. But if there was no portal, that means there's a traitor in Stour! Rudyard lied about the portal. You told me yourself he'd kill to protect the college, yet he forbids you to fight the Dresden magicians. It must be Rudyard. He must be the traitor."

"No!" Arden turned now, leaning back against the vine-clad windowsill and gripping it hard. "I'm sorry about your friend. I liked Rapp, too. But there are bigger things at stake than one man's life. You need to let this go. There are things you don't understand."

"Then tell me! Make me understand!"

"Please, Phil, just leave now. I don't want anything to—"

She saw it again, there on his face, saw just for one unguarded instant that reciprocation she longed for and made herself doubt and secretly believed in with all her heart. Advancing like a pugilist sure of her strike, she kissed him, her arms finding their home around his body with absolute relief. For a heartbeat the world was bliss, and she pressed herself to him, expecting that chimera melding of bodies, that perfection. But his hands still gripped the windowsill, and his body was as inert and indifferent to hers as an alabaster statue.

"Oh," she said, drawing away. *I made a mistake, that's all,* she told herself. *It's not the end of the world. It's not the end of anything, because nothing ever began. He doesn't love me, and of course—of course I don't love him.*

She fled, and even as she ran, she found herself listening for his pursuing steps, for a call that would make the world whole again. But she didn't stop, didn't turn. If she had, she would have seen Arden in his doorway, looking after her in a manner so peculiar that she wouldn't have been able to interpret it at all. Arden was skilled at glowering, a master of the wry and the sardonic, and he had looks of fury down pat. Alas, he had no talent for expressing yearning or regret or love, or for silently pleading for patience and forgiveness and understanding.

Not folding her in his embrace was the most difficult, distasteful thing he'd ever had to do. And mere moments ago, he had done something very difficult and distasteful indeed.

Methodically, he smoothed the disheveled bed and plucked from his pillow one luminous golden hair. He tossed it out the window, but an errant breeze caught it and sent it back to the climbing wisteria, where it tangled and writhed, a serpent in the moonlight.

He stripped and lay naked on top of his coverlet, wishing he could banish the other woman's smell, send the memory of her touch from his skin. Then he called upon the Essence, drawing it up from the ground through the stones of Stour, and through the window he never closed, until the powers of the earth made him pure again.

Chapter 17

Phil's muster was small the next evening. She took them to the firing range they'd devised, but their shots grew sloppy and widely spaced. She turned to boxing instead, but the young masters and journeymen were so dispirited, they seemed to be punching in slow motion.

When most of her muster had left to prepare for the Exaltation and only Arden's loyal young masters remained, she sat them in a loose circle around her. Arden himself was absent, and after her humiliation the night before, she was glad.

Tentatively, she led them to talk of possibilities. They were full of bravado when it came to what they'd do if they caught another Dresden magician on the grounds. Draining, Felton said. No, Hereweald insisted, something worse. Strangle them, like the Kommandant tried to do to Arden. Make his guts boil, suggested the eager, vulpine Master Todd.

"And if magic doesn't work, call on me," Phil said.

"You're a good egg," Felton told her. "If only Rudyard would let you stay in Stour, you'd have a chance of actually being here when they come."

"But I have my own war to fight." She told them about her night of the Blitz, and of all the nights that followed, which she'd heard about on the wireless, of families crushed in their homes, of hospital maternity wards catching fire.

"It's madness," Hereweald said, shaking his head. "Someone ought to stop it."

"Who?" Phil asked. "We're trying, all of England. But it would take heroes, someone with real power—and real love for this land."

And then, though it made her cringe inwardly, she took a piece of advice from Fee. She sighed, she looked kittenishly helpless, she batted her eyes.

"We could do it!" Felton said. "Once we crush these Dresdeners . . ."

"Ah, but that might be too late for the rest of us," she said, heaving another sigh, this time for the express purpose of lifting her bosom into prominence. Bosoms on the battlefield again. It was a wonder no one ever thought of it before. "Stour will be safe, but England will be destroyed."

"Tell us! Tell us what we can do!"

It was better than she'd hoped; on cue, the rising and falling cicada drone characteristic of the unsynchronized bomber engines sounded from the skies.

"There they go, to destroy my city, to kill more of my friends. Magician or commoner, Germans are the enemy of every Englishman. If only—if only you could stop the planes."

"We could, I think," Hereweald said.

"All of them?" Phil asked, face alight, envisioning the bombers disappearing from the skies, sent through a portal to Antarctica, or exploding in a grand supernova.

"Well, no, but maybe one or two."

"I thought the Essence was limitless."

"It is," he explained, "but we're not. It's like electrical power. At least, I think it is. Haven't used electricity since my journeyman days. But if you plug something in, it takes in a certain amount of power and works. But overload it, and it breaks. Poof!" He mimed his head exploding. "We learn to take more and more Essence, use more and more power, but there's a limit. At least, there is if we want to survive it. We've been training, though, and we're getting stronger by the day. We'll be strong enough for the Kommandant if he returns."

"The planes?" Phil prompted. The first of them were overhead, a few Junkers and Dorniers, but mostly the heavy, slow workhorses of the bomber fleet, the glazed, bullet-nosed Heinkels, carrying more than two tons of ordnance primed to drop on civilians.

"I think I could manage to stop one of them. But Headmaster Rudyard couldn't find out. What do you think, brothers?"

They murmured among themselves, while Phil watched the flock overhead. Two hundred at least, bombers and fighters, in a long loose formation. In another minute they would be past, and this might be the last night. She had heard on the radio that the RAF was engaging them farther from London each day, inflicting considerable losses.

The Germans would have to change tactics again soon. Phil desperately needed her magician friends to make this first commitment to fighting her war as well as theirs. After they had a taste of it, she was sure they wouldn't stop.

Explosion, she heard one say. Decompression, offered another. No, if we do anything that uses too much power, the Headmaster might feel it.

"Quick!" Phil said. "It's almost too late!"

"Well, we'll just buy more time," Hereweald said, grinning, his eyes half closed, head tipped skyward. A rich amber light heaved up from the earth, surrounding the magician's body in a glowing golden caul, and the last plane in formation froze in midair.

Phil breathed a sound of wonder as the plane, once so menacing, now seemed no more than a child's toy, a balsa model tethered to the ground on a fine string of Essence. To her surprise, she felt a flash of sympathy for the four-man crew, who must be scared out of their wits. *But what about the hundreds they might have killed tonight*, she reminded herself.

Holding the bomber still in the sky was obviously costing Hereweald some effort, and even in the chill dusk sweat beaded at his temples.

"Felton, will you do the honors?" he asked, his lips barely moving over clenched teeth.

"My pleasure," Felton said, and prepared to summon the Essence.

"What the hell do you think you're doing!" In a moment Arden was among them. Felton's concentration broke immediately, but Hereweald held.

"You do it then, Arden. It's your right." He meant, not that Arden was senior, but that as a man in love—as anyone could plainly see he was—he should bestow this gift on his beloved.

"Let the plane go," Arden growled.

"No!" Phil said. "It's their duty! These men, among all of the college, know what they owe to England, and to humanity. I thought you agreed that violence must be met with violence, whatever your laws say."

"This isn't what I meant. Those planes have nothing to do with us. Hereweald, let it go this instant."

"Arden, you led us so far—it's time we went a step farther. The enemies of England are our enemies. Let the plane and the crew return to the earth." And heedless whether the Headmaster might feel the percussive shock through the Essence, Hereweald called upon his power to dissolve the bomber and passengers into their elemental parts. He had decided, once and for all, that he was at war.

Arden's features steeled, and bright nacreous lightening flashed between the two men. At once Hereweald's jaw gaped and his eyes stretched wide in shock as he clutched at his chest, at a heart that quivered without beating.

"Arden, what are you doing?"

"Killing him," Arden said grimly, "unless he stops this madness."

Above, the Heinkel bomber shivered midair, then began to move.

Hereweald fell to the earth, kneeling, with his forehead to the dirt.

Felton leaped at Arden with a quick left jab and a right hook that—to Phil's immense pride—probably would have resulted in a knockout if Arden hadn't slammed his friend flat with a burst of the Essence.

"Arden, stop it!" Phil cried, grabbing his collar. There were so many other things she wanted to say, logic and curses and patriotic rhetoric, but in the end all she did was cling to him, her parted lips just below his, waiting for him to make everything all right.

He gripped her shoulders, squeezing them beneath the goldenrod wool so fiercely, she hardly knew he meant it for a caress. "You don't understand what's at stake. You don't know what I've had to—" He drew a sharp breath. This was no time for self-pity. "You're playing with the fate of the world like children." How could he explain without giving himself away? How could he ask for her patience, her love, when he hated himself for what he had to do? Still holding her, he glared over her head at his brother masters. "You will launch no more attacks on German commoners. Everything we do—everything!—is to protect the college and guard the Essence. We keep the world alive! Germans or English, it is nothing to us who is here."

She gave him a little shake. "Arden! You don't mean—"

But a shout from Hereweald killed all chance of Phil and Arden understanding each other then. "The plane! It's falling toward Stour!"

They knew so little of the modern world, had so little comprehension of technology, that it never occurred to any of them that a plane magically immobilized in the sky would not merrily continue its journey once released. The bomber stalled and began to fall nose first from the heavens. On board, the pilot desperately tried to get the engine started. It sputtered and caught for a moment, then died.

Phil watched in horror as the bomb bay doors opened and two tons of explosives jettisoned from the doomed plane. Arden didn't understand. To him, the plane was the threat, not the bits of flotsam falling from it, and he focused his exhausted powers on flinging the plane away from Stour. Lighter after dropping its payload, it caught the air and soared in an inexorable downward arc, out of sight, toward Bittersweet.

They couldn't tell whether the plane crashed, though, because from just over the rising parkland, Stour exploded in a fireball. The highest spires were barely in sight, then they were lost in billowing black smoke. When the smoke swirled and cleared for an instant, they were gone.

They stood rooted.

"Everyone was outside, at the Exaltation," Felton said, offering hope.

"Not everyone," Arden said. "Thomas was pestering me about leaving the college. I was annoyed—I told him what the headmasters do to journeymen who refuse to return. He went to his room, refused to join the Exaltation . . ."

"Oh, Fee," Phil breathed. *I did this,* she thought. "You did this," she whispered to Arden, and ran to Stour.

The Gothic extravagance that had stretched its spires to the skies was gone, a pile of rubble and stained glass kissed with flame and wrapped in a shroud of ash and acrid fumes.

No—no, not quite gone after all, for through the smoke, she could see that part of the west end of Stour was still largely intact. The library and some of the classrooms had been spared, though many were now open to the elements, but all of the living quarters had been destroyed.

And Thomas, lovely, poetic, innocent Thomas . . .

Phil's heart broke for her sister, whose own heart would soon follow suit.

Felton's hopes were justified when several hundred magicians, as stupefied as rabbits in a beam of torchlight, staggered up through the withering jungle from the Exaltation grounds.

They don't know what to do, Phil realized as she waited for them to take action. "Take roll, and find out who's missing!" she called, twisting back her hair and pulling her gloves from her back pocket. "Then do whatever hoodoo you do and find the survivors." Stan slipped from the crowd like a disentangled shadow. "Help me, Stan. Help me find Thomas."

She clambered over the mansion that had become a cairn until she found the place where, roughly, Thomas's body might lie. For he must be dead. Not even a magician could survive a hundred tons of rocks, explosion, and fire. Still, because she had to do everything, she called for him and dragged ineffectually at great slabs of stone until members of her muster firmly pulled her aside and persuaded the massive stones to slowly shift themselves.

She stayed past the point of hope, because she couldn't bear to face Fee. Let her have one more night of happy dreams, before life became a nightmare.

They pulled four bodies from the rubble—three magicians who had been ill, excused from the Exaltation, and a young prentice who had been locked in his room as punishment for tying notes to the legs of the castle pigeons, in hopes one would miraculously fly to London and tell his mother he was alive and missing her. Two others were unaccounted for: an elderly master, and Thomas. Parts of the prentice quarters had been reduced to charred dust by a direct hit from one of the tightly clustered bombs. His body might never be recovered.

Arden remained aloof, standing under an elm with Headmaster Rudyard, murmuring in earnest conversation through the night. Rudyard would sometimes issue edicts or examine the carnage, but Arden never joined his brother magicians.

"He's not even helping," Phil said bitterly as she rested with Stan. "Doesn't he care about the men who might be trapped? He claims that the only thing he cares about is the college, but there he stands, with his arms folded, frowning and doing nothing."

"It's not the college he cares about, it's the Essence," Stan said.

"A blind, cold, unfeeling force. It's like fighting for gravity. Empty and meaningless. Do you know what he said? Oh!"

The hints suddenly coalesced into a possibility she didn't want to believe. He's insufferable, he's confused . . . but not that—not that!

He had been in Stour when Rapp was murdered. Washing his hands . . . blood in the basin, from the cut, he said, but what if . . . And when Hereweald and Felton and the others were destroying the German plane, Arden had stopped them. Was he just following the college's pacifist tenents, or was it something more sinister? Was he in fact saving an ally? German or English, it didn't matter, he said. Germans in England? German magicians in Stour? Did he care, so long as the Essence was honored and circulated through the earth?

Was Arden siding with the Germans?

No, it couldn't be. She knew he was angry with Rudyard and the other old masters who were nothing but talk without action. He was defying them, yes, organizing the young masters and training with guns and fists, strengthening his magical abilities, but it was to fight the Dresden magicians, not to overthrow the college leadership and turn Stour over to the Germans. She knew he looked down on commoners, but he couldn't want to rule and enslave them, as the Dresden magicians did.

There had to be something she wasn't seeing. She mistrusted the Headmaster, who had lied about the portal and was a pacifist only when it was convenient. But if he would kill his own journeymen for threatening the order merely with their absence, why on earth wouldn't he move against the Germans? Did he really believe they weren't a threat, or could he be the one in collusion?

She stroked Stan's cheek and gazed into his wise little face. He looked as if he hadn't been young in years. She bit her lip . . . and told him everything.

"I don't know . . . I don't know," he said. "I thought this was a good place. Mother said to stay free, always, but I thought the College of Drycraeft was for learning and peace and . . . is it true? They kill journeymen who won't return? Kill them and lie about it? Then perhaps they are worse than the Germans. My mother was their slave, and she knew it, so she could defy them. Are we slaves here, but never know it until the moment we try to break free? But not Arden, I'd swear it. He's *good*. Like you, and your family, and Hector."

"But maybe he's been led astray," Phil said, grasping for the least damning possibility. "Do you remember when Geoffrey came home a Blackshirt because Oswald Mosley was all about the working class and ending unemployment? He was so proud of his lightning bolt for a day or two—until he realized that the British Union was really a bunch of fascists. You've all been fed so many lies here at the college. Maybe the Germans gave him more lies, and he doesn't understand what it would mean, to England, to the world. He's a little arrogant, sure, but he doesn't want to subjugate the commoners. I know it!"

Stan agreed to watch him and report back.

"Kiss Fee for me, Phil," he said when she departed.

Phil began her weary walk through the cold dawn, to tell Fee her true love was gone.

Chapter 18

At Weasel Rue, the chickens were squawking for release. Seizing the chance for delay, Phil unlatched their doors and evaded their demanding, beady-eyed stares and insistent pecks before finally, with heavy steps, letting herself into the house. Again, she was glad Mrs. Pippin left them entirely to their own devices. She couldn't have borne a lecture.

She snaked her way down the long hallway to their room. The blackout curtains were still drawn, and the room was dusky. She could just see the red-gold glints of Fee's hair spread across the pillow.

"Fee," she whispered.

"Mmm, there you are," Fee replied with a languid stretch.

"Fee, it's . . . it's Thomas."

"Yes, it is, isn't it. I hope you don't mind. I would have sent him away, but since it looked like you weren't coming back tonight . . ."

A golden-haired form unburied itself from the covers. "Hullo, Phil."

Phil threw herself onto the bed and for the next full minute indiscriminately kissed everything she could find — Fee and Thomas, the blankets, the pillows, her own hands clasped in relief.

"I thought you might be cross I was in your bed," Thomas said, and got Phil's last kiss on his forehead.

"What do I care where you sleep — you're alive!"

Thomas, who'd been alive for nearly eighteen years without anyone commenting on it, looked puzzled. She told them what happened.

"They'll be so relieved to hear you weren't killed," Phil said.

Thomas and Fee exchanged a look, and Fee squeezed his hand. "I'm not going back," he said.

"What! They'll kill you! You said so yourself."

"I would have stayed loyal to them forever, if they'd told us the truth," he said. "But it's wrong to kill a person for thinking, for loving, for questioning. Exterminated like vermin, at the will of the Headmaster! Rudyard has set himself up like a god, telling us all the while that magicians must avoid power at all costs."

"It makes you wonder what else they're lying about," Phil said.

"Exactly. I can't stay there. They're sheep, I tell you, blind and gullible, and at the mercy of the Headmaster. Not all of them, though. Not Arden." He glowed with hero worship. "He's got such a following! Not just Felton and the others who want to defend Stour. There are whispers all over the college about a brave new world for magicians, where we're not hemmed in and dominated, where we can think and act for ourselves."

A brave new world. Wasn't that what the Kommandant said? Was the entire college lured by the Dresden magicians' offer of power at the expense of commoners? Or was it just a coincidence, this familiar rhetoric, the temptation to crib from Shakespeare (and Kipling and Huxley)?

"Thank goodness this happened," Thomas went on. "Oh, what a terrible thing to say! But I'm free now."

"You'll have to be careful, though. They can track down the boys they abduct, so what if a journeyman finds you?"

"It will only matter for a little while. Soon enough I'll be out of England."

"Where are you going?"

He looked at Fee, who was suddenly like a statue of Grace Darling, impossibly stoic, the epitome of brave English womanhood.

"He's going to war," she said, pitching her voice low so it didn't tremble.

She was losing her love after all.

Don't do it, Phil wanted to say. *Run away to Ireland and live in a hovel with Fee until the war's over and done with. Go to America and plant corn and make fat happy babies together. Hell, go back to Stour and be a sheep, or a Nazi magician, or whatever they tell you to be. No more death, please.* A few weeks ago she would have sent every boy in England to Europe with a rifle over his shoulder. Now she was like Fee when she saw a desiccated worm, overcome with universal pity.

But: "Thank you," she said. "For England, thank you. You're better than the lot of them. Better than Arden, a thousandfold." *How strange that I'm crying, and Fee's eyes are dry. I'm not at all like I thought I was.*

An hour later they were at the railroad station to see Thomas off. Luckily it was the day the London workers were scheduled to come for the apple picking. It had been an easy matter to smuggle Thomas into Fee's bed for the night, but Mrs. Pippin might finally put her foot down if her evacuee kept a man in the house for several days. He planned to catch the train on its southerly jaunt to the Brighton coast and find an army recruiter from there.

"But you're not eighteen," Fee said, unable to tell him not to go, but grasping for the last possible loophole.

"I can make a birth certificate that says I'm older, or fuddle the recruiter into believing anything. Don't worry, love. Someone needs to stop this war. Just wait until I'm over there!"

What terrible times these are, Phil thought. He was an Arcadian innocent who didn't even know what war was, and now—off to kill. Did it happen to every man, eventually, this bloodlust? She'd been so full of it herself, so bent on revenge after seeing the first pieces of her country destroyed. The closer she got to the war, though, the more real it became. Her gung-ho jingoism faded, and in her heart she wished she could handcuff herself to a radiator and stay in the darkness until the war was over.

The problem with that is, I can shim the handcuffs open, she thought with a mirthless laugh. There was no avoiding gruesome reality, there was only getting through it, with tricks and bluffs if necessary, and putting on a game face. Which Phil did admirably now, watching with a cheerful, reassuring smile as Fee and Thomas bade each other farewell, all the while very deliberately *not* thinking about Arden, not one little bit.

She thought about other things, though. The Dresden magicians hadn't won the war for Germany yet, after a year of fighting. In fact, as England bullied its way to air supremacy and redoubled her efforts by sea, it seemed the tide was slowly turning, if not quite in England's favor, at least not in such a rip current against it. Why hadn't the Dresden magicians killed the king and Churchill, a few admirals and field marshals, thrown the country into chaos, and brought down all of England's planes? And why, for that matter, after that stunning initial display of aggression, hadn't they made an all-out attack on the college?

If they hadn't, it must be because they couldn't. The Dresdeners were milking other, unwilling magicians to get more power, but it still wasn't enough. They needed numbers. They needed the hundreds of magicians at Stour.

If they got them, the war would be over in a heartbeat. England would lose, and though Hitler couldn't know it, he'd lose, too, as the magicians dominated the commoners.

I have to change tactics, she thought. *I have to find a way to keep the college from turning against commoners despite what the Germans say. I have to make them see that they're just people, the same as commoners. Only, how do you convince a man who can tear a plane from the sky that he's ordinary?*

Fee and Thomas came out of the postmistress's office, he looking glum, she with that peculiarly maniacal expression that comes of trying to hide wild elation.

"What do you think?" Fee said. "That bomber of yours came down a couple of miles north of us and plowed up a big length of track. She says London can't spare men or metal to fix it for at least a few weeks. We're a nonessential line. The entire branch line will be shut down." At the last minute she pulled her face into an appropriate expression of disappointment, but she couldn't quite hold it.

Just then Mrs. Pippin stormed down the main street in the greatest huff Phil had ever seen.

"Supposed to meet the London sluts and drunkards today, and what do they tell me? A great bloody big plane took out the railroad last night, and no trains can get through. Don't those damned Germans know I have to get the apples picked? With petrol rationed as it is, I'll never get the workers in by the road, and if I don't have them here in the next few days, I'll lose half the harvest. I'm ruined — ruined!"

Phil had an idea and started to follow Mrs. Pippin.

"You go with her, Fee," Thomas said. "I have a long, hard walk ahead of me."

"What do you mean?" Fee asked, seeing her reprieve fly.

"I'll go on foot until I meet the next connecting line."

"But that's at least thirty miles!"

"I can't wait. The longer I'm here in England, the longer the war will last."

He was as confident as a child on the roof wearing a cape, certain he can fly. But then, Thomas probably *could* fly, if he really put his mind to it.

He took hold of the strawberry tips of her hair and wrapped the tresses around his wrists, binding himself to her. Then, without another word, without a kiss or a farewell, he untangled himself and ran south along the train tracks.

Fee turned away. *I can't watch him get smaller and smaller until he's gone,* she thought resolutely. *It's too prophetic. He's going away awhile, and he'll be back. I have to believe that. I do believe it. If he doesn't come back I'll—I'll go and get him myself!*

But what choice do you have?" Phil railed at Headmaster Rudyard later that day. He'd left his office door open, expecting Jereboam, and was ambushed by Phil instead. "They were freezing last night, and that was when they were working hard. Tonight, without proper shelter, they'll have chilblains and frostbite, and it will only get colder."

"There's room for some in the parts of Stour that still stand," the Headmaster countered.

"This office and the library are the only intact buildings."

"And the rest will use the Essence to construct adequate shelter."

"Ha!" Phil said. "Did you see the hut some of the journeymen tried to erect? It leaned like the Tower of Pisa and finally fell on one of them when he tried to nap inside. He's nursing a broken ankle and a concussion now. They can make tents at best. You're the only one who has any knowledge of architecture, and you'll be busy rebuilding Stour. What's the harm? It will be for two weeks at the most."

After much arguing the Headmaster said, "Very well, then. The younger men may go. They'll be under the direction of a master, and they will perform the Exaltation near their temporary homes. It is close enough to Stour that it shouldn't make much difference. Close, compared to the wide world."

And so, beyond Phil's wildest belief, Headmaster Rudyard agreed that some hundred of his journeymen and masters should for a time leave Stour and live among the commoners, picking apples and assisting with the cider press work by day, and sleeping in the hopper huts by night.

Then another surprise. "Is Mrs. Abernathy still alive?"

It took Phil a moment to place the name. Ah yes, the dear, deaf old woman who, when she'd tried to talk about rationing, thought Phil was hungry and loaded her with food. "Hale as can be expected for a woman of ninety," she said.

"And Mrs. Braeburn?"

Phil wracked her memory and recalled her first day in Bittersweet. "Granny Braeburn? She died not too long ago. Ninety-five, I think she was."

"She was the assistant cook at Stour when I was a boy. She used to save the marrow for me, my favorite. And she had a biscuit cutter in the shape of a sailing ship. Father disapproved, but when I had tea in the nursery, I could always play Navy and Pirates with my toast."

When he'd been captured as a boy, he hadn't tied messages to pigeons—he'd escaped. How had he been turned into such a steadfast, brutally loyal magician?

"Do you know everyone in Bittersweet?"

"When I returned to Stour in my thirties after Mafeking, as a magician, not a lord, I used to sneak out and watch my old friends. They were friends to me, you know. Tenants to my father, practically serfs, but to me . . . I had to fuddle them so they didn't know me, but I looked after every one of them, in the beginning. They were my responsibility as lord of Stour. That didn't change. I couldn't study architecture anymore, but I could give my dependents beautiful homes. I couldn't mediate their disputes or advise them about their farms, but I could use the Essence to make a drunkard decide to be sober, to make the hops and apples flourish. When the Great War came, twenty young men from Bittersweet enlisted the day war was declared. I knew every one of them. Only one came back."

"Uncle Walter."

"I remember him as a baby. When I was lord of Stour after my father died, I attended every christening. Walter spat up in the baptismal font, then grinned like a demonic cherub at the vicar. When I saw what war had done to that baby, I swore none of my former tenants would fight in a war again. What a fool I was."

Phil shook her head.

"You can't stop it," the Headmaster went on. "You can only thank heaven there's a limit to what commoners can do to each other."

"There is no limit," Phil said, certain.

"Oh, you'd be surprised." He stood abruptly. "Enough of this. Memories do no one any good. Three weeks they may help with the harvest."

"You'll have Stour rebuilt that soon?"

"No. But it does no good to plan too far ahead in these times. We'll see what happens in three weeks."

Chapter 19

No, ye daft toff. You cup your palm around it so, like you're grabbing a nice handful of titty, then you give 'er a lift and a bit of a twist, and off she comes."

Mr. Tremlett, one of Mrs. Pippin's orchard men, was giving the new apple pickers their first lesson. He'd been told they were scholars evacuated from their university and sent to Stour. The gossip said the poor blighters were surprised when they showed up with all their trunks and laboratory gizmos and found that Stour was no more than a ruin. Seems it had been left on the surveys as an intact mansion all these years. Now they had volunteered to help with the apple harvest in exchange for living quarters.

And a good thing, too. Besides Mrs. Pippin's vast acres, there were the Finchley groves (Diana's family), not to mention all the orts and jots growing here and there. Every family in Bittersweet had an acre or two, and the land was fertile enough that even if they left their trees mostly to their own devices, they were guaranteed a decent crop for eating, drinking, and selling.

Mostly for drinking. Hops go for beer, and apples go for cider.

"It ain't *really* a tit, Professor," he called in exasperation. "Don't stare at it and caress it. Just yank it off and drop it in the basket. Aye, that's it. Keep up that pace, and you might have the tree bare inside of a fortnight."

When they had the basics down, the magicians (or professors, as they were universally known) were divvied up among Bittersweet's various orchards. Most of the villagers joined in the picking, too, and though they were sometimes baffled by the magicians' peculiar ways, they unanimously pronounced them good eggs.

It was remarkable how spirits had lifted in Bittersweet. They'd found their wartime cheer, the manner the rest of the nation had adopted a year ago, defiance in a smile, stoicism in a joke. Housewives and hostesses put aside old differences to pool their sugar and have grand bridge parties, playing not for coin but for the even scarcer tea and chocolate. They compared the blackout bruises acquired from bumps in the dark. The village, not long ago a somber, deadly place, now rippled with laughter and jokes, all of which they shared like a generous banquet with their guest workers.

The magicians, reserved and diffident at first, found they weren't proof against commoner camaraderie.

"I think them being so worn out makes it easier," Fee said as the sisters walked home from the post office. Still no word from Thomas, and though the postmistress promised to send a bicycle messenger to Weasel Rue if anything came, Fee still had to check at least once, often twice a day. "They tried not to fraternize, but by evening they just don't have the resistance not to laugh at Eamon's jokes."

Probably the biggest contribution to the magician-commoner détente was the tapping of last year's casks.

It was a Bittersweet tradition that when the first apple of the year was plucked, the last barrels of the year before that had been fermented and aged to perfection were opened. Though cider might be ready for general consumption within two months of pressing, the villagers were connoisseurs.

"The Headmaster never forbade it," Felton said, raising his cup.

"And apples are known to be healthy," Hereweald added, tipping his, and so the others followed suit, and before long they went from exchanging civilities with the commoners, to exchanging pleasantries, to exchanging pats on the back and tipsy bearish hugs. That night of celebration set the tone for the rest of the apple picking, and to the magicians' astonishment, they found they rather liked commoners.

All, apparently, except Arden.

He was nominally in charge, even over some of the masters his senior in years and rank, and lived in a hopper hut all his own, the very last in the long row. This caused some resentment among the other magicians, for they were berthed eight and ten to a house, sleeping on pallets on the floor (albeit covered in downy silken cushions they'd conjured up — their dwellings, though cramped, looked like pashas' tents), but most of them had already formed a special bond in training in Phil's muster, and they used their new closeness to try out advanced, occasionally dangerous manipulation of the Essence. Phil quizzed them daily, and all were certain there had been no further incursions from the Dresden magicians, but now free from the Headmaster's eye, they were more determined than ever to be ready. The clique of five had expanded, and every day more magicians were proving themselves perfectly willing to violate everything they'd been taught—as long as no one found out.

From all this, Arden remained aloof. He'd rise early to stalk through the hopper hut village and count his charges. He didn't pick apples, though he would stride through the orchards with his hands clasped behind his back, never admonishing but frowning severely when any of the magicians became too familiar with one of the villagers, particularly the females.

There weren't a great many unattached young women in Bittersweet, but by the second week of the harvest, their numbers miraculously swelled as word reached outlying farms and letters sped to the rare distant cousin who had migrated thirty miles away to a neighboring town. Perhaps no one said in quite so many words that Bittersweet swarmed with unattached, eligible young men, but like bees to a flower (or as Phil said with annoyance, like flies to dung, for they all seemed eager to lay their eggs), the women came.

Phil joined in the picking, but Arden rarely spoke to her. She watched him, though, stealthy and intense, as she'd watch a competing illusionist to ferret out the secret of some unknown trick. *What do you have up your sleeve, Arden?* she wondered. The things she'd briefly suspected—they couldn't be true.

At least Phil's plan seemed to be working. Slightly under a hundred magicians were working side by side with commoners, treating them like equals. They gossiped about the war, and when someone brought a battery-powered wireless to the groves, they clustered around it, shoulder to shoulder with the villagers, gasping when they heard about the latest casualties, cheering at a successful strike by the RAF. They flirted and argued and ate side by side, and their bond with the commoners grew stronger by the day.

Only, it would all be over soon. The plucked apples were sweetening in the shade, and the press works were being greased. The harvest was almost over, and there would be no excuse for the magicians to stay. Would they go back to their cloister and turn their backs on their new friends in their hour of need, or would they stand up to the Headmaster and hundreds of years of tradition, and fight, for themselves and for England?

One night, when all that remained on the trees were those late-ripening stragglers closest to the trunk, Phil went to the hopper huts just after sunset. They had several small campfires going, and some of the village girls had stayed behind.

"Sing us a song!" the magicians begged them, for this too had become a treat. Most only had dim recollections of cradle songs, and a few gleaned on their journeying.

A girl with a cherry ribbon in her dark hair shyly rose and sang a melody as familiar as birdsong, a lament that had been sung in that land for hundreds of years.

Early one morning, just as the sun was rising,
I heard a maid sing in the valley below,
"Oh, don't deceive me, oh, never leave me!
How could you use a poor maiden so?"

Her sweet voice rose plaintively above the fire's crackle, and her face was a mask of practiced anguish, for this was her parlor piece and had charmed more than a few gentleman callers.

> "*Remember the vows that you made to me truly*
> *Remember how tenderly you nestled me close . . .*"

Phil, who ought to have been immune to it, having heard buskers in the tube belt it out with astounding pathos in hopes of a shilling, found her eyes growing warm and felt that peculiar tingle on the upper lip that heralds a good weep. She opened her eyes wide to keep the tears—foolish things—from falling, and knowing she'd fail, she turned quickly away from the firelight to lose herself in the darkness. A few steps, and she was night-clad.

The darkness made her a stranger, forgotten and obscure, while the rest sported in the merry flicker of firelight, bathed in warmth and glowing human happiness. *All they see are the flames, and each other,* she thought. *And I am alone . . .*

Girls sidled close to young men who hadn't been so near a woman in years—or at all, for not every magician had turned to debauchery on his journeying. They were better than recruitment posters, better than Churchill's speeches of dogged fire, these girls. A little more of this, and the magicians would rush en masse to the Continent, forgetting their vows, forgetting the Exaltation, forgetting everything except the tender softness they must protect and the arms they'd be coming home to. Phil only wished she could import a few more women to Bittersweet.

She drifted farther from the light, feeling unwelcome (foolishly, for the magicians adored her, and even the girls were no more jealous than they absolutely had to be, seeing her more as matchmaker than as competition) but unable, quite, to make herself leave. For Arden was there.

She'd seen him, dour as an unlit coal at the edge of the campfire light, and then he'd vanished. She was sure he'd seen her and was, as usual these days, avoiding her. *Perhaps if we had a moment to talk,* Phil thought, *I could find a way through this coldness.* But he never gave her the opportunity.

The singer's voice grew more wistful.

> *Here I now wander alone as I wonder,*
> *Why did you leave me to sigh and complain?*
> *I ask of the roses, "Why should I be forsaken?*
> *Why must I here in sorrow remain?"*

She heard a sound—a sob—choked quickly off. Could it be Arden? Was he suffering too? *If I find him in the dark, without eyes to avert and blushes to shame us, only voices and breath and body, can we find our understanding again? We were so close.*

She crept toward the sound.

Arden was supposed to stay with his fellow magicians at all times, supervise their interactions with the commoners, and, clandestinely, keep tabs on those confirmed or suspected to side with the Dresdeners. All those he was sure of had been included in the apple-picking detail. Rudyard, heeding Arden's advice, thought it better to keep them away from the college. Now they were liberally mixed with the magicians of Phil's muster, the loyal (and rebellious) fighters, so that if things erupted before Arden managed to discover the Dresdeners' plans, he'd have allies.

But the folk tune, sung with such sweet rue, dragged the river of his memories and hauled up such corpses of regret that he had to flee. Still, the haunting music followed him, Ruby's voice, and somehow Phil's, too.

> *Although love's folly is sure but a fancy,*
> *Still it should prove more sweet than your scorn.*

Rudyard had been right—he hated himself now. Playing traitor to the college—and being traitor to Phil. And yet he had to keep up the act, pretend the passion, until he could discover exactly how the Dresdeners planned to bring down the college.

With every breath, he doubted it was worth it.

With every sigh, he told himself it had to be.

Fleeing one sound of sorrow, he heard another and followed it to the hopper hut nearest his own. There it was again, a little breathless sob, and then a man laughing.

He pulled the door open so forcefully, one of the rusting hinges tore, leaving it hanging drunkenly. Inside, in the baleful glow of a kerosene lantern, he saw a flaxen-haired young woman, buxom and soft, with a simple face and oddly dull eyes, stretched limp and indifferent on the ground. Standing over her, his breeches loosened, was the giant Journeyman Bergen.

"What are you doing?" Arden asked, feeling fury rise, welcoming it because at least it eradicated the pain for a time.

Bergen gave a great guffaw. "You of all people should know," he said, beerily convivial. Then he saw Arden's hard face. "Just enjoying myself, master," he said more stiffly. "You know, *droit de cuissage,* as the Fräulein says." His hand still at his belt, he looked defiantly at the smaller man.

"And is the girl willing?" Arden asked through clenched teeth.

Bergen shrugged. "She is now."

Clearly the girl—a local milkmaid, common and pretty as a sparrow—had been fuddled and was in no position to have an opinion of her own.

Arden pushed his way past Bergen and hauled the girl to her feet.

"Leave her be!" Bergen shouted, not quite daring to lay hands on his master—or the man the Fräulein had chosen—but grabbing the milkmaid roughly. "She's a commoner. It's my right to do whatever I like with her."

"Not while I live," Arden said, remembering poor Ruby, so fuddled and swayed by his magical persuasion that she—the girl who'd laughed at his love—killed herself rather than live without him. Never again. No, not even for the sake of the college.

"You have your own woman," Bergen said petulantly. "When we've taken over England, every commoner will be our slave. Why can't I have my fun, too?"

To think of Phil too often was, Arden knew, a very dangerous thing; and yet he could not help but see her determined, set face, the beads of sweat dripping down her chest, the incongruous way that lovely body could throw itself like a demented dervish into a punch, as he recalled her training and prepared to beat Bergen to death with his bare hands.

A biting animal perfume filled the air, soft and sharp all at once, like a white ermine with even whiter teeth. Fingers traced the taut sinews of his neck, and a voice, huskily accented, purred, "Yes, my love, why can't he have his fun, too?"

He turned to behold the most glorious creature created by nature, a marvel of curve and line, of the firm and the yielding, and color, oh, even in the dismal kerosene glow, she blazed, white and gold, crimson nails and coral lips, eyes the blue of Alpine gentians, and around her throat, her wrists, her tapering fingers, and in the sunshine glory of her piled hair, cosmically whirling opals.

Arden had to fight back his physical revulsion at the sight of her. He smiled, silky charm. *How much easier the false emotions are than the true,* he thought. With Phil, the more he felt, the less he knew how to show.

"Fräulein Hildemar, I cannot help but believe that continence is better than defiling oneself with a commoner. Look at her, stupid and vacant. One might as well fornicate with mud."

He gave the girl a gentle shove out the door and unfuddled her as she left. She gave one bewildered look over her shoulder and ran for the safety of her friends.

The Fräulein radiated approval. "How well you put it, Arden. Still, boys will be boys, isn't that so, Bergen?" She blessed him with a look that said, *But for a turn of fate, I'd be yours tonight,* and he renewed his vow to serve her, however she desired . . . But he was beginning to hate the influential young master who had so quickly won the thrilling Fräulein's affections.

She gave Bergen a smart little tap on the cheek, playfully admonishing. "Only wait, dear one, and you will have a bevy of magician ladies in a frenzy to meet a fascinating, powerful fellow such as yourself." She made a little moue. "What a shame only the Kommandant and I are able to make the journey! Once we figure out how to bring all our little group to England, oh, how jolly it will be! Soon enough you will have loyal helpmeets, and darling magician babies to pass your knowledge on to. And then"—she gave a dismissive wave of her hand—"you may have as many commoner concubines as you like. We ladies never mind that. Only, do us the honor of picking pretty ones at least, not rough peasants like that creature. Come. I long to be alone with you." She said these last words to Arden, but she looked at Bergen as she took the master by the arm. Bergen's eyes followed her like a starving cur.

Phil, approaching the house from the wrong side, heard none of that and arrived in time only to see the milkmaid being herded out. Phil waited, pressed to the shadows, certain with unerring female instinct that Arden was about.

Then he emerged from the hut, and she almost called out to him. Before she did more than draw breath, she saw the dazzling blonde with him, and shrank back again. Together the couple walked to Arden's hut next door.

At the fireside, the singer took up a new lament.

> Oh I loved a lad, and I loved him so well
> That I hated all others of him that spoke ill.
> And now he's rewarded me well for my love . . .
> He's gone to be wed to another.

Phil wanted to wail, she wanted to run, but she forced herself into stealth and crept to Arden's window. It was shut against the cold and sooted over with a greasy haze, but she pressed her eye to a clean spot and made herself watch Arden take the woman in his arms, cauterized her wounded heart with the sight of his lips on her throat. She watched until she killed her love, until it dropped like a coursed hart, exhausted, for the hounds to tear apart.

Now it is truly over, she thought, *and I never have to think about him again. Who is she? I've never seen her before . . . no, stop that. It is no concern of yours. Focus on the other magicians. Never think of Arden again.*

But Fee was right, and Phil couldn't think herself out of love, any more than she could think herself into it. Love does not succumb to logic. It simply *is,* or it is not.

Oh God, Phil thought with a low helpless groan as Arden tumbled the golden goddess on the bed. *How I wish love was not, but it is!*

Chapter 20

The harvest was in. Phil expected the magicians to be summoned home to the college, but when she went to Stour for the first time in three weeks, she found it still hardly more than a heap of rubble. Slightly neater rubble, to be sure — the stones had been piled according to purpose and proportions — but very little had been done beyond reinforcing the supports of those parts of the manor left intact after the bombing.

"Another month at least," Rudyard told Phil.

Not that she minded, because it furthered her interests, but she was puzzled. "Even with all of you working, you haven't gotten farther than this?"

Rudyard spread his arms over the schematics and blueprints that littered his desk. "It isn't like in the old tales — would that I could snap my fingers and have a castle! It's still work, girl. Planning and design and work. I can make alabaster grow from thin air, but if I stack it wrong, it will still fall on our heads. It would take a team of architects and stonemasons three years to build Stour anew. Don't grumble if I have it done in months."

He gave Arden a different story. "I'll delay as long as I can. There have been no more incursions into Stour. She's focusing on the magicians who are outside. Easier targets, I'm sure. That leaves me free to plan what must come next."

"Which is?"

"None of your concern, for the nonce. You just keep the rebels identified and away from Stour. Are you certain you have all the troublemakers isolated in the huts?"

"I think so, but she doesn't confide everything in me."

"But you know a dozen of her collaborators. You know she has not yet learned how to get all of her Dresden compatriots to England."

"Yes. There's so little Essence there, they have to gather it, bit by bit. Here, though—I can't believe how powerful she is. We should dispatch her while she's here, before the others manage to cross over."

"No, this threat has hung like a sword above our heads long enough. There can be no half measures. Discover what they're planning, so we can be ready to end them, forever."

"Perhaps they won't ever find a way here." *And if not, if there's nothing more to worry about, I may finally break free of the demonic Hildemar—and strangle her with my own hands.*

"They will find a way, eventually, and perhaps . . . it may be necessary for you to help them with their portal, to push this affair to a crisis."

"What?" Was he mad?

Rudyard rubbed his deeply lined brow. "If they are all here, we can drain them all and have done with it. But nothing is known yet. Speak no more of it."

Arden, having received his dismissal, left, to unwillingly conspire, to plot false treachery, and to caress the lovely monster who believed she had ensnared him.

When he was gone, Rudyard returned to staring at his blueprints, wondering if he could look as if he were making progress, and thus avoid suspicion, yet still delay the rebuilding. He shivered, a deep rheumatic ache settling into his spine. He'd have to ask Mrs. Tingle to ease him when next they met. The leader of the women was so adept at healing. He shifted uncomfortably and hoped he could endure the two days until he saw her again.

And so the hundred magicians continued to live in the hopper huts, cold and cramped and (except perhaps for the dozen or so traitors) in a state of perpetual bliss. Like children on holiday, they reveled in their freedom. Though they faithfully adhered to that daily ritual of drawing up the Essence and spreading it through the world, they began to find joy in using their magic for its own sake. They became playful and made bouquets for their sweethearts and bowers in the snow.

More intently every day, they followed the commoners' wartime travails. They heard with dismay that Hungary and Romania had joined the Axis, and they whooped with pride when Greece made a brilliant incursion into Italy's territory in Albania.

At every turn, the magicians of Phil's muster looked for ways to fight for their new friends, and always Arden, their hero, their leader, shot them down. We have our own war to fight, he reminded them. Yes, they argued, but what are we doing about that? There's nothing to be done, he assured them. It seems the Dresdeners have given up. Then why not fight for the rest of England? they demanded. Because we must be ready to protect the college, first, foremost, and only. The Essence is all. And though they grumbled, they obeyed, while another group of men, to whom Arden was also a hero, laughed at the rest behind their backs and waited for the day when they would assume their place as masters of the world.

Phil retreated, from the magicians and from the Home Guard. She'd done all she could do, and she couldn't bear the thought of seeing Arden again.

"Get out of bed," Fee urged, but Phil only grumbled and pulled the blankets back over her head, staying cocooned until Fee left for her daily trek to the post office.

When Fee was gone, Phil would crawl out of bed and drag herself about the farm, listlessly milking with stiff, chafed hands, mucking the pens, stopping up rat holes, and chopping wood, anything to keep mindlessly busy until she could legitimately get back into bed again. She thanked goodness for the early nights and did her best to be asleep before Fee, scribbling another letter by candlelight, came to bed. So far, she'd accomplished the impossible—she hadn't told her sister what happened. Bad enough that the image of Arden and that spectacularly beautiful fairy-tale creature seemed to be burned into her eyelids, renewing the vision whenever she so much as blinked. To speak of that moment would kill her, she was sure of that.

Relentlessly, she forced herself to enumerate his faults. Ruthlessly, she dissected his face to prove to herself that it was, after all, only another face.

And fighting those things, like a hopelessly outclassed bantamweight who simply won't stay down for the count, was the memory of his fingers on her lips, the wondering way in which he said, "I didn't think it would be possible." And that promise—*tomorrow.* That word stayed nestled in her heart, refusing to believe that tomorrow had come and gone. *Don't worry,* her foolish heart tried to tell her. *There will be another one.*

She went to Stour a time or two to visit Stan, creeping about the place like a thief until she'd ascertained that Arden was still with the others in the hopper huts.

Her only other distraction was the magic show she and Fee had promised for the village Christmas fete. After quite a bit of prodding, Phil finally threw herself into rehearsal. It was more hard work, after all, and that's just what she needed.

They did, as she'd predicted, requisition most of Bittersweet's mirrors, and Joey rigged up a smoke machine, more malodorous than their dry ice contraption back at the Hall of Delusion, but just as effective. Phil got yards of thick rope from an ox driver, oiled her handcuffs, and convinced the constable to donate the straitjacket that had been hanging for years, unused, under a sign stating "IN CASE OF MADMAN."

From pride in her craft, if nothing else, Phil was determined to put on a good show. She and Fee sewed outlandish new costumes from Miss Merriall's bountiful trunks and practiced in their rooms, in the fields, and finally locked inside the meeting hall where the performance would take place, the windows papered over against prying eyes.

"I don't know why the magicians want to come, anyway," Phil said, prickly and nervous.

"They're curious. All they've seen is our close-up magic. Maybe Arden will come, and you two can finally—"

"Don't say his name!" Phil roared, and stormed out.

For Phil to yell at her beloved sister was a character change as worrying as a sudden compulsion to rob liquor stores might be in another person. Fee had no idea what had happened between Arden and Phil—and her sister's stubborn reticence was another worrying symptom—but that moment made Fee resolve to be a busybody.

The next day, the morning of the performance, Fee layered herself in flannel and wool and trudged through ankle-deep snow to the hopper huts. The sky, overcast since dawn, was lowering menacingly, and both the temperature and the barometer were beginning to drop sharply. Fee's loose hair crackled over her shoulders as she greeted the few magicians who were about. Most were either still holed up against the cold or had arrangements to stay with the friends they'd made in the village.

Without making it look like her sole purpose, she made her way to Arden's hut and rapped at the door.

She hardly recognized the man who answered. He looked hunted and harried, with dark circles under his eyes on a face gone gaunt and new lines etched deeply in his brow, which smoothed slightly at the sight of Fee.

"Come inside, out of the cold," he said tenderly, for whatever else might be clouding him, he was full of sympathy for the girl. Even he didn't know that Thomas still lived. It was easy at the moment for Fee to encourage his compassion, for she was indeed melancholy — it had been four days since she'd received a letter from Thomas, and she was half frantic. Had he been deployed? Had he met someone else? Was he dead? Four days was a lifetime, and her fancy whirled with ways he could come to grief.

"Thanks," she said, stamping off the snow. "My, how pretty!" she couldn't help exclaiming when she looked around. The rough room had been lavishly furnished, with a lapis and cream Tabriz carpet in the ancient fish-admiring-the-moon motif cast upon the concrete floor. Tapestries fluttered against the wall when a gust slipped through the closing door, and candles flickered in scattered, rune-bedecked earthenware jars. The bed was deep amethyst and took up half the room.

Fee looked around for a place to sit, but there was only the bed, and somehow its empurpled bulk suddenly made her feel, for all her experience, prim and prudish in reaction. She leaned against the tapestry-covered wall instead.

After a few pleasantries, awkward on each side, she said, "I hope you're coming to our performance tonight."

There was a long silence, and then, "Ah yes, it is Christmas. I'd lost track. I ought to light a candle. My mother always did." He reached for one of the stubby earthenware jars, then pulled his hand back as if he'd been electrified. "Not these, though," he said, shoving it away. A gift from Hildemar, it bore the *Wolfsangel* rune, the wolf trap. *The wolves are lured in with flesh,* she'd explained to him gleefully, *and they are hooked like fish and left to dangle from a tree.*

He jerked one of the candles out and lit it, melting a pool of wax directly onto the windowsill and anchoring the naked candle as it hardened.

"There." The way was lit for her. Only, he knew she would never come. And if she did, he would turn her away. He'd made himself unworthy.

"What did you ask?" he said, as if startled from a dream. "No, I cannot go. I have to . . ." He let it trail off. He didn't have the strength to lie, and now it didn't matter. Fräulein Hildemar had told him last night, amid moans and caresses, that the Dresdeners were ready to descend on Stour.

They will all be back in the manor soon, no? she'd asked. *They must be together for the attack to succeed. We will separate the loyal few, and as for the rest . . .* And she'd folded him in her ivory limbs and thrown her head back, laughing in mad ecstatic passion at the thought of killing the men who'd been his friends, his brothers, for almost as long as he could remember. And he had smiled, too, and reached for her throat, and how he'd turned murderous rage into a caress, he did not know.

"Please come, Arden. I want you to. And you know that Phil wants—"

He made a low, bestial sound of pain and turned away.

Fee knew that sound. She, who lived in constant fear that some army telegram would carry her the news that would make her moan like that, knew it was the sound of a broken heart. "She needs you, Arden."

"What?" He turned.

"She . . ." Fee did not enjoy lying, but she was quite good at it. "She's doing a new escape for the grand finale, and even though she can't quite get it right, she's determined to do it anyway. You know how stubborn she is. She's been doing it with the safeties in place so far, but I'm terrified that tonight, when she does it for real, something will go wrong. If it does, she could die."

A muscle in his jaw jumped, but he remained impassive.

"Please. If you're there ready with the Essence . . ."

"You know the Essence can't touch her."

"But if she fails, she'll be falling on spikes. You can turn the spikes into daffodils, or melt them, or send them to Timbuktu."

"Surely one of the other magicians—"

"You, Arden. You're the only one I trust to keep her safe." Then, feeling as if she might be jinxing herself, she pulled out her big guns. Her chin trembled, her eyes, tear-filled, seemed suddenly twice their normal size, and she whispered, "I lost Thomas. Please don't let me lose my sister, too."

He tried to inhale to steady himself, but his chest tightened and his diaphragm seized, as if a very powerful magician were cutting off his breath. He found no relief until he uttered the promise, "I will come."

He did not know what Rudyard planned to counter the Dresdeners' attack—he hadn't even told the Headmaster yet—but he knew that if anyone was to lead a forlorn hope, or be a sacrificial pawn, it would be him. Even if he survived, Rudyard had said in no uncertain terms that he might be executed so as not to be a blight on the passive, pacifist order. Arden knew he should be raging against death, but if he was to die to preserve the college, to keep the Essence flowing, it would almost be a welcome rest. His only regret was Phil.

His day of reckoning was near at hand. Every man is entitled to a final pleasure, a final torture, rather, to remind him of what he'll miss in death—a last meal, a last cigarette, a shot of whiskey for comfort and courage. Yes, he would have a moment of solace before the war. He would see her one last time, his lovely, gallant shot of courage. But he would not let her see him.

Preparing for her Bittersweet debut, Phil was revivified. How easily she slipped into the familiar old routines of false eyelashes and mica glitter, of limbering up her shoulders almost to the point of dislocation, of chanting a litany of cues and perfectly synchronized timing. *This is my life,* she thought, with very little of the torment of resignation—*illusion, show business, the best kind of life there is.* It was the murmuring anticipation of the audience that made her heart beat, the gasp, the awe-filled silence just before thundering applause, that gave her breath and life. *Love is nothing,* she resolutely told herself as she peeked through the curtain at the packed house, friends that now blurred into that anonymous and beloved thing, an audience. *Even the war—that's other people's business. I was deluded enough to think I could change the course of the war. Let me do what I do best. I was foolish to stray.*

She slithered into her first costume, a dark jade chiffon one-piece that covered as much skin as a Land Girl uniform but managed to be as lascivious as a harem costume, skintight in some places, flowing in others, and astonishingly transparent without revealing a blush of what are known as the good bits.

Fee, embraced in a pale silver-green costume of the same design, peeked out the window as she smoothed on her Paint the Town Pink lipstick. "It's a regular blizzard tonight," she said, pursing and blotting. "We could practically do the Disappearing World."

"Don't say that," Phil said with a shudder. "When I think of that night . . ."

"I know. I always felt like it was almost our fault, for doing that illusion."

"Me too. Silly, isn't it? To think that magic could . . ." She caught her breath and resolutely painted on a sable swath of eyeliner, giving the delicate task her entire focus. *The show. That's all you can think about tonight. And tomorrow, and for the rest of your life.*

Joey, serving as stagehand-of-all-work, exercised his privilege of entering the dressing room without knocking (hoping for a glimpse of something) and told them, "Five minutes till curtain."

Fee pulled her sister up and held her by the shoulders. She longed to tell her that Arden would be in the audience, but she wasn't sure how Phil would react. She might very well storm off into the blizzard and hike back to Weasel Rue in her costume, indifferent to frostbite. Well, better leave it up to Arden, then. Remembering the tiny groan that was the demolition of his heart, Fee rather thought he'd do something.

So she gave Phil her own love, pulling her in their forehead-to-forehead embrace, becoming that chimera creature. "We have each other," she whispered. "Whatever happens, I'll be with you. Never forget that."

Phil felt tears burning her eyes, which, with her copious eyeliner, would have been disastrous. She broke the embrace, opening her eyes wide and rolling her head back, letting the tears dry in their own good time.

"I'm ready."

Chapter 21

Arden trailed behind the other magicians, intending to slip into the back, unseen, and escape the moment the curtain fell and Phil was safe. As he was leaving, a form materialized from among the skeletal hop trellises, a form that swelled from intangibility to generous, fleshy proportions.

"You shouldn't be here in daylight," he said, squinting at her through the molten sunset.

"Ah, what does it matter? In a few days the fools will be huddled back in Stour, and we will destroy them all with one fell swoop." She nuzzled him. "Come, there's time for sport, and then I must go to Stour and mark the layout for the attack. It's a shame we have to destroy the castle along with the magicians. It has been rebuilt even finer than before, though I'd prefer something inspired by the baroque splendor of Dresden. What ill luck everyone escaped the bomb! Did you do that? Come now, the truth! Bergen said you weren't at the Exaltation when it fell."

"It was an accident, I assure you," he said stiffly.

"Such modesty! Well, you'll reap rewards enough for your part in destroying the college. You will be one of our generals!" She began to draw him back toward his hut, but he resisted, which brought a look of faint amazement.

"I have to go to Bittersweet. I'll meet with you tomorrow, once I know precisely when the magicians will move back into Stour."

She tried to persuade him, but when he was adamant, shrugged her lovely shoulders and said she'd go with him.

"Are you mad? A hundred magicians will be there, and most of them would kill you on sight if they realized who you are." *Including me.*

Her lips curled. "They won't have any idea who I am. I can fuddle them all."

"That's not possible. Do you realize the kind of power it takes to sway a magician on his mettle? Even if you try, they'll know someone's meddling with them."

He couldn't shake her. He knew he should give up all idea of seeing Phil one last time, but he thought, *What harm can it do? The Fräulein won't know my thoughts, Phil won't see either of us. I must have this last good thing.*

So he told her, "There is a gathering of commoners and magicians tonight."

She gave a delicate shudder of revulsion.

"While they're together, I'd like you to point out all of those you've swayed to our side. I know you haven't told me all of them."

"Secrecy is essential in these matters," she said.

"Not from me," he said sternly, and noticed she seemed to regard him with renewed respect. She liked to have him under her thumb, true, but it also seemed to give her pleasure when he asserted himself.

"You're right. If you are to be by my side when we rule, nothing should be kept from you." She inclined her head in apparent acquiescence but could not quite hide the hint of a smirk.

She conjured a beaver cloak for herself and set out into the driving snow. Arden, in thin breeches with his fine linen shirt open to the freezing air, followed. When they arrived, just as the performance was starting, he tried to lead her to the back entrance, but she ignored him and continued to the side.

"Why mingle with the plebs?" she said, shedding the cloak, which dissolved to nothingness in the snow. "If it's the audience you want to see, we'll get a better view from backstage. What a paltry place this is. Oh, if you could have been in a box at the Semperoper—the Strauss premieres, under the aegis of Dionysus and his panthers! We will bring such wonders to this backward land!"

"Wasn't Strauss a commoner?" Arden began, but she shushed him and, gathering the Essence to her, opened a door in the wall, through which Arden could clearly see both the massed, eager audience and—oh God, there was Phil, poised and commanding . . . and apparently clad in a green cloud.

"Come forward," the Fräulein said, taking him by the hand and leading him to the wings of the stage. "They can't see a thing. You could spit in each of their faces, and none would know we are here."

It was true—not a single eye was on them, only on Phil and her sister as they playfully palmed cards and made coins dance with false transfers and French drops until the spectators were dazzled. Audience members were called up to have never-ending scarves produced from their noses and trembling white doves from their hats.

That was just the warm-up, the vaudeville part they normally would have left to Hector or Stan. Now Phil was inviting Eamon Dooley to examine a length of rope and proclaim it perfectly ordinary. She uttered something in a foreign language, undulated her arms mysteriously, and tossed the rope high, where it snaked and then stiffened, apparently frozen in midair.

Arden was entranced. He knew there must be a wire, a hook, but for the life of him, he couldn't see it. Then, oh so gingerly, Phil began to climb, feigning tremulous fear, but he could see from the light in her eyes that she was as in her element as an eagle high on an updraft. She struck a flourishing pose at the top and dropped lightly down, to stamping and hoots and boisterous clapping.

"That one, in the red waistcoat. Selkirk is his name."

"What? Oh, yes, I had my suspicions." She was pointing out the other traitors—or by her account, the magicians sensible enough to pick the winning side.

"And Montrose. He hasn't declared, but he certainly knows what's in his best interests, and he's strong, a useful ally. He may not fight for us yet, but he's too smart to fight against us. Arden, are you paying attention?"

"Of course, my dear." But his eyes slid over to the stage, where Fee appeared to be drifting in and out of the visible plane, ethereal and fey in the rising sulfurous smoke. He could see the mirrors this time, but from the audience's gaping amazement, it seemed real to them. Even his fellow magicians looked awestruck, though perhaps that was because, unbeknownst to the Albion sisters, the footlights made their costumes considerably more transparent than they'd planned.

Fräulein Hildemar continued her litany of names, while Arden did his best to pay attention. There were considerably more than the dozen he was certain of.

"And Bergen, of course. He is second only to you in his passionate loyalty to me. To us, that is." She arched her golden eyebrows, and he realized she was trying to provoke him to jealousy.

Fräulein Hildemar, watching the permutations of his face, narrowed her eyes and said, "Bergen has already proven himself. It is time for you to do the same."

"What do you mean?"

"A little thing, really. No more than blowing a speck of dust from your sleeve. Bergen has killed for me, and a magician at that!"

For a moment the Fräulein's exquisite features blurred and transmogrified into the crushed pulp that had been murdered Rapp's face.

"What I ask of you is far, far less," she said, caressing him. "Kill a commoner for me, Arden."

He stood, dumbfounded.

"Any commoner will do," she said lightly. "That fat farmer in the front row, or the ginger biddy in tartan."

"But why?" He fumbled desperately for a reason not to do as she asked. As a follower of the Dresden school, he'd affirmed time and again how he, too, despised commoners, how he'd be their master, subject them all to his lightest whim, and—he'd suggested this himself during one night of debauchery, delighting her—even culling a fair number of them outright simply to reduce their unnecessary, unsightly presence. How could he now say he wouldn't kill one of them?

She waited. When he did not respond, she said, "I've decided to teach you how we in Dresden gain and hold our fearful strength. Listen." Her warm breath tickled his ear as she whispered such blasphemy, it was all he could do not to shout a warning to the rest, to strike her, to weep at the very idea that any magician given such an incomparable gift as the Essence could deliberately misuse it in such a horrific way.

Draining power from a magician, and letting him live afterward, was bad enough — but this?

She saw his look of disgust, though he quickly disguised it. "How is this any different from eating?" she asked. "You kill a beast and eat it. It feeds you, keeps you strong for a time."

He tempered his revulsion to a practical question, always the good spy. "When we drain an animal, its Essence passes through us and back to the earth. Are you telling me that you drain its essence and keep it?"

"This drains more than just Essence. It drains the other thing. That, we can keep for quite a while, held captive in the opals we all wear, the living stones."

"What do you mean, the other thing?"

"We don't name it. The soul, perhaps? The Essence is universal. It is in everything and flows in and out, continuously. This other thing, it is not universal. It is the essence of the individual. We take it, and it makes us strong, stronger than you can imagine!"

A wave of nausea swept over him.

"We have flocks of commoners, like sheep. The rabble who think they are in charge in Germany harvests them for us, pens them, and they are ours for the taking. Ah, wait until you experience it. I will guide you." Her hands snaked over his body. "It is better than the act of love," she whispered.

Onstage, Fee had placed her head in a box, and Phil was gracefully skewering it with an ice pick, a knitting needle, and a bayonet. Such realistic blood flowed that a woman in the front row fainted. Then, above the box, Fee's disembodied, ghostly head floated in a fresh haze of Joey's smoke bombs, sneezed, and broke character long enough to thank the many who blessed her before speaking a few prophetic words. Then the stage went black.

"What is more," Hildemar said, "you can give it as a gift. Drain a commoner, my adored one. Take his life, take everything he is, and give it to me! I will save it, here"—she touched the large opal nestled in the hollow of her creamy throat—"to use against out enemies." She was panting, and Arden saw the opal jump as she swallowed hard, salivating in anticipation.

Arden stood in the darkness, concealed by the Fräulein's magic but feeling as if he were trapped in a horror show, on display and under judgment.

Then the lights snapped blindingly on, and in the glare a figure slowly resolved, luminous and pure as light itself, dressed in a silver-tinged white gown, a crown of yew berries atop the coiled braids of her hair.

What could Arden do? He knew the Fräulein's strength, knew if he challenged her, she could very likely kill him now, with no one being any the wiser. And not just kill him but take his life, take it for her own. He'd always been told that in death, one rejoined the Essence. What, then, if one was sucked up, eaten, then used for evil?

He looked at Phil, strapping herself into a straitjacket, telling the volunteer from the audience to pull it tighter—tighter! Then chains, crisscrossed over her chest, and finally a slinglike harness that seemed held in place by no more than friction and the gradient between her slim waist and lush hips. Eamon and two other local swains hauled her up, hand over meaty hand, until she was ten feet up in the air, the belled skirt held mostly in place by a set of reverse garters she'd devised. They tied the rope to a ring in the wall.

Fee slipped lightly from the wings, almost brushing Arden's arm, but they were in the curtain's midnight velvet folds, and even without magic, they were concealed from her. She carried a large metal plate, from which protruded a half-dozen wicked-looking steel spikes as long as her forearm, and placed it precisely under the serenely dangling Phil.

Finally Fee crouched and lit a candle, adjusting it so the dancing flame licked the rope, sending up curling tongues of smoke. Arden forced himself to remain calm as he realized that, within only a matter of moments, the rope would be burned clear through, sending Phil plummeting down onto the deadly spikes.

"She would do," came the serpent voice in his ear.

He followed her gaze to Phil. "No, that's the descendent of Godric Albion I told you about. The Essence cannot touch her."

"A pity. But it can touch the rope that holds her, no? Or the candle." A shining silver worm of Essence undulated from the Fräulein's fingertips, and the flame jumped and burned brighter.

"No, I won't let you!" He grabbed her arm, expecting to be immediately smitten by her power. But she only cocked her head.

He knew he couldn't stop her attack, so he said, "She . . . desperately wants her powers back. She hates her life, now she knows what she could be, and I know if only I could find a way to restore her link to the Essence, she'd join our side."

"That's the girl who struck the Kommandant. Bergen says she hates the Germans and would do anything to keep England from being conquered. We tried to have her killed, you know. It seemed like she was going to stand in our way."

"She would have, until she understood what she was, what she should have been, if Godric hadn't been stripped of his power. Now it's only commoner Germans she hates. She deserves to have her birthright restored, don't you think?" And though it killed him to say it, he added, "And she's half mad for Hereweald, so she'll follow wherever he leads."

"Hmm. Interesting." The flame returned to normal, but already it had eaten through a chunk of the rope.

From above came a rattle and crash as Phil's chains fell to earth. A cheer rose, but there was still the straitjacket to go, and as far as Arden could see, there was no trickery to it, only skill. And skill might fail.

"So it will be another, then. Have you picked your victim . . . your sacrifice . . . your gift?"

"I'd rather have you," he said huskily, pulling her close so she wouldn't see his anxious glance at Phil. The shoulders of her strait-jacket were definitely looser, but he didn't think she'd make it. Nearby Fee crouched in the wings, watching her sister intently.

Phil had freed one long flopping straitjacket arm and dragged it wrenchingly over her shoulder. Would she make it? Arden began to hope — but no! The sling around her hips was beginning to slip!

The Fräulein pulled herself from Arden's embrace. "Another loyal magician is always welcome. And I think you said she has a sister, too? Yet another soldier for our cause — or else a hostage for her sister's good will. I will have to consider. Arden! Why do you look at her like that?"

Too late, he schooled his expression. The Fräulein's lovely face twisted cruelly, and the candle flame leaped up, consuming the rope until Phil twisted on the barest thread. Arden's hand reached for the Fräulein's throat, even as he began to call upon the Essence to save Phil. Before he could, a shrill whistle sounded from somewhere on-stage as Phil, writhing in her struggle to free herself, was enveloped in a sudden acrid cloud of smoke, and fell . . .

Nothing matters, Arden realized with a terrible numb descent. *Nothing matters but her. Not the college. Not the Essence.*

Now nothing matters at all.

His fingers touched the Fräulein's throat, though he knew it meant his death. He felt dead already.

Then the smoke cleared, and the spikes were empty: no body, no blood. Phil, borrowing a trick from Fee, had vanished.

Whatever it takes to live, he decided, dizzy and light in the incredible new altitude of relief. *I will do what I can for Rudyard, for the sake of the Essence, but now it is for her, above all.* He looked fleetingly at the spiked place where Phil was so astonishingly and absolutely *not*, and again turned his attack into a fierce caress.

"See how clever she is, even without the Essence, Fräulein." he said, pretending indifference. "Won't she do splendidly as your servant, or as a reward to one of your magicians? You say there's such a shortage of women, and you want to keep the line as pure as possible." He pinned her against the wall, shifting the curtain. "What a prize she'll be to you—Godric Albion's descendant! The one who started it all."

He couldn't tell if she was deceived; she melted into him with such practiced abandon.

"Shall we go someplace we can be alone?" he murmured, as the thunderous applause began to peter out. Phil had not yet produced herself, and the illusion hung suspended, incomplete.

"No one can see us here," she said, fondling him, then broke away with a sigh. "But I should go. I have things to see at Stour and must report back to Dresden almost at once, to prepare the attack. You will discover when the magicians will all be gathered in the manor, so we can strike?"

"As soon as I can."

"And then we will rule England, together. But first—you've forgotten about my gift."

"Really, we're both in a hurry—"

She stiffened. "Do it at once, before I doubt your loyalty, Arden," she said, without a trace of her erstwhile softness.

He still needed all the details of the attack, and she'd never tell him if she had the slightest doubt. "I've never done it before," he said, stalling. "Is it difficult?"

Her smile returned, slowly, creeping like a lizard. "You're afraid? Oh, silly boy, I forget how inexperienced you are! You're like a virgin with his first woman, aren't you! I will guide you. Pick one."

The audience should have been begging for curtain calls, standing and cheering bravo, tossing paper flowers. But only Fee stood onstage, baffled, uncertain whether to to follow her generations of training and force the show to go on, even if Phil was lying with a broken neck on the triple layer of mattresses under the hastily opened trap door set just before the mirrored image of the deadly spikes.

"Pick one. I swear, you have never known a feeling such as this!"

Arden closed his eyes and made his choice, reaching down from the stage wings to the first row, where frail Mrs. Abernathy sat, her eyes bright with excitement in their fringe of deep wrinkles. She was the oldest one in the village, Arden reasoned, half blind, wholly deaf, and subject to small strokes at the slightest provocation. If he must do evil, at least let it be the lesser evil. One old woman at death's door, for hundreds of magicians.

Fräulein Hildemar placed her hand on his arm, and he felt a part of her flow through him in a way he'd never before experienced. It was cloyingly intimate, almost unbearable. Her Essence, and as she'd said, something else, some elemental part of her, coursed into his body as he stretched out to drain Mrs. Abernathy. He felt the old woman's Essence enter him in a hot rush, followed by a quicksilver chill as he sucked away not just her life but her very self.

It was incredible. He felt . . . he felt . . . ah, he had no words for it except that he *felt*—everything! Sensation rushed at him as if for the first time, everything in its purest form. The air around him seemed abuzz with energy, colors shifted to new vibrancy, and the Essence seemed to flow into his every pore, making him preternaturally aware of every living thing near him, including, like a drink from a spring, Phil herself, near and safe and alive.

"Now give it to me!" Hildemar breathed as the old woman's head nodded to her breast, gently as sleep.

Arden abandoned himself. *This is not me,* he thought. *Only Phil can return me to myself. And if she won't . . .*

Hildemar sighed, shuddering and ecstatic, then drew herself up, her eyes luminous. "Even an old harridan like her makes me feel a thousand times stronger. Did you taste it?" She licked her lips and touched the great opal that danced with a more vibrant fire. "Now that you have a feel for it, you can do that whenever you like. The commoners—they're ripe fruit for your plucking." She kissed him, and he could feel the Essence swirling in her, unnaturally vibrant, raging like a fever.

If I had that, I could defeat you, Arden thought. He looked across the gathering, and the life forces seemed to tug at his will with a siren song.

No, only for Phil would I do such a thing . . . and in so doing, I would certainly lose her.

"To victory," Hildemar saluted him.

"To victory," Arden echoed weakly as Hildemar took her leave, walking through the wall.

Arden remained, shaking and as empty as if Hildemar had drawn away a part of his own soul, still hidden from all the world . . . except for the pair of wide blue-green eyes framed by tumbled scarlet hair that bored into him for one more instant before she ran onstage to bow, whisper a word into Fee's ear, and dash off into the frozen white night.

Chapter 22

I *should have killed him then,* she told herself as tears froze on her cheeks. *How had I not known who that woman was?* Rapp's description came back to her — the stunning woman with the *Sonnenschein* hair, bedecked with opals. She was the wicked demon who'd tortured Rapp, who had infiltrated Stour to lure gullible magicians with her promises and wiles, who no doubt murdered Rapp for failing to kill Phil. Or — Phil's old suspicions rushed back — had Arden do it for her.

Oh Arden, Arden, how could you do it?

At least he hadn't seen her, and she could place the responsibility into another's hands. She didn't have a great deal of faith in Rudyard's ability to take action against the Germans, but he had a history of secretly getting rid of rebellious magicians. As soon as Rudyard heard this, he'd do what he did with errant journeymen and have Arden eliminated.

The tears came harder, and she swore to herself they were only tears of fury.

I'll tell Rudyard, and then I'm leaving. I'll be eighteen in a few months, and then I can be a Land Girl, or a Wren, or work in a munitions plant. Anything to get away from here. I'll rent a place for Fee and me. She won't care where she lives; her whole life is waiting now, and she can wait anywhere.

If anyone had asked her, she would have said she'd never feel anything again. All the same, after ten minutes of dragging herself through the deepening drifts, she began to shiver violently. She'd only thrown a light evening coat over her stage dress, and her shoes were silver ballet slippers.

I can't get word to Rudyard if I freeze to death first, she thought, as pragmatic as if she'd never felt love's life-altering touch. She changed her course to stop at Weasel Rue, only slightly out of the way to Stour.

He doesn't know I heard him, and he didn't see me, so I have enough time.

He had seen her, though. He had no inkling that she'd overheard any of his plotting with the Fräulein, but he saw her rush offstage into the swirling snowstorm, and without thinking of the consequences, only knowing that he had to, he pursued her, as the wolf leaps for the baited hook strung in the tree, in the lust for what sustains him. He needed to be close to her, needed the reassurance of her presence, after what he'd done. He couldn't tell her anything, of course, but if he could only hint, with a look if nothing else, that she must wait, and all would be well, and if she would only answer that with a look of her own, however banal their conversation might be . . . then he might be able to survive the next few days.

Just out of sight, he trailed her through the snow, a quarter mile behind.

Phil let herself into the farmhouse and collapsed just past the threshold, exhausted from rage and bitter disappointment. She couldn't feel her fingers and wished she couldn't feel her toes, because they were suffused with a pulsing pain. The fireplaces were all out, and the abandoned house was almost as chilled as the outside. She knew she needed to get warm, but she couldn't bring herself to move.

The door swung open behind her, and she looked up gratefully. Phil had never dreamed Fee would follow her, the darling! But it wasn't Fee.

Arden closed the door behind him and watched her, dark eyes intent under winged black brows. Not taking her eyes from him, she reached into the pocket she'd sewn into her costume and pinched the small razor blade between her thumb and forefinger.

"I had to see you," Arden said. "I've been—busy—and I wanted to be sure . . ." He swallowed hard. Phil didn't think he'd blinked once since he entered. "You asked once if we were friends." He moved toward her, looking so tortured, she longed to take him in her arms. But she squeezed the tiny blade more tightly. "I wanted to tell you that I never—"

"What a liar your face is, Arden," she said, and sprang.

She slashed at him, raking his chest in a shallow gash, then grabbed hold of the lace at his throat to pull him into a close embrace, her blade striving for his exposed neck.

It was all going as perfectly as a well-rehearsed stage stunt—to Phil's surprise, because she hadn't really expected to win—and Arden's blood would have been soaking the hay-strewn floor, if not for the fact that her benumbed fingers had dropped the razor in her first attack, and she found herself doing nothing more deadly than caressing his bare skin. Still, luck did not entirely desert her, and Arden tripped as he tried to evade her, hit his head on the mantel, and lay dazed.

Her fingers feeling like potatoes, Phil scrambled for the razor. She could have cut his throat—she knew she could have, then, in the heat of passion. But now, as she climbed on top of him, straddling his chest and pressing the razor to the beating hollow at the base of his throat, she wasn't sure.

I can do it, she thought doubtfully. *I just have to work myself up again first.*

"Clever, am I?" she said, slapping him. *No,* she thought, *it should be a punch. I want to hit him so hard I break my fingers.* "Clever enough to be her servant—or whore to some German magician?" She slapped him again, which for some reason was proving more satisfying after all. *Now all he has to do is curse me or spit or struggle, and in goes the blade.*

But he didn't struggle. He only looked at her, his cheeks cold-flushed, his black hair coming loose from its tight queue. He was memorizing her, possessing every part of her, so that when he returned to the Essence, perhaps some small trace of her might remain with him.

"You traitor! You rotten son of a bitch. We trusted you! I trusted you!" She slapped him again and pressed the knife harder, until the tender hollow welled and filled with blood, a sacrificial spring. "How could you betray England like that?" A renegade tear fell from her eye to his. "How could you betray *me!* Fight, damn it! Fight me so I can kill you!"

"My life is yours," he said softly, and as if the knife weren't digging into his throat, he reached up to touch her temple, her cheek.

"Stop it!" She pulled away.

"It has been yours, since the first day we met. I begrudged it to you, until today. Take my life, Philomel."

The sound of her whole name made another tear escape, to tremble, ridiculously, at the tip of her nose.

"Only promise me you'll tell Rudyard."

"Of course I'll tell him what a foul, scheming cur you are."

"Tell him about the plot. You must have heard, but did you hear all of it? Within a week, when the magicians are all back. They have ten who can pass through a portal, and another twenty magicians from Stour. They're going to destroy Stour with everyone inside."

"Like you almost did? Fool that I was, I thought it was an accident."

"It was, I swear. Please, it doesn't matter what happens to me. Just make sure Rudyard knows. He'll know what to do."

"Confession? You've had a change of heart? It won't win you mercy from me."

"You have to leave. You and Fee. She wants to kill you or enslave you."

"What do you care? You want to give me as a gift to your lover. All that time I thought you cared for me, and I was stupid enough to—"

"To what?" he asked, and perhaps no one in the world, being held at knifepoint, has even looked so radiantly joyous.

"To love you, you bastard!" There, now that she was fully humiliated, she could kill him. Except . . .

"Promise me one thing more," he said.

What now? she wondered. *Give that German bitch your love?*

"Your fingers. They're like ice. You may have frostbite. Get them in warm water, or you might lose them."

Phil rocked back on her heels. Everything she had seen, everything she had heard, told her Arden was a traitor. Every piece of logic her brain sifted through confirmed it. But Fee was right—this wasn't a matter for thought. A man who cared for his executioner's well-being with his final breath simply could not betray England, the college, and most important, her.

She stood up.

"Why didn't you tell me?" She flung the blade across the room. "And why the bloody hell did you have to sleep with her!" she wailed, and covered her face with her hands, shaking in silent, moist dissolution.

In an instant he had her in his arms. She tried to pull away—but she didn't try very hard.

"You were a spy, I realize that now," Phil said, muffled in her own fingers, which warmed with her breath. "And you couldn't tell me, I understand. Oh, but she's so beautiful, I suppose you couldn't resist. Seeing you two together—I hated her, I hated you, but I had to look."

"You saw us?" He blanched.

She nodded, her face still adamantly hidden in her hands. "In your hopper hut. And I know I'm nothing beside her, but—"

"Oh, you stupid, stupid girl!" he said. "It wouldn't matter if you looked like a hag—you'd be a thousand times more beautiful than her, because you're *you,* you silly git. You, Phil, gallant and generous and good. And distinctly unhaglike. You, who I love."

The hands parted a fraction.

"She's loathsome. She's vile."

The hands closed again. "I can imagine, from the way you were fondling her . . ."

"Phil, look at me!"

"No."

"What would you do to save England, eh?" He pried up her pinky and kissed it. "Would you cut off this finger to save your country?" He lifted her ring finger, and a luminous blue-green eye regarded him. "How about this one?"

"Of course."

"Would you die for England?"

"Yes."

"No, you would not, because I would forbid it." He unclamped a third finger and kissed her lightly on the nose. "Would you seduce a Nazi to save England?"

"Yes," she said, and waited for him to forbid that, too. "You would let me?"

He nodded. "Because it is only the body, Phil, and the body can lie just as words can lie. The body does what is necessary."

"Apparently the body enjoys what is necessary," she said archly, remembering their passionate gymnastics.

He very firmly removed her hands from her face and kissed it. "You, Phil. You have my life. Always. Now, shall we be pragmatic a moment and save the college?"

"No. It's terribly selfish of me, and I'll probably get my comeuppance, but please, will you kiss me again first? I wasn't properly prepared the last time and—mmm."

But she still wasn't prepared. Nothing—not her dalliance with Hector nor any of the dozen other boys she'd casually kissed—nothing had prepared her for the stem-to-stern electricity of a kiss given and taken in love. The college had to wait. The whole world had to wait.

"I ought to go," Arden said, stroking her hair.

"You will, very soon," she said, standing on tiptoe to explore the beauty of his trapezius with her lips.

"You *do* have to go," Phil said a long moment later. "But there is tomorrow."

"And tomorrow." He discovered the downiness of her earlobe.

"And tomorrow." She buried her hands in the stygian softness of his hair.

"And . . ." The room felt suddenly chilled.

"*Tomorrow* is the word you're looking for," Phil prompted.

"Phil, what I have to do—I may not come through it alive. If I die, remember that—"

"No!" she said, then forced herself to smile. "You will not die. Because I forbid it."

Chapter 23

It was all Arden could do to seem composed and grave when he met with the Headmaster. The scowl that usually came so naturally deserted him. The world was, after all, a rosy place. Outside the wind howled like a heavenly chorus. *She loves me,* he thought, *and so everything will be all right. It has to be.*

He told Rudyard the Dresdener plan was almost ready and waited for the call to arms, for the old man to finally be ready to pit his best masters against the intruders. There were only ten Germans, and even if you counted the twenty-odd turncoats, a hundred of the college's best should be able to defeat them.

Rudyard interrupted his optimistic musings. "Then we will be ready to leave and disperse. When they come, the college will be virtually empty."

Arden stared at him, dumbfounded. The enemy's plans were in their hands. It would be a hell of a fight, but since they knew the

Dresdeners' strength and numbers, and would soon know the very hour and direction of attack, their victory was all but assured. He must have misunderstood.

"Is dispersal necessary? After the fighting is over, we can always rebuild Stour. It's a good location."

"There will be no fighting," Rudyard said.

Arden felt his temper begin to slip. "You don't honestly think you can reason with them, do you? They're hell bent on ruling England, on killing and enslaving commoners."

"Which we must avoid at all costs."

"Exactly, which is why we must crush them, now!"

"Better to have a score of rogue magicians trying to rule than five hundred. Sit down, Arden. It is time you learned something. If things had gone otherwise, you would have heard it from my lips eventually. I had high hopes for you, son. I thought you might one day follow me as Headmaster. But now you are called upon to make an even greater sacrifice for the college, and it is only right that you know why."

And then, for the first time, he told Arden the truth, and the world's rosiness decayed.

England is a prison for the Essence, Rudyard said, and the College of Drycraeft is a prison for magicians.

Rudyard spoke the litany that had been repeated every generation to the new Headmaster, and to him alone: Once the Essence had flowed freely through all the world, surging and unbound. Any person with the power to control it could gather it up like apples in autumn and use it for whatever he wished. And humans, being human, used it selfishly, foolishly, violently. The weak-willed magicians became the slaves of kings. The bold, the clever, the potent, became magician-kings, taking what they would and subjugating all who opposed them.

"Thus it is whenever there is power," Rudyard told the young master. "But in commoners, there is a limit to the evil they can do. A commoner can kill one man with his hands, a dozen with a gun, a thousand with a bomb. Not so in magicians—there is no limit. Left to band together, they would rule the world—and ultimately, destroy it.

"So the wisest of the magicians, those who understood the dreadful combination of lust for power and limitless access to it, devised a plan. They gathered as much Essence as they could and trapped it in an island fortress bound by wards of terrible strength, from which the Essence could not escape.

"But they could not quite gather all of it, and any ambitious magician still posed a threat. So they rounded up the youngest, those who were still coming into their powers, and imprisoned them, too, on the island. The others they attacked by stealth, though most either died, struggling to keep their last vestiges of power, or faded into obscurity, their link to the Essence so sorely diminished that they were scarcely better than commoners.

"Our ancestors saw what would become of civilization if the magic were left unchecked. We did what we had to do."

Arden still did not completely understand. "What you say makes no sense. Why concentrate the Essence, and then bring magicians to it, if they are such a threat? You're wrong, Rudyard." He looked at his Headmaster beseechingly, begging him not to confirm the terrible thing he felt deep in his bones.

"Because people are gullible," Rudyard said, "even magicians.

Take them young, tell them lies, and they will believe. Tell them the world will be flung from its foundations if they do not perform the Exaltation daily, and they will feel such honor, such obligation, that they will never stray. At least, the vast majority will not. That's why we allow the journeyman year. It weeds out the rebels. Those who return are content to believe in the Exaltation and will never believe it isn't necessary."

"You can't mean . . ." Arden faltered. Nearly his whole life, his entire purpose, had been tending the Essence, being one of the godlike beings that kept the world alive.

"The Exaltation is meaningless, Arden. Busywork for schoolchildren. A task to make their life seem fraught with purpose. *I could be a king,* each lad will think, *but what I do is so much more important.*"

For a moment only, the revelation made Arden feel weak and spent, but rage followed on its heels, ravening for blood.

He controlled himself well, though. His time with the Fräulein had taught him that much, at least. He pretended prostration, as the slave under the lash knows better than to swear vengeance; still, he vowed to be free—and to punish his captor.

A lifetime of lies. *I could have had a life of my own. I could have loved.* He felt, for almost the first time, what Rudyard had called the lust for power. *Yes, I could have been a king,* he thought.

But I would have been a good one.

I should have been given the chance to prove I could. Any man can kill with his hands. Should he therefore be shackled all his days, just in case?

Letting the hurt and confusion through, but not the bitter anger, Arden said, "Then the earth doesn't need us?"

"No one needs you, boy. No one needs me, nor any magician. We serve no purpose. We are unexploded bombs waiting to go off. We must be contained."

"Then why the college? Why gather us and train us?"

"Because magicians will always be born. When they appear in the rest of the world, it is no matter — their link to the Essence is so tenuous, they can hardly accomplish anything."

Except for the monsters who have learned to steal it, Arden thought.

"But when they are born in England, their access to the Essence is so great, their capacity for evil so boundless . . ."

Or for good, you blind old fool. Power can be good, in the right hands!

" . . . they must be guided to a safe path as soon as possible."

"Not killed?" *You've certainly killed enough,* he thought.

"Where's your logic, Arden? Kill them all, and more will be born, and who in turn will control them? The college exists solely as an institution to contain new magicians, perpetually."

"I see," Arden said. "Each generation must be enslaved and fooled, so that they will be willing to enslave and fool the next. How clever — how thorough. And those who rebel are eliminated."

"Exactly. And now you see why I cannot allow any of my magicians to fight."

"No, I don't really."

"Let them taste competition, violence, victory — and they will never look back! I will lose control of them. It is the nature of man."

"You let them train with Phil." Her name on his tongue was a drop of honey.

"Fencing and fisticuffs are nothing. It was like a journeyman adventure — something most can turn their backs on easily enough.

Those who don't—and I know which of your friends have been training to use the Essence to fight—will be drained."

Still, somehow, Arden forced himself to be calm. "If no one fights them, the Dresdeners will be free in England—to do what they will. Isn't that what the Headmasters have been working against for millennia?"

"The Dresdeners will be dealt with," Rudyard said.

"How, if the masters won't fight? Do you mean to use your assassins?"

It was known, among the higher ranks of masters, that errant, rebellious journeymen were drained, but no one knew who did the killing.

"The masters do not carry out the executions."

"Who, then?" Arden asked, swearing in his heart he would kill them all, whoever they were, for executing his brothers just because they yearned to be free.

"Why, the women, of course."

Arden kept himself together by sheer force of will until Rudyard dismissed him, with orders to discover the details of the attack.

He staggered through the halls of Stour like a man in a nightmare, blind to the friends who saluted him.

Look at you! he wanted to scream. *Deluded fools, all of you, thinking the fate of the earth lies with you. Slaves! Dare to have a free thought, and you'll be killed—for the good of the world.*

He stumbled against the great arched entranceway, his thoughts uncontrollable. Was Rudyard right? Were they too dangerous to be allowed to live free in the world? *Look at me—I killed my father, I tormented Ruby—and I think I can be good? I destroyed Stour and killed magicians by using the Essence without thinking. God, I killed Thomas! Maybe I can't be let loose.*

But I can redeem myself. I can free my brothers, he thought. *I can give them a chance to make the choice for themselves.*

He forged out into the blizzard, a burning brand, feeling as if he had died and been reborn. He knew what he had to do. He just needed Phil's help to figure out how to do it.

When he reached Weasel Rue at last, he simply held her, surrendering himself utterly to the right of possession and being possessed. Then he told her, and she listened with tight-pressed lips and never once thought of saying *I told you so,* though she'd known, even with her limited scientific and historical knowledge, that the world's continued existence couldn't depend on a species that has only existed for a tiny fraction of the planet's lifespan.

"They're scattering like rats," Arden said, pacing the farmhouse kitchen. "He's dividing them up among the women, hiding them out until he thinks they can gather again in a new college."

Phil raised an eyebrow. "Tell me about these mysterious female magicians."

"I don't know much. We've been taught they hardly have any power." Phil made a *humph* sound. "But now he says they're the assassins. They kill the journeymen who refuse to return, and he'll be sending them to kill the Dresdeners. How is it that they get to live in the world while we were caged?"

"Perhaps other methods of control work for them."

"Self-control, you mean? Why can't we have self-control? Do they think any man with power is going to wage war and murder everyone who crosses him and keep harems and . . . what are you smirking at?"

"Well, it *is* what men tend to do."

"Not every man," he assured her. But he remembered how he felt when that young soldier she called her brother kissed her. What would he have done to the boy, if not for his strict training in pacifism?

"But you haven't heard the worst," Arden went on. "When most of the college flees, he needs to leave some behind in Stour so the attacking Germans will sense the power inside. He wants to trick them into thinking they've done what they set out to do, so they won't pursue us. That will give the women plenty of time to track them and kill them."

"You mean that, he expects someone to volunteer to die? Who would . . . oh. You. Your punishment for rebelling—and saving the magicians?"

Arden nodded. "Me, and the rest of the muster. A convenient plan, eh? We'll be crushed to dust so the others can escape and never know the truth about what they could be. About . . ." He hesitated to tell her the last thing Rudyard had revealed. Not knowing if it was the right thing to do, he steeled himself and said only, "About what *you* could be."

Phil cocked her head at him.

The women, Rudyard had said, might decide not to drain the Dresdeners but to take away their magic, their link to the Essence, the same way they had with her ancestor, Godric Albion.

"It is a much harsher punishment, and no more than they de-serve," Rudyard had said. "Though I counseled against it. After all, there is the chance, not likely but still a chance, that they'll discover how to reverse it."

His heart barely beating, Arden asked, as casually as he could, how that could be so.

And Rudyard, so cynical, so calculating, so devious, still trusted to the young master's blind dedication and imminent demise, and dropped the bombshell.

"Anyone can become a magician," he'd said. "The Essence is in every living thing already. All it takes to turn a commoner from a passive possessor to an active practitioner is an inoculation, if you will." And then, unbidden, he explained to Arden briefly how to do it. "Should anything happen to me, this knowledge must be preserved, so that you may make absolutely sure no misguided magician re-stores the Dresdeners' powers."

Phil, when she heard, immediately thought of Fee's first meeting with Thomas, when he'd offered to thrust his Essence past her bar-rier, and giggled. No, knowing what those two had been up to in the hayloft, that certainly wasn't how it was done.

"Don't you see what that means?" Arden asked her.

"That we could all be magicians and have a balance of power?"

"No," he said, though the idea intrigued him. "It means I could restore your birthright. What was stolen from Godric, I could return to you. Phil, you could be a magician!"

"No thank you!" she said. "What, be a prisoner?"

"I'm going to change all that somehow, I swear. Every magician will know the truth, and be free."

"Ah, no, but I'd be one of the women, wouldn't I? I wonder what they're really like. No, I'm sorry, I'm not even tempted. Yours is such a tangled lot. I like my kind of magic far better. Do I have to be a magician for you to care for me?"

He answered in a way that put all doubts to rest, and when she emerged, breathless, from his embrace, he picked up her last thread.

"What if we released the Essence from England back into the world? What if we gave everyone the same power? You haven't felt it, Phil, so you don't understand, but all this trouble, all this grief, it's just the human side of the Essence. Yes, most of my life has been a lie, but one thing remains: the Essence is pure. It is life. It is the song of the earth, the soul . . . to feel it changes a person." He took on a visionary glow. "If everyone could feel it, there would be no war, I know it. It is only when some have it, and some don't, that the problems start. If we could—"

"First things first," said pragmatic Phil. "Shall we save you and our friends, and kill the Dresdeners, and then go about rehabilitating the world? Because you see, I think I have an idea."

They discussed it until after midnight, when it was Fee's turn to come home and find a man in bed with her sister, though in this case he was fully dressed (albeit a bit mussed in the hair, with his shirt untucked) and perched chastely atop the bedclothes. They apprised her of the situation, and of course she promised to help. They needed her, because Phil was certain only magic—*their* kind of magic—would save all the magicians of Stour.

Fee, after making a few sketches and doing something suspiciously like trigonometry, admitted that yes, it could work.

"But we're going to need an awfully big mirror," she said. "And you'd better pray we don't have a thaw."

Arden slipped out of the house near dawn.

"It will be hard for me to see you again for a while," he said.

"As hard as for me *not* to see you again?" she asked, plaintively.

"I'll be going back and forth between my hut and the Fräulein, and Stour."

"Which the farmhouse is conveniently between."

"If she sees me with you—"

"Oh, I know," Phil said with a pout. "Only, are you going to have to—you know."

"I'll try not to, beloved, but if she suspects I'm playing her false, she'll change her plans, and we'll be lost. I have to keep her convinced, and if it means—doing *that*—well then, I must." Thank goodness she didn't know what else he'd done to keep the Fräulein convinced. He would never tell her about Mrs. Abernathy, traces of whose life still seemed to tickle his nerves.

"You must," Phil echoed. "Oh, Arden! I know it's only a body." She gave him such a bold caress that he almost had to carry her back upstairs and politely but firmly evict Fee from the bed, unless the hay in the cowshed might do. "But don't you see?" she asked, lingering maddeningly. "It's *my* body now!"

Then she sent him off into the frozen world, to lie, as he'd been taught.

Chapter 24

The battle (or as the Dresdeners knew it, the attack) came together exactly like a premiere. Early on, there was Phil and Fee's audacious plan, the guarantee of resounding success, the confidently sketched diagrams that bade the laws of physics to stand aside ever so slightly . . . followed by grueling work, and then, at the last moment, a flurry of confusion bordering on absolute hysterical pandemonium.

As always, though, the show went on.

"Impossible!" Arden told Rudyard when the Headmaster suggested evacuating Stour days ahead of the attack. "The Fräulein said they'll strike immediately after the Exaltation on the first day the magicians return. Everyone has to be there."

"Then how do we escape? They'll detect a portal, and anyway, half our magicians aren't advanced enough to create one. We need to let the Germans believe they've won so we can continue our work."

"They will see us going into Stour—but we won't actually be going inside."

Arden explained, but Rudyard didn't like it. "More commoner interference," he snapped automatically, which made Arden briefly lose his tightly checked temper.

"Drop that codswallop, Rudyard. I know better than that now. Everything we do is for the commoners. At least let one help us."

Reluctantly, he agreed. "Only be sure it will work," Rudyard cautioned. "I will let the men die—all of them—before I let them fight. What have you told those who will stay behind, inside Stour?"

"Only that they must do their duty to the Essence."

"Be sure they do. And as for you—"

"I will be with my brothers, never fear. Now mind you, the Germans know our routines. Everything about the Exaltation must go exactly as usual, or they'll scrap their plans, and then we won't know when they'll attack."

"And that would be disastrous," Rudyard said. "Can you imagine a world where boys grew up with free use of their powers?" He shuddered. "Arden, I've changed my mind about something. Your willingness to sacrifice yourself has proven to me once and for all that no one but you can succeed me. You were so willing to die for what is right—a lesser man might not have understood. Send the others in, instruct them well—but you, Master Arden, you may live. And one day you will be Headmaster in my place."

Rudyard beamed at his young master, awaiting gratitude, and when he gave it, patted him like a good dog.

The snow, mercifully, held, coating the world in thick white drifts that blurred form.

Arden stood on the hill and watched the final Exaltation that the College of Drycraeft would ever perform. He could still feel the miraculous currents of Essence rise and fall, and that marvelous sense of plunging into a warm viscous pool of *everything*.

Casually, he glanced at a thick plantation of hemlock trees, their weeping, needled boughs caressing and overlapping each other in a coniferous orgy to make a dense thicket, in the center of which waited Phil and her Home Guard. Their faces were whitened with stage greasepaint, the gunmetal shine of their weapons was dulled. Swathed with whatever incongruous and unseasonal white clothes they could find to cover their winter work clothes and make them all but vanish in the snow, they waited, primed and silent, for the invasion Phil swore was at hand.

Silent, except for Mrs. Enery, her hair under a crocheted ivory tam-o'-shanter, who exclaimed, "Blimey, they *have* rebuilt Stour!"

Phil had told them the Germans were attacking a secret military installation built on the old Stour grounds.

"Was that what them professors were really about?" Eamon had asked. "I knew something fishy was afoot."

Phil had been vague about how she knew, and insisted there wasn't nearly enough time to summon help from London.

They were soldiers now, and they didn't question their commander. Tensely happy, they would have been joking if not for the strict command for quiet.

Phil, who knew what they were up against and what was at stake, wasn't so sanguine. But the Home Guard was only a single arm of a many-tentacled attack, and she hoped they would need to be little more than a distraction.

Belly-crawling from one to the other, she reviewed their part one final time and was about to make her way to her own position to the rear of where the Germans would gather, when a crouching figure slipped into the thicket and, with the regrettable grace learned in a barbed-wire youth, dropped to his elbows.

"Uncle Walter!" His rifle strap was twisted tightly about his left forearm to brace it for deadly accuracy, but from his right wrist dangled handcuffs, one cuff clamped, the other loose.

He saw where she was looking. "Just in case I can't stop," he said with a rueful wink.

She fell beside him. "How did you know we were here?"

"Fee was fretting too much to lie well. The lad with her told me the rest. He was sensible enough to think I might be of some use." That would be Stan, at Weasel Rue with Fee for safekeeping. "And your tracks are fresh in the snow." Damn. It was still falling steadily, though, and with half an hour yet to go, she was sure they'd be covered. The Dresdeners were planning to open their portals in one tight cluster, and not scout around, Arden said, so they should be safe either way.

"We don't need you," Phil said. "Fine thing if you go off your nut in the middle of battle. Go home."

"I've seen them shoot," he said flatly. "Trust me, you need me."

And since it was impossible to shift him, he stayed.

Phil crept to her own position and used a compact to catch the sunset rays and flash a confirmation of her location to Joey, crouched with an abundance of matches in a small hoary defile. She found her own store of weapons, hidden the day before, and unwrapped a rifle and her good old tulwar from their waterproof oilskin. There, everything was in place, and now she was free to have a small and private panic.

Ah, but there was Arden, walking across the white open meadow between Stour and the timber. Her panic didn't quite leave at the sight of him, but it suddenly had a companion at its side, bolstering it to a more useful sort of panic, the kind that makes people think swiftly and act even faster, the kind that keeps soldiers sharp. Standing staunchly beside the trembling fear of death was the thing for which she was willing to risk her life—the love of Arden, and love for Arden.

He was to take a position between her and Stour, where the Dresdeners would soon gather.

What the hell was he doing? The moment before curtain is no time for improvisation, and Arden was rewriting the script by walking straight to her hiding place.

He didn't see her until he was almost on top of her, and then it was her aquamarine eyes he spotted first, their pre-Raphaelite luminosity peering from under a furry white Russian *ushanka*. The rest was cloaked in white wool and fur, invisible. Ah yes, there was another part of her he could see now—a slender bare hand, pink with cold, clutching the hilt of her curved tulwar. He could not stomach the thought of Phil's body, Phil's smile, Phil's sweet, soft hands roiling in the middle of a fight. For though the Dresdeners' magic could not harm her, the men they were bringing with them certainly could—and certainly would, if Arden didn't keep Phil out of the fighting.

He'd learned about it that very morning, when the Fräulein slipped into his hut at dawn to make sure everything went as planned. Then lightly, but holding his eye all the while, she said, "I'll be bringing a few commoners along, too, and you mustn't let your appetites tempt you, dear boy." For he'd let on that, beguiled by what she'd taught him, he was wreaking havoc among the local commoners. "They are what you would call a necessary evil. Two soldiers and a champion duelist."

"What on earth do you need them for?"

Now she didn't bother containing her malicious glee. "We'll be eliminating the Albions. Whatever their lineage, they are, after all, only commoners now, and their peculiarity makes them a threat. The one who colors her hair such an improbable hue in particular. Bergen tells me you fancied her, once."

So that was it—he'd played his part of devotion to the Fräulein perfectly, but he hadn't been able to hide his adoration of Phil. The unguarded instant in the moment she fell to the spikes—yes, that was when the Fräulein knew. And Bergen, the swine! Now he had two scores to settle with the traitorous journeyman—Rapp's death, and this.

"Before you opened my eyes, Hildemar," he said. "Would you rather I kill her for you? I don't see why loathsome commoners should be involved."

She looked at him for a long moment, her eyes serene azure poison. "No, this way is best." And of course, with everything hanging on that evening, he said nothing more. In a few hours the Dresdeners would be killed, all the college would know the truth—and the brave new world would begin.

But there wouldn't be a world for him without Phil at his side. He feared—he knew in his soul—what kind of man he would become if he lost her.

"Do you love me?" he asked Phil now.

A little part of Phil crumpled inside. She knew he was going to use her love as blackmail. "Maybe a bit," she said, all the love in the world radiating plainly from her worried face.

"Then you have to stay out of the fighting. They're sending assassins to kill you."

"They've done it before," she said, shrugging a small avalanche of snow from her shoulders.

"More than one—and professionals this time."

"I can take care of myself."

"No, you can't. You're an astonishing woman, Phil, but you're not a soldier, nor a killer. They are, and they're coming for you. You have to take Fee and leave, now. Leave Bittersweet, leave England if at all possible."

"Nonsense. Just like a man, thinking that because I love you, you can order me around. You're fighting—so will I. Do you honestly think I'd leave you?"

Desperate, Arden fell to his knees and tried another dirty trick. "Think of Fee, then. She can't defend herself at all, and the assassins will be coming after both of you."

This almost worked. "But if they're coming at the same time as the Dresden magicians, we'll be able to knock them off, too. They have no idea we're here. We have eight fighters, plus me, and a few extra surprises. Between us and your magicians, we should be able to wipe them out in the first salvo."

"But if we can't? The Fräulein is more powerful than I am, and your Home Guard—they're not proven. If one magician spots them, they're dead. If only one assassin gets through, *you're* dead. If not now, then they'll hunt you down."

"It's war, Arden. No one is safe, ever. It's what the rest of us have been living with for more than a year. I'll be careful."

"It's not enough!" he cried, anguished. "I *need* you safe. Safe and waiting for me, so when this night is over, we can stand hand in hand and change the world. We can, Phil—we can free the Essence, free the magicians, and one day make every human a magician in his own right. But I need you, or . . ."

"Or what, Arden?"

"You know what I've done," he said in a low growl. "I'm not good—not on my own. My father, Ruby—hell, even you. And the things I've thought . . . Phil, the Fräulein taught me something, and I can't stop longing for it." He pounded his thighs with his clenched fists. "It's like a drug, rising in my blood and demanding that I have more and more."

Barely whispering, he told her about draining the life from Mrs. Abernathy.

"When I felt it, it was like I'd been thirsty all my days and only then discovered water. I only had it for an instant—I gave it to her—but I want more. Oh, help me Phil, I want more!"

She held his head to her breast.

"I won't, though, I swear it. I hate myself for what I feel. As long as you're with me, I can control it, but without you, I'll become what the old Headmasters feared. I'll be the reason all magicians are shackled and chained."

"I can't run away now," she whispered into his sable hair. "I have a part to play. The Home Guard is counting on me."

Arden rocked back on his heels, and Phil shrank from his grim, set face.

"Then you give me no choice."

She thought it was an embrace, at first, the deliberately light-hearted *good luck* and *until we meet again* parting of people who know they'll jinx themselves if they acknowledge the terrible possibilities by saying something as final as *goodbye.* He held her arms just above the elbow; he kissed her lightly on the brow.

Then he stabbed her in the heart.

No, it can't be real, she thought, suddenly rigid and powerless. There was another stabbing, and another, a thousand all over her body in an instant, rending her with something that was not exactly pain, not yet, but somehow worse for the fact, like plunging your hand in scalding water that for the first second feels cold, knowing the agonizing damage is done, irrevocably, before you can feel it.

Then through the pain that was not pain came a sweetness, pure and eternal, rising from a time before worry, an age before suffering. She heard a throbbing and knew it was her mother's heartbeat from within. Gravity abandoned her, and direction; color and form fled from her wide-staring eyes, and she returned, ah, with such blessed relief, to a place she'd almost forgotten, a memory older than her own body. She was herself, and she was everything . . . and it was bliss.

She knew what she was feeling, as surely as a child knows with wonder and certainty what he sees when he first beholds himself in a mirror. Arden had restored the Albion birthright. He had given her the Essence.

And not just the Essence, she realized, settling into the surprisingly soothing sensation of being every molecule in her immediate vicinity yet hardly remembering her own name. Arden had given her something else, too—himself.

Thomas in his research had provided the first clue. Fräulein Hildemar, in corrupting him, opened up the secret pathways through which life along with Essence can be drained. Rudyard, believing him loyal, gave him the theory, granting knowledge only to prevent its use. Now he knew exactly how to awaken the power of the Essence in a commoner: he had to give a bit of his own life.

She could feel him in her, small and potent as a single grain of salt on the tongue. Then Essence, power, Arden, all of it, rose within her like a great wave and crested, drowning her.

She fainted against Arden's chest, and he laid her tenderly in the snow.

This wasn't exactly what he'd been expecting. He thought, after the transfer and her awakening, he'd be able to quite calmly and logically explain that, now that she was magical—and no longer immune to the Essence—she absolutely had to go home. After all, she was only involved in any of this because she had special protection against the Dresdeners. Now that this was removed, she had no business here. And now that she was a magician, too, she could, even without training, easily protect herself and Fee from the assassins. Since his ultimate plan was to return the Essence to all humans, she couldn't really complain that he'd done anything but act a little prematurely. Against her will, he knew, and she'd have every right to be furious, but fury he could overcome; death, he could not.

All that did little good if she was unconscious.

He shook her, then tried the Sleeping Beauty method, to no avail. There wasn't time to move her, and already weak from transferring a portion of his life (which left a tickling, empty space in some part of himself he couldn't quite pinpoint; would it regenerate itself, like lost blood?), he wasn't sure he could open a portal for her. He needed all the power he could muster to fight the Dresdeners — and they'd be here any minute.

Making a hollow for her head, he covered her with snow and left her there, snug as a badger in its den. *She'll be safe,* he told himself. *No one will know she's there.* If she woke, though, she'd be vulnerable to the magicians. *Ah, but they won't know that,* he realized with a self-satisfied grin. Even if the worst should happen, they'd leave her to the assassins, and she'd be able to handle them easily, now that she could draw from the Essence.

And he left his love, alone and insensible, to meet his lover at the rendezvous point.

For a time, Phil knew nothing. When the body is given more than it can handle, it surrenders and waits. While Phil slept, dreaming impossible dreams beneath her snow blanket, the Dresdeners came.

No more than a rifle shot away, they stood arrogantly on the low lawn, watching the magicians file into Stour. The sinking sun cast sharply angled rays over the snow, making the world strikingly white, blinding as a noontime desert. The Kommandant was there, the man everyone assumed was the leader, but now he yielded place to the Fräulein.

While strange visions filled Phil's slumbering head, the magicians passed through a precise arrangement of huge mirrors, crafted by Rudyard himself and placed by Fee, that made it seem as if they walked in solemn single file through the high arched doorway.

The traitors, on one pretext or another, had stayed an extra day in the hopper huts, and now they materialized through portals to join the Dresdeners. Together they stood on the exact spot Arden had marked out for them—the only position from which the illusion would work—and never knew that the magicians all passed behind Stour and began a long trek through the snow, to emerge an hour later at a roadside where a convoy of omnibuses collected them. All except the dozen or so of Phil's muster, who were to sacrifice themselves to save the others; they walked through the real doors.

When nearly all the magicians were through, Arden told the Fräulein, "I will gather them in the great room. That way you can be sure no one escapes. Give me ten minutes. I'll come out with a present for you." He gave her a wink and a familiar caress and saw Bergen fume.

In the rigid protocol of college rank, the lowliest entered Stour first, while the loftiest, the Headmaster, always entered last. Arden reached the line just as Rudyard prepared to pass through the mirrored escape and took him firmly by the arm. "Quick, come inside!" he hissed. "There's been a change of plan. I have to tell you!" Rudyard tried to pull away. "Don't worry, we have ten minutes, but you must hurry. This is crucial!"

Reluctantly, the Headmaster allowed himself to be led to the library, where Arden shoved him unceremoniously into the darkened room.

"What is the meaning of this?" he cried, as from all around him, savage faces appeared from the shadows.

"Secure him," Arden said, and the Headmaster felt the Essence surround him, felt coils of magic and steel chains both writhe around his body and hold him fast. He struggled, and against any other magicians of the college, he would have been victorious, but these dozen had been training, fighting, increasing their power in ways that had been forbidden time out of mind. Finally, exhausted, he stood panting as they circled him.

"The old ways are done," Arden said, forcing himself to remember only the lies, the generations of betrayal and subjugation, not the man who had been a kind teacher and gentle master, the man he—and every other magician in Stour—had looked to almost as a father. *It has to be done,* he told himself. *There is no other way. He will never see reason, and the others will follow him. Leaderless, they have a chance.*

"From this moment on, all magicians are free. There is no more college, no more prison."

"Are you mad? Do you know what you're saying?"

"We know perfectly well, you son of a whore!" Herewead spat, and would have struck the bound and helpless Headmaster if Arden hadn't stopped him.

"This isn't revenge," he said. "It is simply . . . what is necessary." He gave a sardonic smile. "You've served the magicians and the world as well as you knew how. I don't blame you—you were lied to yourself. But you were wrong. You can't imprison people who have committed no crime. You can't preemptively punish them for what they might do. We believe in the purity of the Essence, and the goodness of men. All men, magician and commoner. There is no difference—you told me yourself."

"I beg of you, let me go," Rudyard pleaded. "You've lived a sheltered life. You don't understand what people are capable of. They're wicked, Arden; lazy at best, and that's just as bad, because they allow the wicked to flourish. I've seen the wide world, and there is no good in it!"

"There will be," Arden said softly. "Now your duty is almost done. In a moment they will destroy Stour, and then we will destroy them. It will be over, and both magician and commoner will be safe. Unless, of course, they cannot detect power within the walls. Then they'll abandon their mission and escape this neat trap we've set for them, and we'll never know where they'll strike. They'll pick off your magicians one by one, however well they hide. You say you know human nature? How many do you think will join them, to save their own skins? Your worst nightmare, Rudyard—magicians running amok with all of England's power at their disposal. Commoners won't stand a chance."

He had to turn away from Rudyard's ashen face. *I can't doubt I'm doing the right thing,* he thought. *Not now.*

"We're walking out of here. You'll be the only one left. It will be up to you draw up the Essence, to create a mask of power to fool the Dresdeners. A noble sacrifice, to save the world. You could save yourself, perhaps, but then you'd be dooming the commoners."

He turned and bade his allies to follow, shutting his ears to Rudyard's echoing cries: "You'll doom them too, if you free the magicians. I've seen war, Arden! I've seen what people are! Don't give them power—don't give them freedom! You don't know the malice and stupidity of them, Arden! You don't know the horror!"

Even with three slammed doors between them, the Headmaster's words reverberated through the stone halls.

"Will he do it, do you think?" Felton asked.

"He will," Arden said grimly. "What we offer is the lesser of two evils. He knows his duty."

Phil's visions turned molten; red, uneasy things pried their way into unexplored places, and her dreams became tormented. Beyond her the gates of Stour swung open, and Arden drove a dozen men, apparently half paralyzed and utterly cowed, across the open field toward the Dresdeners' lookout.

"It's an ambush!" Bergen cried, but before he could test his powers against Arden, the Fräulein stopped him.

"Wait," she said.

Arden called out cheerfully, "These are the ones who plotted to fight you, Fräulein." With a rush of Essence, he forced the men to their bellies. "Commoner lover!" he shouted with contempt, and shot Felton in the back. "Fool!" He shot Hereweald, and moved along the line, pausing only to reload.

Their masquerade was rendered all the more effective by the fact that the blanks he fired, though nonlethal, had a cardboard wad that was expelled by the gunpowder explosion with considerable force. The magicians were struck hard enough to bruise them, and their convulsive twitches upon being hit, and even a few unfeigned groans, added verisimilitude.

Arden made an elaborate bow, and Hildemar cried, "Bravo!" then whispered to the black-clad Kommandant, "You see, he cannot resist me. Old feelings still linger, but he knows the winning side."

Arden joined them and looked with satisfaction over the still corpses, to Stour, practically pulsating with power. "If I may do the honors?" The Fräulein nodded, and first Arden, then the Dresden-ers, then—some having the decency to look ashamed but not quite enough to protest—the traitor magicians sucked the Essence from the earth, loosed it from the witch-fire opals they all wore, and with a blinding, brilliant, utterly silent streak of color, unleashed doom upon Stour and all it contained.

For a second time Stour fell, not with the ravaging of bombs but with a quiet physical dissolution of the supporting walls, the geological decay of millennia all in an instant. The end result was the same, though. There was a low grinding and crack like an ice-bound river's first thaw, the deafening crash of a thousand tons of stone, and dust, rising in a cataclysmic plume and spreading in billowing dervish skirts over the twelve fallen men on the lawn.

Through even this, Phil slept, and now her dreams became erratic, terrifying. Something huge below the earth . . . no, it was a heaving sea, ancient and boiling, and she was in it, surrounded by something vast . . . now becoming something vast . . .

The Dresdeners and their cohorts whooped in victory. Fräulein Hildemar, in the passion of success more alluring than ever, swayed toward Arden, who had made this all possible.

For the first time, he did not eagerly meet those splendid coral lips, did not reach to caress the alabaster cameo of her shoulders. He did smile, though, and it was enough to make the Fräulein take a step back, for she realized, suddenly, that it was far different from any smile he'd ever bestowed on her before. This one was real.

Puzzled, she tried to dismiss it—after all, everything had gone perfectly—and turned to the Kommandant. "Send the assassins, and as soon as we've rested we'll—"

Her breath was choked off in a golden whip of the Essence, and she reeled, pointing an accusing finger at Arden as she convulsed and gaped and bared her small sharp teeth at him. An instinct that it would cause a hurt more lasting than death prompted him to cast her roughly aside, and he crouched by her as she gasped wheezing, ragged breaths and said, "Your body is garbage, your mind a cesspool. You are filth." From behind him, the executed magicians leaped up and attacked. They would finish off the Fräulein.

With a wild cry, Arden braced himself for attack and searched for the assassins. They were masters of their craft, though, and had slipped the leash as soon as it was loosed, melting into the woods to follow the directions they'd received earlier to Weasel Rue. That magic nonsense back there—that wasn't their sort of fight.

But when bullets ripped through the skeletal tree limbs around them, when a petrol bomb in a jelly jar, hurled by a slingshot, exploded nearby, the fight became theirs, too.

Weary from their efforts though they were, the Dresden magicians were vastly more powerful than Arden could have believed. The element of surprise had served his allies well, but only a moment later the tide turned. Jasper was down and Felton was struggling as the Dresdeners rallied.

Then one of the traitors fell, his skull leaking scarlet, and the Dresdeners had a new enemy.

"Look out!" the Kommandant shouted, holding off both Arden and Hereweald as they struggled to drain him. "Commoners, with guns!"

The Dresdeners could ward themselves against bullets, but it took concentration and sucked away power they needed elsewhere. "Bergen, Lightbody, take them out!"

Hidden in his crevice, Joey, thinking this was all as good as a play, struck a match and lit the long fuse. A moment later a fusillade of bullets apparently flew from a row of red-berried hollies twenty yards from him, and Bergen said, "There!" as he and two comrades proceeded to drain the Essence out of every living thing within ten yards of a row of firecrackers.

Joey chuckled. Just wait till they got a load of the stink bombs he'd concocted, which, he was sure, smelled exactly like mustard gas. His childish laugh carried even above the din of fighting, and one of the commoner assassins, raising himself on his elbows, triangulated the sound and shot at the sliver of flesh he could just glimpse through the sharp-toothed evergreen leaves.

Through this too, Phil slept, though by now it was more delirium than sleep. She thrashed in the snow, freeing her bright flaming hair, and moaned. One of the other assassins caught the sound and crept away from the fighting until he saw crimson in the snow. The Fräulein had been very precise in her description. Who else but his target could have hair of such a fiery hue?

Huddled in a hollow not far away, the first assassin had the same thought when he spied a ruby-haired woman peeking from behind a rough hemlock trunk. He'd assumed the Fräulein was sending him after a younger woman, but perhaps it was only the distance, the hard lines of fear, that made the woman methodically firing the gun (with great accuracy, at targets that, mysteriously, never fell) seem older. He stilled his breath, slowed his heart, and lovingly eased back the trigger. He never missed.

Nor did Uncle Walter, not even when he was shaking with hopeless fury at the death of the woman who'd been his childhood crush, before she'd fallen head over heels for Enery. *Quicker than he deserves,* Walter thought as half of the man's head scattered in a snowdrift, and he looked for another life to end, entirely forgetting his dangling handcuff.

One of the assassins was a champion duelist, with knives strapped to his arms and legs. His favorite, though, was the heavy saber with which he'd dueled at the university. He ignored the battle around him and made his way straight to Weasel Rue.

The last assassin left on the field looked down at the girl, his quarry. She couldn't be sleeping, though the gunfire was sporadic now, and snow-muffled. He stepped back, out of spatter range, and took careful aim.

At the touch of his finger on the trigger, Phil's eyes opened, and she screamed.

At the first pressure of his finger on the trigger, the assassin melted.

And Phil continued to scream like a whipping wind, because she could *feel* him melting. She could feel everything around her—the rocks, the dirt, the microscopic life. The very air tingled with the Essence, and she was engulfed in a deluge of awareness, of power, that stretched to the earth's core but found its terrible focus in her.

She stood, only peripherally conscious of the fighting nearby. It was part of the background in her Essence-trance, neither more nor less important than the dread of a small seed sprouting subterraneanly at her feet as it was inexorably consumed by a creeping fungus. The world was sentient now, and everything was pain and fear, moments of victory when one animal ate, quick sorrow then nothing as it was eaten in turn, and always, through it all, the Essence, blind and indifferent, flowing from earth to air to being without preference, without pity.

"Arden, retreat!" Hereweald shouted from across the field. The fighting had been going on only a moment, but already it was clear that Arden and his allies were doomed. They were brave, they were strong, but their lives had been dedicated to tranquillity, and they simply could not make themselves be merciless.

The commoners were faring little better. The Dresdeners had begun with mere defense, focusing their attacks on the other magicians, but as the inevitability of their victory became more and more apparent, they began to pick off the commoners whenever they could spy them. They drained their Essence, their lives, and became all the stronger. Henshawe the grocer, dashing from trunk to trunk, was caught; his friend the baker died trying to drag his lifeless body to safety.

Arden, pallid and shaking, was holding off the Kommandant and two other Dresdeners at once, but he couldn't last much longer. Hereweald called him again. "Back, Arden! We can't take them!"

"We can't abandon the commoners!" he cried. "Felton, circle round and cover their escape!"

"They're nothing, leave them!" Hereweald shouted, and tried to drag his friend away. "Our duty's to our brother magicians. We have to live to tell them the truth."

"No!" Arden struggled against the hands that pulled at him. He saw another commoner, the tavernkeeper who'd brought barrels of ale to the hopper huts on donkey-back every Saturday, crumple as Bergen ripped his life from him.

Then Arden's concentration broke, and he lost his hold on the Kommandant. Across the gap the man grinned as he began to crush Arden's skull.

Through the chaos and the numbness of universal pain, Phil heard a sound. All else fell silent. The screaming of trees as the sap in their twigs froze, the crashing of molecules, the ripping of dividing cells—they all fell back to the farthest reaches of her preternatural awareness in deference to the one sound that had any real meaning to her: the sound of Arden suffering.

She stood, and felt like she moved swiftly, though around her everything seemed to be suspended in a viscous web. Outrage rose, roiling and boiling, and she could not tell if she was drawing it from the world or producing it herself. She frowned, and the world frowned, and decided unequivocally that Arden, of all the tormented organisms writhing on the planet, must live.

She'd saved Arden from death before, from the same adversary, and had done her mortal best with her fists alone. This time too she did her best, and it was volcanic.

She killed, she burned, she rent and tore everything that was not Arden. Impassive, she saw—and again, felt—humans die, and none of it mattered to her, so long as Arden lived. For a moment, she was more than a magician—she was a god, cruel and indifferent as the cosmos.

Then, her body at last coming to its senses and shutting down, she fell in a limp heap, a flash of flame on sunset-touched white.

Chapter 25

Don't get too near her," Felton said, but Arden paid him no heed. He pulled her into his arms and bent close, whispering inarticulate pleas, salting her face with tears.

When at last she opened her eyes, the three magicians who remained cringed back, but Phil's tragic face cracked in a radiant smile when she saw Arden safe and whole. The rest of the world, everything that touched the Essence, was still there, but it murmured unobtrusively in the background now, and for the moment at least, she could devote herself to Arden.

"Is it over?" she asked.

"God, is it ever!" muttered Hereweald. Slowly, what she had done came back to her, and she looked beyond Arden to see the cataclysm of her own making. There was a great scar in the land, utterly devoid of life. Not a plant, not a microbe, not a magician or commoner remained.

"Did I do that?" she asked, fragile as a fledgling, knowing the answer.

"I don't know what happened," Arden said, helping her to her feet. "I gave you your powers back—your family's powers. At least, I thought I did."

"How could I do . . ." She made a helpless gesture toward the carnage. The tide of Essence ebbed further, leaving memory on her mind's shores. "Eamon Dooley—I killed him."

"And all the Dresdeners," Felton said encouragingly. One must look on the bright side.

"Nearly all," Hereweald corrected. "I saw that blond bitch crawling away, and Bergen was with her."

"The Stour fighters?" she asked.

"Gone, all but us."

"The Home Guard?" she asked, shaking. "Uncle Walter?"

"Everyone who was close to the fighting is dead," Arden said gently. Only those near him had been spared.

Dead, Phil thought bleakly. Put like that, it seemed simple, an on-off switch that happened to be set to off. *What I did was murder. What I am is a monster.*

"What did you do to me, Arden?" she wailed. The *everything* loomed again, and she had to fight off the myriad voices and sensations, the endless eddies of the Essence that plagued her.

"I gave you a piece of myself. It was supposed to renew your link to the Essence."

"It did, oh, it did!" she said hysterically, feeling a man have a heart attack in Manchester, a flea biting a cat in Jaipur, a copepod in the

North Sea beating its antennae like oars. "Make it stop, Arden. Please. I can't bear it!" She covered her ears, but that did nothing. She covered her face, beat her head against the snow, and felt the Essence rising in her again, blessing her with unwanted connectedness, threatening to take over her mind, drive her to madness. *And if I go mad, I'll lose control again, and—*

"Arden, take it away or kill me. I'll hurt you. I'll hurt everyone. I can't stop it!"

But somehow, with his loving hands in her hair, his warm breath on the back of her neck, she found she could. Moving very carefully, as if her whole body were a reservoir full to the brim that any sudden move might cause to overspill, she stood once more. *I am Phil Albion,* she thought. *I am myself. I am not this thing that was put inside me.*

"Do what they did to Godric Albion, please. I do not want magic."

He tried, reaching out with his own Essence, but nothing worked. Her power clung to her, greedily.

"It's just like before. I'd swear the Essence isn't touching you." He gathered the last vestiges of his strength and lifted a single strand of her hair, trying to change its color. "Nothing. You're still immune to the Essence when it is wielded at you." Awestruck, he said, "Phil, your power is incredible. Try something else. Show me what other things you can do."

She made the slightest gesture with her fingers, at the ruined land, the blight she had caused. "That is what I can do," she said, closing her fingers in a fist. "And I will never, never use magic again."

"You'll learn to control it, Phil. I'll help you. It will get easier. There's just so much power in you—no wonder it exploded like that. Generations of potential, all waiting to ignite. I know you're shocked. What happened—it's horrible. But if you hadn't stepped in, my friends and yours would have died just as surely, at the hands of the Dresdeners. You still killed the enemy, and that's the important thing. We'd have been lost without you. England would have fallen if the Dresdeners had won. You saved England, Phil! Isn't that what you've been fighting for all along? Just think what you can do now!"

"You don't understand, Arden. You told me the Essence is good, pure. You can't have felt what I'm feeling now. It *hurts!* If I blink, if I flinch, it will take me over again—and I don't know what I'll do! I don't want to kill. I don't want this. Oh, Arden, you ruined me!" But she clung to her seducer, the man who had ushered her from innocence to experience, and loved him still.

There came a small, bright note in the shape of Joey, who staggered out of the holly bushes covered in gore.

"Did I do that?" Phil asked as she hugged him tight.

"Naw, bullet grazed my forehead. I'm a right mess, ain't I? Hardly hurts, though don't let on to Tilda." Tilda, a plump, nurturing sort, his chosen sweetheart after he'd given Phil up as a lost cause, could be counted on to make a very pleasant fuss.

"Blimey!" he said, wiping the blood from his eyes and getting his first good look at the carnage. "Did I do *that?* Must have used too much gunpowder. Where are the others?"

If there's one small consolation to being given near-godlike powers and slaughtering a good many of your friends, it should be the undisputed privilege of telling your story first and receiving unlimited sympathy. But when Phil and the others dragged themselves back to Weasel Rue, she had only to take one look at her sister's stricken face to think that her own troubles must be fairly trivial, after all. She sent the weary men into the house with Stan and caught her sister's hand.

Fee perched on the porch, holding two pieces of paper. One, the featherweight airmail parchment, was obviously from Thomas; Phil could see his large, loopy scrawl. The other was a half-sheet telegram.

Fee took a long, shuddering breath. "They regret to inform me . . . missing in action."

Grief, Phil could have handled, somber depression or wild weeping. What she could not bear was to see Fee diminishing before her eyes until she became a shell, a shadow. Fee's great blue-pearl eyes were empty, as if everything dear to her had fled—all hope, all love, every tomorrow.

"No," Phil said gently, taking her by the shoulders and leaning into her. She knew what it felt like to be losing yourself. "I won't let you go." She pressed her forehead to Fee's deathly cold one and tried with all her will to use their old familiar embrace to revive her. Their hair entwined, their eyelashes brushing, Phil reached out to her, seeking that alchemical blending that had solaced them so often before. *Stay with me, Fee,* she begged. *Don't give in to grief. It will pass, it will join the great sorrow that is life.*

She felt something electric pass between them and pulled back sharply, gasping. In giving herself to Fee, to be her prop and her support, she'd very nearly passed on a thread of her life, which would have awakened the dormant Albion power in Fee, too.

Fee, emerging slightly from the void of her woe, examined her sister. If there was anything that could drag her from her misery, it was the need to succor her beloved Phil. "What is it?" she asked, slipping easily into the role of comforter.

Phil told her, doing her best to be brave, but Fee knew her too well.

She regarded Phil solemnly. "I've never had a burden that you didn't gladly bear with me," she said. "What you feel, I feel. We will always be together, in everything." She took Phil's hands, her own surprisingly strong. "Share it with me, Phil. I don't know if it will make your weight lighter, but at least we will bear it together." She pulled Phil to her again, but her sister fought her.

"No, you don't know what you're saying. It's a curse. I feel like I'm going bonkers, like I'm about to fly in a thousand pieces. I killed our friends, Fee! I killed Uncle Walter, and Eamon, and—"

"Shh . . . hush, dear. It's not your fault."

"But it is! I—"

She pulled Phil to her one last time and repeated, very firmly, in exactly the tone Mum used, "It's not your fault."

Phil stayed in her embrace, but she kept the Essence, and herself tightly in check. "Fee, no," she said weakly.

Fee, playing as dirty as siblings always do, whispered, in a hurt tone, "Would you really deny me the power that might help me save Thomas, if perhaps he's still alive?"

Abandoning herself to the inevitable, Phil let go.

When the magicians returned a few minutes later, they found Fee burnished with an inner luminescence, grinning at all the world like it was her best friend.

"Oh, Phil, it's lovely!" she said, staring at nothing with a look of absolute adoration. "I can feel things under the snow, waiting." Her face lit up even more. "A worm, Phil, so cozy—can you feel him? And my, it just goes on and on, doesn't it? How do you keep track? Ah, that's what you meant about the crazy part, I see now. But it's like a symphony, all playing together. What does it matter if there are twenty instruments or a billion? It's all the same song."

The flaw's in me then, Phil thought bitterly. *Why do I feel the struggle and suffering of life, while she feels only the joy? Why did I slaughter, when she sits there like Buddha under the bo tree?*

She felt a seed of jealousy, but it had no time to sprout, for:

"He's alive! Oh God, Thomas is alive! I can feel him!" Fee's face flushed with excitement, and she was neither desolate nor enlightened, but just herself again—though with all the power of the Essence. "I can find him, Phil. I can bring him home!"

She handed Phil the other piece of paper. "Maybe I can figure out where he is. Too bad the Essence doesn't have a homing beacon. Or does it, once you get closer? Read it, Phil, and tell me if you find a clue."

Dearest, beloved Fee,

I can't tell you where I am, pet, and if I did, they'd censor it and throw me in the chokey for treason. I volunteered for something special, thinking it would be so easy for me, with the Essence to help me. Only, I didn't realize . . . You see, we all knew England held the greatest concentration of the Essence. It's the heart of the world. But I never dreamed that there's hardly any Essence at all over here. I left England, and I felt as if part of me had been ripped away. I can sense it here, just barely, and if I exert myself I can draw up a trickle (I healed a razor slice this morning — army razors are so dull, I might as well use my bayonet), but not enough to do any good. So I'm stuck here, a common soldier. A commoner soldier. But I'm still fighting for the same thing. I'm still going to help make this world the peaceful and beautiful place you deserve, darling Fee. It just might take a little longer! I really don't mind . . .

Seemingly from nowhere, the last assassin slipped to Fee's side and whipped the saber blade to her throat. Fee, half elsewhere, glanced up at the last instant—and dropped him with a thought almost before anyone else realized he was there.

"If he's alive, and missing, that means he's captured, right? He must be in Germany. Do they treat their prisoners well? They better."

"Fee!" Phil cried, staring aghast at the dead man at their feet, then at her sister, who utterly ignored him. "You feel sorry for worms, Fee. You shed a tear and apologize if you slap a mosquito. How . . . how . . ."

Fee regarded her sister serenely. In the back of her mind, she could still feel Thomas, somewhere. Could he feel her? She sent pulses of love through the earth's crust but couldn't tell if they reached him. "Would you rather I let him kill me?" she asked. "I don't *like* swatting mosquitoes, but I'd be a fool to let them bite me." She looked down to the corpse at her feet. "I'm very, very sorry," she told it, utterly sincere.

Phil took her sister's slim hand. The Essence had changed her. She was still Fee, but she was something else, too, something vast, with a frozen place that had never before existed in her gentle soul. Or had it? Was it in everyone, waiting to emerge as soon as the power was there? The ancients were right to keep it in a cage. Maybe they were right about keeping magicians imprisoned, too. Phil could feel the power in herself, throbbing just below the surface, begging for release. *Maybe if I train for twenty years, I can be like they were at Stour, swirling the Essence in meaningless currents, doing nothing more wicked than making exotic flowers and gentle tigers. Or I can chain myself like Uncle Walter. Only, how do you chain power like this? How do you beat back the knowledge that you can do anything?*

She bent her head to hide her tears, and read the last lines of Thomas's letter.

I really don't mind dying, Fee, you must believe it. Everything comes, and everything goes. Of course I'd rather have a hundred years with you, but the important thing is that I had a moment. Our lives are such small parts of everything, really. They seem so big, but the Essence has taught me that a moment, an aeon, an inch, the world, are all the same. A moment's as good as a century, if it's the right moment. If I don't come back, hold on to that, Fee. Hold on to our moment.

Phil looked up at Arden through tear-hazed eyes, gazing at him, loving him like a ceaseless ache, but however she tried to fill her thoughts with that dark, handsome face, however she tried to recall the feel of his fingertips, the smell of his hair, it was all blurred somehow, and the image of dead bodies in a ruined landscape rumbled behind it, a juggernaut threatening to wipe out everything that was good.

He kissed her and turned to consult with the others before he noticed her tears.

"Which moment is mine?" she whispered after him, but he could not hear her.

"We should go," Arden said, coming back to her, taking her free hand, the one Fee wasn't holding, a bit possessively. "We need to track down our brothers and tell them the truth. They were heading to London, to disperse from there. It will be hard for them at first, but together, we'll give them a better life. The Fräulein and Bergen—do you suppose they went back to Germany?"

"With their tails between their legs!" Felton said triumphantly.

"Then England belongs to the good magicians again."

Except for me, Phil thought.

She wasn't sure if she shared Arden's beliefs anymore—but she believed in Arden, and that was enough. "You're coming with us, right Fee?"

"For now, until I can figure out how to rescue Thomas. You'll help me?"

"Always, in everything."

"To London, then," Arden said, giving Phil's hand the slightest tug, freeing her from Fee's hold.